THE BASTARD OF SAINT GENEVRA

Diane Gallagher

Also by Diane Gallagher

Greenwich List (2011)

Mancia di Sanu: A Canadian Expat's Take on Sicilian Life and Cuisine
(2016)

The Bastard of Saint Genevra

DIANE GALLAGHER

Island2Island Press

Duncan, B.C., Canada

Island2Island Press
Duncan, B.C., Canada
island2islandpress@outlook.com

Printed in the USA
First printing 2017

Gallagher, Diane, 1961-, author
    The bastard of Saint Genevra / Diane Gallagher.

    ISBN 978-0-9951839-2-6 (softcover)

        I. Title.

    PS8613.A45933B37 2017   C813'.6   C2017-900687-8

This book is for Miyuki who taught me how to love,

and for Nick who taught me how to love myself.

"The universe is not just made up of electrons and atoms and molecules.
It is made up of stories, interconnecting and expanding."

-Nicola Cacciato

Synesthesia

syn·es·the·sia (sĭn′ĭs-thē′zhə)

Noun:

a sensation that is experienced in an unexpected way when a stimulus is applied, such as the involuntary visualization of colour in concert with particular sounds.

Sicily

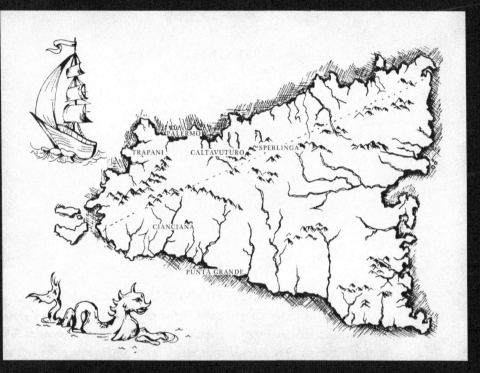

Chapter One

FIRST STEPS IN TRAPANI

~AGOSTO 2011~

THE HEAT WAS A FUZZY ORANGE COLOUR but the light was a
sharp yellow as Elena stepped through the grey hiss of the sliding glass
doors to the sidewalk outside Trapani Airport. The rental agreement felt
cool in her hand. The Eurocar sign was a good 200 metres to the end of
the parking lot. Before she was halfway there, Elena's forehead was
damp with sweat and her white cotton blouse had attached itself to her
chest and back. To make matters worse, her sweat-dampened shirt had
made her cheap, knock-off leather bag leave a large pink stain down one
shoulder and across one breast.

"Shit." Elena tried to adjust the purse strap but it was too late to
save the blouse.

Two Eurocar employees leaned against the carwash, and
watched as she trudged through the wavering heat, openly admiring her as

she stepped up to the car wash station. Elena handed the paperwork to one of the men. As he carelessly flipped through, the younger man ran his hazel eyes over her and she realized her blouse was now entirely transparent and her bra was not only visible, but the lacy pink flowers were now completely discernible. The young man grinned at her and said in Sicilian, "*Bedda.* Beautiful."

"*Signurina,* your keys." The older man was standing next to a Fiat Panda.

"Wait. That's not the car I booked. I asked for a smartcar. You know, a little car." Elena reached for the rental agreement and pointed to the word 'smartcar'.

"*Mi dispiace signurina.* I'm sorry." The older man shrugged and joined his counterpart in staring at her chest.

"Fine, fine. *Va beni.*" Elena sighed. It had been a long day. Vancouver to Frankfurt sitting next to an exhausted mother with her screaming child – every shriek causing sharp brilliant white lightning bolts to cross her vision and bore into her brain; two hours from Frankfurt to Trapani wedged into discount airline seats. She grabbed the keys and loaded her bag into the trunk of the tank-like Fiat. As she climbed into the car, the younger man winked at her and said, "*Grazii signurina.*"

"Whatever," she muttered and pulled out of the parking lot, grinding the gears in the process.

Chapter Two

FAMILY SECRETS

~MARZO 2011~

ELENA STARED AT THE DARK CIRCLES UNDER HER EYES. Inside the medicine cabinet was the bottle of aspirin that become her friend. In the quiet squeak of the hinge was the familiar pale pink tinge that spread across her thoughts. Elena was grateful for the synesthesia that had been her companion for as long as she could remember. But even the comforting colours could not ease the ache in her heart when she thought of her father, now lying under the grass next to her mother.

Elena's memories of her mother no longer brought her the sharp pain they once had–Maria had died so long ago. Her father was a different matter. She had grown up surrounded by aunts and uncles and more cousins than she could count, but at the end of family gatherings, she and her father went home alone. He had never remarried in spite of the urgings of his sisters – he had always said his wife was the first love of his life, Elena was second and there would never be a third. He was a wonderful father and Elena loved him. At Notre Dame High School, she listened with sympathy but not much comprehension to the complaints of her girlfriends about their parents.

"Elena, you home?" It was the voice of her cousin, Lucia.

"Here, in the bathroom" Elena answered. "I'll be right out." Elena popped two aspirin into her mouth.

"You look like hell, girl." Lucia stood with her hands on her hips. "You should take some of the money Uncle Sal left you and go lie on a beach somewhere."

"Thanks. You're a laugh a minute."

"No problem coz. That's what family's for."

Elena groaned as she lifted the ancient cardboard file box, edges held together by fraying duct tape. "Here, can you look for anything that could be important? Insurance papers, old family stuff, those sorts of things. I think Dad kept every paper from every letter he ever got."

Lucia sneezed as she brushed the dust off the box. "No kidding. Must be a family trait–my dad is the same."

The two women drifted into silence as they took one file after another, opening, skimming and depositing them in one of three piles: important, not important but keep, and toss. They had grown up together– their birthdays were days apart–and they had lived next door to each other all their lives. When the ambulance had taken Elena's father to the hospital after his first stroke, it was Lucia she had called to drive her. When her father had his second stroke, it was Lucia that had sat with her, watching the silver blip of the monitors. When the doctors had suggested turning off the life support, it was Lucia that held her while she cried and helped her realize there was no other decision to be made. And it was Lucia who had held her up through the appalling week that followed with the wake, the funeral, and the well-meaning relatives. The reading of the will brought the reality of her father's death crashing around her, and when she fell apart that night, it was Lucia who arrived, unbidden, with chocolate, ice cream, and a pile of chick flics.

A deep orange cut through Elena's wandering thoughts as she heard a sharp intake of breath from Lucia.

Elena looked at her cousin. Her face had turned white and she was staring at an official looking document. "What is it?" Elena twisted and leaned forward towards her cousin.

Lucia's were wide. She whispered, "Elena... you were adopted."

"What? That's ridiculous. Of course I wasn't adopted."

"But...I have the adoption papers right here." Lucia stretched out her arm, a slight tremor shaking her hand.

UPON THE APPLICATION OF SALVATORE ALCAMO AND
CARLA ALCAMO COMING BEFORE ME
THIS DAY IN THE PRESENCE OF ANTONIO BARONE,
OF COUNSEL FOR THE PETITIONERS, AND THE
REQUIREMENTS OF THE ADOPTION ACT HAVING BEEN
COMPLIED WITH;
THIS COURT ORDERS THAT THE CHILD
WHOSE PARTICULARS OF BIRTH ARE SET OUT
IN THE ABOVE-DESCRIBED BIRTH REGISTRATION AND
WHO WAS BORN IN VANCOUVER, BRITISH COLUMBIA,
ON THE 16TH DAY OF APRIL, 1980,
BE AND IS ADOPTED
AS THE CHILD OF THE SAID APPLICANTS,
SALVATORE ALCAMO AND CARLA ALCAMO
THIS COURT FURTHER ORDERS THAT THE CHILD SHALL
ASSUME THE SURNAME OF THE APPLICANTS AND THE
CHRISTIAN OR GIVEN NAME OF ELENA ANGELINA.

As she read the words a murky green rushing filled her ears and her vision narrowed. A voice, drifting in the air above her called, "Elena, Elena!" She felt a sharp shake and looked up to see Lucia holding her shoulder.

"Elena, you didn't know anything about this?"

Elena shook her head. "No, nothing." She paused. "But how could they hide this from me all along?"

"I don't know…but I know who would."

"Who?"

"Dad. He knows everything that goes on in this family. Let me call him." Lucia reached across the box of files to pick up her cellphone. "He's always at Scarpone's playing *scupa* and guzzling coffee with his cronies."

Lucia dialed a number and waited for it to ring. *"Ciau,* Guido! *Sugnu* Lucia. Is my dad there? Great. Can you send him up to Elena's house? It's important. *Grazii."*

Lucia dropped her cellphone. "He'll be here in ten, coz. Let me put on some espresso. Leave those papers and come in the kitchen with me."

Elena sat as Lucia made coffee and chattered away, trying to distract her.

She listened to the deep burgundy bubbling of the *espresso* pot, concentrating on the colour of the sound, so she wouldn't have to think.

"You're seeing colours, aren't you?" Lucia was one of the few people who knew about Elena's internal life of colour.

Elena nodded. She pulled her fists to her heart, trying not to wonder if her father was truly her father.

"I was thinking the only people who knew about the colours are…were… you and Dad. And now I'm not sure Dad was even my father."

"Whoa, Elena. Don't get ahead of yourself. Uncle Sal was your dad no matter if it was his sperm that made you or not. Let's wait till Dad gets here. If anyone knows it'll be him. You know how close he and Uncle Sal were."

Elena took a deep breath. "You're right. Thanks, Lucia. I'm not sure what I would do without you, and Uncle Tony, and Aunt Laura."

They sat in silence, sipping their *espresso*, until the sharp grey sound of Tony's boots hitting the wooden steps announced his arrival at the kitchen door. As always, he opened the door without knocking but instead of his usual deep *'Bon giornu!'* or *'Bona sera!'* he strode to the kitchen table, sat opposite Elena and took her hands in his.

"Well, *bedda mia,* it seems we have some things to talk about."

Elena looked into his kind brown eyes and nodded; only nodded and waited.

"This is a story my brother should have told you but couldn't. Perhaps when I finish, you will understand why." Tony turned to his daughter, "Lucia, *il cafè.*"

"*Sì Papà.*" Lucia poured the steaming *espresso* into a tiny demitasse.

"*Grazii.*" Tony settled himself into the kitchen chair, and looked into Elena's hazel eyes. The wooden seat squeaked as he shifted.

"Now, you need to know your father and your blessed mother loved you more than you can every understand."

Elena took her lower lip between her teeth. "I think I know that."

Tony sighed. "Elena, you do know it. Sal told you often enough.

Now, here is the part he should have told you.

"Your mother and father got married young, and they tried and tried to have a baby, right from the day they got married. But your mother, she had ladies' troubles, all the time. They didn't want to tell the *famiglia* –they were ashamed–but Sal told me."

"Ashamed?" broke in Lucia. "That's crazy! That's not her fault. Anyhow, Mom had all kinds of trouble and she talked to everyone about it." She turned to Elena. "Do you remember? We'd come home from high school and there she'd be, talking to Mrs. Rossi or Mrs. Di Luca or cousin Antonietta about menopause or her hysterectomy. It was gross."

"I know, I know. But your mother was born here. Sal and Carla had only been in Canada a few months. Back then, Cianciana was a small town with old ideas, and they brought those ideas with them.

"When your father came to me he was so worried about your mother. The doctor told her she would never have a baby and she might need to have…Lucia, what was that word again. That thing your mother had."

"Hysterectomy, Dad."

"*Sì, sì.* A hysterectomy. Your mother couldn't stop crying, Elena. One day, I heard in my shop someone talking about a Sicilian girl, pregnant with no father in sight, who wanted to find someone to take her baby. I didn't know how to manage it, but your Aunt Laura, *grazii Diu,* she is a smart woman. She found someone–I don't remember her name–who was working in the hospital helping girls who wanted to give up their babies. This girl insisted they find an Italian family for her baby. You know, Elena, for an Italian man to say he can't father a baby is a shameful thing. This woman was having a hard time finding an Italian family to take the baby. But, your Aunt Laura told your mother, and she was so excited that Sal agreed. Reluctantly, but he agreed.

"Your father had one condition, though. He made Laura and me promise not to tell anyone that the baby was adopted. We told the family that Carla was pregnant, and she had kept it a secret because of all her female troubles. When the time got closer Sal told everyone that the doctor had insisted that Carla stay quiet at home and in bed as much as possible. It was hard for Carla to stay in the house and only be visited by Laura and me but for her, it was worth it to have you.

"Finally, they got a phone call from Laura's friend. The baby–

you–had been born. Sal and Carla rushed over to the hospital and there you were. A perfect, beautiful baby girl. Blue eyes–you know you were born with blue eyes? And curly black hair, so much all over your head. They brought you home that day. The girl signed the papers right away. We never knew anything about her, except that she was Sicilian, and even that we weren't supposed to know.

"As you grew, Carla decided you should know the truth and convinced Sal they should tell you but your mother got the cancer and died. Your father was terrified of losing you too, and he forbade us to tell you."

Silence settled back over the room. Elena thought about her kind, loving, proud father. She thought about his soft moss green voice. She thought about how she had begged for a pony–she had wanted so much to be a cowgirl. He couldn't afford a pony so instead he had found a place she could ride a pony once a month until her cowgirl phase had passed. She thought about all the swimming lessons and picnics and how he surprised her at twelve with her first guitar, and had taught her, long hours, until she knew more than he. She thought about how he had scraped together enough money for piano lessons, and how he had stood and cheered when she walked across the stage, and got her degree in music when all the other parents sat and clapped politely. And with every thought, the warmth in her chest grew and she realized it would take more than words 'adoption certificate' on a piece of paper to believe her father had not been her dad.

She looked up from the tabletop and saw Uncle Tony and Lucia peering at her. She gave them small smile and sighed. "You know, Uncle Tony, he could never lose me. He was my dad."

Lucia let out her breath, and reached over to hug her cousin and whispered, "You always were a smart cookie."

Chapter Three

THE DECISION

~APRILE 2011~

"ELENA. ELENA!"

Elena started and looked up. "Sorry Gerry. What did you say?"

"I said, let's take it again from the beginning but *pianissimo* from the fourth bar."

"Oh, okay. Sorry Gerry."

Elena tilted her head from side to side, stretching her neck, and straightened out the sheet music. She placed her slender fingers on the keys, rubbing the smooth, soft ivory, and tried to let the music and the colours fill her as she restarted the piece. She closed her eyes and swayed to the music, and watched the colours move before her like they were floating in a lava lamp. As the lyrical notes filled her, she could feel the satisfying energy of the music throughout her chest and the dingy walls of the recording studio faded. The light airy notes and the beautiful colours surrounded her and lifted her like the sun crossing the line of the horizon on a clear summer morning. The grief she had been carrying dissipated and the relief music always had given her, returned; her frown-lines smoothed and her shoulders dropped.

As the final notes of the piece and the beautiful colours faded, Elena opened her eyes to see a grinning Gerry walking into the recording room.

"Finally! I've been waiting for you to break through your blue funk!" Gerry caught his breath. "Oh Elena, forgive me. That was so thoughtless."

"It's okay, Gerry. You're right. This was the first time I've been able to cut through the sadness in my playing." Elena cast her eyes down. "Too much to process, I guess."

Gerry gave Elena a tight squeeze. "No sweat kiddo. You're the best session musician I've ever worked with. You're worth the wait."

Elena smiled back up at him. "Are we done, Gerry? I have a couple of things that I have to do today."

"All done. That last set was exactly what I wanted."

Elena picked her backpack up off the floor, and slipped it on over her shoulders, tightened the straps and strolled out of the recording studio into the wan March sunlight. Gerry watched her leave and thought to himself, 'Elena's back.'

~|~

Elena carried two coffee cups in her hands as she tip-toed across the close-cropped lawn, passing the floral displays and stepping around the granite plaques lying flush to the ground. Her eyes scanned the lush lawn, frowning until she found the two she was looking for.

"Salvatore Giacomo Alcamo. Carla Giovanna Scavone Alcamo." The Italian syllables rolled off her tongue like water. She closed her eyes and repeated them. The soft lavender swirl that always accompanied her voice settled like plum blossom petals in her mind, and she could almost smell the sweetness of the colour.

Elena settled herself on the grass next to the graves, and placed one of the cups next to her father's plaque.

"Dad, I brought you *cappuccino*, just the way you like it. *Mamma,* I'm sorry, I don't remember what you liked to drink. I thought we could share mine." Elena sipped on her latte. "Dad, I found out. About the adoption, I mean. I kind of understand why you didn't tell me– it wouldn't have changed how I feel about you at all. You were so great; you always did things for me. And you always stood up for me. I'm glad you got to see me become a professional musician–to know I made good use of all those lessons you paid for." Elena blinked hard and turned her head away to watch a woman in black cleaning a headstone. A widow. The woman finished, made the sign of the cross, and leaned forward to kiss the stone. Elena thought of all the times she and her father had come to this place to do the same thing. How they had sat on this spot so many times and he would tell her stories of Sicily and her mother. He would kiss her plaque and whisper *"Ciau Carla. T'amu bedduzza.* I love you darling."

Elena tipped her head back to look up to the clouds. "Dad, I've made a decision. You and Mamma, you will always be my parents, but I want to meet the woman who gave birth to me. I want to hear from her why she gave me up. Please understand, I am not being ungrateful, I just need to know." Elena placed her latte on her mother's plaque and she leaned forward to kiss it. *"Mamma, t'amu."* Kissing her father's plaque she whispered, *"Miu papà."*

Elena sat in silence; listening to the lemon-coloured chirping of the birds, watching the clouds drift past across the azure sky. In the distance, the grey rumble of the cars as they sped along Boundary Avenue infringed into her thoughts. Finally, she pulled her feet under her, and stretching her legs as she stood, said. *"Ciau mamma, ciau papà.* I love you both."

Chapter four

PINA HAS THE KEY

~APRIL 2011~

ELENA SAT WITH LUCIA, sipping a single glass of Uncle Tony's brutally potent homemade wine. Uncle Tony's powerful wine had been known to be responsible for several drunken escapades amongst her male cousins and everyone in the family over twenty had learned to say '*no, grazii'* to his offer of a second glass. Aunt Laura had placed a plate of steaming *arancini,* the delicate rice dumplings stuffed with cheese, and ham, and spinach, in front of the two cousins before sitting with her own glass of wine.

"So. Elena. I am guessing you want to talk about the adoption."

Lucia winced. "Ma! Do you have to be so blunt? Maybe Elena doesn't want to talk about it yet."

"No, no, Lucia," Elena put her hand on her cousin's arm. "That's exactly why I came here." Elena turned to her aunt. *"Zzia. Zzio* Tony said it was a friend of yours that arranged the adoption?"

"Yes. We worked at the hospital together. She was a social worker."

"Are you still in touch with her? Do you think she could tell me anything about the adoption?"

Laura's lined face crinkled into a smile and she reached out to caress Elena's cheek. *"Bedda mia.* I knew you would ask this one day. I've kept in touch with her so when the time came you could speak to her. Now, you both, eat the *arancini* while it's still hot. I'll call her and see if she can join us."

Lucia leaned over and grasped Elena's arm. "Are you ready to do this?" Lucia asked. "This is a lot to handle in a few months."

"I want to know. No, I have to know." Elena answered back.

"You know who your mother and your father were. And whoever this woman–your birth mother–is, you may not want to hear what she has to say. If you can find her, that is."

"But what if there's something I should know about my biological family? Some kind of medical condition. Or what if I meet someone, fall in love, and find out we're related? No, I need to know." Elena's brows met at the familiar little vertical frown lines above her nose.

"Okay," Lucia answered, "Just be careful, and don't get your hopes up too much. Chances are you won't ever find her. The rules about adoption were pretty strict."

"I know… but I have to try."

Lucia picked up her wine glass, "Here's to finding absent relatives."

The two women clinked their glasses together, and drank their wine in thoughtful silence as they waited for Laura to return to the kitchen.

"Listen!" Lucia poked Elena's arm. "Ma's talking to someone."

Both women held their breath to try and hear the conversation happening in the next room. Laura laughed, paused, and responded in Sicilian.

"Dammit, my Sicilian isn't good enough – she's talking too fast. Do you understand?" Lucia whispered.

"Shhhh." Elena answered. "I can't hear her."

Laura spoke once more, and ended with *"Ciau, ciau."* She walked into the kitchen, her housedress swishing as her shoes clicked across the shiny linoleum floor. "You girls. You haven't eaten a single bite!"

"Come on, Ma. You know that's not what we're waiting to hear. Give it up. What did you find out?" Lucia leaned towards her mother.

"Well, Elena. I called my friend Pina who was the social worker when you were adopted. She said she would come over to talk to you, but she can't promise too much." Laura picked at one of the *arancini* and put a morsel of the fried rice into her mouth.

"Elena. You've let the *arancini* go cold. Here, I'll heat it up for you." She popped the plate into the microwave, and pinched Elena's cheek. "Look at how skinny you are. Your mother would make you eat something before she would let you do anything else."

"Ma, leave Elena alone. Anyhow, isn't Dad going to be home soon?" Lucia turned and winked at her cousin. "You want me to help get his dinner ready?"

Elena leaned back into the kitchen chair, grateful for the quiet moment. She watched as Lucia and Laura prepared a baked aubergine. The scent of fresh basil and dried oregano filled the kitchen, and her mouth watered as Laura added homemade tomato sauce and anchovies and sprinkled it with cheese. The scene was so familiar to her, played out over and over throughout her childhood, her teen years, and now as an adult. Tears edged along the corners of her eyes, and a small smile of gratitude for her *famigghia*–her family–played on her lips.

Chapter five

SECRETS REVEALED

LAURA WAS BUSY WASHING THE DISHES, and Uncle Tony was drying when the knock came at the back door. Both Elena and Lucia jumped. Laura wiped her hands on her apron, and turned towards the door. She stopped at the table on her way to the door; she stroked Elena's hair once, twice.

"Don't worry, *bedda mia,* All the questions that should be answered, will be answered."

Uncle Tony frowned, dropped the tea towel, and growled, "I'm going to Scarpone's." He grabbed his coat and made a beeline for the back door.

Laura waved her hand at him. *"Vatinni.* Go!" She turned to Elena. "Don't mind your Uncle Tony. He cares, it's just nothing gets in the way of his scupa game!" She chuckled, and answered the door.

Standing there was a roly-poly woman with a huge grin showing teeth–crooked, tobacco stained, and most certainly her own. Her hair was a curly mop of silver, and she wore big gold hoops that poked out from beneath the frizz. Her cane was covered with bright skateboard stickers, including one prominent yellow and black sticker that read 'Take it easy, Life is short.' She waddled to the table, huffing and puffing and plopped her wide derriere into one of the wooden kitchen chairs. Elena smiled, and sat back with a relieved sigh at the jovial woman Laura introduced as Pina.

"So," she said leaning both dimpled elbows on the table. "You are Elena." Her voice was a bright neon pink and the final few trepidations vanished from Elena's mind.

Elena nodded. "Thank you for coming over to talk to me."

Pina waved her thanks away. "Laura told me you would want to speak to me some day." She slurped from the cappuccino Laura had put in front of her. *"Grazie,* Laura. So, Elena, tell me what you want to know."

Elena was taken aback at the sudden question. What did she want to know? "Well, I guess my first question is, why was I given up for adoption?"

Pina scrutinized Elena. "All right. Your birth mother was Sicilian. Her parents had brought her here a few months before she got pregnant. She was a good girl by the standards of the old country. She went to mass, she helped out her family by taking a job, she never spoke to boys–well, she barely spoke English when I met her."

"Then how did she get pregnant?" Lucia broke in.

"Ah, well, tragically, it was as happens with so many young immigrant girls. They get lonely; they have no one to talk to. There was a man, an Italian man, who was much older than her, and he convinced her they were in love. She was only seventeen, and she was so innocent. It didn't even occur to her she might get pregnant." Pina paused, and sipped her *cappuccino.*

Elena was leaning forward into the table. "Do you know who the father was?"

"No, your birth mother never told anyone. At first when she realized she might be pregnant, she was terrified. All she wanted to do, even before we'd confirmed her pregnancy, was to go to church and confess. But after…" Pina paused and ran her fingers through the curly mop on her head, "…I always thought it was strange. The moment she confessed, everything changed. She became calm, confident. It was as if she grew up ten years in the space of a few spoken words to the priest. Just like that," Pina snapped her fingers. "She knew what she wanted to do. No questions, not a single worry if her plan was right."

Elena couldn't hold herself back. "What? What did she want to do?"

"She decided to give you up for adoption. There was no discussion; she didn't ask any questions. And, she refused to involve the father. She kept saying, 'She needs to stay here.' And that was the other strange thing. She knew before her pregnancy was even confirmed you would be a girl. She never once referred to you as he or it or the baby–it was always she or her. Strange."

Pina paused to take one of several golden biscotti from a plate Laura placed on the table. "The priest, Father Ignazio, and I met with this poor girl to tell her family what had happened. Her father couldn't have taken it any worse. He was ready to throw her out of the house. She was young but she handled it as if she were a woman of thirty. Her father, your grandfather, was a brute of a man. Violent with his wife, and would have been violent with your mother, I think, if the priest had not been there. But she stood up to her father as did her mother–something I had not expected. I arranged for her to stay in a foster home and she wrote to her nonna in Sicily who agreed once the baby had been born she would take her granddaughter in. I phoned her before the birth and she had some choice words about her son, I must say." Pina chuckled at the memory. "In any case, both of them insisted we find an Italian Catholic family for the baby. That's where your Uncle Tony came in. Laura was working as a nurse in the hospital. Your Uncle Tony had heard through the grapevine at his shop that a Sicilian girl was looking for an Italian family to adopt her baby. He told your Aunt Laura, she talked to me. And voila! You had a family."

"Well, Pina, it wasn't that simple," Laura interjected. "Sal and Carla had lots of paperwork and hoops to jump through."
Pina waved that away, "Window-dressing. Trappings. The important thing was you had a good home to go to."

Elena was looking at the table, the characteristic frown line between her brows. "So, she went back to Sicily."

"That's right."

Elena looked up and into Pina's eyes. "So I have no chance of finding her."

Pina's animated face grew still. "I never said that."

"But, if she isn't here, how can I possibly find out her name?"

There was a heavy pause, before Pina replied. "I remember her name."

"You do? But, but, I thought you weren't allowed to tell me."

The movement came back to Pina's face as she winked at Elena. "What are they going to do to me, fire me? I've been retired for years. Take away my pension? The union wouldn't let that happen. Anyhow, I know people, and I can see in your face what I say here will stay here. I believe you can keep your source to yourself, can't you?"

Elena nodded, eyes transfixed on Pina.

Pina leaned forward and cupped Elena's chin in her soft hand. "Your mother's name is Cristiana Esposito and she went back to live in Sperlinga."

Chapter six

ALBERGO DI SCALE DEI TURCHI

~AGOSTO 2011~

ELENA PULLED OVER TO THE SIDE OF THE ROAD. She had taken a turn towards Menfi as she drove to Agrigento where she planned to spend the night. As she stepped out of the car the hot, dry air wrapped itself around her and immediately droplets of sweat appeared unbidden on her forehead. The road was deserted, but not desolate. The sky was the same azure as the sea. In brilliant contrast were the golden hills of dried soil and durum wheat. Beside her were rows of olive and almond trees and huge prickly pear cactus. Other than the distant sound of cars on the *autostrada* and the occasional bee, it was silent, but warm and full of life. She gazed with wonder around her–wonder that she had never seen this beautiful island, and yet it had only taken a few words on a Canadian government document half the world away to put her on the road to her homeland. She breathed, filling her lungs, and smelling the richness of the land around her.

Elena stretched, and looked at the ruined blouse she was wearing. She pulled it off what had been a white blouse, and from her carry-on, grabbed the Japandroids t-shirt Gerry had given her at the airport when she left.

"That's my favourite band–I want that back when you get home." He warned her.

She pulled the t-shirt on over her head and tucked the ruined shirt into her bag. As she did that, she noticed a ziplock bag peeking out from under her clothes. It was the GPS Lucia had lent her. She had forgotten all about it.

"Well, you will be useful." Elena commented to the GPS. She climbed back into the car and plugged the GPS into the cigarette lighter. She scrolled through the voice settings, and settled on 'young female'. She set the GPS to Agrigento and started up the car.

As Elena pulled forward onto the rough, cracked road, the GPS voice spoke its first sultry, sienna-toned words. "Go straight for two kilometres."

"Hmmm." Elena wondered aloud. "I wasn't expecting an Italian accent. Must have installed when Lucia downloaded the Italian maps."

The rolling landscape inched by. The stunning orange hills seemed to glow from within in the rich Mediterranean sunlight. Every now and then she would get a glimpse of the brilliant sea, sunlight sparkling like precious gemstones on the calm surface. The air conditioning in the car felt like an icy disconnect from the warmth all around her. She pushed the button switching off the AC and opened the windows to feel the breeze. Immediately sweat appeared on her upper lip but Elena was grateful to feel the authentic richness of her homeland, and a little sweat seemed a small price to pay.

"Turn left in 200 metres."

Sure enough, a sign reading 'Agrigento" pointed to the left. Elena followed the turn and found herself on a road lined with vineyards on each side. The broad grape leaves and ripening purple grapes swayed in the gentle breeze drifting across the land from the Mediterranean. A faint, sweet musk touched her nostrils, then turned and fled.

When the GPS told her to turn right onto the autostrada, Elena almost didn't turn. The backroad was so peaceful. But the *autostrada,* smooth and modern, would take her to her hotel. The posted speed limit was 110 kilometres per hour, but the few cars sharing the smooth highway with her, passed her by as if she were caught in some ancient time warp. She pressed her foot harder on the gas and watched the speedometer needle creep up until she and her Fiat were keeping time at 150 with the other cars.

The landscape changed. Houses made of stone and tile appeared more frequently and wine grapes, olives, and orange trees stood in the fields adjacent to the houses. When the GPS told her to turn right she and the little Panda left the *autostrada,* happy to be back on the narrow state road. Elena pulled into a gas station and up to the pump at which the attendant stood waiting.

"Fill please." She said in the same Sicilian she used with Mr. Sarducci, the owner of the gas station near her house. The sunburnt attendant grunted a gruff *"Si"* as he wiped his forehead with a handkerchief stiff with his sweat and dust that blew across the Mediterranean from the Sahara.

Elena pulled out her guidebook and searched for the hotel at which she had planned to stay. *Albergo di Scale dei Turchi.* The Turkish Steps Hotel. It was given a high rating in the guide and, even better, was relatively cheap. She punched the exact address into the GPS as the grouchy attendant finished filling the Fiat.

"Sessanta euro. Sixty euro."

Elena counted out the unfamiliar bills, and handed sixty euros to the attendant. As she pulled out onto the road, the smooth Italian tones of the GPS gave her instructions.

"Turn left in 200 metres... curve to the right in 150 metres. A sharp left in 100 metres." Elena followed the instructions meticulously until at last the GPS said, "Destination in 50 metres." Elena pulled over and got out of the car. Lifting her hands to shade her eyes, she gazed about trying to spot *Albergo di Scale dei Turchi.* The buildings around her wore no signs and none appeared to be a hotel. Sitting on a folding chair was a black-clad elderly woman dozing in the shade. Elena drew near the woman, almost tip-toeing, not wishing to frighten her.

"Ma va scusari signu. Unne' Albergo di Scale dei Turchi? 'Where is the Turkish Steps Hotel?'"

The woman jumped and then opened her eyes wide like a yawn, shook her head, and stared up at Elena with curiosity.

"Ccà non c'e' Albergo di Scale dei Turchi. 'There is no Turkish Steps Hotel here.'"

Putting her hand to her forehead, Elena turned her back to the old woman. She sucked in a frustrated breath and pulled out her Lonely Planet guidebook, opened it and handed it to the old woman.

"This is the hotel I'm looking for." Elena spoke the round Sicilian syllables once more in case the woman had misheard her.

The woman secured a pair of taped, black-rimmed glasses on her nose, and peered at the book.

"Ah! Here is your problem. *Albergo di Scale dei Turchi i*s in Porto Empedocle near Agrigento!" The woman slapped the pages of the book together as if in triumph.

"So, where are we?" Elena shook her head. She thought she had been heading to Agrigento.

"Punta Grande of course!"

"Dammit." Elena muttered in English. The elderly woman focused a sharp gaze on Elena.

"You are not Italian?"

"No."

"Where are you from?" she asked, her eyes narrowing.

"I'm Canadian." Elena replied.

"Why is your Sicilian so good?" The old woman tilted her head away from Elena, scanning her.

"My parents were Sicilian. My first language is Sicilian. I didn't speak any English until I started school."

The change in the woman's face was immediate. "Ah, so you have come home to visit!" She heaved herself to her feet. She motioned Elena to follow her. "Is this your first night is Sicily?"

Elena nodded.

"You can't stay in a hotel your first night here. Where did you land, Catania? Palermo?" She didn't wait for Elena's answer. It was as if Elena had correctly answered some magical question that gave her the keys to a by-gone kingdom. Elena followed the old woman into the entrance foyer with a surprisingly beautiful marble floor and staircase. The outside of the building was plain stone and mortar, arranged at random, with no ornamentation save a wrought iron balcony on the second floor.

"This is…beautiful!" Elena stammered in surprised Sicilian.

"Grazii," answered the old woman, tossing a warm smile back at Elena, as she laboured up the stairs, "My husband's father put in this marble when my husband was a little boy. Come, come."

Elena followed in awe up the lovely staircase.

"My name is Francesca." The old woman turned down a narrow hallway. "The bathroom is here. We don't have much water so the town turns it off in the daytime. It is back on now." She continued a few steps farther, and turned in at another doorway. "This is the bedroom." She padded across the dark room to the window and pulled the blinds.

Elena gasped as the light brought visibility to the room. It was huge–easily double the size of her own bedroom at home–and filled with antiques. Over the bed was a sad-faced Madonna in the requisite blue robes. Above the window, running the length of the room, was a shelf adorned with ancient household goods–Venetian glass vases, a cast iron clothing press, a stoneware jug, blue Italian patterned plates. But when she turned around, Elena caught her breath with excitement. Against the wall leaned a gleaming antique cello beside an equally ancient and well-maintained piano. Music that Elena recognized as Verdi sat on a wooden music stand close by.

Francesca was busy brushing invisible dust from the already spotless white bedspread. Elena gestured to the instruments. "Do you play?"

Francesca looked up and gave Elena a distant smile. "Oh, now and then. Not so much since my husband passed away."

Elena looked at the sad smile on Francesca's face. She reached out her hand to the elderly woman, and said with heartfelt and gentle words, "Thank you so much for welcoming me into your home."

Francesca stopped at the tenderness in Elena's voice, and gave her a surprised smile. "*È nenti.*" She replied. "It's nothing."

Chapter seven

A GIFT OF MUSIC

FRANCESCA BUSIED HERSELF IN THE KITCHEN. As the sauce simmered, Elena's mouth watered at the amazing garlic and oregano fragrances wafting across the kitchen. She sat and sipped home-made wine and listened to Francesca talk about Agrigento, Sicily, and her life with her husband Antonino.

Elena had showered and napped before dinner–grateful that Sicilians ate so much later than she was used to in Canada. She felt refreshed and most definitely hungry.

Francesco placed a plate of *antipasti*–olives, cheese, *salami,* and vegetables–on the table.

"Now, I have talked too much. I want to hear about you. Where in Canada are you from? Toronto? Montreal? My late husband's cousin lives in Montreal."

Elena had just bit into the sharp, strong flavour of a piece of *provolone* cheese, and had closed her eyes to appreciate the wonderful taste before answering.

"No, I'm from Vancouver, on the west coast, but my whole family, are from a small mountain village near Sciacca–it's called Cianciana."

Francesca nodded, "That explains your Sicilian. You speak Sicilian like someone from forty years ago. Each village has its own dialect. Yours is different from mine, but not so different I can't understand you. But I could tell it was from the mountains." Francesca paused to pour herself some more wine. "So, are you here to meet your relatives–see your homeland?"

"Well, yes," Elena replied, "But not in the way you think."

Francesca spooned plump eggplant pieces onto their plates, added sauce and sprinkled grated *tumazzu* cheese on top. As she sat she said, "We have all evening. If you would like to tell me, I would like to hear."

Elena paused to gather her thoughts, then told Francesca the story of her adoption, and why she had come to Sicily. Along with her tale, she poured out her fears and trepidations about finding her birth mother. "I want to meet her but what if she doesn't want to meet me?"

Francesca reached across the table, and patted Elena's hands. "Your mother will want to meet you. Mother's never forget their children. I know. I lost my first baby when I was eighteen years old. That was seventy years ago."

Elena scrutinized Francesca's face, astonished. This woman was 88 years old? Elena would have placed her at no more than 60.

Francesca continued, "My Antonino missed his son until the day he died. He said to me before he went to our Lord, even though he was sad to leave me, he was happy because he was going to join our son. And I know I will feel the same."

A quiet pause fell over the kitchen as both women withdrew into thoughts of those lost. Elena shook off the momentary sadness and asked Francesca, "How did you learn to play the piano and cello?"

Francesca gazed out the window at the golden glow of the setting sun, and sighed. "It was after the war ended. My parents sent me here to work and send money home. I washed clothes, and cooked, and cleaned for a family that had lost their mother and grandmother in the bombings. Next door there was a young man, a very handsome young man. Everyday I would see him coming home from work, and then I would hear beautiful music floating through the open doors. I used to wait to sweep the living room just so I could be next to the door when he played. I didn't know it at the time, but he was playing the cello."

Francesca rose and shuffled across the room to pick up a small framed black and white photo. She gazed at it for a moment then handed it to Elena. In it Elena saw a serious faced young man with curly dark hair hanging below his ears, unusual for what must have been the early 1950s. One hand held the neck of a beautiful cello, and the other hand held the end of a bow tucked under his arm.

"This is Antonino?"

Francesca nodded.

"He is handsome–and serious." Elena handed the photograph back to Francesca.

"He was serious about his music, but he had a wonderful sense of humour too. One day, he began to throw pebbles at my balcony. I would go out to sweep in the morning and I would find them everywhere. I thought they were from the birds, or perhaps the two boys I was taking care of but they denied it, and I never saw a bird drop anything on our balcony. At first there were one or two, then a few more and a few more until there were handfuls every evening. One day, I decided to hide behind the curtain to catch the rascal who was making all this mess for me to clean up. I waited until it was late and well after dark, and then I heard it."

"What?" asked Elena leaning forward.

"The sound of pebbles hitting the balcony. I burst out onto the balcony and shouted 'Ah ha!'. He jumped back, and put his hands behind his back looking very guilty indeed."

"What did he say?"

"Well, he admitted it had been him all along, and he was doing it to meet me. After, we spent time together secretly–back then unmarried women never spent time alone with men but his mother caught us talking. To cover up he told her that I was asking him about music lessons. Suddenly we had the perfect reason for spending time together. He taught me cello and later piano, and we were married a few months later. My father was not happy because I could no longer send money home but my mother was relieved to have me married."

Elena nodded. "My father was the same–he encouraged me to go to school, but I know he wanted me married so he wouldn't have to worry about me. Instead, I became a musician."

Francesca sat up. "You are a musician? But why didn't you say anything? What do you play?"

"Guitar and piano mostly. Sometimes I sing or play the banjo or organ. I played the organ in our church when the organist was away or sick."

Francesca clapped her hands. "We must play together! I haven't had anyone to play music with since my dear Antonino died! Come!" Francesca stood up and grasped Elena's hands. Elena smiled at

Francesca's enthusiasm as she allowed herself to be pulled into the bedroom where the piano and cello sat. Francesca let go of Elena's hands and rifled through a tidy pile of sheet music and music books.

"Here!" Francesca cried out. "This is what we will play!" She opened a music book and placed it on the piano. Elena looked at the piece–Franz Liszt's Liebestraum.

"I've heard this one, of course, but I've never played it. I usually play jazz or pop, but I can try if we go slowly at first." Elena looked over at Francesca's empty music stand. "Don't you need music as well?"

Francesca waved her hand dismissively. "I have played this so many times I will probably be playing it on my way to heaven! And Antonino used this to warm up before he had a performance...did I tell you he played at the Opera House in Palermo? He was celebrated for his playing here in Sicily." Her eyes crinkled with joy. As she listened, Elena could imagine Francesca playing piano or cello along side the serious faced young man in the picture.

Francesca settled the bow against the cello strings, and played a few practice notes. "Ready?"

Elena nodded, and soon the sweet coral sounds of the cello mixed with the deeper, honey colour of the piano, and the two of them were swept away–one by her memories, the other by the colours, and both by the beautiful sounds of the instruments.

Chapter eight

FAREWELL TO FRANCESCA

A WARM STRIPE OF SUNSHINE walked its way across Elena's cheek, and lay across her still closed eyes. The rich, insistent scent of *espresso* tickled her nose. A yawn, a stretch, and Elena opened her eyes to gaze at the graceful lines of the cello in the corner of the room.

She smiled at the thought of the wonderful musical evening she had spent the night before. She had imagined many things when she planned her trip to Sicily, but an evening playing piano to a stranger's cello was not one of them.

Elena rose and pulled on her clothes, anticipating the first sip of the rich coffee. She could hear Francesca in the kitchen singing Sicilian folk songs Elena recognized from family get-togethers back home. The sound filled her with silver memories of Christmas, and Easter, and weddings, and birthdays. Taking great care, she smoothed the lovely bedspread before she turned and left the bedroom.

"*Bon giornu!*" Francesca cried out.

"*Bon giornu,* Francesca. How are you this morning?"

"*Stupendu!* Wonderful! I have not felt so happy in a long time. I think," she said as she placed a cup in front of Elena, "it must be the music. The last time those two instruments were played together was before my husband died." Francesca pushed a plate of biscotti in front of Elena. "*Mancia, mancia.* Eat, eat."

"*Grazii.*" Elena reached for an almond *biscotto.*

"So, where does your journey take you today?" Francesca asked.

"It's a small town–only 700 or so people live there. It's called Sperlinga." Elena finished a sip of *espresso* and looked up to see Francesca's mouth drop open.

"Sperlinga? You didn't say your mother was from Sperlinga!" Francesca gasped.

"I didn't think you would have heard of it–it's so small." Elena leaned back at Francesca's surprised reaction.

Francesca grasped Elena's arm. "I am from Sperlinga!"

It was Elena's turn to look astonished. "But…" Elena ran her hands through her thick hair, "…this is remarkable!"

"When was your mother born?" Francesca asked.

"I'm not certain," Elena replied, "But I think it would have been around 1962."

"Ah, much after I left." Francesca shook her head. "I wouldn't have known her. But here! I can still help you." Francesca reached for a note-pad.

"Take this paper, and ask for this woman–she is my cousin–she has never left Sperlinga. If anyone would know, it would be her."

Elena picked up the scrap of paper and in Francesca's spidery handwriting, she read the name 'Angelina Lo Bianco'.

"Tell her you stayed here with me, Francesca Lo Bianco. She is getting old and forgetful, but if you give her my name she will be happy to help you." Francesca took both of Elena's hands in her own and squeezed. "If your mother came from Sperlinga, it is possible we are *famigghia,* family." Francesca's eyes watered a little. "Tell Angelina your story. She will know if we are related."

After breakfast, Elena carried her single bag out to the car. After she had tucked her duffle into a corner of the trunk, she turned to Francesca, and gave her a tight Canadian style hug. She stepped back but Francesca caught her, and kissed her on each cheek. Elena's voice caught in her throat as she tried to thank Francesca. She cleared her throat, and managed to squeak out, *"Grazii* Francesca. *Grazii pi tutti cosi,* thank you for everything. I will call soon and tell you how my travels are going."

Francesca swatted Elena's arm. "Now go on–you have a long drive." She pressed a paper-wrapped package into Elena's hands. From the strong scent Elena knew there was warm *provolone* cheese and from the shape, a loaf of bread, and a bottle of wine.

"Grazii, Francesca. *Grazii milli."*

Elena climbed into the Fiat, placed the package on the already warm seat next to her, and started up the car. She set the GPS to

Sperlinga, tooted the horn, and pulled out into the road as Francesca waved in her rear-view mirror.

Chapter nine

AN UNEXPECTED DISCOVERY

AS IT HAD BEEN THE DAY BEFORE, the weather proved to be bright and hot. Elena drove away from the coast, and into the mountains of central Sicily, hoping the elevation would bring a cooler temperature. Instead, as she wound up the mountain roads, the dry earth was baked harder, and it was hotter than she had expected. Elena was still determined to not give in to the necessity of air conditioning. The breeze blew hot on her face, and with amber bursts, the cicadas' humming filled her eyes and ears beneath the rush of the wind. The soft, dark Italian voice of the GPS whispered to her, "One hundred metres, sharp curve to the right." The Panda hugged the cliff face, tires complaining with a silvery whine, and as the road straightened Elena found herself pitched head long into a darkened tunnel. She scrambled to turn on the lights as she opened her eyes as wide as she could, blinking hard. She slammed on the brakes as two unexpected, but placid cows appeared in the dim, cool light, seeking relief from the hard heat of the day. She skidded to a halt with several feet to spare. Heart pounding, she swore, "*Minchia!*"

Elena leaned out her window and yelled, "*Andiamo!* Let's go!" The cows just blinked. She tooted the Fiat's horn–a non-imposing 'meep-meep' which did nothing to the cows, but make them shake their horns at her. Finally, Elena edged forward, honking until she was a few inches away. With a disdainful shake of her head, one of the cows moved into the other lane allowing Elena to edge by.

As she drove out of the tunnel, she gasped. On her right, there was a steep rocky slope dotted with huge flat-leafed cactus sprouting brightly coloured prickly pears. On the left, the slope eased to a gentler incline spreading out with fields of golden wheat surrounded by rows of green olive and almond trees. Not a house could be seen in the fields—only the occasional ramshackle stone shack. Ahead of her, the road wound up the steep rock face to a group of ancient stone buildings clinging like still mountain goats, and melting into the grey stone face of the mountain.

She inched the car forward, cutting back and forth along hairpin turns. The road straightened, and she drove between the first of the bleached stone buildings to a small piazza where she slowed to a stop. Along one side there were stone benches in the sliver of shade from a building. Perched in the shade, like ancient olive trees, were three elderly men, leaning on their canes, hands twisted and knotted with arthritis, buttoned shirts open at the neck, and all wearing peaked hats. The man on the end had oxygen strapped under his nose. His eyes were half closed and Elena wondered for a moment if he were breathing at all. But, as the other two men discussed the business of the town, the crops, and their children, the third man nodded in agreement, and Elena realized with relief he was alive.

She stepped out of her car and stretched. The men stopped their conversation, and stared at her openly. She nodded, and said a pleasant *"Bon giorno,"* and the suspicious looks broke into wide grins.

"Bon giornu, bon giornu. Where are you from? Palermo?"

Elena laughed, and walked towards the men. *"Grazii,* thank you for complimenting my Sicilian. I am from Canada."

"Ah, Canada. Giulio, didn't your son go to Canada?"

"No, no. He went to Marsaille."

"Bah, Canada, Marsaille—they all speak French."

And the other two nodded at the wisdom of what he had said.

"Signurina. The bar there is my grandson's. Tell him Giulio said to give you a *gelato.* My treat."

"Oh, I couldn't possibly accept." Elena answered following Italian custom. It would be impolite to accept on the first offer.

"Don't be ridiculous! It's only a *gelato,* and his *gelato..."* Giulio kissed his fingers and raised his eyes to the sky. "I taught him to make it myself. But ask for *cicculatta,* a chocolate. It is the best. His *pistachio* is shit."

Elena grinned and said, *"Grazii Signuri* Giulio. If you taught him, I will enjoy a *cicculatta."* Elena walked into the bar and a wall of air-conditioned cool.

"Bon giornu!" she called to a bent over back she assumed was Giulio's grandson.

The back straightened and turned to reveal a burly young man. *"Bon giornu, signurina.* What would you like?"

Elena felt an arrow of fear shoot through her. Under a mop of wildly curly hair, his frowning eyebrows–or rather eyebrow as it was really only one–shaded his one blue eye, a gift, undoubtedly, from some long past Norman ancestor, the other eye covered by a black patch. Snaking out from under the patch, a scar slithered its way down his cheek, curving back and coming to rest beneath his earlobe. His face was whiskered–it seemed he had not shaved that morning nor perhaps the morning before. His face was fearsome.

"I'm sorry to bother you. An elderly gentleman, Giulio, in the piazza, suggested I try your *gelato."* Elena stammered.

The fearful face transformed as it broke into a wide and open grin.

"Giulio? That's my *nonnu,* my grandfather. Did he tell you my *pistachio* is shit?"

Elena nodded in relief as the young man chuckled, and shook his head.

"It's not shit. It's just not as good as his. Do you like chocolate? The chocolate is my best."

"I love chocolate, *grazii."*

He chuckled again. "What woman doesn't like chocolate? Especially a beautiful one." His good eye appraised her under his raised brow.

Elena blushed, and looked at her dusty sandals.

Giulio wobbled into the bar behind her, gripping his wooden cane with white fingers. Elena jumped forward, hand outstretched, fearful the old man would fall. Waving her away, he tottered to a worn wooden chair.

"Marcello, give me a *gelato* as well–none of that *pistachio* shit." The young man, Marcello, grinned and handed her the *gelato* with a wink of his good eye.

"Now, I'm paying for that. A stranger who speaks Sicilian is a rare thing, and in this town, the stranger never pays." Giulio motioned to a chair next to the window. "Sit, sit! I want to hear why a Sicilian-speaking Canadian girl would want to come to a town like Sperlinga. We have no beaches, no cathedrals, and no museums. All we have are the caves and the castle."

Elena wiped her face with a napkin, cleaning off the last sticky drops of the sweet chocolate *gelato*.

"Actually, it's a person I'm looking for." Elena paused. "Her name is Cristiana Esposito."

"Cristiana Esposito? I don't know her. Nonnu?" Marcello turned to his grandfather and raised his voice a little. "Have you ever heard of her?"

Giulio tilted his head to one side, squinting his eyes as he peered up to the ceiling. "Yes, I think I remember her."

Elena's body tensed, and leaned forward.

"She went to America I think. Or maybe England. I'm not sure. She came back to visit her *nanna* for a while but she left here a long time ago. I don't know where she is now."

Elena's shoulders drooped, disappointed.

"But I know who could tell you." Marcello finished wiping up the brown drips of *gelato* from the counter, and threw his rag into the sink. He untied his apron, and said, "*Signura* Lo Bianco. She keeps the history of Sperlinga locked safely here." He tapped the side of his head. "I'll take you there."

"Do you mean Angelina Lo Bianco?"

Not a flicker of surprise crossed Marcello's face but Elena's mouth dropped when he answered "*Sì, certu.* Of course."

How could it be that she would be directed to the same woman in a tiny mountain village twice in the same day? She felt a shiver in spite of the heat that hit her like a wall as she stepped out of the bar.

"*Nonnu,* I'll be back later. You should stay in the cool while I'm out."

"*Vatinni.* Go, go." Giulio waved his grandson away. "I'll be fine."

Marcello shut the door to the shop, and hung a sign reading "*chiusu*" –closed–from the doorknob.

"Follow me. *Signura* Lo Bianco lives in the caves. We have to walk. Your car won't make it there."

Elena skidded to a halt. "She lives in a cave?"

Marcello called over his shoulder "*Sì.* She's only one of two people left who do."

Elena ran to catch up with him. "What do you mean she lives in a cave?"

"You don't know about the caves?" Marcello questioned her, his single eyebrow raised in surprise, as he slowed his pace to allow her to come abreast with him. "Most foreigners who come here do so because they have read about the caves." They turned a sharp corner that led onto a street with a view of the hill to their left. "Look up there." Marcello pointed.

Elena's eyes followed his gesture. She could make out what seemed to be rows of... "Doors? Are those doors in the side of the mountain?"

Marcello laughed out loud at her astonished look.

"*Sì.* The people of Sperlinga have lived in caves for generations. I heard from my grandfather that before there were the caves there were houses that were demolished in an earthquake. To make safer homes, they dug into the sandstone and built the caves. My father says it was to hide from invaders - Greeks, Carthaginians, Romans."

Elena was staggered. If that were true, the cave homes had been there since before the time of Christ!

The steep hill Marcello was following soon precluded any conversation. Sweat ran down Elena's back, and she wiped her forehead with her arm to keep the salt from running into her eyes. They wound back and forth up the hill until, without warning, Marcello took a sharp right turn and stopped. Elena found herself standing, panting, on the precipice of what seemed to be a cliff edge.

"Careful. If you trip here there is no way to stop yourself from falling."

Elena's stomach dropped as she looked over the edge and out across the valley. Marcello stepped forward, and Elena gasped, sure he was stepping off the cliff. Instead of falling to his death, he turned back to give her a quizzical look. Hidden from her view, were steep stairs traversing the edge of the mountain, taking them to what she could now see was a ledge below. Elena edged her way closer to the steps. Marcello offered his hand, and Elena gratefully accepted it. Slowly, step-by-step, they descended the stairs onto a wide ledge. Elena's mouth dropped open. What she couldn't see from above was a trellis covered with vines–wide flat leaves and green not-yet-ripe grapes. Flower boxes filled with plumeria and snapdragons brightened the sun-bleached stone with amber, pink and red. Next to the weathered boxes was an equally weathered door flanked by two open windows from which crisp, white curtains fluttered. Along the ledge was another door–this one propped open, but with a wide wooden board leaning across the lower section. From the open door, Elena could hear...chickens? She shook her head, trying to clear her ears, thinking she must be hearing things.

Marcello grinned at her. "Chickens," he said. "Chickens, two goats, and maybe a pig." He gestured towards the door. Elena walked over and peered into the darkened space. It took a moment for her eyes to adjust but when they did, Elena was dumbfounded. Carved into the stone was a cave, easily 20 feet deep and 15 feet wide. The walls had pictures painted by a childish hand, but most startling were the placid eyes of the two goats staring up at her, and the soft snoring of a sleeping sow in chorus with the suckling of eight little piglets. The pungent odor of the pigs made her ease back from the door. From behind Marcello, the door in the stone wall creaked open and a slight, elderly woman, back bent forward– a sign of decades of hard work and osteoporosis–stepped onto the ledge.

"Bon giornu, Marcello! *Como stai?* How are you?"

"Stupennu, Signura Lo Bianco. May I present *Signurina* Elena? She is looking for someone who came from Sperlinga. I've never heard of her, but I thought perhaps you might have."

Signura Lo Bianco's face seemed to light from within as she beamed at Elena. Her teeth were crooked and yellowed from years of espresso and smoking but her eyes were gentle and kind. "Come in, come in! I was just going to make some *cafè!"*

Marcello handed her a paper package he had carried from the shop. "Here, these are a few *biscotti f*rom the bar. My grandfather sends his regards."

"Grazii, grazii. These will go well with our *cafè." Signura* Lo Bianco turned, and walked into her home. Elena followed, and gazed, dumbfounded. The room was much the same size as the cave with the animals but in this one the walls and ceiling had been scrubbed clean and

whitewashed. The spotless floor was covered with a large throw rug on which sat a wooden table whose top had been polished to a high sheen. On the right, was a traditional stone pizza oven in front of which sat several loaves of freshly baked bread, their fragrant aroma carrying Elena back to her Aunt Laura's kitchen. On the wall, next to the oven, hung a large framed portrait of the Virgin Mary wrapped in blue with an otherworldly expression on her face. What most surprised Elena, however, were the electric lights, the electric hotplate, and the small refrigerator. If she were to ever imagine a home in a cave, she certainly wouldn't imagine a cozy, spotless cave with electricity!

"Your home," she said, "It's...amazing!"

"Would you like to see the other rooms?" *Signura* Lo Bianco's eyes crinkled.

"Oh please," Elena answered, "I've never seen a home in a cave before."

Signura Lo Bianco gestured Elena through a small low archway. She ducked her head, and shuffled her way into a bedroom. A soft looking bed took most of the space but a small dresser with a mirror, polished and without a smudge, was tucked into a corner. Between the mirror and the bed, carved into the wall was a depression with a piece of doweling across, from which the elderly woman's clothes hung evenly and neatly. Along the walls, framed and in precise rows, were black and white pictures, some yellowed with age: a young man looking stiff and uncomfortable in his suit with an ill fitting collar, two young women in long skirts sitting next to a table with a vase of flowers, an old couple, the man, face lined with sun and hard work, knotted arthritic hands holding tightly to the head of his cane, stared, proud and serious, at the camera. His wife, dressed all in black, stood close yet not touching, eyes gazing softly down, her face also lined with work and sun and the grief of lost family, and lost time.

Elena jumped when *Signura* Lo Bianco said from behind Elena's shoulder "They were my parents. They lived a long time–everyone in my family does. They both lived into their nineties. My mother was still washing clothes by hand the day she died. She had a stroke–dropped to the floor like a stone. My father was hit with cancer. Fortunately, it was quick. He believed he was cursed with *malocchio*–the evil eye."

Signura Lo Bianco kissed the tips of her fingers and reached up to stroke the face of her father, crossed herself, and kissed her fingers once again.

"Now, let me make you that *cafè* that I promised you. Come back to the kitchen."

Elena and Marcello sat at the table while *Signura* Lo Bianco fussed around in the kitchen. She and Marcello talked about people in the village, how the olives, and almonds, and the wheat crop were doing this season. Moment by moment, the table filled with food—a large gourd-shaped *provolone* cheese, fresh bread, garlic-scented *salami*, glistening olives, cold, grilled peppers soaked in oil. And the *biscotti*. As the room filled with the scent of coffee *Signura* Lo Bianco turned back to the table.

"Eat, eat! After walking all the way up here you must be hungry." She poured the *cafè* into three tiny, gleaming white cups and served Elena and Marcello before sitting down to join them.

"Now, what is it you want to know?" She placed her hand over Elena's, and with her warm smile Elena felt safety in telling this elderly woman the whole story.

"I'm looking for a woman named Cristiana Esposito—she should be about forty-five. I think she might be... my mother." Elena told the story as she had been told, and finished with "Do you know anything about her?"

Signura Lo Bianco stood and turned from the table. Elena watched her take a handkerchief from her pocket, and raise it to wipe her eyes. She reached up to a shelf below the portrait of the Virgin. She took a small cookie tin, and placed it on the table.

"I didn't ever think this day would come. I knew she had a child—or at least I suspected she had—I wondered if I would ever meet you." *Signura* Lo Bianco opened the tin to reveal a small pile of photographs. She shuffled through them and handed one to Elena. It was a woman, likely in her thirties, caught in the midst of hanging laundry; she was laughing as she brought a small towel up to her face. The photographer had snapped the picture just before her face was covered—her black hair was pulled back but a few stray strands hung on either side of her oval face. The beginning of a few wrinkles were showing themselves, softening the expression but outlining her eyes. Her eyes—these drew Elena's gaze the most. They were crinkled and joy-filled and... familiar. Elena had seen those eyes in every picture that had been taken of her since she was a small child. If nothing else, the eyes convinced Elena this was indeed a picture of her mother. Her hand trembled. She was sitting with strangers who were possibly family, seeing a picture of her mother for the first time.

"This is my...mother...," Elena stammered a little.

"Yes," *Signura* Lo Bianco said simply.

Marcello gazed at the picture over Elena's shoulder. "She looks like you... or, I guess you look like her."

"Yes, I do, don't I?" Elena looked up at them with an enormous grin on her face. "I do look like my mother." She turned to *Signura* Lo Bianco. "May I keep this photo?"

"Of course you may," *Signura* Lo Bianco said to Elena gently, "But you should know, she is no longer in Sperlinga. In fact, she left here about ten or twelve years ago, not long after that picture was taken. When she came back to Sperlinga she lived with her grandmother, helping her around the house–she took in washing, to bring in extra money–but when her grandmother died she packed up her home, sold the few things her grandmother had, and left Sperlinga."

"Do you know where she went?" Elena asked.

"She said she was going to Messina. She'd heard of a job there, working in a restaurant. She wrote me once after she arrived, but that is all I know. I haven't heard from Cristiana since."

"And you don't know the name of the restaurant?"

"No, but I think it was a small place, near the water. She talked about walking to the harbour on her lunch break. She said in some ways it reminded her of where she had lived in Canada." *Signura* Lo Bianco paused. "There is one more thing I should tell you. Cristiana's grandmother and my dear late husband, Massimo, were siblings. He was your mother's great uncle–which means I am your great-great aunt."

Elena froze, her eyes locked onto *Signura* Lo Bianco. The elderly woman patted Elena's hands and said kindly, "I suppose this means you should call me *Zzia* Gina. That is what all my nieces and nephews call me."

Elena blinked hard and turned her head away for a moment, pursing her lips together.

"When I started this journey I thought I was looking for my mother. It never occurred to me I would find family."

Signura Lo Bianco rose to her feet, came around the table and took Elena into her surprisingly strong arms and held her. "Of course you are family." *Signura* Lo Bianco released her hold on Elena, only to step back and take Elena's chin in her right hand. "Sicilians, especially Sicilians from the villages, have long memories. You look like your mother–Cristiana has the same eyes, the same profile. I suspected when you walked in here you were looking for Cristiana. I always hoped you would come looking one day. Blood must find blood." The women held still, mesmerized, looking into each other's eyes.

A small sound interrupted the silence between them as Marcello cleared his throat. The women pulled back and *Signura* Lo Bianco turned her black eyes to Marcello.

"Marcello, can you show Elena the road to Messina?"

"Of course, it isn't difficult. Do you have paper?"

Signura Lo Bianco handed Marcello a lined piece of paper. While he drew a map, the elderly woman, Elena's newfound aunt, rifled through a drawer in her kitchen. She pulled out a small, shiny coloured coin and handed it to Elena. When Elena turned the coin over she saw the enameled face of a serene young woman, eyes up-cast, branches of almond blossoms in her arms. Her dark hair framed her illuminated face and in her hand, she held one white lily. Below her face were the words, '*Santa* Genevra'. Elena looked up at *Signura* Lo Bianco with her eyebrows raised.

"This is *Santa* Genevra. She is not the patron saint of Sperlinga– in fact I don't believe she is the patron saint of anywhere–but I always believed she should be ours instead of John the Baptist. She left her home, and her wealthy family to live in Sperlinga, but she disappeared from the town when the Virgin appeared to her and told her to go and walk–walk until the Madonna told her where she should stop and build a shrine in honour of Her. A Marian shrine–do you know what a Marian shrine is? Any shrine built for *Santa* Maria is a Marian shrine. She suffered so much–she had the stigmata. Keep her with you. She will protect you from all harm. I believe she has a special fondness for all young women and all cave dwellers."

Signura Lo Bianco crossed herself, and kissed her fingers once again.

"*Grazii*. I will keep her with me always," Elena replied. "Thank you for everything. Thank you both." She took *Signura* Lo Bianco's hands. "You have been wonderful."

Chapter ten

DETOUR

ELENA CLIMBED INTO THE CAR, and perched the map on the dashboard in front of her. She edged the car along the narrow lanes leading out of Sperlinga, increasing her speed as she moved out into the golden countryside. It was not far, however, before she found herself stopping the car, and frowning at the map Marcello had drawn.

"What the hell is this?" she muttered. Marcello's squiggles seemed to have no relation to the road she was travelling. Turning the map upside-down, she frowned again, and threw the map on the passenger seat. "Right. GPS, it is." She set the GPS, put the little Fiat in gear and pulled out onto the narrow road.

The road corkscrewed away from the ancient stone buildings and cliffs of Sperlinga and in the space of only a few minutes she was travelling along an empty road, large cactus flowering with dark pink fruit on either side. Elena glanced in the rearview mirror–her eyes were glowing, a wide grin splitting her face. She raised a hand to her cheek and realized her facial muscles were sore from smiling most of the afternoon. Had she only been in Sicily for two days? It seemed like so much longer.

"Destination in one kilometre."

"What? That's not right!" Elena said to the GPS. She reached with one hand to reset the GPS but a curve surprised her and Elena had to grab the steering wheel with both hands. Just then her stomach made a disgruntled noise.

"Time to find a place to eat," Elena told herself. "Then I can reset this GPS." *Signura* Lo Bianco had also provided her with a bag full of bread, cheese, olives, and wonderful *arancini* stuffed with *succu di ragù,* a delicious meat sauce, as well as other mysterious paper packages. All she needed was a place to spread out the little blanket she had brought and she could have a picnic.

"Easier said than done." Elena commented to the cows she saw in the fields. The roads in Sicily were so narrow and winding there was nowhere to pull off safely, and park.

The GPS continued to count down to what it considered the destination. At 100 meters, Elena spotted a dirt road leading off to the right, up the hill. She slowed as she approached it, preparing to turn. The road, if it could be called that, was lined with deep ruts and large rocks, and she pulled off into a farmer's field dotted with olive and lemon trees. She turned up the hill, and followed the rough lane a short 50 metres until she found a spot she could pull off, and not block the road.

"Stupid machine," she muttered at the GPS. Grabbing her blanket from the back, the paper bag full of food, and the bottle of water Marcello had given her before he waved her good-bye, Elena made her way to a shady spot under a large lemon tree. She spread the blanket on the grass, and sat facing the large sun as it dropped bit by bit closer to the horizon.

'I'm going to have to find a place for the night soon.' Elena thought to herself. She had been with *Signura* Lo Bianco far longer than she had realized or intended–it was close to seven o'clock now. She had planned to stay in Sperlinga but the tiny town did not have a *pinsione* much less a hotel.

"I'll eat a little something before I find somewhere to stay," she declared to her lunch bag. She pulled out a paper parcel. Opening it, she found delicately sliced *prisuttu,* cured ham–tantalizing pink with lacy edges, and a wonderful aroma. Another packaged contained a cheese she didn't know, which tasted warm, and strong, and rustic. Fresh bread was in another paper parcel, and a fourth contained two warm, fresh peaches with an aroma that almost made Elena believe in the old gods of Sicily. And finally, the ubiquitous *arancini*–found everywhere in Sicily but nowhere else. A light clanking sound revealed a surprise–two bottles of dark red homemade wine. Elena looked at the wine longingly, but decided to be safe and drink water for the time being.

As she ate the delicious food, Elena watched the sun as it inched its way across the horizon. The light transfixed her. The light in Sicily was different than in Vancouver. More orange–older, wiser. It had seen more. It deepened into a blood red, darkened, and turned blue-black. The slow reveal of stars, moment by moment, mesmerized Elena.

"I'll watch them for a while," she whispered, and lay back on the blanket to watch through the leaves of the lemon tree. As she gazed up at the night sky, she felt the heavens stretch, dome-like, above her. The warmth of the earth seeped through the blanket and into her limbs. The scent of the lemons blended with the dark musky scent of the rich Sicilian earth and the warmth in her body. It felt as if the earth were curving up to meet the sky. She lifted one hand and stretched it up. A soft breeze caressed her and whispered in her ear. For a moment, Elena imagined her father was sitting beside her.

"Papà," she whispered, "Did you bring me to Francesca and *Signura* Lo Bianco? Are you trying to help me find Cristiana?" Her eyes drooped and she struggled to keep them open. The stars, one by one, seemed to enter her and as she closed her eyes she could feel herself moved by the earth's gentle rotation. *"Bona notti, Papà,"* she whispered.

~|~

A soft snuffling sound and a sudden tug on her shirt nudged Elena from a deep sleep into sharp awareness, and she bolted upright. Shaggy, white goats surrounded her. The goat that had tried to taste Elena's clothing had jumped back when she moved, and was now shaking his long, twisted horns at her menacingly.

"Here you, get away from her!"

Elena turned, as much surprised as she was by the American accent as she was by the voice itself. She shook her head when she saw a thirty-ish, blonde woman, sporting a cowboy hat, riding up on a sturdy bay horse.

"Are you okay? I wasn't sure if you were alive or not. I came down the hill and saw all these monsters around you. Don't worry, he won't hurt you. He's just establishing his territory. He's a big baby. Guido! Get away from her!"

Elena eased herself to her feet, carefully testing each of her joints.

"Hello. I'm fine. I didn't intend to fall asleep here last night.

I'm sorry."

"No worries. I doubt the goats minded much. At least you didn't fall asleep in the field with the bull. He's not so sociable." The woman swung herself out of the western saddle and dropped the reins to the ground. She pushed her way through the crowd of goats and held out her hand. "Hi. I'm Annabelle."

"I'm Elena." There was a friendly warmth as she took the hand and looked into the frank green eyes. "How did you know to speak English to me?"

Annabelle's laugh echoed through the fruit trees. "The first clue was the rental car and the second was the 2010 Winter Olympics t-shirt you're wearing. I've been here a few years, but if I'm not mistaken, it was in Vancouver? And third, young Sicilian women don't generally sleep in a stranger's fields."

Elena looked at her shirt. "I guess I wouldn't make much of a spy."

"You want some coffee? I can whip up some *espresso* in a few minutes and you are welcome to have a wash if you like. Then you can tell us how you came to be sleeping in our field," Annabelle grinned.

"That would be wonderful. I would kill for some coffee right about now."

"Can you ride? I don't think your car will make it up the hill but you could climb on behind me if you like. John Wayne, here, has carried two people more than once."

A grin crossed Elena's face. "I don't know if you would call it riding, but I used to get led around on a pony a bunch when I was a kid. I'm game if you think your horse will put up with me. John Wayne, was it?"

"Yup, John Wayne it is. Climb on, pilgrim!" Elena threw her blanket in the car and grabbed her backpack. Annabelle held out her hand and helped Elena scramble up on the back of the horse behind her.

"John Wayne is a San Fratello. They are the only wild horses left on Sicily. My husband's uncle came across John Wayne's mother about five years ago. She was injured and had to be put down, but she had this beautiful foal. I raised him from the time he was about two weeks old. He follows me around when I'm not riding him. He thinks I'm his mother." Annabelle chuckled.

Elena ran her hand along the rump of the beautiful horse, and he nickered back at her.

"He is beautiful. Why do you call him John Wayne?"

Annabelle laughed. "I first met my husband when I came to work here on his family's *agriturismo* about ten years ago. He was dying to keep his English up, and we both loved watching movies. So, in the evenings we would take turns watching English movies and Italian movies, and talking about them in whichever language the movie was in. After we got married, and he took over the *agriturismo* from his parents, we started naming animals after characters or actors from the movies we liked. The goat that woke you up? He's named after Guido from Fellini's 8 ½. Our dog is Ebenezer, and our cats are named after the Von Trapp children."

Elena looked over her shoulder. "Guido is following us."

Annabelle looked back too. "Yes, he'll follow us all the way up. We raised him with a litter of puppies, and now he thinks he is a dog. We have a lot of strange animals on this farm."

As they rounded the hill above the orchard, Elena caught sight of an enormous ancient house in the centre of a busy farmyard. The stone house, covered in luscious pink bougainvillea, seemed to grow out of the landscape.

As if she were reading Elena's mind, Annabelle commented, "The house is about 400 years old, as best we can tell. We've kept it as traditional as possible but we have also modernized a good deal of it, much to my in-law's chagrin."

There were several cars parked in the yard. Between them ran goats, geese, cats, and two or three dogs – Elena wasn't sure as they were twins, or triplets, obviously from the same litter. Two work-hands rode past with chattering tourists on placid ponies.

Annabelle raised her hand and waved, calling out "*Buon giorno*! Have a good ride!"

They stopped close to an ancient barn. "Slide off here." Annabelle said.

Elena managed an awkward landing from the back of John Wayne, and watched with envy as Annabelle gracefully dismounted. Waving Elena towards the farmhouse, the two walked across the yard, avoiding the farm menagerie along the way.

Elena brushed her feet carefully before entering the house, not wanting to tread dirt on the beautiful volcanic stone tiles. They entered a huge open room serving as a kitchen and a living room. The marble countertops gleamed a pale pink, and framed a huge gas stove and an old-fashioned pizza oven. The table in the kitchen was huge, and covered with bright blue, red, and orange tiles.

"*Buon giorno!*" Elena jumped and turned to see a man lying on the couch with his leg in a cast.

"Aldo, this is Elena. She fell asleep in our lemon orchard last night so I invited her up for coffee, and to let her get cleaned up. Elena, this is my husband. He had a disagreement with the barn roof, thus the cast. There is a bathroom through the door at the back. You can get cleaned up there while I put some coffee on."

"Thank you. I won't be long."

Annabelle waved her off. "Take your time. All the guests have already eaten, and taken off for the day."

Chapter eleven

A NEW COUSIN

ELENA STOOD IN FRONT OF THE MIRROR, and groaned at the matted hair and dirty face staring back. The bathroom was modern and beautiful. She was a shocking contrast to the polished pink marble countertop and thick fluffy white towels. She scrubbed her face and hands until she was sure she wouldn't leave any dirt on the pristine towels, then pulled a brush and elastic from her bag, and brought a semblance of neatness to the tangled mess of her hair before rejoining Annabelle and Aldo.

"Did you find everything you need?"

"Yes, thank you. I feel much more human now," Elena answered.

Annabelle placed two cups of coffee on woven placemats, and sat down next to Elena. "It's so kind of you to do this for some stranger who fell asleep in your field. You don't know anything about me."

A chuckle came from the couch. "Annabelle is always picking up strays. Our dogs, our horse, about half the cats in the yard."

"Like you ever complained." Annabelle answered.

"True." Aldo answered. "And you, Elena, is it? What is your story?"

"Aldo!" Annabelle rebuked him. "That is none of our business."

"No." Elena protested. "I don't mind. The coffee and the wash make it well worthwhile as far as I'm concerned."

Over the next half hour, Elena shared her story. When she got to the end Aldo suddenly leaned forward.

"You are related to Angelina Lo Bianco?"

Elena nodded. "It appears so."

Aldo laughed. "She is my mother's oldest sister. You and I are cousins. The restaurant your mother went to work at is my aunt's restaurant in Messina."

Elena's mouth dropped open. "But how can this be? Of the people I have met in the last three days, I'm related to three!"

"It is less surprising than you might think. Your birth mother is from Sperlinga. Sperlinga has a population of only 700 people–most of us are related in some way. Some nearer and some farther, but many of these small mountain towns are the same. Today, there are good roads, but even sixty years ago the roads were not easily passable, so people married according to who was available in their towns. It means we are all related." Aldo waved his hand at Annabelle. "Situations like us, Annabelle and I, are rare. Most Sicilians are suspicious. We have been invaded so many times, and we have long memories. The Greeks, the Arabs, the Romans, the Normans, the Spanish, the Germans, the Canadians, the Americans, the British, and more. They all came. Fortunately, I went to stay with my uncle who had immigrated to New York. I lived with him for a year to go to school and learn English. So, when Annabelle came to work here for a summer, the idea of falling in love with an American was already in my head. I don't think many Sicilians living in mountain villages would feel the same."

"You know, at home in Vancouver, I always felt like I was part of a small group–there are not many Sicilian-Canadians in Vancouver. Lots of Italian-Canadians, but not so many Sicilians," Elena replied. "Our world was so narrow compared to the rest of the people I knew. But here, the world seems much narrower. It makes me wonder if my birth mother was capable of living in such a big city. She didn't speak English. She didn't know Canadians. She didn't know how to protect herself, and her parents wouldn't have known how to protect her either. No wonder she ended up badly."

A soft silence fell across the room. Elena could hear the charcoal sounds of the goats in the yard bleating back and forth to each other, and she could picture her mother as a girl tending those goats.

"Would you like me to call my aunt? She might have some information that could help you."

"You wouldn't mind? That would be wonderful." Elena replied.

Elena and Annabelle moved to a table on the terrace at the back of the house, sipping their second *espresso,* and waiting for word from Aldo. A black and white shaggy dog lay at their feet, nose pointed toward the scent of a warm brioche. Elena scratched the top of the dog's head. "Who is this sweet dog?"

"That is Robin Hood. And I would watch your brioche, if I were you. We called him Robin Hood because he steals from everyone." Annabelle laughed. "Don't you, Robin."

The dog looked up and tilted his head to the side at the sound of his name. Behind them, Elena heard a man's laugh. She turned to see Aldo standing on crutches. "He steals everyone's heart too." He hobbled across the flagstones and Annabelle pulled out a chair for her husband.

"Here *miu preju,* my joy. Put your leg up, and tell us what you found."

Aldo settled into the chair. Annabelle kissed the top of his head, and rumpled his hair before helping him set his leg onto a cushioned stool.

"Well, I spoke to *Zzia* Vittoria. Cristiana did work in her restaurant for two or three years. *Zzia* said she became good at baking and making desserts. She had an opportunity to go to Palermo and start her own bakery. I guess she jumped at the chance and *Zzia s*ays she is still there. Her bakery is called *Panificio Cristiana* but she didn't know exactly where it was, and she didn't have the telephone number.

Elena could feel the excitement building in her gut. She felt so close to meeting her mother. She wanted to jump up and run but didn't want to be rude to her newly found cousin and his wife.

"Grazii. That is a huge help." she responded.

Annabelle tilted her head and looked at Elena with a grin. "That's it? That's all you are going to say? Come on, be honest. You want to jump up and run, don't you?"

Elena looked at her feet. "Yeah, I kinda do."

Annabelle and Aldo responded in a harmony of purple laughter.

"Go, go! If you leave now you can be in Palermo and looking for the bakery by lunchtime." Aldo waved at her. "Call us from Palermo!" he said handing her a card.

Elena stood up and took her bag. "Thank you, thank you so much." She held her hand out to Annabelle who brushed her hand aside, and instead took Elena into a bear hug.

"Come on, I'll ride you back down the hill."

Chapter twelve

A FORK ON THE ROAD TO PALERMO

ELENA JUMPED INTO THE PANDA. The comfortable fit of the bucket seat moulded around her like a friend even though this was only their third day together. The car coughed and started as if in indignation at being left out in a field all night. Elena leaned to wave at Annabelle.

"Thank you! Thank you for everything."

"Drive safely! Traffic gets crazy the closer you get to Palermo." Guido bleated his agreement, and shook his horns. Both Annabelle and Elena laughed. "Come back and visit before you go home! We always have extra space for family."

Elena waved and called back, "I will! Thanks." She put the solid little car in gear, and bumped her way to the road. She tooted the horn and turned right, accelerating along the narrow, winding road to Palermo.

The sun shone just as brightly, and perhaps even a bit hotter than the day before. Once again, Elena pondered on what seemed to be an incomprehensible series of coincidences. 'How could it be almost everyone I've met here in Sicily is a relative? Surely, even in a remote place like Sperlinga, that must be unlikely.'

The road took her back and forth along the rough Sicilian hills. Innocuous Italian pop hummed a quiet taupe from the radio, and Elena found herself bouncing her head gently from side to side. The drive was relaxing–no cars behind her, none in front, and thankfully, none barrelling towards her on the narrow road. In fact, other than the occasional cow or donkey and the sounds of birds and cicadas, Elena could have been alone on the ancient island.

The road to Palermo was straightforward. Or at least it was until

Elena found herself stopped at a "T" intersection with no clear sense of which was the correct way to turn. She reached into the glove box, pulled out the GPS Lucia had lent her.

"Your turn little TomTom. Time for you to show me how to get to Palermo. Although with the instructions you've been giving me so far, I don't know why I should trust you." Elena said to the GPS.

In the same sultry Italian-accented English Elena heard, "Because without my instructions, do you think you would have met Francesca or Angelina or Annabelle and Aldo? And without them, you would still have no idea your mother was in Palermo."

For a fraction of a second, the GPS voice speaking back to her seemed like the most normal, natural thing in the world. And then the reality of what she heard came crashing down.

"What the hell!" Elena pushed the button on the radio and killed a whiny pop song in mid-wail.

"Oh, *grazii.* That music was terrible. I can't stand Italian pop music. Classical, rap, opera, folk, R&B–they are all fine. I especially like American country music. Just don't play pop *pi favuri.*"

Elena stared at the GPS with her mouth open, unable to respond.

"Do you not answer when you are spoken to? Is that how your father taught you?" the GPS continued.

Elena jumped out of the car and slammed the door shut. She stared at the GPS through the window. She turned away from the car and ran her hands through her hair.

"What the hell is this?" she muttered pacing back and forth. She turned back to the car. "The GPS can't be talking to me." She peered through the open window. The TomTom looked no different. Elena put the back of her hand to her forehead. "Maybe I'm overheated. Maybe I'm only hearing things."

"You know the window is open, and I can hear you." The GPS responded. "And it isn't hot enough for you to have heat stroke. Are you sweating?"

In spite of her shock, Elena answered, "Yes, yes I am."

"Then it can't be heat stroke. And you wouldn't be hallucinating unless it were."

"Are you the GPS?" Elena took two steps back. "Oh my god, I'm talking to a GPS."

"You are NOT talking to a GPS. I may be using the GPS to talk to you, but I am not just a piece of metal and plastic and computer chips. Now get back into the car so we can talk properly."

Not sure why, Elena climbed back into the car. She squinted at the GPS. "Wait, is this some sort of trick? Did Lucia set this up?"

"Now how could your dear soul sister Lucia set this up to work half a world away? And when did Lucia show you any type of technical skills at all?"

Elena looked around and into the back seat. "Where are you? Who are you?"

"My name is Genevra. I am in what, I suppose, you might call an alternate universe, or the ethereal plane, heaven, the God place. Many people have called it different things over time. I am using your GPS so you can hear me. Because, càra, we need to talk."

"You are in an alternate universe," Elena shook her head. She felt dizzy. "This is crazy. How can this be happening?"

"If you drive, I will tell you the story and explain why I am here talking to you."

Elena sat for a few moments with both hands tightly on the steering wheel, not sure what to do. She took a deep breath and answered. "Okay. But don't throw any other surprises at me or I might just drive off a cliff."

The dark, Italian voice gave a throaty laugh.

"Well, Elena, hold tight to the wheel because there may be a few surprises in store for you."

Chapter thirteen

GENEVRA'S TALE

~1130-1160~

I WAS BORN IN THE YEAR OF OUR LORD, 1130, in a town near Palermo. Today if you look on a map, you might find Santa Genevra di Mare, however in my time it was known as Palazzo di Mare. My father, Calogero, was a Norman lord. My mother, Rosaria, a Sicilian by birth, was forced to marry my father as he was wealthy and the marriage was advantageous for my grandfather. I was told, after the death of my brother, she retired to a contemplative life with Basilian nuns. Many people have since written I, too, was a member of the Basilians but that story is not true. This is the truth.

I was a spoiled child. I had a slightly older brother who had died–drowned in the pond in our garden. As a result, *Papà* had the pond filled and I remember I cried more about the pond than about the death of Carmelo, my brother. I was, in my child's mind, certain Carmelo would come back but the pond, I knew, was gone. When I cried over the pond *Papà* struck me and called me selfish. I stamped my feet in anger and ran to the skirts of my nurse, Agata, who always comforted me and gave in to my tempers.

My mother had always been too busy running my father's household to spend much time with me, but after Carmelo died, *Mamma* withdrew from everyone. She prayed and wept all day. Finally, my father dragged her from her room into the kitchen to force her to take up her work again but she fell to her knees and threw herself prostrate on the flagstones and begged God to forgive her. *Papà* pulled her up and struck her across her face and stormed from the room. My father, whom I had never seen strike any woman or girl, had hit the two he loved most in the same week. After that, my mother left to join the nuns.

Zzia Marcella, Mamma's older sister, took over running the household. I did not like her much, although I didn't hate her. She was strict but not unkind and I could see what she did was for our benefit. She put an end to the spoiling and made sure I had the training I would need to be a good lady of the court, as well as wife and mother.

When I was thirteen, *Zzia* Marcella presented herself to my father. Curious, I crept after her, and listened at the door.

"Calogero, it is time to present Genevra in court. She is becoming a shapely young woman, and if you don't marry her off soon, you will find all too many young dogs sniffing around."

"Marcella, she is still a baby. It is too soon to present her. She needs two, maybe three years before she is old enough."

"Ha! You do not pay attention to your own child. She is already thirteen, and the monthly flow is upon her."

"Is this true?"

"Yes, and if you had paid attention, you would see her breasts are like plums and her hips have widened, and all the boys and some of the old men watch her when she enters church to give confession."

In an impatient voice, *Papà* answered. "Well, what do you suggest, Marcella?"

"After the harvest, King Roger will be hosting the lords and counts as he always does. That would be the time to present Genevra. I will have the seamstress make an appropriate gown. If we quietly spread the word of her beauty and her value, the tongues will wag, and the suitors will be lining up to speak to you. You can have your pick of husbands."

Papà must have nodded as my aunt made quick steps to the door. I scrambled back, and hid around the corner. Once outside his door, she called out "Genevra."

I came forward, shame-faced.

She took my chin in her bony hand. "I suppose you heard the conversation I had with your father?"

"Yes, *Zzia* Marcella."

"Then you must realize it is not appropriate for a young woman on the threshold of being presented to the king to be on her knees–either listening at a door or for any other reason."

I flushed. "Yes, Zzia Marcella. I won't do it again."

She let go of my chin, and patted my cheek instead. "No matter. Now, let's go and speak to the seamstress. You need a gown that will make every girl green with jealousy, and every man pink with lust."

~|~

That afternoon, when most of the household was asleep in the torpid heat, I rose and went to the garden to sit in the shade under the orange tree. As I sat listening to the humming song of the bees and the cicadas, there was a rustling of bushes behind me. I turned to see a brown mongrel wander into the garden. He stopped and looked at me, tongue lolling out, tail wagging.

"*Bon giornu*. What a handsome fellow. Would you like a drink?" I said to the dog.

"Why yes, thank you. That would be most appreciated, *signurina*."

Behind the dog, a tall man stepped out from the bushes. His black hair was cut above his ears and swept back gracefully from the crown of his head. His eyes twinkled and flashed. I jumped to my feet, and tripped, landing hard on the flagstones behind me.

"*Signurina*, are you hurt? Let me help you up." He strode forward and held his hand out to me.

"I am fine," My pride had been more hurt than anything, so I brushed his hand away. "And who are you to trespass on my father's land?" I replied, the haughty tone covering the blush creeping across my face.

"Forgive me, *signurina*. I did not mean to alarm you. My name is Landro. I work with horses to earn my meals. If there is work I stay, when there is no work, I travel on." He gestured towards his dog, "And this is Aberto, although he is not so noble as his name implies."

I realized my rudeness, and my aunt's lessons took over. "There is nothing to forgive. I will have a servant bring you water. The household is resting, but I suspect my father may wish to employ your services–there are several colts waiting to be broken." I walked into the house, but not before catching a glimpse of his handsome profile from the corner of my eye.

~|~

My father was proud of his stable and was glad of the assistance of a talented horse-trainer. I, of course, had my own lovely mount, Bella. She was a beautiful dapple–an unusual colour–fine bones and sweet of disposition, and I believed she was the loveliest horse in my father's stable. I would visit her every morning, bringing her an apple or carrot from the kitchen. And each morning I would bring some treat from the kitchen to Beppe, the boy whose job it was to take care of Bella. Every instruction from my father, Beppe carried out fastidiously. He worshipped *Papà*, with good reason.

The previous winter, my father and I had been out riding together–it was a rare treat for me. As we approached the stone hovel of the family of one my father's workers, I could see the door wide open.

"Strange." My father frowned. The weather was cold. Steam rose from our horses' necks. My father urged his horse to a canter, and I followed with Bella. As we stopped, I could hear crying.

"Wait here, Genevra." My father's tone brooked no contradiction. Shortly, my father emerged with his arm around a young boy, perhaps ten years of age who seemed to be nothing but skin and bones. I opened my mouth to ask who he was, but my father gave me a warning look. *Papà* lifted the boy on to his saddle, and mounted up behind him. We rode slowly back to the stable, my father and I silent while the boy wept.

"Genevra, go inside," *Papà* said once we reached the stable. "Tell Marcella to have the housemaids bring some hot food." I did as I was told, but my curiosity raged about in my head.

One of the advantages of the old stone house in which we lived was that there were many corners and hiding places with small windows, and I had found them all. I had spent hours eavesdropping on the servants' conversations. I tucked myself into a convenient corner with a piece of needlework in case *Zzia* Marcella found me, and waited. They didn't keep me waiting long.

"Did you hear?" This was Velia, the scullery maid. She was the most outrageous of gossips in the kitchen, but her gossip was unerringly accurate. "About the boy the master brought in?"

"Is he the reason you carried food out to the stable?"

"*Sì*. He is so thin you can see every bone in his face and his eyes..." At this Velia spat and I could picture her make the sign to ward off the *malocchio*, the evil eye.

"What happened?" came a chorus of shocked voices.

"His parents worked out in the fields. They caught the fever. Such suffering as you cannot imagine. And then they died! They up and died, and left that poor lad not knowing what to do." There was a pause and I heard some scuffling of feet. Velia resumed her story but at a whisper. I had to strain to hear her words.

"I heard him say he was in the hovel with his dead parents for a week before the master found him. No food, just sitting and crying beside his dead mother. I heard the master say the boy was holding her hand to his cheek when he went in their hut."

I crossed myself. What a terrible thing! No wonder my father had been so gentle with the boy.

From that day, Beppe lived in the stable, worked with the horses, and ate with the other servants. Beppe was a skinny, wisp of a lad, at first terrified of the large beasts towering over him. But I had watched him scrunch up his face, and close his eyes to gather the courage to brush the horses. He would do anything my father asked.

One morning, I was standing in the stable rubbing my forehead against Bella's neck as Beppe was picking out her hooves. I had managed to sneak away, and was planning to take her for a ride before Zzia Marcella called me back. I heard footsteps–human and equine– behind me and I turned to see Landro leading one of my father's colts.

"*Bon giornu, signurina*," he said with a deferential bow.

"*Bon giornu*, Landro. Is my father's colt behaving himself?"

"*Sì*. He will be a good mount. Are you taking your mare out for a ride?"

"*Sì*," I kissed Bella's nose and pulled on her forelock to which she nickered back. "I do not ride her enough now that my duties in the house have increased. I thought I would take her up through the hills this morning."

Landro frowned at me. "There are bandits in the hills, and the terrain is rough. Are you sure you should be riding there?"

I laughed. "I have been riding in these hills since I first learned to control a horse. Besides, Bella is itching for a hard ride, and a leisurely stroll through the olive trees will not satisfy her."

"Please allow me to accompany you, so I can be sure you are safe."

I paused. If my father were to know I had ridden into the hills unescorted he would be furious, but he would be equally furious if he knew I had ridden alone with a man–any man. But I was headstrong and foolish.

"*Grazii.* Your company will be a pleasure."

I glanced at Beppe, hoping he would keep his tongue, but he was in deep concentration as he bent over the final hoof, taking great care, as he always did, with Bella. Landro frowned at Beppe.

"Boy, go. Find some other horse to work on."
I didn't like his cold, dismissive tone, one I had never used with Beppe. But when Landro turned back to me his warm smile had my stomach tied in knots. Could I be ill?

Landro quickly saddled both the skittish colt and Bella. His hands were worker's hands, calloused and strong, but surprisingly gentle on the two horses. The strange feeling rose from my stomach to my chest. I had been kept from the company of eligible young men, however servants and old men were not considered off limits–the old men were too frail to be a threat and the servants were too frightened. Landro was different. Strictly speaking he was a servant, but not like any I had met before. His family did not depend on my father for their livelihood, and if my father chose to send him packing, Landro could find work anywhere. This made him dangerous–a servant with no fear. It also made him fascinating. I knew I was entering treacherous territory.

Our ride into the hills was pleasant. Landro was soon telling me tales of his wanderings in Sicily and Calabria–riding a wild tempered stallion along the sandy white beach at Eraclea Minoa, visiting the temples in Agrigento, standing on the Calabrian coast and watching the island volcano spew into the dark night sky. I found myself catching my breath with every exciting story he told and I would gaze at him through my dark lashes and giggle at his jokes. It was a thrilling, heady rush.

Soon Landro and I were riding together two or three days a

week. I would leave early in the morning, before most of the household, save the servants, were up. We would ride through the hills together, and we would split off to arrive back home separately. As much as I told myself these rides were innocent, I knew were we seen riding back together, there would be hell to pay.

September came and with it the heavily laden fig trees and grape vines and the fields filled with workers. I had always loved this time of year; the grape vines fecund with their luscious purple fruit. When I was younger, I helped pick the grapes and watched the women crush them under their feet. Later I would visit the oaken barrels with my father and his vintner as they conferred over which wines were ready to bottle or to be opened. But this year I resented the harvest and the missed rides with Landro.

One week, towards the end of September, we missed all three rides and *Zzia* Marcella took me aside.

"Genevra, I have been working hard to prepare you to be the lady of a household, wouldn't you agree?"

"Yes, *Zzia*, and I am grateful."

"Do you watch what I do as well as listen to what I say?"

I nodded.

"Then, show your gratitude by learning your lessons. Have you ever seen me lose patience with a servant?"

"No *Zzia* Marcella." I hung my head. I knew what was coming next.

"You have been sharp with the servants all week, and this morning I heard you boxed the ears of Velia. She is a sweet girl, even if she is a gossip. As the lady of the house, it is your job to lead by example. If you are disrespectful to the servants, they will have no respect for you. You must be firm, clear about what you want, but kind," She looked directly into my eyes, and with a softer tone said. "Is there any reason you have been so cross this week?"

"No *Zzia*. I promise I will treat the servants better." I answered. A flush of shame had crossed my cheeks, but my aunt took it to mean something else.

"I think I understand, Genevra. You are almost fourteen–you are becoming a woman. You must be anxious about the match your father will make for you. But do not be in haste to find a husband. Enjoy this time–this may be the last harvest you can go and ride freely in the mornings. This time next year you will likely be wed."

The slight flush turned to bright red as my aunt's guess hit nearer the mark than was comfortable.

Chapter fourteen

A DANGEROUS ALLIANCE

THE NEXT MORNING, I rushed to the stable earlier than usual. At first it seemed I was the only one there, and I felt my heart drop into my stomach. But I heard the clop clop of horse's feet, and I turned to see Landro leading Bella and one of the colts, both saddled and ready to ride. My cheeks hurt as I grinned stupidly at him.

"Shall I help you onto your mount, *signurina?*" His formality flustered me as we had been using first names for some time now.

"Please."

He chuckled and grabbed my waist to lift me onto Bella. "I have found something in the hills I would like to show you, Genevra."

The smile on his face gave me the courage to place my hand over his. "I would love to see it."

We rode into the hills in silence, me following his lead. I watched his back. The muscles made from horse-breaking moved under his shirt. I let my gaze run from his thick black hair, along his shoulders and down his arms. I was much more fair than he and for the first time I wondered how my paler skin would look next to his darkly tanned olive arms.

Instead of taking the direct route to the top of the hill, Landro turned and plunged through some bushes. I gasped as I thought he would fall from the cliff. I stopped and waited, afraid to call his name in case my voice carried to the house below.

I heard a whistle–the sign we had agreed to use if we became separated. With trepidation, I directed Bella towards the bushes and pushed slowly through until we came out the other side on a wide ledge. Landro had already dismounted and came to help me.

"If we walk a few steps around this edge here, you will see what I have been wanting to show you." He took my hand–shivers shot up my arm, into my chest and to parts that made me blush. I clutched his hand as he led me around the edge, and as we turned the corner to an opening in the cliff face. It was a cave! A large, dry cave in which I could see blankets and a basket filled with bread, cheese and wine.

"I found this cave early last week and brought up a picnic for us for today." He stood close to me; I could feel his warm breath on my face. His hands slid up my arms and he squeezed me to his chest. His face came closer and closer until he kissed me softly on the lips.

"Oh Genevra. I have wanted to do this since that first day I saw you out on the *tirrazza*."

I hesitated, and he kissed me again. Everything disappeared. All that existed were his lips against mine and the lighting that was shooting through my body. I gasped for breath when he stopped.

"Kisses are wonderful, *amuri*," he whispered. "But after a long ride, wine and bread should come first."

We sat on the blanket–quiet and a little awkward at first–not touching but close enough that I could feel the heat of his body. We spoke of nothing, I don't remember what, and then, as I turned my head, his lips were again on mine. And, like the first moment he touched me, I was filled with a storm. Powerful lightning and thunder rolled through my body. He pulled me down onto the blanket. I knew I should resist, but his warm lips convinced me otherwise and I yielded.

Landro was a gentle lover. He took his time. When he entered me, his kisses and caresses distracted me from the momentary sharpness, and then I felt nothing but the supreme ecstasy of being in his arms. When we had finished, he poured more wine for me and told me how wonderful I was.

"Genevra, I will take my savings, and buy some land near here. I will show your father, even if I am not rich, I can take care of you." he whispered in my ear. And, like so many other foolish young girls, I believed him.

~|~

One morning, in the middle of November, I took the lead and

trotted up the path before Landro.

Landro followed, jumping off his horse after me, laughed and said, "Are you in such a hurry, my saucy wench?"

I turned to him, dancing, and grabbed his hands. "I have something tremendous to tell you!"

"And what is it? Are they making all horse-trainers into noblemen?"

"No silly. Much better," I whispered as I put my arms around his waist and embraced him. "Landro, I think I am with child. I wasn't sure before, but my woman time has not come twice now." I could feel my eyes filling with tears. Now Landro would buy the land and he would marry me! A strange look came across his face, almost–fear. But he as fast as I had seen the fear, he replaced it with a smile. He held me and whispered his love. I was filled with pure happiness in that moment.

We didn't make love that day. Instead we talked about plans for our lives and the life of our baby. And when the time came for us to return, he kissed me soundly, and suggested we ride separately. He would go first, and speak to my father and I would join him later.

"I love you."

He kissed the top of my head and answered "I will see you at the house."

I waited for about half an hour before riding carefully home, enjoying the feeling of having a wonderful secret.

As I rode into the stable, I looked for my father's colt–the one Landro had been riding. I didn't see him. I wasn't concerned. Landro may have let him loose in the paddock. Leaving Bella with a stable boy, I walked into the house to wash and wait for my father to call me.

~|~

The house grew quiet for afternoon rest, but I could not sleep. I paced back and forth. I picked up my needlework and my sewing, and put them down. I glanced out the window. I lay on my bed and rose again. Finally, people began to stir. I left my room and settled myself in a chair on the *tirrazza*. How could it be taking this much time? *Zzia* Marcella came yet said nothing. She gave me several tasks, which I managed to stumble through. Finally, dinner came, and father descended from his rooms to join us for the meal. Surely he must say something now!

We murmured grace and as we were about to eat, Beppe came to the door, a worried frown darkening his face.

"Excuse me, my lord, I'm very sorry to interrupt your meal."

My father looked up with some irritation. "What is it, Beppe?"

"I was wondering if you had sold the colt, the one that is brown with the white socks?" Beppe looked terrified–he had never been in the big house in his brief life as a stable boy.

"Sold my colt? No, of course I haven't sold my colt."

"It's missing signuri. It has been missing all day."

"Well, ask Landro about it. He probably has it off training somewhere." My father waved at the boy as if to chase him away. But Beppe, in spite of his trembling, continued.

"I tried to ask *Signuri* Landro about it, but we can't find him either."

My heart skipped a beat. "But you have spoken to Landro today, haven't you father?"

"Me talk to Landro? No, of course not." With a curse, father pushed away from the table, and strode out of the house.

I stared at my plate. Around me I could hear the muttering of servants and my aunt as she gave them orders, but the words meant nothing. The colours in the room swirled around and I could see little but the plate in front of me. Landro had not spoken to my father. Landro and my father's colt were missing. But Landro was going to buy some land and ask my father for permission to marry me. I couldn't understand.

"Genevra. Genevra!"

I looked up to see *Zzia* Marcella peering at me.

"What are you dreaming about girl?" She thrust a wine skin and a cloth bag with food into my hands. "Take this out to your father. He is going after that scoundrel, Landro."

"He's going after Landro?"

"*Mamma mia*, Genevra. Have you not been paying attention? He's stolen your father's good colt. Your father and some of the men are going after him." *Zzia* Marcella stared at me sharply. "What is wrong with you?" Her voice had a suspicious tone.

"Nothing. Excuse me *Zzia*. It was the shock of the colt being stolen. I will give this to father." I stepped outside quickly. Father was shouting instructions as they saddled the horses. *"Papà.* Here, food and wine for you."

"Grazii, daughter." He took the food and wine and tied them to his saddle.

"Papà…"

"Si?" He gazed over my head, frowning at the men. "Faster! If we want to catch him, we must hurry."

I wanted to tell him. I wanted to say that I loved Landro. I wanted to tell him he was going to be a grandfather, and Landro would be his son-in-law. I wanted to tell him it would be all right. But it wouldn't. Landro was gone with my father's horse, and it could never be all right.

"Be careful *Papà.*" I choked the words out.

Father looked at me, and ran his hand along my cheek. "Don't worry Genevra. I will catch that thief. He can't hurt me."

I stepped back, my hands clasped tightly at my breast. All I could think was 'That wasn't what I meant *Papà.* That wasn't what I meant.'

~|~

I didn't see *Papà* for a week. Then, late one night I heard the hooves clattering across the flagstones. I climbed out of bed and rushed to the window–expectant, fearful, excited.

"Merciful Mother," I whispered to the Virgin, "Please let Landro be with them." I sank to my knees, clutching the curtain. My father was there. His men were too, and the colt was tethered to his saddle, but there was no Landro. In the bright moonlight, my father dismounted slowly and handed the rope to one of his men. He turned and I saw, in the light, my father put his hand to his side and wince. The shirt under his hand was stained.

"Marcella!" he called to my aunt. One of the servant girls ran out of the kitchen door. He grasped her shoulder, and I heard him say, "Help me in. Send for *Signura* Marcella."

I stayed on my knees, my hands tight together; whispering prayers, nonsensical and rambling but I hoped the Virgin understood them nonetheless. I heard footsteps running up the stairs and a sharp knock on my aunt's door.

"*Signura*, come quickly. The *signuri* has returned and he is injured!"

"Quiet girl, you'll wake the whole house. Now, what is it?"

"The *signuri* has returned, and he is bleeding!"

"Oh, *miu Diu*. Take me to him."

I froze where I was. I couldn't move... my legs shook. My hands clenched into fists and I pressed them against my mouth to keep from screaming. My whole body quivered. I knew what had happened. *Papà* had found Landro. Landro was dead and *Papà* was injured. I stuffed the end of the curtain into my mouth and wailed my pain to the moon.

Chapter fifteen

A PROBLEM AND A SOLUTION

IN THE MORNING, I awoke on the floor. I blinked and squinted at the early morning sun. Why was I on the floor? I gazed out the window. It was late November, and the harvest was finished. I would soon be presented to the court. I rolled onto my back–the movement was excruciating. And, like a sharp knife to my heart, I remembered why I was on the floor. I sat up slowly, carefully moving each part of my body, grimacing. I felt as if I had been beaten–beaten hollow–that all my insides had been shaken and crushed until they were liquid, and I had cried them all away. My head pounded and my eyes felt like I had rubbed them with sand. I pressed my palms against them.

Soft footsteps padded up the hallway, and the door cracked open a little. Agata peered through the crack and then rushed in, skirts swishing across the stone floor. She knelt awkwardly–I knew it pained her–and put her arms around me. "Oh *mia dreva,* my child, are you all right?"

I buried my face into her skirts, but there were no more tears. I was empty. "No, I will never be all right. Never again."

"Child, child. Your father will be fine. The wounds are not deep and he is resting now. That thief, Landro, was no match for your father."

At the mention of Landro's name the anguish I believe had all drained away rose up again, and I sobbed.

"What is this? These are not tears for your father, I think. You had better tell me what is what." Agata took me by the arm and helped me up. We sat together on the bed, Agata patting my hand, me with my head down in despair and shame.

Agata was patient but persistent, and bit-by-bit she drew the story from me. She grasped my chin, the way *Zzia* Marcella did, and stared me directly in the face until I blushed with discomfort and humiliation.

"It is not just love we are talking about here. You have been with him and carry his child, am I right?"

The frank words started my tears afresh, even though her tone was concerned. All I could do was nod.

"We must take care of this quietly, Genevra. Here is what we will do. I will tell your aunt you heard your father return last night, and out of fear for his safety you have fallen into a fever. You must stay in bed and I will bring you a tea that might make you lose the child if you are not too far along." I dropped my head and nodded, wiping tears from my eyes. "Lady Marcella is busy with your father, she will be quite happy to have me take care of you."

Agata helped me lay back into bed. Before she left, she ran her fingers through my hair and kissed my forehead, and I was grateful.

When Agata returned, she carried a tray with two large steaming cups. Handing me one, she said, "Drink this first. It will cause you to bleed." When I was finished she handed me the second cup. "This will calm you. You will sleep and it will ease your mind." This one I drank gratefully. Sleep would be welcome. I didn't want to cry anymore.

"Close your eyes, child. I will take care of you." Agata whispered, and I knew she would.

~|~

Over the next two weeks or so I drifted in and out of sleep. Strange and terrifying dreams preoccupied me; dreams of bouncing babies held by a bloody Landro or Landro being swallowed by a cave and calling for my help, my father delivering my baby, dead and bloated. Finally, I woke. It was a cool afternoon and the sky through my window was overcast. I turned my head and saw Agata sitting next to my bed sewing. She looked up and smiled.

"So you have decided to awaken. You have had a long sleep, Genevra. How are you feeling?"

I struggled to sit up, and Agata rushed to help me. "All right I think. Weak."

"Hmph, no surprise. You haven't eaten in almost a fortnight. It was all I could do to get you to drink a few sips of water or tea when you woke."

Agata arranged me on my pillows. "Agata, I don't remember much. What happened?"

"What happened? Well, you weigh less than I thought, so the sleeping draught I gave you kept you sleeping for almost two weeks!"

"No, Agata." I said, staring into her eyes. "What happened to the child?"

"The child is still with you," Agata whispered. "But don't worry child. I have a plan."

A pair of footsteps echoed outside my door.

"Genevra, you're awake," my father grinned as he came in my door. His one arm was bandaged and he winced as he leaned over to kiss my cheek. "How are you feeling my girl?"

"I'm…I think I will be fine *Papà.*"

Agata stepped forward. "She is still a little weak as she has just woken. She will need to eat and drink a little and rest for a few days more, but I am sure she will recover and be up and back to herself."

My father turned to Agata. "Thank you. This house has seen too much death and despair; we don't need to see more."

Zzia Marcella and Agata gasped. "Calogero!" my aunt cried out, "Don't say that! You are inviting bad luck and death into the house!" My aunt and Agata both spat over me and made signs to ward off *malocchio*–the evil eye.

My father crossed himself. "Well, child, you must get well soon. We have been invited to King Roger's court next week, and you are to be presented." With a curt nod, he walked gingerly from the room. *Zzia* Marcello followed behind.

When the door closed behind them, I turned to Agata and gasped, "What am I going to do? I can't be presented if I'm carrying Landro's child!"

"Calm down, Genevra. You will go to court, and you will be presented. You will press your father for a quick marriage, and you will tell your husband you delivered the child early."

"But he will know I am not a virgin, if I don't bleed!" I cried.

"Don't worry about that. I know how to handle such a problem." She winked at me.

Chapter sixteen

A DANGEROUS PLAN

"HOLD THAT STEADY, NOW," *Zzia* Marcella chided the servants balancing the polished metal mirror. "What do you think, Genevra?"

I turned back and forth. The damask dress the seamstress had created was revealing not so much in the amount of flesh it showed, but more in the amount of flesh it alluded to. The colour was pale peach. It gave a warmth to my skin, a suggestion of my breasts. I blushed.

"That's right, Genevra." *Zzia* Marcella told me as she gazed at me. "Tonight, you will be hitting the right balance between temptress and virgin. You will make your father a richer and more powerful man, and you will make your suitors fall to their knees."

"But I've lost so much weight! I look like a child."

"There are many men out there who would rather bed a child," Agata answered.

"That is true," *Zzia* Marcella nodded. "As long as he is rich and powerful, his tastes in bed don't really matter. Come child, your *Papà* is waiting."

As we rode towards the castle I turned to my father and spoke. "*Papà*, I know *Zzia* has talked to you about my age."

He looked at me and raised an eyebrow.

I was a little nervous to discuss my future with him, as it had always been his domain to decide. "I am fourteen. I think it is time for me to find a husband. Surely there will be eligible men at court!"

"So, you think, *passaru*, little sparrow, I should be marrying you off, do you?" My father grinned at me.

So much depended on this night, I couldn't make any mistakes. I took an offended tone. "Do you not think I am ready? Do you not think

Zzia has trained me well?"

My father guffawed. "Well, Marcella, I think you may have done a little too well. It seems she is ready to take on any man.

My aunt turned away with a snort. "She still has much to learn about taking on a man, much less a household. But she is right. It is time to marry her off."

My father eyed me closely, but simply said, "We will see."

I had not been to court before. I had always thought our home was lavish, and it was compared to the farmers' huts that lay in my father's domain. But this castle was… opulent. Rich tapestries hung from the walls. Rugs from the northern coast of Africa lay on the floor. Gold and jewels were everywhere. As my father led us into the great hall, heralds proclaimed our entry. Their long trumpets gleamed gold, and the bright blue shield waved gaily from the long narrow bells. The hall was filled with people–other Norman lords and ladies in splendid robes; Saracens with their heads wrapped in turbans of brilliant colours; Sicilians and Byzantines with their dark eyes and olive skin. I could hear six or seven different languages. I was excited and terrified at the same time. I was well aware of the importance the evening held.

We reached the royal receiving line and my father bowed low to King Roger. Following his lead, both *Zzia* Marcella and I curtseyed even lower. The king was a handsome man, dark-bearded with piercing grey eyes–an homage to his Norman heritage.

"So, Calogero, this is your daughter. She is lovely. I see why you have chosen to bring her to court. To leave such a fetching girl without a husband would be to invite all the young mongrels to come sniffing."

I drew a sharp breath but kept my eyes firmly downcast. The king was far too clever for me to allow him to examine my expression after a comment like that. I hoped he would not see beyond my façade of deference.

"Let me look on your face girl. Raise your eyes. I'm sure your father told you to show reverence, but I want to see you." Damn. I calmed my face, rose and gazed at the king with all the demureness and chasteness I could muster. He stared into my face eight…nine…ten seconds. I wanted to squirm but I slowed my breathing and gazed back as calmly as I could. I could feel a slow drip of sweat drawing a line down the back of my neck. Thank goodness it was my neck and not my forehead. After what seemed like an inordinately long time he broke his scrutiny and turned to my father with a grin and said, "Yes, Calogero, you need to marry this one off quick."

Papà took my elbow and steered me away from the king. "He liked you, Genevra. He is a wise man–perceptive. That will stand you well. He will speak highly of you to the single men here tonight."

Zzia Marcella snorted, "As long as he doesn't suggest her as a wife to one of those Mussulmen or add her to his harem."

"That is enough Marcella. It is not wise to speak of our king that way. It may not be our way to keep more than one wife, but it is not for us to criticize our sovereign." *Papà*'s voice was quiet, but sharp as steel.

~|~

The evening passed in a riot of colours, laughter, music, food, and drink. I danced when I was invited, chatted demurely about art and literature when I was addressed. All in all, I did everything I could to make myself appear to be the ideal wife: accomplished, intelligent, and above all, humble. When the evening drew to a close, *Zzia* Marcella herded me towards the entrance of the castle where *Papà* waited with a wide grin.

"I have news for you daughter. Climb in the coach, and I will tell you of your good fortune as we ride home." My father climbed in ahead of us, and the driver helped *Zzia* Marcella and I climb the two steps up and settle in amongst the cushions.

I sat, hands clasped tight in my lap. Would this be the answer to my problem? Had he found me a husband? My breath sat heavily in my chest as I waited. He leaned back with his hands behind his head, beaming. I could wait no longer.

"Papà, what is it? What is the news?"

"What child, so quick you cannot wait? I suppose not, and I suppose I should not call you a child anymore, now you are to be a wife."

It felt like my heart had jumped from my chest into my mouth. I wasn't sure, for a moment if I could speak.

"A…a husband? Who is it, *Papà*?"

"His name is Roberto del Vasto, the cousin to Enrico del Vasto."

My father made his announcement with a flourish. I understood immediately why *Papà* looked so immensely pleased with himself. I had not heard of Roberto del Vasto, but Enrico del Vasto was a name known to every Italian of any standing. He was the son of Manfred del Vasto, a margrave, or military nobleman, of western Liguria and the nephew of Countess Adelaide of Sicily. Both the countess and the margrave had died but her nephew was well known in Sicily. Countess Adelaide had gifted Enrico with two cities–the most important was Paterno on the east coast of the Island of Sicily. Not only that, he had married Flandina, the daughter of King Roger I's second marriage. By marrying his cousin, Roberto, I was marrying into a favoured branch of the royal family in Sicily! I couldn't believe my good fortune.

"You made a good impression on the king. The family has been looking for a husband for Roberto for sometime now, and the king has chosen you." My shoulders sagged and I leaned back against the cushions, relief flooding through me.

"When will Lord del Vasto host the wedding?" *Zzia* Marcella asked.

"As soon as we reach Firenze. I think we can leave in about two weeks."

I sat up sharply, my breath catching in my throat. "Firenze? Why Firenze? I thought he was part of the Sicilian royal family?"

"He is, Genevra. But Enrico del Vasto was born in Firenze and that is where he lives. But don't worry, daughter. The king assured me he comes to Palermo every summer."

I managed a smile for my father but inside my head was spinning. Firenze! It would take weeks and weeks to get there! By the time we arrived my pregnancy would be showing! What could I possibly do? My father reached over and patted my hand in a comfortable way.

"Thank you *Papà*. I'm sure Firenze will be wonderful. It was just a shock to hear we would be leaving Sicily."

Papà smiled and patted my hand again.

"*Zzia*, how long does it take to get to Firenze?" I murmured.

"I have never been, but I would guess at least a month." she answered. "Don't worry, child. The time will come soon enough."

A month! I furrowed my brows as I calculated the time. A month plus the two weeks in preparation to leave, two more weeks to prepare for the wedding, would mean eight weeks until I married, and with the two months I calculated I was already pregnant that would mean I would be almost half way through the pregnancy. *Santa Maria*! I squeezed my eyes closed in prayer as we drove home. Perhaps if I prayed hard enough I would wake up in the morning to find it was all a mistake.

It was late when we arrived home–too late for me to speak much with Agata–and I climbed into bed to fall asleep, exhausted.

~|~

The sun rose and filled my room with light. As exhausted as I had been, I had only been able to sleep a short time. The remainder of the night I had stared at the ceiling, trying to think of some escape from the terrible place in which I found myself. Landro seemed so far in my past his face barely flitted across my consciousness. There was no time to look back, I had to keep moving forward… just which direction was forward, was a blank to me.

There was a light tap and Agata entered my room.

"*Signura* Marcella told me what happened last night, *carina*." Agata ran her knuckle across my cheek. "I'm so sorry. Who would have thought the king would want you to marry someone in Firenze?"

I sat up, swallowed, and ran the back of my hand across my eyes. "I don't have time for tears. I need to act, not to cry. What do you think? What would you do?"

Agata was a servant and had never been educated. She could neither read nor write, not even the Bible, but I had seen her make sharp decisions in the past–finding solutions to problems no one else had thought of. She rose, deep in thought, and walked to window looking out over the hills through which Landro and I had ridden so many times. I watched her shoulders set, and her chin lift.

"You will be your mother's daughter," she said simply as she gazed out the window.

"What? You want me to go to a convent?"

Agata turned. "No, not quite." She smiled at me. "You will tell your father you had a dream in which Our Lady came to you and told you that you could not leave for Firenze. She said she wanted you to live in contemplation and prayer in a cave for the winter to prove your chastity and devotion to God and the Church. After, you would be fit to marry Lord del Vasto. In the meantime, I will take you to stay with my cousin in Sperlinga. They live in caves in the mountain walls, but they are dry and warm. You can have your baby, leave it with my cousin, and return after. No one will be the wiser, and you will be honoured by your new husband as a pious young woman!"

I shook my head. "*Papà* will never let me go."

"True," Agata smiled at me. "But your father won't know until after you've gone. Write him a letter today, I will pack a bag for each of us, and as soon as the house sleeps we will be off. By the time they awake we will be long gone."

I nodded. Because my mother had run off to a convent, it did seem more likely I might run off as well.

"The servants are already collecting and packing for the journey. Spend today gathering the few things you need for the journey. Don't leave your room. I will tell your father you want to spend the day in prayer and fasting. I will bring you paper and some food later." Agata walked to the door. "You must be steadfast in your resolve Genevra."

"*Sì*." I stared into her eyes. "*Sì*. Only with that will our endeavour succeed."

Agata nodded then left the room.

I looked up at the picture of the Blessed Mother hanging on my wall next to the crucifix. I knelt before them, and clasped my hands together, and prayed.

Chapter seventeen

THE JOURNEY BEGINS

AGATA SLIPPED INTO MY ROOM CLOSE TO MIDNIGHT. The moon was bright and round in the clear sky. It would be easy to find our way with so much moonlight, but it would also make it easy to find us, if our departure was discovered.

"Have you prepared your bag, *bedda mia?*" Agata whispered.

I held up a small, rough woollen bag I had filled with a few coins. I knew there was little point in bringing many clothes with me; soon they wouldn't fit anyhow. I had dressed in a rough woollen dress, and had a thick shawl wrapped around my shoulders. My shoes were old and coarse–later I realized they were the shoes I had worn riding with Landro but at the moment all I could think of was to get out of the house quietly and get away.

We made our way to the stable. I had already decided I could not take Bella. I truly loved her, but she was too fine a horse for me to be riding if I were dressed as a peasant. She nickered a greeting as I approached. I stroked her lovely soft nose and whispered to her.

"Goodbye, my Bella. Be well. I will be back soon, and we will ride again." I blinked back a tear and turned to Agata. "We will take the donkey. We won't be noticed with her."

I placed a rope bridle over the little creature's head. She shook her head a little, and snorted. I scratched under her forelock and whispered softly in her ear, "Shhhhhh little one. We need your service tonight and your quiet." Her ears flicked forward at my soft words. There was no saddle to fit her small back, so I tied our bags together and hung them across instead.

"Sperlinga is in the mountains to the east and a little south of here," Agata whispered. "We must take the road that travels around the hills. We will meet fewer people if we follow such a narrow, lonely path." I nodded, and the donkey and I followed her out of the stable.

The sky was clear. The light from the moon kept us from stumbling. I shivered as I walked, and wrapped my shawl tighter about me.

"There is no snow here, but up in the hills it is colder, and there will be snow," Agata warned. "We needed to travel east. As long as the sea remains on our left side we'll be fine, at least for a while."

The moon cast sharp shadows across our path. At first, I jumped at every sound, but as one step followed behind another, and as the excitement and fear decreased, sleep kept sneaking up behind us. At one point Agata stumbled.

"Agata, climb up on the donkey's back. You're exhausted."

She nodded. "I will. We need to reach Termini Imerese before we stop."

"Termini Imerese! But that's miles away." I gasped.

"It will give us enough of a head start, and your father would not expect we could make it that far."

~|~

As the night tiptoed on, Agata and I took turns riding on the patient donkey. We walked on aching feet, eyes open, but I was not awake. I did not know where my feet fell, nor could my eyes see the path before me. I stumbled forward when Agata grasped my shoulder.

"Look, *bedda mia*. The sun."

I shook my head, and looked up. A bright light burst across my eyes, and I squinted against it before I realized it was the morning sun.

"Morning?" I croaked. "We should stop and eat."

Agata shook her head. "No, if we stop now we won't be able to start again. We can eat as we walk, but I don't want to stop until we reach Termini Imerese."

Exhaustion boiled over into anger. "Are you mad? That is at least another four hours of walking!"

"Nonetheless, it will be Termini Imerese." Agata and the donkey moved on.

"Agata, my father will never believe we could have walked as far as Termini Imerese in one day. He will never look for us that far away. And it doesn't matter where he looks for us if we have died from exhaustion!"

Agata continued on. With a curse, I followed. The cold of the night before lifted, as the sun warmed the ground beneath our feet. Occasionally, the path would rise up, and we would find ourselves in sight of the Tyrrhenian Sea. The sun cast diamonds back at us from the tiny waves the wind blew across the water. It was a beautiful sight, but by the time the sun had risen half way up the morning sky, all I could think of was each excruciating step.

It must have been close to ten or ten-thirty when we saw the outline of Trabia. I stopped on the path. Immediately, I could feel heat radiating from my lower legs. My feet throbbed mercilessly. From the back of the donkey, I heard Agata moan. Her determined words were gone. Her face was white; she was shaking, and I knew we had to stop. I cast my eyes about.

"Agata, look!" I pointed at a small stone hut nearby in the field next to us. I turned my face towards the hut. Half pulling and half leaning on the donkey's neck, I stumbled through the field, past a small well, to the door of the hut. I pushed the door open, and the three of us–Agata, the donkey, and I–stumbled in across the threshold. I helped Agata slide from the donkey's back, my exhausted arms straining to keep her from falling to the ground.

"Agata! Agata, can you hear me?" Her eyes rolled back and I could only see white. She slid from my arms, and fell to the ground. I grasped around, frantic for something to help me. An old wooden bucket lay on its side in the corner. I grabbed the bucket, and ran for the well.

"*Grazii Diu.*" I whispered. The farmer who used the field had left the well in good order, and I dragged the bucket of water back to the hut. Pulling Agata up against me, I poured cold water on her face. Wheezing and gasping, Agata leaned forward coughing and wretching. I held her back against my chest.

"Water." Agata rasped. I held the bucket for her and she gulped the cold water. I lowered her to the ground before I drank my share. I left the remaining water for the donkey. Then, I lay down next to Agata, and slept as if I were dead.

Chapter eighteen

A DEVASTATING TRUTH

AGATA AND I CHOSE TO STAY a few days in the hut. When I say 'chose' it was our feet and legs and backs that chose for us. After the second day, I stumbled off to Trabia and bought bread, and cheese, and oranges and brought them back. I longed for some olives, but only the rich could afford olives, and it would look strange for a peasant to be buying them. The nights were still cold, but sleeping in the hut with the donkey made the temperatures bearable. After the second day, Agata sat scratching the donkey's nose.

"Does she have a name, this one?" she asked me.

"I don't think so. I've never heard her called anything more than 'the donkey'." I answered.

"I think we should change that. She should have a name."

I ran my hand along her rough mane. "I think you should name her. This trip was your plan. I would be in a terrible place if it were not for you."

"I think she should be Graziella. We need to be grateful to her. She brought us this far."

"Graziella it will be. I think that is a perfect name."

It was mid-day, and the hut was warmer than I would have expected. I felt the grey stone pressing into my back, and my eyes drooped lower.

"*Bedda mia.*" Agata murmured.

"*Sì?*"

"We still have a long walk in front of us."

"*Sì.*"

"Before we leave, I have something I think I should tell you. It's about your mother."

I peered at Agata. Her tone was serious.

"Go ahead."

"After your brother, Carmelo, died, you know of course, your mother chose to leave for a convent."

I opened my eyes and sat up. There was an undertone to Agata's voice–a sadness and, perhaps regret, I had not heard before.

"*Sì*, I remember."

"That wasn't quite true. You were small. What you remember is what you have been told, over and over."

"What do you mean?"

"I tried so hard to help your mother, but she was battling forces much stronger than either she or your father could manage."

"What forces? What are you talking about?"

"This is not an easy story to hear, so you must be sure you want to know the truth."

I nodded, not at all sure I wanted to hear it.

"After your brother was born, your mother took to her bed. She stayed there for weeks, crying, refusing to eat. And when she wasn't crying she was talking to people–do you understand, Genevra? People who weren't there." Tears ran from Agata's cheeks, and dripped into her lap. "Your *Mamma*, she said the apostles were visiting her. When your father accused her of looking for attention, she refused to speak to him."

I could not imagine anyone ignoring my stern father. "What did he do?"

"Of course, I had been given Carmelo to take care of. I would take him to her to nurse. One night, perhaps a week after your mother had stopped speaking to your father, she had just finished feeding Carmelo. Your father came into the room, and took Carmelo from her. He handed your brother to me and told me to leave. Your mother screamed at your father–saying vile things I had never heard come out of any woman's mouth before. Your *Papà* pushed me out the door, and I fell to my knees. He slammed it behind me." Agata pushed the heels of her hands against her eyes. I could hear soft, muffled whimpers as she bent over, and lay her head against her knees.

"Agata, Agata. What is it? What are you trying to tell me?" I knelt beside her and lay my head against her back.

"Inside the bedroom, I could hear your father shouting at your mother. She shouted back. I heard a slap. Then, I could hear nothing for a moment but her crying. She screamed 'No! No!,' and another slap. After, it was silent until your father came to the door. He strode past me, as if we weren't there. I took Carmelo, and crept into the room. Your mother lay twisted on the bed; her nightdress was ripped–pulled up around her waist. She was…bleeding, a little. I called to her but she didn't answer. At first I wasn't sure she was even breathing. Her eyes were wide, staring at the window. I went and knelt beside her, but she didn't seem to see me. I don't know what she saw. I straightened her clothing, and covered her with the blankets. I brought a cloth, and wiped her hands, and her face, and, well, the rest of her. She didn't speak. She didn't move."

"But, was she all right? Had *Papà* hurt her?" A growing, burning knot beat in my breast. I pressed my hands against the spot but I felt no relief.

"No, your mother was not all right, and yes, he had hurt her. Do you understand what he did to her?" Agata looked hard into my eyes.

I shook my head. I didn't want to know. I did want to know. I covered my ears, and shook my head hard. "No, I don't believe it. *Papà* wouldn't do that. He loved us."

Agata took my hands, and gently lowered them from the side of my head. "*Carina*, it was not even a year later you were born."

"NOOOOOOO!" I wailed. My vision blurred, hot tears ran from my eyes, and I closed them, not wanting to see or hear any more. My stomach roiled and churned, and I felt as if I would be sick. I clutched my belly, and rocked back and forth. I collapsed face down, and a heavy weight held me there. Through waves of anguish, I cried and screamed into the pile of loose hay until my eyes and throat were raw, and I had no more tears left. The pressure that had held me down lifted and I realized it had been Agata holding me in my paroxysm of grief. She pulled me into her lap and swayed from side to side, stroking my back, and singing softly as she had done when I was a child.

We stayed together like that for a long time–how long, I am not sure, but the light grew long and the warmth left. Agata wrapped my shawl around me. I leaned back against the wall, looking at Agata without speaking. Finally, I asked, "Did *Papà* not love us?"

"Of course he did. He still does." Agata took my hand. "You have to understand, *bedda mia*. Your father is Norman. Serious, not emotional. Even when he killed Landro for stealing the horse, it was not out of passion, but because he knew it was necessary–necessary for all his peasants, and servants, and the other nobles to see him as a powerful man, a man in control. Your mother was Sicilian, passionate and hot-blooded. He didn't understand her. What he did to her was no different than what he did to Landro. He was showing his dominance."

This I could understand. I was a mix–half Norman, logical and serious–half Sicilian, passionate in love and loyalty. And then it hit me.

"Wait. You said my mother was Sicilian. Was. Is my mother dead?"

Agata held me tighter. "Yes, *carina*, your mother is gone. Let me finish the story, and you will understand."

I nodded and wrapped the shawl around me more tightly.

"After that night, your mother rose from her bed, and took up her tasks as the lady of the house, but all the passion had left her. She no longer talked to people who were not there, or so your father believed. But in the evening, when I took Carmelo to her to be fed, she would speak to the Blessed Mother and to the Apostles as if they were in the room with us. I begged her to stop, but she said it was the only time they would speak to her now. Over time, her pregnancy began to show, and almost exactly nine months from that terrible night, you were born. Your mother didn't show much affection to you, save the evening you were born. She held you so gently, fed you, and then she handed you to me and told me to find a wet nurse. So, I did.

"You and your brother grew well. I gave you both as much love as I could, trying to make up for your mother's lack. She became more and more obsessed with her secret conversations. She would call me to her room, and demand that I tell her I could hear them too. I didn't know what to say. I was terrified, sure the voices were demons.

"One terrible, evil day, when you were three and Carmelo was four, I heard him playing in the courtyard. I heard your mother's voice. There was a splash, but no other sound. I had a terrible feeling and rushed outside, and there I saw... I saw...," Agata stopped.

"What? What did you see?" I grabbed her arm.

Agata was crying again. "Your mother was holding Carmelo.

Holding him under water." A sob broke free from her throat. "I ran and grabbed him from her. She kept saying the Blessed Mother wanted him. I shook him, and called for help, but it was too late. Your father came running, and in the chaos, I didn't say what I had seen. I didn't want the other servants to know. But later that night, I went to your father and told him the whole story. Your mother left the next morning. Everyone was told that, stricken with grief over the death of her son, she had joined a convent. This was not the truth. Your father sent her away. To a convent, but not to live a contemplative life; instead to be exercised of the demons that had been speaking to her since your brother was born. About a week after she arrived at the convent, the priest sent word your mother had succumbed to the demons, and had taken her life by jumping from a cliff."

We sat in silence for a long time. The long light had disappeared and the silence was covered in darkness. I was empty, hollow, and my head throbbed. "Why did no one ever tell me this?" I finally asked.

"Your father swore me to secrecy. He was afraid if it became known your mother was possessed, no one would marry you. He kept it from you and everyone else so that you would have a normal life."

I snorted derisively. "Normal life? Not one thing in my life has been normal."

I heard a rustling sound, and felt Agata wrap her shawl closely around the both of us. She tightened her arm around me, and pulled me into her lap. As she stroked my hair, she whispered, "Genevra, you are meant for greater things than 'normal'."

Chapter nineteen

A STRONGHOLD OF VULTURES

I WOKE TO A TICKLING of donkey whiskers. Graziella was sniffling my face. "Get off me, you foolish donkey." I pushed her away as I sat up. Agata was already up with a bucket of fresh water.

I dipped my hands into the bucket. My eyes were still aching from the tears of the night before, but neither Agata nor I spoke of it. I splashed the icy water onto my face, and dried it on my shawl.

"Genevra, I think it is time for us to move on. With luck, we can make it to Caltavuturo." Agata shivered and crossed herself. I knew why. I had never been to Caltavuturo, but the meaning of its name–a stronghold of vultures–conjured up terrifying images. I shivered at the thought of it, and the thought of the steep mountain climb we had before us.

"Is there any other way to your village than Caltavuturo?"

Agata shook her head. "No, we must pass by there."

"Then come, hand me the bags, Agata. You should ride Graziella first."

~|~

That day passed more easily than our first walk. We stopped and bought bread, and cheese, and wine from the market in Termini Imerese before we followed the road southeast away from the sea. The road rose slowly–rocks and stubbly grass gave way to small sharp shrubs. We saw herds of sheep and goats and as the road narrowed to a pathway, the shrubs became pine trees. We wound our way back and forth around the hills and rocks, and our progress slowed.

Evening fell—the sky turned bright pink, and orange, and deepened into indigo. The stars twinkled above us. I didn't want to stop on the path—it was too cold, and I was fearful of the bandits I had heard wandered the Sicilian mountains. Agata was riding, and I held onto the neck of Graziella, trusting her to keep us on the trail.

As the moon rose, we came around the side of an outcropping and found ourselves face-to-face with the overhanging shadow of the foreboding castle tower of Caltavuturo. I shuddered.

"Look Agata, we are here. Perhaps we can find someone who will let us use their barn or stable to sleep in."

Agata crossed herself and I did the same, but I gave her the bravest words I had. "Look, Agata, I think it is safer trying to find a bed in a place of vultures, than to follow a dark path of bandits."

"Yes," Agata nodded. "There are good people everywhere in Sicily. I'm sure we can find one here."

It was dark, but not so late the people of Caltavuturo had retired to bed. As we approached the heart of the village we found the *piazza* lit with torches and filled with people—old men sitting and discussing the weather and their expectations for their wheat crops next year, grandmothers, cuddling their grandchildren as the mothers scolded. Young men and women stood in groups on opposite sides of the *piazza*, eyeing each other and either strutting or giggling, depending on their sex. As we walked toward the small fountain in order to give Graziella a drink after her long walk, we were approached by an older woman: not elderly, but old enough her childbearing years were likely gone.

"*Bona sera*! You are new to Caltavuturo." It was not so much a question as a statement.

"*Sì*, we are travelling to Sperlinga to visit family." I answered.

She looked at the two of us curiously. I realized too late my educated speech made my peasant dress unlikely. She shrugged, and I was grateful she did not question us.

"We were hoping to find a hut in which to spend the night." I asked. "Do you know of someone who might let us stay until tomorrow?"

She looked us over carefully, and answered, "My daughter has married and moved to her husband's house. I have an empty bed. You are welcome to share it if you like. My name is Valentina."

"*Grazii*. I am Genevra, and this is my... this is Agata. We are grateful for your offer. It has been a long walk for us today." Agata nodded in agreement from Graziella's back.

"How far have you walked?" She asked.

"We left Trabia early this morning." Agata answered.

Valentina gasped. "Trabia! You have walked from Trabia today?" Valentina stood with her mouth open in astonishment. Another woman caught the surprised tone in Valentina's voice and came to hear the conversation.

"Where did they come from?"

"Trabia."

"They came from Trabia?"

"How could you walk from Trabia in one day?"

We suddenly found ourselves surrounded by people, men and women, wanting to know about the long trek we had made. The one question they did not ask, thankfully, was why. The mountain peasants of Sicily had learned it was in their own best interests to not ask too many questions, or to not ask the wrong ones. Asking how we had done the walk was one thing, but the reasons why might be information they didn't want to know.

We answered the questions as best we could. "We left early in the morning. No, we stopped in Termini Imerese. Yes, we have been travelling several days. Just cheese, and bread, and a little wine." With the last answer, a great clucking of tongues and wagging of heads broke out, and Agata, Graziella and I were swept along until we reached what turned out to be Valentina's home. Our little donkey was led into the ground floor, and left in the hands of a young boy to feed and water her.

"Ivo, come up and stoke the fire when you're done."

The rest of us, Valentina, Agata and I, along with a great crowd of chattering women, climbed the outdoor stone stairs to Valentina's living area.

As the child of a nobleman, I had only had limited opportunity to visit the homes of the peasantry, but Agata, as we walked, had told me about the houses in which she and her family had lived, in the mountains around Sperlinga. It was normal for families to live with their donkeys, sheep, goats and other animals on the ground floor, and the family to live above. Having spent a few days in the hut in Trabia, I could appreciate the warmth, if not the odour, the animals gave to the house. Valentina's house, simple and, small as it was, filled with people as we entered. Valentina waved us to sit in two rough wooden chairs, and she pulled out the ingredients for a hearty peasant meal of pizza. The dough had been sitting on a shelf, covered with a cloth. Valentina, ignoring the advice and instructions of the women around her, pressed the dough out into a thin, flat, round shell and poured oil over it. The women clucked with approval.

An elderly woman grasped my elbow. "Her son makes the best oil in Caltavuturo." she whispered conspiratorially. She kissed her fingers as if to place a definite exclamation mark on the end of her statement.

"Ivo, away from the oven!" Valentina called to the boy who scrambled to the other side of the room. Valentina slowly slid the dough into the oven, onto the cooking stone. The women chattered with each other. I stood and let my mind drift, surrounded by the warmth of the oven, the delicious smell of the bread, and the gossip of the women.

The aroma of the bread mixed with the sweet smell of the straw below and the pungent scent of Graziella wrapped around me like a shawl. I felt myself slip into an odd dream state. The room faded, and my father's stable surrounded me instead. My father stood to the side, and behind him stood Landro. But it wasn't either of them that caught my attention. Directly before me was my mother. Even though I had long forgotten the look of her face, I knew it was her. Her face was gentle, soft, content. The thought crossed my mind she must have truly been exercised of the demons when she died, and, in spite of everything I had been taught about suicide by the priest as I studied for communion, our Lord must have forgiven her for taking her life in order to rid herself of the evil that had chased her to her death. She beamed and reached her hand out to me. She, my father, and Landro disappeared into a swirling mist, and I felt myself drifting as if I were about to fly. I was so grateful for the moment with my mother, I tried to make the sign of the cross to thank our Lord and the Holy Mother. A cry and the sudden feel of hands gripping my arms and shoulders shattered my moment of gratitude. I felt my body lowered to the straw floor, and I opened my eyes in surprise. A floating crowd of shocked, female faces circled above me. Confused, I tried to sit up. A chorus of "No!" met my attempts.

"Genevra," it was Valentina's voice, although I could not pick her out in the gathering of women's faces. "You fainted. Don't try to get up too quickly or you will faint again."

I heard footsteps, and the faces moved away. It was Agata. "*Bedda mia,* are you all right?" Her face moved closer. My vision slowly cleared to see the room around me.

"Yes Agata, I am...I will be fine." I sat up. Agata grasped my hand, and put her arm around my shoulders. The women did not challenge me this time. They stepped back, deferential. Clearly, Agata was in command.

"We have walked too far today." Agata spoke to the women but focused her gaze at me. "She did not take her fair turn on the donkey, and she has not been eating properly. She is exhausted."

Valentina stepped forward, and helped Agata get me to my feet. "Here, sit in this chair. You should not be on your feet." She turned her head to the women and said, "Someone take out the bread, *pi favuri,* and put it on the table. Now, this young woman needs food and rest. She will get neither with all of you busybodies here. *Scio!* Shoo! Leave her be. You can ask your questions tomorrow."

The women grumbled their way out and into the street. Valentina ignored their complaints, and instead sliced two large pieces of bread, and poured three large cups of wine. She sipped hers and watched Agata and I devour the delicious bread, and drink the rich, red wine. When we finished, she sliced another piece for each of us, and smaller ones for herself and for Ivo. He had crept up the stairs, and was watching us with big dark eyes. She handed it to him, and waved him back down the stairs.

We ate and drank in silence. I had few words left to answer any questions. Agata, however, seemed to have recovered and when they had finished their meal, she and Valentina chatted quietly while I sipped the last of my wine. When I finally placed my cup on the table, Agata stood up and said to me firmly, "Genevra, you will take the bed, and I will sleep with Graziella."

I nodded. I knew I could not argue–I did not have it in me. Agata and Valentina each took an arm, and led me to the straw ticking. I lay down and immediately drifted that valley between sleep and wakefulness. In the silence of the evening, the murmurs of Agata and Valentina floated around the room. Valentina's voice had the gravel sound of someone used to cooking at a wood stove, breathing in the rich smoke. The last thing I heard before I finally succumbed to sleep was Valentina's deep burr asking, "Your mistress, she's with child, isn't she?"

Chapter twenty

VALENTINA AND LUIGI

I GRUMBLED TO MYSELF as the distant sound of Graziella braying pulled me to the surface. Odd, she sounded too far away. Were we not still in the farmer's hut in Trabia? I cracked one eyelid open. This was not the farmer's hut. I bolted upright and gazed around the room, empty but for me. Right, this was Caltavuturo. I swung my legs around but my stiff muscles and joints screamed in pain. Slowly, I rose, my bare feet on the grey stone, polished from so many years of footsteps. I could hear movement outside, and I wobbled my way to the door. My mouth dropped open. A thin layer of snow lay on the ground, and my breath came in wisps before me. I shivered. I had never seen snow. Agata had told me about it as I grew up, but I didn't realize how lovely and clean it looked.

"Genevra! What are you doing! *Scio*! Into the house with you and put on your shoes!" Agata glared up at me from the piazza. Rather than face her wrath, I stepped back inside.

I pulled my stockings back on, and slipped my feet into my now worn shoes, Valentina came into the room carrying a bowl of warm bean and lentil soup.

"Sit, eat!" Valentina gestured for me to take my place. "Agata, you too. There is plenty of food." She winked at us. "My son has a good farm, you know."

Valentina poured a generous dollop of olive oil over the soup, and passed a plate of warm bread. Valentina was truly a *maistra* in the kitchen. After the past week of dried bread, cheese, and water, these flavours were ambrosia. Valentina carried a steaming jug to the table, and poured mugs of warm wine with honey, cinnamon and herbs. I could feel the strength of the drink course through me.

We all sat and ate in silence, even Valentina, until our mugs and bowls were empty and the bread was gone.

"*Grazii, Signura* Valentina. That was...I can't say how wonderful that was."

Valentina waved my words away, but there was a glint of pride in her eyes. "Now, we have much more important things to discuss than our lunch." I glanced at Agata. How much had she told Valentina?

"If you are planning to make it all the way to Sperlinga in the snow, whether you walk or ride your donkey there, you will not keep that baby of yours. Now, don't jump up. Sit, sit. Your 'cousin', Agata, did not have to tell me anything. I have been delivering babies in this town for too many years to not know when a woman is carrying one."

My heart pounded. Our whole plan depended on the secrecy of this pregnancy. "Please, *Signura*, please don't tell anyone about this."

"Oh, don't worry child. You are not the first girl to find herself in this way. You could tell from the women who followed you here last night, gossip is one of the chief pastimes in this town." Valentina chuckled. "So, you can't stay here to have your child, but I have a plan. I'll need to bring my son into our confidence but you don't have to worry–he is as closed-lipped as they come. I have sent Ivo for him."

I opened my mouth and she, once more, waved my words away. "There is plenty of time to discuss this later. For now, rest. We will decide our strategy tonight over dinner and wine."

~|~

The sun set early in the mountains. The moon had already risen when Valentina's son, Luigi, arrived at her door. She hustled him into the room, closing the door, and the cold, behind him. A taciturn young man, he nodded to us silently. Still, there was a glimpse of the fire I could see in his mother's eyes.

"First, we eat." Valentina said, placing dried meats and apricots alongside a steaming risotto, and for a time there was no talking–we were too busy eating. The flavours and scents overwhelmed me. After finishing a second bowl of risotto, I sat back with a satisfied sigh.

"*Grazii, Signura* Valentina. I don't believe I have ever eaten anything so delicious. At least not since lunch!"

Valentina chuckled and nodded graciously as she returned to the table with a plate of sliced blood oranges and dried figs. "*Pregu.* But you must eat some of these. They are the last of the oranges from the fall. They will give you strength for... they will give you strength and thicken your blood."

I glanced over at Luigi–he hadn't caught his mother's near slip.

"Luigi, Genevra and Agata have a problem. I think you can help them but the reason for it must remain a secret. It will take you away from the farm for a few days. Will you help them?"

It was hard to read Luigi's face. He glanced over to us and answered, "*Sì, Mamma.*"

"*Va beni.* Good. These two must reach Sperlinga before the weather gets too bad. They have been walking many days but Genevra's health is... delicate. I think walking, or even riding their donkey would be unsafe for her. Can you take them in the wagon? If you leave tomorrow and there is no more snow, you could get to Castellana Sicula tomorrow, then Gangi, and be in Sperlinga by the end of the third day."

"*Sì*, that would be possible. I can take some of my oil to sell." Luigi answered.

"*Bonu*! Then none of those bleating sheep will have stories to tell." Valentina nodded her head with satisfaction. "I will pack food for all of you."

Luigi stood up, and placed his woollen cloth cap on his head. He nodded to us, and kissed his mother on each cheek. "I'll be here early with the wagon," he said and turned and left us behind in the warm room.

I watched him go, worried that my secret would be safe. I could feel my brows come together in a frown.

Valentina looked over at me and shook her head. "You needn't worry about Luigi. As you can see, he says very little. Even if I had told him your secret, he would never tell. Not even his wife will know more than that he is taking his last load of oil to sell, and that you happen to be travelling in the same direction."

Agata took Valentina's hand and said, "*Signura* Valentina, we trust your son because we trust you. I can never thank you enough for your kindness and your help. I have been so worried Genevra would take sick or, God forbid, lose her child on the road. I am so relieved we will be in Sperlinga at my cousin's home in three days, rather than spending another hard week walking through the mountains."

I nodded, then impulsively threw my arms around Valentina. Valentina, surprised at first, returned the warm embrace. After a moment, Valentina stepped back, flushed and brushed invisible crumbs from her skirt.

"You two still have a long journey, even if the wagon is shortening it for you. You need to rest–tomorrow will be a hard day. *Scio!* Off to bed with you." With that Valentina hustled the leftover food and dishes from the table, leaving us to prepare for bed.

Agata and I climbed into the soft straw bed. I was grateful for the comfort of this woman whom I had known my whole life. This adventure which had seemed so simple and straightforward at my father's house had become much more difficult and complicated. I heard Agata's regular breathing as she drifted into sleep. Shortly, I closed my eyes and joined her.

~|~

I felt Agata's hand on my shoulder shaking me gently. "*Bedda mia*, we need to get up."

I opened my eyes slowly to see sunbeams crossing the room. It was cold when I rose, so I pulled on my stockings and shoes quickly. I wrapped my shawl around me tightly. I was sure the temperature had dropped from the night before. As if reading my thoughts, Valentina commented, "The sky has cleared. It is always colder in the mountains when there is a clear sky, but at least we can be sure there won't be snow for a few hours."

The ice-cold water Valentina had set aside for us shocked me into wakefulness. There was a sharp knock at the door and Luigi slipped into the room.

"The wagon is ready. I tied the donkey to the back."

"*Bonu!* Genevra, you should take your things to the wagon." I picked up my bag and followed Luigi out the door, but before I could descend the stone stairs, I heard Valentina whisper to Agata, "Here, take this bag. These are things that will help if the baby comes while you are on the road." I shuddered at the thought.

Agata hurried behind. Luigi helped us into the wagon, half filled with large ceramic bottles of Luigi's famous olive oil. In the rest of the space, Luigi had spread straw over the floor and covered it with thick woollen blankets. Agata plumped up the straw so that we could lean back against it and I separated the blankets so that we had two under us and two over. We settled ourselves, and leaned in together for warmth.

"God go with you!" Valentina called to us.

We waved in return and called "Grazii!" as Luigi clucked at his mule.

Chapter twenty-one

A RIDE IN A WAGON

THE CRAGGY, GREY MOUNTAINS stood out sharply against the beautiful, clear blue sky. Our breath made little fog trails as we moved along the road that took us further up into the mountains.

"It is good it is so cold today," Luigi said over his shoulder. "Otherwise the road might have become impassable with the snow."

Agata lifted her eyebrow at me. This was the most we had heard Luigi say at one time.

"*Grazii*, Luigi, for taking us to Sperlinga. It must be causing you such trouble to do so." I answered.

"No."

Agata and I glanced at each other again. It was hard to read this uniquely inscrutable Sicilian farmer. After a moment Luigi spoke again.

"I mean, no, it is no trouble. Now I can sell what remains of the extra oil from last year's season."

Agata and I, used to the temperament of the Normans, found nothing disagreeable in the silence, but Luigi, living in a Sicilian family, must have expected his silence would be taken as rudeness or surliness.

"I'm sorry, I don't talk so much. Don't misunderstand, I'm not angry. My mother always says I must be angry when I don't speak."

"Oh please, don't worry. My father could be quiet when he wanted to be. Both Agata and I are used to silence." I answered.

Luigi paused again.

"I'm the youngest of eight. The rest are girls. They never stopped talking. I could never get a moment to speak. Now, the family expects me to be quiet, even if I have something to say."

"Is it the same with your wife?" I asked, curious.

"No. She waits to hear what I have to say. Even if it takes me a long time." His voice softened.

"Do you have children, Luigi?" Agata spoke up from beside me.

"Yes." He looked back at us with a grin. "I have four, and my wife will give me another in the spring. They are all boys, so she is hoping for a girl this time, to help her in the house. The oldest, he is seven, then five, four, and two." He puffed out his chest as he spoke of his boys.

"They are all strong, and the oldest two help me in the fields. In the spring, the third one will follow me to the fields…"

I leaned back and listened as Luigi rambled on about his boys. Once he began to speak of his children, it was like a clear frozen mountain stream that had thawed. I placed my hand over my stomach and wondered when I would feel my child move; if I would become as passionate as he over a child I was planning on leaving behind. I closed my eyes, and felt the rocking of the wagon. The clip-clop of the mule and donkey hooves on the stones lulled me to sleep.

Chapter twenty-two

A VISITATION

I WAS IN A DARK HOUSE, leaning back on a birthing stool with straw spread beneath me. I was panting, and sweat covered my face. Women, I'm not sure how many, were gathered around me but their attention was not on me–it was on a small bundle held by a slight woman with grey streaks in her hair. She looked up at me with a glowing smile on her face. It was my mother!

"It's a girl, *bedda mia*! You have given me a granddaughter!"

I was puzzled. I didn't remember having a baby. I raised myself up, and looked into the face of the child; a sweet cherub with long dark lashes, grey eyes and wisps of fine dark hair. But those eyes–they stared at me with far more knowledge and comprehension than any baby I had ever know. Accusation glinted hard in those eyes. She knew what I planned to do! She knew I planned to leave her here, and return to my father's home to be married into the royal family. I didn't know who would care for her, if she would have a good life, or even if she would have a life at all! I stared back in horror that I was possibly condemning this child–my child–to a life of want and misery. I couldn't do this. She was born of my womb, and even if Landro had left me, I had loved him. She had been conceived in love. She deserved so much more than this. I reached one hand out to touch her soft hair, ran a finger along her pink cheek, and with that touch I knew I would not leave her behind. Relief washed over me. The tension I had been carrying from the day Landro had disappeared lifted and I felt as if I could fly. I glanced up at my mother only to see another woman, a breath-taking woman, standing next to her. Who was she? A soft glow surrounded her, and serenity rolled off her in waves and lapped over me. She could only be the Holy Mother, the Virgin. I scrambled to my knees in supplication. Smiling softly, my mother placed my daughter in my arms, and I felt a warm breeze blow through us; a breeze of peace and contentment.

As I looked into my daughter's face, it changed and drifted–it took the shape of another baby and another and another, flashing forward into the future. Each one gazed back at me with grateful eyes. Each one was thanking me for my decision, a decision making each one of them possible for a thousand years or more.

Tears streamed down my cheeks with the momentous realization of the mistake I might have made. I clasped my new baby to my breast and made a prayer of thanks to our Gracious Mother. I would name her Amadora for she was a gift of love. The Holy Mother reached out, and placed one hand on Amadora's tiny head and one hand on my cheek. As She whispered a benediction, Amadora, my mother and the Virgin faded into a mist and drifted away. I wasn't alarmed. I knew Amadora was still with me, and my mother and the Madonna had never left. I drifted deeper into a dreamless sleep.

~|~

I turned and stretched, but the jugs of olive oil stopped my feet. I squinted up at the sky. The sun didn't seem to be in the right place. I sat up and gave Agata a bleary look. She smiled back at me.

"So, *bedda mia*, you've decided to join us again. You slept like an old woman." Agata laughed.

I smiled back. "*Ó cchiù bello d' à vita è ó ddurmi.* The best thing about life is sleeping!" I looked up at the sky. The sun was past its zenith, and had started its path downward to the afternoon.

"We stopped for lunch a while back. Luigi wanted to wake you up, but I thought we should let you sleep." Agata handed me some cold bread, and cheese, and a jug of wine. "*Mancia.* Eat. You shouldn't miss meals."

I chewed contemplatively on the cold food. The decision I had made in my dream still sat with me. Should I tell Agata? I knew she would have to know. My decision would affect her. I swallowed, and laid my hand on this woman who had taken care of me my whole life.

"I need to tell you something, Agata."

She said nothing as I confided in her, but her eyes opened wider and wider.

"*Bedda* Agata. I know this will change your life. Can you live with this?"

Agata sat for a moment, staring at my face, eyes welling over. Suddenly she threw her arms around me, and held me so tightly I could barely breathe.

"Oh, *bedda mia*, I have wanted to return home for so many years but I couldn't leave you! We can live in Sperlinga together and raise your little *bambino*, or *bambina* if your dream is true." I returned her embrace, then lay my cheek in her lap. I knew that it was the right decision.

~|~

The next two days passed quietly and without incident. Our luck held as the skies remained clear and the roads were dry. As the end of the second day grew near, we found ourselves following sharp and craggy rock faces. Agata, who had remained peaceful since my revelation, seemed suddenly restless.

"Are you uncomfortable, Agata?"

"I'm fine." She looked at me as a wide grin split her wrinkled face in two. "As soon as we round that next sharp cliff face, we will be able to see Sperlinga!" Her eyes were twinkling as she pointed ahead.

I looked in the direction she was indicating. The road twisted tightly along the cliff and as it sheered to the right it seemed to disappear off the edge of the mountain.

"Luigi, is the road up there safe? It looks very narrow."

Both Luigi and Agata laughed. "*Carina*, it is clear you were not raised in the mountains." Agata shook her head as she chuckled. "That road is the best one into Sperlinga!"

"We couldn't get the wagon on the other one." Luigi added. "It is barely fit for riding horses. Even donkeys and mules find it difficult."

I gave them a smile I hoped would convey my confidence in them, but inside I was making my prayers to the Holy Mother. As the wagon rolled forward, I found myself clutching the rough wooden sides, knuckles white. Luigi's brown mule made the turn, and I could feel the wagon lean. I closed my eyes and tiny beads of sweat prickled the back of my neck. My prayers were no longer silent–I muttered them over and over. 'Make the turn, oh wagon, please make the turn.' I held my breath and... nothing. I opened one eye and squinted around. We had made the turn. I waited for the drop, the crash and... and... we were still on the road! I looked over at Agata, sure she would be about to tease me for my fear of the mountain roads, but Agata had a glowing expression on her face. A wide smile took years away from her. Up ahead, built into the rock face, I could see row after row of doors. Agata had said her people lived in sandstone caves. I don't know what it was I expected, but a mountain covered in doors astonished me. Agata grasped my hand.

"Do you see that door almost at the top? The one with the vines? That is my cousin Maria's home. It has been so long! We were girls together–like sisters in fact! Oh, I have missed her so!"

I could hear Agata's excitement, but inwardly I was afraid. Agata had not been home to Sperlinga in my lifetime. What if her cousin was no longer there? What if she didn't want us? I did not know what I would do if that were the case. Perhaps I would have to throw myself on the mercy of a convent after all.

Luigi drove the little cart into the piazza. It was too early and too cold for many people to gather outside so it gave me a few moments to look around. Stone buildings surrounded the square yet all the way up the mountain, doors were built into the rock face. Agata's eyes jumped from place to place, exclaiming how little it had changed. She turned to see an elderly man step out into the street. Agata watched him hobble painfully over the cobblestones. She squinted at him and squealed like a small child.

"*Zzio* Enzo! *Zzio* Enzo! It's me, Agata, your niece!" She ran over to the old man who peered at her, confusion crossing his wrinkled face. Then his face broke into a radiant smile.

"Agata! *Diu miu*! I never thought I would see you again! Why are you here? Have you come home to stay?" Before *Zzio* Enzo could wipe his eyes, Agata threw her arms around him.

"Oh, *càru zzio*, I am home to stay."

I stood in the background and watched, open-mouthed, the tender moment between Agata and her uncle. I had known Agata for almost fourteen years and yet it had never occurred to me she might miss her family. In fact, until she mentioned her cousin Maria, I had never considered much that she would have family. I wondered how many of the servants in my father's house were separated from their families. How many worked day after day, year after year, and never able to ask for a few days to visit their parents or cousins or siblings? I knew for a fact most of our servants could neither read nor write, as my father preferred it that way. Agata was no exception even though, as a nurse, she enjoyed more privilege than most of the servants, and was given more leeway. My eyes welled for I knew my decision meant I would not see my father or *Zzia* Marcella again. Even if I tried to return, my father would likely banish me for causing him such shame. No, I could never return to the only home I had known. My throat, aching, choked closed as I fought the tears.

Agata brought her uncle in tow, over to where I was standing.

"*Zzio*, this is...." At that moment Agata saw the tears on my cheeks. "Oh Genevra. Of course, this would be hard for you–we have come to my home and left yours behind. But don't fret. My family will always be your family. Isn't that right Zzio?"

The elderly man looked at me with such kindly eyes as he nodded I dropped my head and my shoulders shook with the pent-up emotion of the past few days. Soon Agata joined me, and all three of us stood in the *piazza* crying as Luigi tried, nonchalantly, to unload his bottles of oil.

It took very little time for people in the surrounding buildings and the closest cave dwellings to realize there was some kind of disturbance out on the street. Slowly, then faster and faster, people came out into the *piazza* to exclaim over and embrace Agata. Did they all remember her? Did this mean perhaps my own *Papà* and *Zzia* Marcella would not forget me either?

Soon the *piazza* was full and Luigi was benefitting from the good feeling and well wishes in the crowd. His olive oil was either sold or traded in a short space of time. As he packed the goods he had received in trade, I trod across the cobblestones, and placed my hand on his arm.

"Luigi, you well may have saved my life. I can never thank you enough. You have been so kind."

Luigi gave me a lopsided grin. "If my wife needed some help, now she is with child, I would hope someone else would be good enough to help her too."

My mouth dropped open. "But, I mean, how did you know? It was meant to be a secret!"

Luigi smiled gently. "You and Agata may have thought you were whispering, but you were not as quiet as you might think." He gave me a serious look. "You don't need to worry. I may speak more than my mother thinks, but I am good at holding my tongue."

I beamed back at him. "In any case, thank you Luigi."

Agata came up and grabbed both our arms. "*Zzio* Enzo would like you to stay in his home for the night, Luigi. He has room for your mule as well. And Genevra, I want you to meet my cousin, Maria."

I looked into the face of a woman that could almost be Agata's twin. Her hair was greying, and there were more lines on her face, yet there was no doubt they were related. She grasped my cheeks between her two hands and squeezed.

"Genevra! Agata has said you have come home with her. You are welcome at my home for as long as you wish to stay with us. Forever, if you like. *Grazii* for bringing Agata home to us! *Grazii milli!*" Maria took our bags and the rope that held Graziella. "Come, we will pull you away from all these people and we will go to my house up the hill. *Vene ccà!* Come!" She waved to Luigi. "Join us for breakfast tomorrow, *pi favuri!* I want to thank you for taking such good care of these two!" And with that, Maria led us up the hill.

We followed Maria along the narrow paths switching back and forth up the mountain. Her home was close to the top, and when we reached her door, I was grateful I had no more climbing to do. Maria had two caves side by side. From the first one, I could hear the sound of chickens. She opened the door and led Graziella inside. She fed and watered our sweet and patient donkey.

"There, she will be warm and dry if it snows tonight. Even the chickens didn't want to come out!" Maria laughed. "This way, my home is through this door."

Maria led us into a dark room. She lit a candle, and I could see the room clearly. For a cave, it was spacious, and an opening led into another room behind. Maria carried our bags into the second room, and placed them on a straw ticking that half filled the room.

"You and Agata can share that bed. I will sleep in the main

room. It was such wonderful timing you came home now. *Miu maritu*, pig of a husband that he was, got drunk and fell down the mountain last summer. My son–you haven't met him yet, Agata–took over the flocks of sheep. I make cheese and I trade that along with the eggs to support myself, and my son and his wife share their bounty with me too! It has been good, but too lonely. I am so glad you are here." Maria hugged us both, one after the other.

"Now, I was making pizza when the word came you had arrived. I have enough here for the three of us to share if we are careful!" Maria placed a plate of pizza and a bowl of dried figs on the table. She poured wine into ceramic cups–one for each of us. *"Va beni. Mancia, mancia.* Eat, eat!"

We each sat with our own thoughts, eating the delicious food Maria had given us. I was exhausted. I had no reserves left as I thought about my father and *Zzia* Marcella. Slowly, one tear made its way down my left cheek. I tried to wipe it away so neither Agata nor Maria would see, but it didn't matter. It was followed by another and another. I hung my head over my plate and let the tears flow. A sob rose in my chest. As hard as I tried to hold it back, it fought me and fought me until it burst. I put my head in my hands and cried and cried.

"Cry, cry it all out *bedda mia*. It has been a long journey and you have a difficult road in front of you. But you are made of strong stock. Sicilians have weathered much more than this over the years and the Normans are strong, intelligent people. You have the best of both and you will take this and turn it into something wonderful. I know you will."

I turned to Agata and buried my face in her skirt as I had done as a child. She stroked my head until my tears were gone. I sat back and grasped Agata's hand.

"I think I need to sleep now, Agata. Please forgive me Maria. I am not being a gracious guest. Today, I have nothing, but tomorrow I will start again." I stood and bowed my thanks to Maria and made my way to the second room and lay on the straw ticking. I was asleep in moments.

Chapter twenty-three

A NEW LIFE

IN THE MORNING, Agata shook me awake.

"Genevra, wake up! Come look outside!"

I sat up and rubbed my eyes. Agata had slipped out the door to the next room. This room was chilled, but I could feel a warmth coming from the front room that called to me.

Maria had a bright fire burning in the oven, but neither Agata nor Maria were there. Confused, I looked about. The door swung open and a rosy-faced Maria called, beckoning.

"Genevra, come, you should see!" I stepped out the door and stopped, stunned. There was snow. Not just a little like we had seen in Caltavuturo, but several inches blanketing the entire mountain. Even in the valley below, we could see wisps of snow drifting from the top of the fields.

"Oh, this is so beautiful!" I exclaimed. "Wait! Luigi! Will he be able to travel in this?"

"Oh, I think so," answered Maria. "This snow is dry. It is when the snow is wet the wagons can't make the road. Anyhow, I was in the village already, and he left early this morning. He should be fine."

I whispered a little prayer he would get home safely and crossed myself. I couldn't forgive myself if he didn't reach his home and his children.

"Now, come inside. It is cold, and we need to discuss your future." Maria waved me inside. Agata paused to look at the view once again, and slowly returned to the cave.

"It has been so many years since I last saw snow!" Agata declared. She sat at the table with a big grin crossing her pink cheeks.

Maria placed a plate of sliced bread and soft cheese on the table in front of us.

"Genevra. Agata has told me about your situation. Perhaps you should tell me what you wish to do."

"At first, I had hoped to give the baby away and rejoin my family, but...," I hesitated to say anything about the visions especially since my mother's end had been so tragic.

"But?" Maria asked.

"I want to keep my baby, take care of her. If, I can stay here, that is."

Maria made a sort of derisive snort. "That is not even a question. If Agata brought you here you are family, not a stranger. How many of your woman times have you missed?"

"I think it is three. But I may have lost count." I answered.

"Yes, and with a young mother, the women times are often irregular." Maria frowned and counted on her fingers. "I think we should plan your baby will be born in late *Aprile*. And, of course you have nothing set aside yet for the baby." This was a statement rather than a question and directed more at Agata.

"No, nothing. We didn't have time to do any sewing before we had to flee her father's home."

"That shouldn't be a problem. We have almost five months to sew and we can borrow some if we need to. The more important issue is what will we tell people in Sperlinga? We can't have them knowing who your father is. We are remote, but not so far your father cannot find you here if he chooses. I understand he is a man of considerable influence."

"Yes, that is true." I answered.

"I have given it a lot of thought." Agata broke in. "The simpler the story the better. I think we should say you were a servant in Palermo. You had married last summer but your husband was drowned while out fishing. No one here will know anything about fishing, and they will not ask you any questions. I will say that I had heard that Maria's husband had died and I came home to help her and brought you with me as you had nowhere else to go. There. Simple."

Maria nodded. "Yes, I agree, simple is better." Maria cleared the rough wooden table. "Now, enough talk. We need to prepare for *la Festa di San Silvestro* tonight." Both Agata and I looked up in surprise.

"Is it already New Year's Eve?" Agata asked.

Maria placed her hands on her hips as she looked at Agata. "Of course it is! How can you ask that? We have so much cooking to do, Agata. We will eat with *Zzio* Enzo. We will bring the food to him, and eat before the festival." Maria answered.

I was stunned by Maria's answer. Somewhere in there, Agata and I had missed Christmas, and neither of us had even noticed.

Maria lifted a large pot of lentils soaking in water onto the table.

"*Suppa di linticchia*–lentil soup? Is it your mother's recipe?" Agata asked.

"*Uffa*! Of course, it is. What else would I make for *la festa*?" Maria answered in an impatient voice. "But, you can help with the preparation.

~|~

We spent the morning cooking. I felt like a bumbling child. *Zzia* Marcella was teaching me how to manage a kitchen, but our servants had done all of the cooking.

"So, **Genevra**," Maria asked me, "Do you know why we eat *lenticchie* at New Year's Eve?"

I bristled a little at the question. "Of course I do. The lentils represent wealth to come to us in the New Year."

Agata laughed and shook an onion at me. "Don't be so indignant. You have so much to learn about running a household here. It's not the same as running your father's house filled with servants.

Over the next few hours, I chopped onion after onion until my eyes were streaming and I could not see. I minced garlic, and chopped basil, and oregano, and sage. I sliced leeks. I watched Maria as she cooked them all in Luigi's oil. Maria and Agata had set me to work scooping and sorting the lentils, so there would be no stones accidently left in the soup. As I worked, Maria and Agata talked quietly about their family–stories of births and deaths, of young men leaving to find work elsewhere, since the mountain had little extra land to support them. Life was difficult for the peasants of Sicily–hard winters, crops failures, farmers falling to accidents and children to diseases. It made me even more certain the path I had chosen–staying here with her–was the right one for my child.

~|~

The soup sat simmering all afternoon. Before the sun disappeared, Maria placed the pot on the floor to cool. The wonderful scent made my mouth water. When I reached the point where I thought I could no longer wait to taste the delicious-smelling soup, Maria brought out two empty oil jugs and filled them.

"We will carry these to *Zzio* Enzo's home." Maria told me. "We will take the donkey, what did you call her? Graziella? She will be more sure-footed than we will be, and she will help us get to the *piazza* safely."

The mountain path was slippery. We clutched on to Graziella she plodded along, making her own way–we trusted her balance far more than our own. Far below, there was a huge bonfire in the *piazza*. My shivering face and hands looked forward to its warmth.

~|~

"*Bona sera, Zzio!*"

"Ah! *Bona sera*, Maria. Agata, Genevra, come in!"

Zzio Enzo waved us in. A fire crackled merrily and the heat wrapped around us like a warm blanket. Maria was already pouring the soup into a pot to reheat by the fire. There were three other old men sitting with their cups of wine in front of them. They nodded as we entered.

"Sit, *Zzio*, sit," Agata hung her shawl and mine next to the fire. "We will have soup for you as soon as it's warm."

"*Zzio*," I was examining a beautiful carved and painted board hanging on the wall. "What is this?"

"Ah, just a little something I did when I was younger."

"He was a cart-maker, when he was younger," Maria called over her shoulder.

"Not just a cart-maker–one of the best in Sicily!" One of *Zzio* Enzo's cronies piped in. "You don't know the story?"

"No. Would you tell me?"

The two other old men settled back, expectant looks on their faces. Certainly, this was a familiar story, but one they obviously enjoyed.

"Enzo's father was a cart-maker, and his grandfather and his great grandfather before that." the eldest of the old men started. "The carts were solid and well made, but the best thing he did was to carve figures onto the sides and the traces of his carts. Some were religious, some were animals he imagined, whatever people wanted. His carts ended up in Palermo, and princes and dukes would send for him to come and make them carriages."

"That's right," *Zzio* Enzo stepped in. "He lived in Palermo for a long time. He would send money home us, until his hands became too twisted to keep working. *Mamma* saved the money, only using what she needed, and when he returned he bought this house with their savings.

Maria dished out the soup for all of us and continued the story while we all ate. "*Zzio* Enzo learned from his father, but he was even more talented. No, *Zzio*, don't deny it."

"Did you work here in Sperlinga or did you go to Palermo?" I asked between spoonfuls of soup.

"Oh, I worked for the same family my father had in Palermo. I did just the same thing except my wife came with me." Enzo crossed himself at the mention of his wife. "I still miss her every day."

"I'm so sorry, *Zzio*."

As the old men rattled on Maria leaned over and whispered, "They both got sick, a strange fever. It left *Zzio* Enzo with a withered leg and his wife never recovered. He couldn't live in Palermo anymore so he came home and traded his woodwork for food."

I nodded at the other men. "Are they relatives too?"

Maria laughed. "No, just other old men like *Zzio* Enzo, who no longer have wives to cook them lentil soup on New Year's Eve. *Natale con I tuoi, Capodanno con chi vuoi*"–Christmas with the family, New Year's with whom you want, as they say."

The room filled with laughter as the men recounted stories of other festivals of San Silvestro when they were young men and full of vigor. As the wine cups were filled over and over, the stories became more and more ribald.

"All right," Maria said after one particularly bawdy joke, "I think it is time for the three of us to join the bonfire outside."

We wrapped our woolen shawls around us and joined the crowd. The raucous music had a wilder sound than the music in King Roger's court. The *ciaramedda*–bagpipe, *friscalettu*–flute, and *marranzanu*–jaw harp, were harsh but still made beautiful harmonies. And with the music, people had begun to dance the traditional folk-steps they had been dancing for hundreds of years.

I had never learned these steps, of course, but soon most of the crowd was dancing and a young man grabbed my one hand and a young woman grabbed my other and I was pulled up into a *tarantella* that was different than anything I had seen before. Laughing, I stumbled along with them until the song came to an end.

Wine was being poured as fast as we could drink it. One song followed another and another, and everyone who could dance, did. Even *Zzio* Enzo lumbered from hand to hand in the circle dances. The temperature was cold, but the wine and the dancing and the bonfire kept us all warm. The night whirled away in a frenzy of singing and dancing, and laughter.

In the early hours of the morning, just before the sky was tinged in gold, the musicians packed up their instruments and the women who lived near the *piazza* came out of their homes with fresh brioche, cake, and warmed wine. The bonfire was now embers and the whole village stood close to it, eating their treats and drinking the wine.

Maria touched my elbow. "Did you enjoy yourself Genevra?"

"Oh *si*! It was wonderful."

"Not tired?" Maria asked with a slight grin.

"Yes, I am so tired. Will we be going back up the mountain soon?"

"*Si*, I think we should go up now. Agata has already fallen asleep." Maria gestured to the side of the *piazza* where Agata was sleeping on a wooden bench with a brioche about to fall from her fingers.

"Poor Agata," I laughed. "I don't think she is used to late night parties anymore."

We helped Agata up on to Graziella's back and Maria led the donkey through the narrow pathways back up to the cosy cave waiting at the top of the mountain. Agata dozed all the way up, and Maria and I whispered back and forth.

"I spoke to my son last night. He will bring us a load of fleece later today for us to turn into yarn. We will need to start working right away if we are going to make enough cloth for this *bambino* of yours."

I was a little out of breath from our journey up the hill as well as struggling not to slip on the path.

"I'm afraid I have never made cloth." I panted. "Of course I have seen it made, but I was trained to oversee and not so much to do."

Maria shook her head. "How can a girl learn to run a household without knowing how to do the basics of cooking, and weaving, and sewing, and cleaning? Even if you only oversaw these activities, if you can't do them, your servants will cheat you! Steal your cloth and your food and you would never know!"

I could see the wisdom in what Maria said. When I was living in my father's house, it never seemed necessary to learn to do the work myself. Now, more and more, I was regretting my lack of knowledge.

When we entered our friendly little cave, Agata stumbled into the back room and fell, snoring, into bed.

"Even as a child she could sleep anywhere, anytime," Maria laughed. She unwrapped a cloth on the table revealing more of the delicious cakes. "Here, eat some more. You are carrying an extra person, and you need the extra food."

I sat and picked up a slice of cake and nibbled on it absentmindedly.

"What will we need to make for the baby, Maria?"

"Ah, well, you will need diapers of course with fleece to line them. A christening gown, several gowns to wear during the day and at night. You will need little shirts to go under the gowns. You will need small blankets for under and over the baby. I will make you a special sling so you can carry the *bambino* while you work. And we will make a little hammock for the baby to sleep in. The bed is too small for you, and Agata, and the baby as well."

I was counting the items as my head.

"Do we have enough time to finish all this before the baby comes?"

Maria nodded. "From what you have said, and from looking at you, I don't think you will be due until late spring. And Agata and I will show you how to do all the other things–making cheese, killing chickens, lambs, and pigs, curing meat. It won't take you long to learn what you need to know to run a house on your own, if you ever need to."

I looked at the delicious cake in my hands and felt, once again, overwhelmed at the kindness of this woman and of Agata, without whom I would have been lost. "Thank you, Maria. You didn't need to take me in, but I am glad you did. I appreciate everything you are doing for me."

Maria waved my thanks away and laughed. "See if you still want to thank me after I have put you to work."

Chapter twenty-four

GENEVRA'S CONFESSION

THE NEXT FEW MONTHS danced by in a whirlwind of weaving and sewing, cooking and curing. I lost track of the days as I prepared for the arrival of my baby, but every morning I checked out the window to see what the weather brought. Once the milder weather arrived, the almond trees growing in the valley below blossomed with a pale blushing pink. The fields grew riotous with the bobbing and brilliant blossoms of the wildflowers. The grass was lush and verdant after the winter rains. Maria and I walked to the valley, or rather, I waddled and Maria walked, to pick wildflowers, which we brought back and dried for medicines and dyes.

The wildflowers were not all that had been growing by the time spring arrived. My stomach swelled as the temperature climbed. My clothes stretched over my expanding belly, so, when the snow was gone, and the rain had diminished, Maria, Agata and I made our way down the mountain to attend Ash Wednesday mass, and to visit Maria's niece. It was the first time I had been to the village since it became obvious I was with child. I was embarrassed and shy, but I didn't want to complain to either Maria or Agata. The closer we got to the village, the quieter I became. Agata and Maria chattered away, discussing whom they would likely see, and what they could trade for their homemade cheese. About halfway, Agata looked at me with a raised eyebrow.

"Genevra, you are so quiet. Are you feeling well?

"Yes, I'm fine. I'll be fine."

"What is it?" Agata probed. "I know you. You are only this quiet when something is wrong."

I bit my lip and blurted, "I'm so big. What will everyone think of me! I'm a girl with no man who is about to have a baby!"

Maria stopped and stared at me, mouth open. She threw back her head and laughed until tears ran down her face. "You are worried they will find out you are pregnant? Genevra, they have known since the day you arrived! Do you think there are any secrets in a small village like this? The gossip has gone round and round like that spinning wheel you have mastered until it is no longer interesting for the old crones in Sperlinga. And as for not having a man, we told the village your husband drowned, but they have never believed it. They have already chewed your story about like a piece of gristle until it became tasteless. They are no longer either interested or surprised by your pregnancy."

I stood stock still–my face and chest flushed with shame and mortification.

"Genevra, do you think you are the only girl to have a baby without having a husband? It happens in every village!" Agata said as we resumed walking. "You are more fortunate than some–you have Maria and I to help you deliver and you and your baby will always have a place to live as long as we are alive."

I grabbed Agata's hand and squeezed it. "Thank you, both of you. But I think, to be sure, I should give my confession to the priest." It had been months since my last confession, but now, my fear for my baby's soul was much greater than the fear of the wrath of the priest.

"Father Nicolo will be there for confessions today. You can go before we see Marietta."

I entered the church early. There were only two other people waiting. A young dejected-looking man sat next to his *nanna*. She was whispering angrily at him, and he nodded contritely as she ranted. I sat a few pews behind them, not wishing to hear the angry accusations as I waited my turn. As I made my now considerable girth as comfortable as possible on the hard, wooden bench, I looked about me. The mother church in Sperlinga was not as grand as the one I had attended with *Papà* and *Zzia* Marcella in Palermo, but I preferred the smaller building here. The walls were close yet instead of feeling oppressive, I felt embraced.

I drifted in a wordless prayer, and my fear dissipated as if it were a wispy cloud floating around the rocky peaks on which I now lived. A warmth spread from my belly, almost, but not quite replacing the evil humiliation that had taken root.

A small scuffle broke through my revere. While I had been lost in thought, the contrite young man had been in to give his confession, but when he stepped out of the confessional his *nanna* was clearly not satisfied. With a smack upside the head, she followed him out of the church with a diatribe of reproachful words.

I rose awkwardly to my feet and took a deep breath. The confessional was small, and it was difficult for me to reach over my stomach and pull the door closed. By the time I had managed and settled myself on the small, uncomfortable stool I was panting with the effort.

"Are you all right, my child? You don't sound well."

"Yes, father, I'm fine. I am with child and it is difficult for me to get into the confessional."

"So, you are close to your time? Do I know you? I don't remember any of my parishioners being in your situation."

"No Father, I have been in Sperlinga since just after Christmas and this is my first time to church since then." I stared at my hands as I conceded this to the Father.

"That is far too long to go without the absolution of the confessional."

"Yes Father, I know, but I have been afraid to give my confession."

"Afraid? But child, our Gracious Lord already knows what you are about to confess. There is nothing to be afraid of, just the relief and grace of forgiveness to look forward to. Come child, I think it is time for you to confess."

"Yes Father." My hands were shaking, yet not from the cold inside the church. "Forgive me Father for I have sinned. It has been… I'm not sure… months since my last confession. In that time, I have dishonoured my father and my family, I have not attended mass as I should, but more than that, I… I lay with a man without the sanctity of marriage." With that I began to tell him the story of Landros, my love for him, and the baby I now carried.

"Father, I was so afraid to come and make confession because I was terrified you would tell me I could not be forgiven. I have felt the burn of shame deep in my belly, so strong I was afraid it would leave no space for my growing child. I am afraid my child will be born with my sin upon her head, and she, too, will never be forgiven. Father, please tell me I will be forgiven."

I sat with my hands clasped together against my whispering mouth, praying I hadn't condemned my child, my eyelids squeezed together hard trying to stop the tears fighting to burst forth. The priest didn't answer for a moment, and I felt I could scream in the pause before he spoke.

"Child, I can't say you have not sinned, and sinned egregiously. However, as John told us, if we truly and honestly admit our sins, so will our Lord forgive us our sins and cleanse us. There is nothing you have done our Lord cannot forgive..."

My head fell back and my mouth opened with a sigh from the depth of all that I was. I was forgiven. The burning shame that had been deep in my belly rushed from my mouth and was given to Christ to be swept away in his ultimate sacrifice. My relief was so great I missed what the father said was my penance. I didn't care. I would pray every day and night, attend mass every week, give to the church as best I could, and be the most devout woman in Sperlinga in gratitude for the forgiveness with which my child and I had been blessed.

"Give thanks to the Lord for He is good." I caught the words the father intoned.

"For his mercy endures forever." I responded.

"Now let me hear your prayer of sorrow, my child."

I responded to the kindness behind the priest's words with the most heartfelt prayer of contrition I had ever made.

I exited from the church to feel the most wonderful late morning sunshine shimmering on my face. I turned my face to the sky, raised my arms and twirled around in joy. Behind me, I heard Maria calling.

"Genevra! You, silly girl, come, *Zzio* Enzo has invited us for lunch!"

~|~

After lunch, Maria made her way from house to house to see what she could get for the cloth and the cheese. After we had loaded up

Graziella with flour, dried onions, oranges preserved in oil, garlic and shallots, we turned our direction to the home of Marietta, Maria's niece and namesake. Marietta was a jolly woman with five children, all boys. She opened the door at Maria's knock with a wide smile.

"Come in! Come in! *Zzia* Maria, it is so good to see you and Agata, and you too, Genevra. You have been holed up in your little cave all winter. I was worried you wouldn't be warm enough!"

We stepped into her house and were wrapped immediately in a blanket of the warm, fresh scent of bread.

She gestured to three chairs she pulled up to the table.

"Sit, please! *Mancia*!

She laid a plate of the fresh bread on the table and placed a bowl of warm olive oil and dark vinegar next to it. Agata and I both reached for the bread but Maria took Marietta's hand.

"Marietta, do you think you will be blessed with any more *bambini*?"

Marietta's warm laughter filled the room. "If I do, it will be a miracle and the priest will have to make me a saint!"

Agata looked at Marietta in shock, and Maria shushed her.

"What? It is only the four of us here, and what would the priest do if he heard me? I bake bread for him, and my husband gives him enough cheese, and prociutto, and olive oil so he never wants. What would he do if he excommunicated me? He would starve!" Marietta shook her head. "But I'm guessing you aren't here to talk about the priest. Genevra, you are bursting out of your clothes. Would you like to borrow the clothes I wore in my pregnancies?"

I nodded. "Would you mind lending them to me?"

"Of course, of course. I won't give them to you, because if I do, I certainly will become pregnant again, but I will happily lend them to you." Marietta went into the backroom and returned with a wooden box. "Here you are, whatever you think will fit, you are welcome to."

I reached into the box and pulled out a dress with a loose waistline. I felt the fabric with awe. It was the softest wool I had ever felt, softer even than the most expensive fabric in my father's home. After the weeks of carding, spinning, weaving and sewing, I was impressed.

"How do you make this wool so soft?" I asked. "I can never

make my weaving feel like this!"

Marietta smiled. "How many times do you card your wool?"

"Well, just the once I suppose."

"That is your problem. I card the wool, wash it in cold water and soak it in olive oil. When it has dried, I card it again, soak it in vinegar, wash it in cold water again, dry it, and spin it into the finest thread I can without breaking it. It makes a finer, softer cloth." Marietta picked out an apron and handed it to me. I rubbed it against my cheek and marvelled.

"If I can make cloth like this, it will make beautiful baby clothes!" I exclaimed. I reached into the box and pulled out another dress. "These are all so lovely, I don't know which to choose."

"Well, don't choose. Take the box! When you have recovered from your childbirth, bring them back." She pulled out a beautiful green skirt with a blue apron. Red and white embroidery trim edged both the bottom and top of the apron. "Try this one on and see if it fits."

I pulled it over my own and dropped my skirt to the floor. Agata tied the lovely green skirt at the back and help me settle the apron over the new skirt and my white blouse. Agata took a pale, yellow scarf and laid it over my head. The skirt fit comfortably, compared with the skirt I had put on that morning which was now much too tight.

Maria clapped her hands. "Genevra, you look charming! Marietta, that embroidery is gorgeous. Your clothes are always the most beautiful."

"Thank you, *Zzia*. Genevra, I have some baby clothes in the box I can lend you as well. It would save you some work."

We carried the box out of the house and tied it to Graziella's back. Before we could finish, *Zzio* Enzo came hobbling out of his house and calling to us.

"Eh! Maria! *Aspetta*! Wait!"

We turned to watch him cross the cobblestones.

"I have something for Genevra. You must come to my home to see it." *Zzio* Enzo insisted.

We followed him back across the street and into his home. As we stepped across the threshold he stood pointing, chest puffed and a wide grin across his face. What we saw he was pointing at was an exquisite baby cradle. The ends of the cradle were carved with an intricate relief of birds, and lambs, and other tiny creatures.

"You like it?" he asked me with a gruff voice.

"Oh, *Zzio* Enzo, it's perfect! Did you make this for me?"

"Ha! For you? You wouldn't fit–for your baby, not for you." He said, laughing at his own joke. "Do you want it? I think you don't have a bed for the *bambino* yet."

"No, no I don't. Thank you so much."

He waved my thanks away. "Maria, send your son to see me, I will get him to bring this up to you."

Impulsively, I threw my arms around him in a tight hug. "*Grazii, Zzio* Enzo. *Grazii milli.* A thousand thanks."

He grunted gruffly, and returned my hug quickly. "*Pregu.* You're welcome."

Chapter twenty-five

ON THE EVE OF EASTER

THE MONTH BEFORE THE EASTER CELEBRATION was a whirlwind of activity for me. As I had promised myself, I made the trek to the church as often as I could in spite of the protests I heard regularly from Maria and Agata. As my time got closer, of course, I found it was more and more difficult to get to the church especially as I insisted Maria and Agata did not have to accompany me every time. One day, I slipped and fell. Father Nicolo happened to be stepping out of the church, and he rushed over to help me.

"Genevra, are you all right?" he said, an echo of his first words to me.

"Yes Father. I am clumsy now that I am so big."

Father Nicolo led me into the church and to a pew.

"Genevra, why did you come without Maria or Agata?"

"They are so busy, preparing everything for the coming of spring and Easter, as well as the baby, I hate to ask them to come with me."

"I am going to say something to you I don't think I have ever said before. Stop coming to church. At least, stop coming unless you have someone with you. That child inside you is our Lord's child too. Don't do anything to endanger him or you. Now, I am going to find someone to walk you back up to your home, and you will stay there as I have told you. Do you understand?" he said sternly.

I smiled–behind the stern words, I could see kindness in his eyes. "Yes Father, I will do as you say, but I will spend the time I would have been at church making cloth and cheese for you."

"That will be perfectly acceptable, thank you Genevra."

Later that day, I pulled out the bag of sheep's wool I had been working on. I followed Marietta's instructions with the next batch most carefully. After I had spun the wool most slowly and carefully into the finest thread I had yet managed to accomplish, I wove it into a piece of cloth I could use as a scarf to wear over my head now, and as a wrap for the baby later. I marvelled at how soft it was with the few extra steps. I worked everyday, creating new cloth and new baby clothes, setting aside some, of course, for the church.

"Genevra! This cloth is wonderful–so silky. It is at least as good as Marietta's." Maria declared as she picked up the new piece of fabric I had finished. "I think you can trade this cloth for almost anything you want."

"Thanks Maria, but I need to finish making baby clothes first."

"You have made plenty of baby clothes! And, I think after the Easter celebration, you won't be going anywhere for a while. You'll have at least another week or two for sewing before your time, but you won't be in much shape for walking."

I set my needle and thread on the table. "Have we got all the food ready to take down the mountain tomorrow?"

Maria counted off on her fingers. "Marzipan shaped like apples, oranges, lemons and lambs, three *cassata* cakes, a basket of red painted eggs, and tomorrow morning Agata will make *fritella,* and I will make the *sfincione.* I think that is all we need."

After what had been a long winter, I was excited to gather with everyone in the town, enjoy the end of Lent, and to see how Easter in Sperlinga would compare to the grand celebrations in Palermo my father had always insisted we attend. I had washed all our best clothes, and so I busied myself pressing them and putting them away until the next morning. I was tempted to ask Maria what the festivities would be like, but I decided I would hold my questions and enjoy the surprise.

The day dragged on as if it would never end but finally we finished our evening meal and the clean up afterwards. As I returned the last plate to the shelf, I felt Agata's hand on my shoulder. I turned to look into her eyes and was astonished to see tears glistening there.

"Agata! What's wrong?"

"The next Easter, you will meet it as a mother." Agata wiped her eyes with her apron. "I always expected I would see you become a mother, but I never thought it would be here in Sperlinga or under these circumstances. I can't help thinking I have let you down."

"Oh Agata, that isn't true! What would I have done without you? If it hadn't been for you, my father would have shipped me off to a nunnery and they would have taken my baby away from me! You have saved our lives, and I will make sure my baby knows what you have done for us."

Agata squeezed me and pushed away, gently saying, "Off to bed with you, *bedda mia*."

~|~

The next morning Maria and Agata rose early to make the final preparations of the food we would carry to the *piazza*. I rose to help but Agata waved me back to bed.

"You will have precious little time to rest soon enough and I think you will find three days of celebrations exhausting. Sleep a little longer *carina*."

I snuggled back under the blankets and revelled in what I rarely got to enjoy anymore. At my father's home, only *Zzia* Marcella would have dared to wake me when I slept late. Here I never slept late, not because Agata or Maria woke me, but because I knew my hands were needed to accomplish the day's tasks.

As I lay surrounded by the warm ticking, I listened to the soft sounds of Maria and Agata's work and conversation. Slowly I drifted back to sleep and into the dream world I had not visited since our journey into Sperlinga.

Chapter twenty-six

"YOU ARE THE ANCHOR"

I WAS SITTING AT THE TABLE holding Amadora. I looked out the window and saw mist floating around the mountain. The mist swirled around the open door and leisurely drifted inside. The mist had a warm, sweet scent, and I breathed in deeply. As the mist filled my lungs, my eyes darkened, and soon I could see nothing around me, yet I wasn't frightened. I closed my eyes, and opened them to a faint light. The faces of children drifted in and out of the light. Together we watched, knowing these faces were the children, grandchildren and great grandchildren of Amadora. As we watched the procession of faces, the sweetest, most soulful voice I had ever heard, whispered to me, "You are the anchor." The faces came into focus, moved along and stopped before us. This face was not Amadora's great grandchild; she was much more distant. Her name became clear to me–Maria-Anna. She was a little girl, playing in the field below the village with her brothers and sisters. She had lovely dark hair and bright hazel eyes. Just as I was able to understand who she was, she faded away and another face took her place. This face was of a young woman, Angelina, several generations later. She was heavy with child. She was standing at the stove, in this same kitchen, dishing out a bowl of *succu di ragù* as her husband watched her lovingly from the table. The mist swirled again. This time the faces moved hundreds of years forward. It stopped with a lovely young woman named Cristiana. The place was unfamiliar. She was giving birth in a stark white room. Curtains hung around her bed and she was surrounded by women in short white dresses showing their legs up to their knees. One man also stood at the bedside. At first, I thought he might be her husband, but I realized he was a kind of healer and was helping her deliver her baby. When she finally delivered, the women in white took the baby, wrapped her in a clean cloth, and took her away. Cristiana lay back in the bed and cried. She turned her head towards me, eyes widening, and said, "You are the anchor, you must not forget." The mist and the faces faded, and I opened my eyes to see Amadora gazing up at me. I held her firmly, and I cried too.

Bang! I woke with a start. It was Agata pounding at bread dough. I lay back and brought my hands to my face. My face was wet.

Maria had drawn the curtain between our bedroom and the main room. The shutters were open wide and fingers of late afternoon light caressed the walls around the bed. The golden sunlight cradled me. I could hear Maria and Agata chatting and laughing in the next room. My stomach gurgled to the delicious scent of the Easter bread. I rolled onto my side and shut my eyes–the golden sunlight was so bright. Patterns of black, and red, and white bounced across my closed lids, forming shapes and images that arose unbidden. I caught my breath as the sudden figure of Landro appeared and disappeared. For the first time in weeks my thoughts settled on Landro and how he had abandoned me. A needle, hot and sharp, pierced through my chest, and a red-hot rash prickled and spread. My mind turned to the moment I'd left my home, and a monstrous, evil wave of regret washed over me–not because I had left, but more because I had not been truthful with *Papà* and *Zzia* Marcella. I had not been the good and faithful daughter I had always intended to be.

No! I would not let the past drag me down! Instead, I thought about the dream. I knew I was doing the right thing, and my mother, my soon-to-be daughter, and I were the beginning in a long line of strong and determined women stretching through time.

"*Carina*, are you awake?" I jumped at Agata's gentle words. "It is almost time to leave. We don't want to miss Maundy Thursday and the removal of the Blessed Sacrament."

"Don't worry Agata. I am up." With a groan, I pushed myself up into a sitting position. My huge belly filled my lap, and I grasped at the mattress as I wobbled precariously.

"Here Genevra, I think you should wear this. You look lovely in it and it will make Marietta happy to see it on you." Agata handed me the green skirt, clean and smelling of the spring breeze, with a white blouse and the pretty blue apron Marietta had lent to me.

'Thank you, Mother.' I thought as I crossed myself and kissed my fingers. It was a silent prayer of thanks to the Holy Mother–Marietta had been so generous with me, and I now had clothes that would fit around my great belly. Agata helped me on with the skirt and tied the apron around my back.

"Genevra, before we leave, I have something to give you," Agata held out her hands. In it was a cloth bag. "It is your birthing bag– I've filled it with herbs and a blessed amulet from Father Nicolo. It is to help you have an easy childbirth."

"Thank you Agata, but do you think I will need it this soon?"

"Only God knows when your child will be born. It is best to be prepared."

I smiled my gratitude at Agata. I opened my mouth to speak but Maria interrupted us.

"Come on you two!" Maria called from outside. "Graziella's ready and waiting to carry you and your bulging middle down the mountain, Genevra!"

I pulled a brown scarf of my own soft wool over my head and waddled after Agata. Outside I was greeted by our ever patient Graziella. Yet one look at me and Graziella made a loud, braying protest. Running my fingers through her bristly mane, I whispered, "I'm sorry, sweet Graziella. I wish, for your sake, I was lighter." I leaned over, as best I could, and kissed her between her gentle, liquid eyes.

Maria stood with a lantern in one hand and the other firmly on her hip. "Well, I am not at all sure how we are going to get you up on that donkey, but you can't make it down the mountain waddling like a duck."

Agata snorted. "Maybe we could sling her across like one of the sheep from the fields."

Startled, Maria looked at Agata for a moment. Her face twisted, her shoulders shook, she covered her face with her hands and giant guffaws burst from her, echoing across the valley. Agata grinned, chuckled and collapsed into laughter. Maria and Agata leaned against each other howling at the thought of my rotund body stretched out across Graziella's back like some errant ewe.

"Ha ha. Very funny. Just lead Graziella over to that rock and I will climb up on her back." I stood on the stone and put my backside against our little donkey. With Maria pushing and Agata pulling, the three of us managed to get me on Graziella's back, despite howls of laughter from all of us, and complaining brays from Graziella.

~|~

"Oh Maria! The *piazza*!" I clapped my hands at the wonderful red and white decorations strung all around the square. It was as beautiful as anything I had seen in Palermo. Brightly lit lanterns hung between the streamers, chased back the darkness. At one end of the *piazza*, a crucifix had been erected. Christ's face was twisted in torment. I felt tears pricking at the corners of my eyes as I looked at Him and thought of the anguish He had faced on that day over a thousand years before. At the other end of the *piazza* stood the Madonna. My stomach flip-flopped as I gazed up at Her. Her face, now so familiar, gazed back at me. I jumped. Her face, carved to look terribly sad, had suddenly turned up the corners of Her mouth and smiled at me. I stared intently at Her face. Yes! It was there. A smile. I looked to either side of me to see if Agata or Maria had noticed but they were busy adding to the armfuls of spring flowers the children of the town had gathered. I shook my head and looked back at Her face. The smile was gone. Had I truly seen it?

The children continued to bring wild flowers to hang in flower chains from the statues. Soon, they would be covered, as would all the statues of the saints in the church. Agata and Maria stepped back and the three of us watched.

"Surprise!" Marietta had come up from behind and thrown her arms around us in a tight hug. "Quick, let's tie up your donkey and head off to the church." Marietta helped me slide from Graziella's back.

The candlelight in the church danced and flickered off the walls, making warm shadows in the normally dark corners. We settled ourselves next to Marietta and her family, close to the back, excited to worship and enjoy the symbolism of the emptying of the church.

I took a deep breath and grasped Agata's hand. She squeezed back as we watched the ceremonial removal of the Blessed Sacrament and the covering of the saints.

"This is always the best part," Agata whispered. "Knowing that life will fill this empty church tomorrow. Every time, it gives me such a thrill to see it."

Father Nicolo stepped forward to wash the feet of twelve lucky men. Even though I had seen this event many times, it was shocking to watch the priest lower himself to that level before mere farmers. In Palermo, it was always high members of the court chosen for this honour. Not even my father had been amongst the fortunate twelve.

As we reached the end of the ritual, we all rose in silence and filed out of the church one by one. Held in rapture by the wonder of the moment, I fell in step with the other townspeople as we moved quietly through the town until we reached the *piazza*. The Christ and the Madonna had both been covered at their respective ends of the *piazza*, but the bright lanterns and candles and the red and white streamers lifted our mood as did the tables groaning with food–roast lamb and *mpanata* or lamb pie, wonderfully fresh *pupi cu l'uova* or Easter breads, *frittella* made with peas, fava beans and artichokes all freshly picked, wild greens soaked in olive oil, and of course, for dessert, both a "flock" of martoran– the marzipan shaped like lambs–and the traditional *cassata*, a delicious cake made with *ricotta*. Next to the food was a second table equally laden with red wine. As each of the worshippers reached the square a shout of appreciation rose up around the now covered crucifix and we all crowded the tables to taste our share of the delicacies.

"Maria, is the *pupi cu l'uova* yours?" a matronly woman I hadn't yet met called across the crowd.

"Of course it is Gina! And some of the *mpanata* and *frittella* too!" Maria shouted back.

Laughter and shouting filled the *piazza* and we took our bowls full of food to find an edge to perch upon while we ate.

"*Signura!*" I heard a young girl call to me. It felt an odd thing to be called *signura*–I still felt I was a *signurina*, but now I was so heavy with child it was to be expected. The girl gestured to me to take her seat, which I did with gratitude.

"*Grazii.* Thank you for the seat."

"*Pregu, pregu.*" The girl waved off my thanks and disappeared into the crowd.

Music played and voices raised in the country songs of the farmers. Across the *piazza* I caught a glimpse of Father Nicolo. He looked back and nodded at me with a smile and turned to a group of old men to join in the singing.

I had learned a few of the songs and sang what I knew. When the young people got to their feet to dance I clapped along in time with the music. I glanced at my rotund belly and sighed, wishing I could join them.

"Come *carina*, on your feet!" I looked up to see Agata standing before me with one hand outstretched.

"Are you mad, Agata? I can't get up and dance like this!"

"Oh, I think you can. Take my hand, you and I will dance together."

I lifted an eyebrow at Agata, but she didn't give ground. "Fine." I answered, heaving myself to my feet and taking her hand.

We danced slowly, but still in time with the music. After a few moments, we were joined by *Zzio* Enzo and Maria and later by Marietta, her husband, Giovanni, and Maria's son Giacomo. The next thing I knew, Father Nicolo had joined in. We circled joyfully, if slowly, our timing dictated by what I could and couldn't do.

The song drew to a close. I clapped my hands together gleefully. I heard a huge "*Brava!*" and I looked around to see the crowd had stopped to watch us and were now clapping and smiling at our slow *tarantella*.

Father Nicolo laughed. "You may be as large as a horse, but you still blush like a maid."

I lifted my apron to my face. I was embarrassed to be so huge and to still be dancing.

"If *Zzia…* I mean, my old family had seen me, they would have been shocked!" I said. 'But,' I thought to myself, 'The old Genevra nine short months ago would have been too proud to behave this way.' I waved at the crowd and they all laughed and then turned to dance.

A little out of breath, I sat and fanned myself. Agata joined me panting. Father Nicolo stood beside Maria smiling at our little group. He turned to *Zzio* Enzo.

"So, Enzo, this is quite the little family you have now. A few months ago, you were complaining about being alone, now look! You are surrounded by women!"

Laughing, he answered, "Ah Father, it is much better to be

surrounded by women's chattering than by memories that can't talk to you. I like this." He turned to Agata and me and waved a gnarled finger at us. "When this baby comes, I want to have many visits. I can't make it up the mountain anymore so that little donkey you spoil so much will have to bring you every week!"

"Yes, Genevra, we will have to arrange the baptism as soon as your little one is born. And you could arrange your visits to Enzo on Sundays when you come for mass."

"Yes, Father. And when I come next, I will bring the cloth and the cheese I promised you."

"That is kind of you Genevra, but there is no rush for that. Take care of yourself and your baby first."

With that, Father Nicolo nodded and turned to greet other parishioners and to join other dancers.

"Maria, you will be sleeping at Marietta's house and Agata and Genevra, you will come with me tonight." *Zzio* Enzo stated emphatically.

"Yes, thank you *Zzio*. It is kind of you."

Giacomo clasped Enzo around his shoulders. "Thank you *Zzio*. With our children all home sick, we didn't want Genevra to get sick as well, and my wife is run off her feet trying to take care of them and get all of her work done as well."

Zzio Enzo gave Giacomo a dismissive gesture, but self-satisfaction was written all over his face. "I have a lot of space so it is an easy thing for me to do."

We finished our delicious Easter food, and made our way to *Zzio* Enzo's house. The revels continued, but Enzo, Maria, Agata and I were worn out from the celebrations and needed to sit and rest.

As I sat, my head drifted to the side. My eyes were closed and the sounds of the party outside and the voices telling stories inside became a slow buzz distant in the background. I felt a hand, a very small hand, take mine, and other hands place themselves on my shoulders. The child's hand squeezed mine, but I could not squeeze back. Women's voices, different from Maria, Agata and Marietta, whispered to me, telling me their own stories–stories of love and motherhood. Finally, the women's voices stopped, and there was silence. Quietly, through the silence, a soft voice whispered to me. "I'll be there soon. Don't worry."

I jumped slightly, and looked up at everyone.

"So you decided to join us, eh Genevra." Marietta chuckled. "We thought you were gone for good!"

"I, I'm sorry. I guess I was more tired than I thought."

"Not to worry, the partiers outside seem to be quieting, and I think we should head off to our own beds." Marietta pulled herself to her feet. "Sleep well, all. And come over for breakfast in the morning!"

Maria stood and followed Marietta and her husband out the door, waving a tired good night to us all.

Zzio Enzo had been hunting through a wooden box and came out carrying several blankets that he handed to us.

"If you take the boxes from the corner over there, you'll find a bed with a straw ticking underneath. Throw these blankets on the bed and I'm sure the two of you will be fine."

"*Grazii, Zzio. Bon notti.*"

"*Bon notti.*" *Zzio* Enzo nodded and left us to our bed down below.

Agata and I moved the few empty wooden boxes onto the floor to reveal a beautifully carved bed. Once again, *Zzio* Enzo had outdone himself with his carving. The headboard was covered with trumpeting angels playing their music to the Madonna that sat on a cloud above them on the top edge of the headboard. He had taken some paint and coloured her gown blue and the angels' gowns white yet tinged with a sunrise pink. It seemed to me, we would be sleeping at the gates of heaven.

The boxes had flattened the ticking so Agata grabbed one side and shook it out. I reached for the other side, but Agata shooed me away.

"You will be doing enough lifting soon enough, Genevra," Agata scolded. "Get yourself ready for bed."

I turned away to remove my dress, and fold it carefully–I didn't want to wear a wrinkled dress to church the next day. I ran my fingers around the curve of my belly and felt a small kick against my hand. There was nothing I had ever experienced like the deep feeling of contentment and growing excitement about this child–this daughter, I was certain–growing within me. The kick was a message from my little girl to me. A simple message she would soon be with me, and I was grateful. I hugged my belly tightly and whispered '*bon notti*' to my little Amadora.

Agata had already climbed into the bed, so I lowered myself carefully, if awkwardly, onto the ticking Agata had fluffed out on the low wooden bed. Agata had created a warm pocket under the blankets so I leaned up against her back.

"*Bon notti, bedda mia.*"

"*Bon notti*, Agata."

Chapter twenty-seven

THE BIRTH

ONCE AGAIN, I FOUND MYSELF slipping into sleep, warm and comforting. For a time, I drifted in a kind and gentle darkness as if I were wrapped in soft wool–for moments and epochs–it felt like both. One by one, pinpoints of light broke through the darkness. As I saw the lights shine against the deep indigo background; I knew each one was a prayer from a mother to the Madonna to protect her child. This light was a young mother praying for an ailing baby. That light was an older mother praying for a good marriage for her daughter. Over and over, these lights whispered their prayers in the hopes the Madonna would reach out Her hand and grant their deepest desires... prayers for their children were the deepest desires of all mothers. The darkness lifted and after a time I saw clouds drifting past over a pale blue sky growing lighter and brighter by the moment. I raised my hand to my eyes at the brilliant light.

"Genevra, why do you hide your eyes from Me?"

"The light–it hurts my eyes."

"Uncover your eyes and look at Me."

I pulled my hand away from my eyes and found the light, while still brilliant, did not burn as it had. I blinked once, twice, and looked into the pale blue. The sky was enormous, both wide and tall. As I opened my eyes wider, I discovered the blue of the sky fell in folds and in truth it was not the ether but a robe. I followed the folds of the robe up until I saw the face–the serene face–of the Madonna. The brilliance I had seen had not been the sun but the Madonna's radiant face. I fell to my knees and prostrated myself before her. I reached out to bring the hem of her robe to my lips in order that I might kiss it, but no matter how far I stretched out my hand, she seemed to move that much farther away.

"Child, stop reaching for My robe."

I felt a hand touch the top of my head and I began to rise–floating slowly to my feet.

"Stand before Me, Genevra. Do not prostrate yourself before Me. You will soon be joining Me in the ranks of all mothers, the most honoured of women. Take the hands of My cousin, Elisabeth, of Salome, Hannah, and Rachel. Stand with Jochebed, Rebekah and Sarah. Our Lord looks on all of us with favour."

As the Holy Mother spoke, I felt a joyous jump in my belly.

"Can you feel that, Genevra? Your daughter hears My words and knows they are true. She will be blessed thusly, as well. You are the anchor, the root. Amadora will continue your line, and on, and on, for a multitude of generations."

One hand on each side of my protruding stomach, holding my blessed child with my palms pressed tight, I gazed in wonder at the face of the Madonna.

"Mother, you honour me."

"And you, Genevra, you and all your generations of daughters will honour Me as well. It is time now that I leave, but know My child, I will visit you again. I will stand with you as you raise your daughter. Know that I walk beside you."

As She spoke her final words, the Holy Mother faded. Lighter and lighter, She became a beautiful pale wisp until She disappeared into the sky.

I sat up with a gasp. I was no longer in the sky with the Holy Mother–I was in *Zzio* Enzo's house, sharing a bed with Agata.

Agata rolled towards me, and sat up sharply. "Is it time?"

"No, not that."

"What made you jump so?" she asked.

"Agata…I was visited by the Holy Virgin."

"What? Don't be foolish Genevra. All women have strange dreams before they are delivered of their child. I'm sure you are no different."

"No Agata, this was different than a dream."

Agata pulled the blanket up and settled back against the headboard. "All right, tell me about it."

I could hear scepticism in her voice, but I plunged in to the story in spite of the disbelief I was sure would follow. But as I spoke, Agata was silent. Her eyes grew rounder, and her eyebrows crept up her forehead. When I came to the end of my story, Agata was silent. She climbed out of bed to make a fire.

"Agata, you haven't said anything! What do you think?"

"Shush. Let me think girl. Give me a moment and I will tell you."

I watched Agata build the fire for a moment, and I got up to straighten the bed. As I rose, an ache in my back stopped me and I leaned on the bed, and with one hand reached behind and pressed the sore spot on my back.

"Are you in pain?" I was surprised to see Agata beside me. I had not heard her cross the floor.

"It will pass. I have been getting back pain off and on since yesterday." In a moment or two of pressing on the painful spot, it stopped. I straightened up and grabbed the bed quilt to straighten it.

"Off and on since yesterday?" Agata squeezed my arm. "*Carina*, you are a foolish girl. You are in labour!" Agata grabbed my shoulders and pulled me to her.

Labour? I was in labour? It didn't feel like I was in labour–I had a sore back.

"Are you sure it's labour? I don't feel unwell at all." I pushed back to look at Agata.

A pained smile settled on her old lips. "I was there when you were born–your mother was the same. Back pain for several days and a short but hard labour. It will be difficult, this delivery, I think."

"I'm not afraid. The Holy Mother will be beside me. She told me She would." I ran my hands along my belly. "I know I will suffer, all women do, but She told me I was the anchor for my line, a line of women starting with Amadora. I will live, and so will *mia bambina*."

"And you believe the Madonna visited you?"

"No, Agata, I don't believe it. I know She did. I have always had faith in the Holy Mother, but this is more than faith. She was here. She touched me. She spoke to me."

Agata held me at arms length, a frown deepening on her face.

"*Bedda mia*, if this is true, if the Holy Mother has come to you, you must tell Father Nicolo."

"I will. Once the Easter celebrations are over, I will."

Agata embraced me again. "Do you feel well enough to attend church this afternoon?"

"I feel fine now. It is just a sore back from time to time." I picked up my clothing to dress. "Besides, I wouldn't miss the veneration of the cross. I always feel so–I'm not sure–at peace perhaps, when the cross is uncovered."

Agata nodded. "I know, I feel the same way. It reminds me of how much I have to be grateful for." She put her arms around me, and hugged me tight.

~|~

At three o'clock the bells called us to the church doors. People from the town, from the caves, and from the fields all joined together in the pews of the empty church–every statue and cross covered–to commemorate the death of Our Lord on the cross. The uncommon sight of the walls bare of everything but colourless sheets left me with the same uneasy feeling I experienced every year at this time. I was filled with a sense of fear, for those few days before Our Lord was risen, I was left vulnerable and unprotected. My hands moved unconsciously to my belly in protection of my tiny Amadora. She was much smaller and more defenceless than I, and I felt the deep need to protect her.

Finally, Father Nicolo uncovered each of the four crosses within the church. His face was serious as he moved from cross to cross.

"Behold the wood of the Cross on which our Saviour was hanged."

Upon each cross, as it was uncovered, he laid his lips and kissed the blessed wood. As he continued his way about the church, the worshippers followed him, each kissing the cross before them.

Agata, Maria and I had sat at the back of the church, so we were amongst the last to approach each cross. I watched Agata and Maria curtsey before the first cross and kiss it reverently. I stepped forward, curtseyed and bowed my head humbly. I felt a hand press my shoulder. Without looking, I knew it was the Virgin who stood next to me, reminding me I, too, was blessed. I was filled with an overwhelming feeling of thankfulness, so strong I nearly stumbled.

"*Grazii, mia Matri, miu Diu.*" I whispered as I leaned forward to kiss the first of the crosses. As my lips touch the wood upon which the form of Our Saviour hung, a deep, transcendent warmth spread rapidly from my lips down my body to the depth of my belly and I felt warm liquid gush from the core of my womb and puddle on the floor below me.

I stood, shocked, unsure what I should do as I looked at the clear fluid on the floor at my feet.

"*Miu Diu*, Genevra! Your water has broken. We need to get you home." It was Marietta. She had come up behind me, unheard. She waved anxiously at Agata and Maria, and grasped me tightly by the shoulders. "I'll take you to *Zzio* Enzo's house. He has already said he would be happy for you to birth there."

Maria hurried over with Agata panting behind her. "What is wrong? Is it your time, Genevra?" Maria whispered.

"Her water is broken–there below the cross." Marietta made the sign of the crucifix. "If that is not an omen, I don't know what is."

Maria and Agata both crossed themselves.

"I will take her to *Zzio* Enzo's house. Agata, can you clean up? *Grazii a Diu* Genevra was at the end of the line for the veneration."

"*Sì, sì.* Go, I will clean up." Agata answered. "I will come soon to help with the birth, as soon as I can."

Marietta held me around my shoulders and directed me towards *Zzio* Enzo's house by the *piazza*. I had taken only a few steps when the pain I had felt earlier in my back returned. I grabbed for Maria's arm and clutched hard. This pain was darker, duller and insistent. It gripped my pelvis and held on, promising much worse later. It terrified me.

"Breathe." Maria's voice seemed to come from far away. I heard her but for the moment couldn't understand or respond. Finally, the pain receded and I was able to breathe as she had told me. I wanted to tell her what had just happened, but I had no words I could share with her.

"Are you all right to walk now?"

I nodded, shaken by the pain.

"You were not ready for that first contraction, were you?" Marietta asked as we walked again towards the house. "Many women are shocked by the pain with their first child. If the water breaks first, the labour can be hard."

"Will… will it be much worse than that?" I gasped, still trying to gain my breath.

Marietta laughed. "Genevra, this is just the beginning. Now you have time to breathe between the pains but as you get close to the birth there will be no relief. You must make sure you breathe. If you hold your breath, the labour will be much more difficult."

"Marietta speaks the truth. After five children, she knows about birthing." Maria chuckled.

"That is true. Still, you are a fortunate girl Maria is such an experienced midwife. She birthed all my children and you have seen what a healthy and noisy bunch they are!"

I listened to Marietta's words but did not find them comforting in any way. I wasn't prepared for this.

"Come, let's get you home before the next pain hits." Maria said.

Marietta and Maria hustled me along the cobblestones, holding my arms firmly. Once again I keenly felt the loss of... Landro? No, in truth, other than the fleeting image in my mind the day before, I had not thought of him in a month or more. It was the loss of a normal life. If I had not met Landro, if I had married as my father wished, at this moment I would be labouring in my husband's home, surrounded by the women of my husband's family. Gifts would be bestowed on us, and grandparent gifts on our parents. After the birth, I would be gifted with a *desco da parto*, a birth tray, beautifully painted on both sides to show the joyous entrance of my child into the world. Joyous entrance... my poor daughter. None of these things would be hers. Fatherless, she will be alone in this world.

Just as that thought crossed my mind, I was hit, unprepared, with another pain. Angry, dark waves wrapped themselves around my stomach and pelvis. Was I being punished for bringing a child into this world with no family and no name? The pain was so strong my knees buckled. Where was I? I couldn't see anything before me—my vision was grey—and all I could hear was the dark, angry rushing of pain.

As the pain diminished, I realized Maria was holding me on one side and Marietta on the other. I was kneeling on the doorstep of *Zzio* Enzo's house.

"Come, inside with you." Maria insisted. "Sit in this chair here until we get everything ready."

Already exhausted, I watched Maria and Marietta work. The

first thing they did was to build a fire in the hearth.

"It is not good for you to get cold when you labour, and the room must be warm for the baby when it is born." Maria explained.

Marietta brought a knife from *Zzio* Enzo's kitchen. "This will help cut the pain," she told me as she placed it on the floor in front of the hearth.

Maria came bustling into the room carrying a bundle of hay from out back of the house. She spread the hay on top of the knife, creating a thick mattress that would absorb any fluids.

"Have you got the birthing bag Agata made for you?"

"Yes, Maria. I have it tied on my belt...," As the last word came out of my mouth, I was gripped once again by the same pain. This time I remembered to breathe as both Maria and Marietta had told me. I grasped with one hand for the birthing bag and with the other for Maria.

"That's good, keep breathing, breathe the pain away."

I breathed as deeply as I could and focused my mind on the objects in the little bag as I rolled it between my fingers. The pain was intense and was spread wide through my lower back and groin, yet, even though the pain was no different than before, by rubbing the herbs and the amulet in my birthing bag, the pain seemed slightly more bearable. I kept breathing until I could feel the pain dissipate.

"Good girl, that was much better than before." Maria patted my shoulder and rubbed her hand.

"Oh Maria, did I hurt your hand? Forgive me!"

"Don't be foolish. A strong grip simply means you will push this *bambino* out much more quickly! It is much less work for me."
Marietta chuckled, "And we can relax and share some wine all the sooner! So, push! Push!"

"Stay sitting there, we are almost prepared, and I can check to see how you are progressing." Maria turned away from me and moved back to the pile of straw she had laid before the hearth. "Marietta, hand me the birthing stool from under the stairs."

Because I was born and raised in nobility, I had never had the chance to attend a delivery, but I wished now I had. Marietta handed a strange chair, about one foot tall, to Maria. It had four short legs and a back but the seat was odd, nothing I had seen before. Instead of a round seat, it was V-shaped. My best guess was I would sit on the chair, my legs along each part of the V, so the baby would be delivered onto the straw that would lie between my legs.

Marietta had gone to each window and closed the shutters and pulled the curtains. She had lit several candles, and as she was bending over to fill the keyhole with a bit of cloth, the door pushed open and knocked her off her feet.

Agata's head appeared around the open door. "Oh dear, did I do that? I am sorry, Marietta."

"Never mind, never mind. Come in so I can get the keyhole plugged up."

Agata came in quickly, and closed the door behind her.

"The church floor is all clean, and I spoke with *Zzio* Enzo so he knows to go to your house, Marietta, until the baby is born." She turned to face me. "How are you Genevra? Have you had much pain yet?"

"Some, but the birthing bag is helping."

"Good, I'm glad I gave it to you before we left. Something told me you might need it before we made our way back up the mountain."

"Agata, enough talking. I need some help."

"Whatever you need, Maria."

"Agata, I need you to help me get Genevra settled on this stool. Marietta, I need my bag that I left at your house."

Immediately, Marietta ran out the door, closing it tightly behind her. Agata helped me to stand.

"Should I take off my dress?" I asked.

"No, you have already got your waters all over the skirt. You might as well keep it on–we will have to wash it anyways." Agata answered as she put her arm around my waste and guided me to the stool.

"Now, Genevra, it will be difficult for you to lower yourself onto this stool so I want you to put one foot against mine and one foot against Agata's, take each of our hands and we will lower you onto the stool. Are you ready? On three–one, two, three…"

I found myself dropping slowly. Surprisingly, even with the space between my legs not supported, it was far more comfortable than I was expecting. Agata placed a rolled pillow low behind my back. The pressure there felt good.

Marietta opened the door and slipped back in, handing a bag to Maria.

"Marietta, can you chop and grind the lavender and chamomile in my bag, and Agata, can you warm a bowl of oil." Maria turned to me. "Genevra, I am going to raise your skirts so I can examine to see how far you have come."

I nodded my head, my cheeks fully reddened. No one had ever looked at this part of me before–not even Landro. I turned my head away as Maria gently pressed my thighs apart and gazed between.

"Good news, Genevra! You are well opened. Not enough for the baby to come yet, but still well along. This is good because it will let me rub oil on you which will help you open completely and will help the pain be less." She turned to Agata and Marietta. "Here, hand me the herbs and the oil."

Marietta and Agata gave both to Maria, which she mixed together. The combined scents of the lavender and chamomile filled my head, and my muscles slowly released the tension built, brick on angry brick, by the pain. Maria dipped her hand into the bowl and reached her dripping hand between my legs and rubbed the oil carefully around my opening. As she massaged, I could feel the muscles relax and release. She had not been massaging more than a few minutes when another wave of pain hit me. This one was hard, and even though I remembered to breathe and to hold my birthing bag, the pain was dull and sharp at the same time, and I had the overwhelming feeling I was about to be ripped in two. Maria kept massaging between my legs but it didn't help.

"Agata, quickly, massage the oil into her belly. Genevra, keep breathing!"

I wasn't able to pay attention to anything said or done to me. The pain rolled over me in powerful waves. As I reached the crest of the pain, I tipped back my head and screamed as loud a sound as I had ever made. The pain slid into the background and I was, once again, aware of the things around me.

"That was strong, wasn't it? That is good. If you keep having strong pains like that, you will deliver quickly."

Marietta stoked the fire, and, in spite of the pain, I felt comforted by the warmth both from the hearth and from the support of the women with me. I slipped quickly from intermittent pains with relief in between, to constant dull pain marked with sharp peaks of agony, taking me from a quiet constant moaning to sharp screams that sliced through the air like the knife that lay in the straw beneath me. Through it all, Agata rubbed my belly with the sweet-smelling lavender and chamomile oil. Marietta stood at my shoulders, rubbing them, and supporting me through the worst of the excruciating pain. Maria continually monitored my progress and gave me words of encouragement, reminding me to breathe and to focus on the birthing bag she thrust into my hand when the strong pains came.

I do not know how long I laboured that way, but suddenly, in the midst of one of the strongest pains, I found myself bearing down. It was the strangest feeling, and in spite of the pain, I wondered at it. It was as if I had lost the ability to control my body. Without any decision on my part, my body had begun to strain and push, to thrust the baby from my womb. I groaned and grunted with the effort over which it seemed I had no jurisdiction. The moment I began to groan, Maria leaned forward quickly.

"Ah, *bedda mia*. Your body is telling you to push. This is the hardest work but you needn't worry, your body will tell you what to do." Maria held my legs apart. "Marietta, when she pushes, hold her forward and don't let her tip her head back. Genevra, when you push, hold your breath while I count to ten."

I nodded my response. The intense pain relinquished its hold and I was able to breath again. I expected I would have at least a few moments to recover, but the pain and the pushing came on again, much faster than before.

"Push, Genevra. Hold your breath. *Unu, dui, tri, quattru, cincu, sie, sette, otto, nove, deci.* Now breathe. And once more... *Unu, dui, tri, quattru, cincu, sie, sette, otto, nove, deci..* Excellent!"

I could feel sweat dripping with the effort. I gripped the birthing bag and prayed to the Madonna. She had told me I would live to anchor a line of strong women, but the pain had become so intense I was not sure I would survive it.

I pushed and pushed. I could feel the body of my sweet *bambina* moving inside me as she slipped into the birth canal.

"I see the baby's head–oh, such dark hair! Not brown like yours, Genevra, but black like a raven." Maria cried out.

At that moment, I was struck with such a strong urge to push I called out to *mia Matri*. It felt as if I were being torn in two.

"Oh, Madonna, help me, help me please!" My vision clouded over with the agony of this, the last instant of the birth. I knew either my Amadora would be born or we would both die in this moment.

"Do not despair, *bedda mia*." I heard a soft whisper in my ear. "I promised you a long line of powerful women. I will not let you die. We will fill you with our strength. Push this child from your womb." I looked up to see from whence the voice had come–it was neither Maria, Agata, nor Marietta. My vision cleared and I saw, past Maria's worried face, a group of women filled with light. I knew I gazed upon the countenance of the Madonna and with Her were Elisabeth, Salome, Hannah, and Rachel, Jochebed, Rebekah and Sarah. These were the other mothers the Virgin had spoken of in the vision I had seen earlier in the day–had it been the same day? I wasn't sure.

I watched as the light surrounding them spread and stretch forward to encompass me. It replenished my strength, and I found myself able to gather all my power in my belly and I bore down with the fortitude of all these women surrounding me, and I felt Amadora's head break free from my body.

"The head is out!" Maria cried. "Stop pushing for a moment, Genevra. I have to clear the baby's mouth."

Marietta held my shoulders higher so I could see the face of my baby for the first time. She was red and wrinkled and covered with birth fluid, and she was the loveliest baby I had ever seen. Maria swiped a finger in her beautiful mouth.

I knew she was well, and I gazed once more into the faces of the women standing behind Maria. This time it was Elisabeth that spoke to me.

"One last push, Genevra, and your child will be born. We will help you."

I gathered all the strength they offered to me and pushed once more. I felt Amadora's shoulders break free, one after the other, and she slipped from my body into Maria's arms with a mighty and angry roar.

"It's a girl! A beautiful girl!" Maria cried.

She was beautiful–strong and beautiful. My exquisite Amadora. I looked up at Agata and saw she was crying. I took her hand and she kissed the top of my head.

"You did well, *bedda mia*. She is a lovely child.

I looked up to thank the Madonna and the other women who had given me the strength to make the final pushes, but they had gone. I was not surprised. They had given me what I needed at the moment I needed it. Still, I whispered a grateful *grazii* for the help I had received.

"Marietta, hand me one of your cloths please." Maria held her hand out and took the cloth Marietta passed her. "Here you go, you sweet little *carina*." She rubbed Amadora briskly–my daughter was not pleased with these ministrations and continued to yell her displeasure.

"Agata, can you get the knife? We need to cut the cord." Agata reached under the stool and pulled the knife from beneath the straw.

"May I cut the cord?" Agata wiped her eyes with the back of her hand.

"Of course." Maria smiled at Agata. She held up Amadora so the cord hung free. I watched Agata cut the cord with a sharp motion and tie a knot close to Amadora's belly. Maria wrapped my baby tightly in a clean cloth and handed her to me.

"She is hungry–you need to feed her."

I awkwardly pulled my breast from my shirt and took my darling girl and held her to my nipple. Immediately she stopped crying and latched on. My breast tingled as the milk released. I looked at the perfect little face pressed against me. It was bliss–sweet bliss–holding this child that had grown within me for the past nine months.

"How much your life has changed…," Agata stroked the tiny back. "Forgive me for saying this, Genevra, but less than one year ago you were a spoiled nobleman's daughter. You had few skills but your arrogance. Look at you today! You are a mother with a beautiful daughter of your own. You make some of the best woollen fabric in Sperlinga–you know how to cook, to clean, to take care of animals. You are not a spoiled child anymore–you are a woman now, and a far better person than you might have become if you married as your father arranged."

"You are so right, Agata. When I look back to that time it feels as if it were a lifetime ago, and it were another person living that life."

"What will you call her?" Marietta asked.

"The only suitable name, I think, is Amadora." I smiled gently at my child.

"Gift of love–I think that is a most fitting name." Marietta stroked my head softly.

I nodded, looking at the women around me who would gift this tiny being with much love all of their lives, but more I was thinking of the gift of love the Madonna and my mother had given me by convincing me keeping Amadora was the best thing for me to do.

"Agata," Maria broke through my revere. "She is about to deliver the placenta–I need you to massage her stomach."

As Agata rubbed and pressed on my belly, the placenta slipped from me with much more ease than Amadora had.

"Good, it is intact." Maria handed it to Marietta. "Take a piece to mix into the caudle for Genevra to drink. Put aside the rest to plant under Amadora's birth tree."

Marietta mixed wine, sugar, eggs, and a small slice of the placenta and cooked it over the fire in the hearth.

"Genevra, can you sit up? I want to wash you." Maria took a cloth and dipped it into a bowl of warm water. Gently she washed all the blood and fluid from my legs as I cuddled Amadora.

"Genevra, hand me the baby. Agata, there are clean clothes on the bed." Marietta took Amadora and nodded towards the gown spread out on the coverlet.

Agata's hands gripped my shoulders and helped me stand. She untied my skirts and let them fall to the ground. I grabbed for Agata as my legs wobbled and threatened to collapse.

"Whoa, Genevra, let's get you sitting before you fall." Agata lowered me carefully onto the bed. She pulled the clean gown over my head and I settled into the bed we had shared the night before. Marietta lay Amadora, now sleeping happily with a full belly, next to me on the bed. Turning around onto my side, I curled around my quiet babe. With one finger, I touched the pink, rosebud lips, the tiny cupid nose, and the blue tinged lids. My finger ran back over the top of her head and through the black curls drying there. I pressed my nose close to her head and breathed deeply. The wonderful baby scent filled my lungs and seeped into me from every pour. I couldn't remember ever feeling more content, and, exhausted, I drifted off into a dreamless sleep.

Chapter twenty-eight

IL DESCO DA PARTO

"GENEVRA, WAKE UP. You need to eat."

I opened my eyes, unsure how long I had been asleep. Maria, Marietta and Agata were all standing over the bed grinning at me. I slid myself to a sitting position in the bed, careful to not disturb my sleeping babe.

"What is it? Why are you all looking at me that way?"

"Well," Agata began. "You need to eat, and Marietta made you some caudle to drink."

"But why are you all grinning so?"

Maria held out the drink on a tray. "We thought you might want to see this."

I looked at the tray. It was a *desco da parto,* a birthing tray. Rich and noble women were usually the only ones gifted with these fine art works on delivering a live child–most often a son. I felt tears prickling the edges of my eyes.

"Where did you get this? I mean, how... but... I'm not a noblewoman...," I caught myself before I said 'anymore.' "Besides, I had a daughter, not a son!"

Marietta took the drink from the tray and handed the tray to me. "*Zzio* Enzo made it. *Zzio* Enzo gifted all of us–that is, all of his nieces and grand-nieces and the wives of his nephews and grand-nephews–with one when we delivered our babies."

I ran my fingers over the fine carving around the edges. At each quarter point of the circular edge there was an image carved in relief: a baby at the top, a little girl running along the right side, her hair streaming behind her, a young woman knelt at the altar with her groom along the bottom, and finally the same woman sat, rocking her own baby on the left side.

"But how did he know I was having a girl?"

"I don't know how he does it–he has been right on every birthing tray I have seen him make. Now, before it gets cold, here is your drink. This will make your milk thick and good for your baby. *Vivi, Vivi!*" Marietta handed me the steaming drink.

For the rest of the weekend, I rested in bed and listened to the sounds of the Easter celebrations outside. It was my first Easter in Sperlinga, and I expected to be disappointed to be missing the fun, but instead I felt a warmth in my chest that spread to my extremities whenever tiny Amadora tugged on my breast to feed and I was left instead with peace and contentment. I sent Maria, Agata, and Marietta out as much as possible so I could allow myself to slip gently into my new role. The evening Amadora had been born, *Zzio* Enzo came to speak to me.

"Ah, she is a beautiful one, that *bambina* of yours. She will make you happy in your old age."

"*Grazii, Zzio.* I think she is beautiful too."

"I wish to speak to you, Genevra." *Zzio* Enzo dipped his head and ran his hand threw his hair, scratching his head roughly. "I know you were planning to go back up to your cave when Easter was done, but..." He lifted his reddening face, "...but I think you need a longer lying in than a few days. I think you should stay with me for a proper lying in. You could have Agata stay with you." He rushed through his speech and stood staring at his feet.

What an effort it had been for *Zzio* Enzo to make that speech! Childbirth and lying in were topics usually reserved for women. He stood head and shoulders bent more than usual and arms tight to his sides as he waited for me to reply. I lay Amadora carefully on the bed to hug him.

"Of course we will stay, *càru Zzio.*" I bit my lip as I stepped back from him. "I'm sure Agata will be happy to stay too."

"Good! It is settled!"

"Almost." I answered. "*Zzio*–I have something important I wish to ask you."

His gentle quizzical look gave me the courage to ask him a question I had been thinking about since before Amadora was born. I almost lost my nerve, but his gaze was steady, so taking a deep breath I went ahead.

"You know I have asked Marietta and her husband to be Amadora's godparents, but Amadora does not have any grandparents. I know both Agata and Maria are more than happy to take the place of her *nanna* but she has no grandfather. I know that you are not my uncle, even though I call you *Zzio*, but would you be willing to act as Amadora's *nonnu*?" I held my breath. I knew what I was asking was a tremendous favour and responsibility. To accept a child with no real family as his own *niputi*, little granddaughter, was not something most men would do.

Zzio Enzo's face broke into a broad, beaming smile. "*Certu*! Of course, I will! How could I say no to such a sweet *pupa*, your little baby!"

Chapter twenty-nine

AMADORA'S BAPTISM

AGATA, AMADORA AND I stayed with Zzio Enzo until the warmest part of spring arrived and the crops were peeking their green heads out of the rich earth. The time of lying in was a time of rest and a time for the new mother to be cared for by the other women in her family. For me it was Marietta and Agata, with Zzio Enzo keeping me company while they went to church or to the market. But it was not long before I felt restless and wanted to make my way outside.

"Genevra," Agata scolded me, "You will end up catching a cold and your milk will dry up. Do you want that?"

Finally, after I had been inside for three weeks or more, I decided, on a warm and beautiful day, I would wait until Agata had gone to the market and convince Zzio Enzo to walk outside with Amadora and me.

"Oh, *Zzio*! Look at the sunshine! What a perfect day to introduce Amadora to the world!"

"Have you wrapped her well enough? What if there is a breeze?"

I tipped my head back and laughed to the sun. "You sound like Agata! Amadora is as healthy as the lambs in the field. Besides, look at her little face. She's smiling! I think we should take her out to meet everyone, and this Sunday is her baptism. She won't be inside much longer."

"I suppose that is true." *Zzio* Enzo's gaze softened as he looked at Amadora's sweet smile.

The sun was bright in the brilliant azure sky. The warm brown of the mountain behind us and the rich raw pistachio green dotted with specks of colourful wildflowers in the valley below reflected against the buildings and streets of Sperlinga. After weeks inside, I spread my arms to accept the fresh air and golden sunshine. I threw my head back and grinned at the sky. Amadora seemed to agree with me as she gurgled and sighed when I picked her up and walked towards the *piazza*.

"*Signura* Genevra! It is good to see you out in the sunshine! And let me see this little cherub of yours." I looked up to see Father Nicolo approaching us from the *piazza*. "Ah, she truly is a cherub. And her eyes! They have that beautiful dark brown of good loamy soil, but with a hint of amber! So lovely."

"*Patri*! Do you want someone to curse her with *il malocchio*?"

I jumped, both at the surprise of hearing Marietta's voice and at the thought that someone might curse Amadora with the evil eye. Without hesitation, Marietta and I both spat on Amadora's head.

Quickly I answered Father Nicolo, "But she is so dirty!" thus turning away the compliment the Father had given.

Both Marietta and I sighed with relief. We had acted quickly enough to ward off the evil eye.

"I am sorry, Genevra. I wasn't thinking." Father Nicolo frowned, shaking his head. "I will not make the same mistake tomorrow at the baptism."

"I'm glad to hear that Father." Marietta glowered at the priest and turned to shake her finger at me. "And you, Genevra. You should know better! I saw you walking outside through my window with no protection and brought you these."

Marietta produced two strings of dyed-red wool; one tiny for Amadora and a longer one for me. She tied one on each of our wrists.

"To come outside with no red string is asking for *il malocchio* to come! Foolish girl!"

I hung my head and held my precious daughter close to my heart whispering, "Forgive me little one." I was filled with shame that I could invite such harm to Amadora.

Marietta turned her fury to *Zzio* Enzo who, throughout this encounter, had been quietly trying to slip away.

"*Zzio* Enzo. I blame you the most. It was your job to keep Genevra and Amadora safe. How could you let them come outside without any protection?"

Poor *Zzio*. His face had reddened and was screwing up, brows drawn together and mouth squeezed tight.

"Oh, please don't blame *Zzio* Enzo! He has been so good to both of us, and I convinced him to let us come out in the sunshine."

"Wife, what trouble are you causing now?" Giovanni called to Marietta across the *piazza* as he strode towards us. He was a tall, powerful man covered with the muscles that come from years of working with cattle.

"Genevra brought Amadora out with no protection from *il malocchio!*"

Giovanni gasped and made the sign of the *mano cornuto* or the "horned hand" to protect himself.

"Well, I think no harm has been done—we cancelled out the *Patri*'s words soon enough." Marietta continued.

Tears pricked at my eyes. *Zzio* Enzo looked thoroughly chastised. Giovanni glanced over us and said to his wife, "*Basta*, Marietta. I'm hungry. Make us some lunch, woman."

Marietta harrumphed and turned her back to us. "Fine!" she called over her shoulder. "Don't take me seriously. At least come for some *gnocchi*—you can appreciate my food even if you don't appreciate my advice!"

Giovanni gestured in dismissal at his wife. "That woman can talk you to the grave if you let her. *Zzio*, ignore her—she is never happy unless there is a fuss. Father, you'll join us for lunch?"

"*Certu*! Marietta may like a fuss, but you can't deny she is one of the best cooks in Sperlinga." Father Nicolo chuckled.

~|~

The next morning, Agata, *Zzio* Enzo, and I rose early to prepare for church and Amadora's baptism.

"Genevra, I have something for you from Maria and Marietta." Agata held out a small woollen bag. "She has been working on this for some time and she asked me to give this to you today. She is at Marietta's house cooking for the celebration after the baptism and knew she wouldn't see you beforehand."

"*Grazii,* Agata." I took the bag and slowly turned it over. What could it be?

I opened the bag and brought out a tiny, white christening gown. It was the softest wool I had ever felt; softer, in fact, than anything I had touched of Marietta's as well. The sleeves were long and gathered at the top and bottom. The dress was gathered under the arms and flowed beautifully. I looked closely at the skirt and gasped! It was covered with tiny white embroidery stitches depicting little birds and lambs frolicking around ornate crosses. At the back were little buttons carved into bird shapes from bone. With the dress was a tiny matching bonnet."

"Agata! This must have taken weeks to make! How did they do this?"

"Marietta made the gown and bonnet–she has had so many children she's become adept at making christening gowns." Agata chuckled. "Maria did the embroidery. She sat up at night when you were asleep to finish the last of it."

"And the buttons?"

"Well, that was *Zzio* Enzo of course. No one else could have done such a good job on those."

I jumped up and threw my arms around *Zzio* Enzo. "Oh *Zzio*! They are lovely! *Grazii milli.*"

Zzio Enzo gruffly pushed my arms away. "Don't be foolish girl. Without buttons the gown would fall off. What else would I do?" In spite of his gruff words I could see a twinkle behind his eyes and a pink flush spread across his face.

I kissed him on the cheek. "Well, thank you anyhow. I love them and Amadora will too when she is old enough to appreciate them."

"Don't make us wait, Genevra, put her in the gown!" Agata insisted.

I wiped a protesting Amadora with soft damp towel, pulled the dress over her head, and tied on the bonnet. They fit perfectly. The gown flowed long below her toes and the bonnet framed her sweet face. Amadora, less enamoured with the bonnet, fretted and fussed and finally broke into a loud howl.

Zzio Enzo chuckled. "I think perhaps she takes after Marietta, even if you are her mother!"

As we walked towards the church, I held Amadora tightly in my left arm, as was the custom. So many people hailed us on our way it took us twice as long to walk the few blocks to the church. I had carefully retied the red string on Amadora's wrist and Agata had tightened mine to protect us from *il malocchio*. Each person who stopped us spoke of the weather or asked after my health. All of them looked at Amadora with a smile, but none commented as no one wished to accidently cast her with *il malocchio*.

"Genevra," Agata said quietly. "Don't forget to keep your eyes forward."

I nodded seriously. Mothers who looked over their shoulders on the way to the church would guarantee that their child would grow up to be full of fear. I was determined Amadora would be a strong, courageous young woman and not timid at all, so I carefully kept my eyes forward and never glanced back, not even once.

As we approached the church, I saw Marietta, Giovanni, and Maria standing waiting for us. I walked carefully up to them and hugged the two women tightly.

"Thank you for the gown, it's beautiful!" I whispered to each one. They hugged me back, but shrewdly said nothing about Amadora.

"Genevra? It is time." Father Nicolo called to me.

"*Sì Patri.*"

I stepped forward into the narthex of the church with Marietta and Giovanni next to me. Father Nicolo stood before us as the crowd hushed around us.

"Giovanni, Marietta, what do you ask of the Church of God?"

"Faith." They both replied.

"And what does Faith offer you?"

"Life everlasting."

"If then you desire to enter into life, keep the commandments. 'Thou shalt love the Lord thy God with thy whole heart and with thy whole soul and with thy whole mind; and thy neighbour as thyself'."

Father Nicolo leaned forward and breathed softly three times onto Amadora's head, making the shape of the cross. "Go forth from her, unclean spirit, and give place to the Holy Spirit."

With these words, he made the sign of the cross on Amadora's forehead and breast. As I watched, a shiver ran through me. I could feel a breath on my neck, yet I could see where Maria, *Zzio* Enzo, Agata, and of course Marietta and Giovanni were standing. In spite of this I could feel someone standing behind me.

"Receive the Sign of the Cross both upon your forehead and also upon your heart; take to you the faith of the heavenly precepts; and so order your life as to be, from henceforth, the temple of God.

"Let us pray. Mercifully hear our prayers, we beseech Thee, O Lord, and by Thy perpetual assistance keep these Thine elect, Giovanni and Marietta, signed with the sign of the Lord's cross, so that, preserving this first experience of the greatness of Thy glory, she may deserve, by keeping Thy commandments, to attain to the glory of regeneration. Through Christ our Lord."

The sound of 'Amen' rippled through the crowd. I, again, felt a breath on my neck, and heard a woman's voice whisper in my ear, "She is blessed" yet I couldn't turn to look backwards to see who it was–I was still afraid if I turned and looked back I would make Amadora a nervous and anxious child.

Father Nicolo placed his hands carefully over Amadora's head and intoned, "Let us pray: Almighty, everlasting God, Father of our Lord Jesus Christ, look graciously down upon this Thy servant, Maria Amadora, whom Thou hast graciously called unto the beginnings of the faith; drive out from her all blindness of heart; break all the toils of Satan wherewith she was held: open unto her, O Lord, the gate of Thy loving kindness, that, being impressed with the sign of Thy wisdom, she may be free from the foulness of all wicked desires, and in the sweet odor of Thy precepts may joyfully serve Thee in Thy Church, and grow in grace from day to day. Through the same Christ our Lord. Amen."

Again, the crowd responded with a respectful "Amen".

This time as I looked at my daughter, I felt hands on my shoulders, as Father Nicolo placed his hands on Amadora's head. Again, I refused to look behind me, but I felt a calm flow through me, even though I was convinced someone was trying to make me look back.

Much to Amadora's loud and very vocal displeasure, the *Patri* placed a little taste of salt on her tongue to make God's love seem all that much sweeter. Father Nicolo made the sign of the cross on Amadora's forehead and Giovanni stepped forward and did the same.

"Maria-Amadora, receive the salt of wisdom; let it be to thee a token of mercy unto everlasting life. May it make your way easy to eternal life. Peace be with you."

Marietta and Giovanni responded, "And with your spirit."

With that, Father Nicolo raised his hands, palms facing outward, and prayed for Amadora's soul. With the sign of the cross over her little head, he exorcised her from any unclean spirits and admitted her into the church. I shivered again at the thrill that my daughter was nearly safe. As Father Nicolo called out "Maria-Amadora, enter thou into the temple of God, that thou mayest have part with Christ unto life everlasting!" I responded with a heart-felt "Amen!"

Father Nicolo turned to Marietta and Giovanni and in a fierce voice I had never heard from him before, questioned them seriously.

"Do you renounce Satan?"

In fearful and trembling voices, they both answered, "I do renounce him."

"And all of his works?"

"I do renounce him."

"And all his pomps?"

"I do renounce him." A tear escaped onto Marietta's cheek.

Father Nicolo anointed Amadora with oil and in his powerful voice declared, "I anoint you with the oil of salvation in Christ Jesus our Lord, that you may have everlasting life." And we all replied with a subdued "Amen".

Finally, Father Nicolo took water from the font and covered Amadora's forehead three times, saying "In the name of the Father, the Son and the Holy Spirit. May the Almighty God, the Father of our Lord Jesus Christ, Who hath regenerated thee by water and the Holy Spirit, and who hath given thee the remission of all thy sins, may He Himself anoint thee with the Chrism of Salvation, in the same Christ Jesus our Lord, unto life eternal." The exotic scent of balsam drifted up from the Chrism and filled my nostrils with its sweet aroma.

Handing a pure, white cross and a lit candle to Marietta and Giovanni, he ended with "Maria-Amadora, go in peace and the Lord be with you. Amen."

With that, there rose a cheer and a clapping of hands, and I was embraced by Marietta, Maria, Agata and of course Zzio Enzo.

"Who was standing behind me?" I asked each of them, but they all gave me a puzzled look.

"No one was standing behind you, Genevra." Agata leaned in

and whispered, "Did you feel like someone was there?"

I nodded but didn't say much more–there were too many people milling around. As we left the church, Marietta and Giovanni tossed sweetened almonds at the waiting crowd outside.

"Hurry up and bring out the food! You have a hungry village here!" I turned to see one of *Zzio* Enzo's cronies with a merry grin on his face.

"Pah, Guido, you are always waiting for someone to feed you!" *Zzio* Enzo called back, to much laughter.

There was no worry about the food, however. There was enough to feed three villages, and a real party atmosphere broke out in the *piazza*; laughter and joking and music, and through most of it, Amadora slept.

Towards the end of the afternoon, I took a quiet spot along the side of the *piazza*. The sun moved down the valley–I knew it would soon be time for us to head up the mountain. I had not been in our little cave home for weeks and I missed it.

"Well, Genevra. How are you feeling this afternoon now that the baptism is over?"

"Oh Father, I am so grateful that I can stop worrying!"

Father Nicolo chuckled. "It has been my experience, Genevra, once a woman becomes a mother the worrying goes on and on. But take your girl home tonight, and enjoy her."

"*Grazii*, Father, I will." I looked out over the valley that lay below. "My life has changed so much in a few months. Had I been given the opportunity to plan my life out, I never would have chosen this path."

"Are you disappointed with the direction your life has taken?"

"Oh no, Father! How could I be disappointed with this?" I looked at my girl, and into the priest's kind eyes. "Father, there is something I need to ask you."

"Go ahead."

"Do you believe our Holy Mother takes a personal interest in the lives of unimportant people like us? Not just grand and wealthy people like the king and all the people in his court?"

"Did she not mother a child that was simply a carpenter? Of course, she cares about each of us! She takes a personal interest in each one of her Son's children. Why are you asking, Genevra? Is there something worrying you?"

I paused, watching all the people visiting in the *piazza*. "Over the past few months, the Virgin Mother has visited me–several times in fact."

"What! Have you seen her?"

"Yes, sometimes in a dream and sometimes while awake."

Glancing around to make sure no one was close enough to hear, I told Father Nicolo everything. I could see his eyes getting larger as each visitation passed my lips, yet when I told him the most recent one was during the baptism he paled and grasped my wrist.

"You mean to say that you heard the Virgin's voice while we were in the church baptizing Amadora?" he whispered incredulously.

"Yes, not only did she speak to me, she laid her hands on my shoulders."

"Genevra, have you told anyone else of any of this?"

"Only Agata."

Father Nicolo hand tightened on my wrist. "I need to speak with the Bishop about this. Please, don't tell anyone else until I do."

I felt the blood drain from my face. "No Father! No, I don't want you to speak to the Bishop. If you do, Amadora and I will never live a normal life again–the Church will never leave us alone. That is not any way for my daughter to begin her young life. Besides…" I breathed deeply, "besides, you know the reasons I have to not want attention on us."

"I understand, of course I do. But, this is a huge responsibility. If I were to keep this kind of information to myself, I would be afraid the power of these kinds of visions and visitations would be too much for you to bear. If you were to collapse under the weight of this, I would not be able to forgive myself–especially if I thought I could have done something."

"Father, please. If you go to the Bishop, I will have to take Amadora and leave Sperlinga, and I don't want to do that. The people here are my family now, and, even if it would hurt each and everyone of them, if I have to run to protect my girl, I will." I could feel my chest tighten and tears prick at the corners of my eyes.

Father Nicolo looked hard into my face. I stared back just as intently. Finally, he dropped his eyes.

"*Va beni.*" His voice had a sharp edge to it. "But if I, at any point, think this is becoming something bigger than you or I can handle, I will be forced to visit the Bishop. Are we clear on that?"

"Perfectly Father."

Father Nicolo gave me the gravest look I had ever seen cross his face. He turned on his heel, his cassock flaring out in the breeze, and strode quickly back to the church.

"What's with the *Patri*?"

I turned to see Marietta walking up to where I stood.

"He didn't like something I said to him." I answered quietly.

"You know, Father Nicolo is a wonderful priest–we were lucky when he came here–but he is still young. As he gets older, he will become more like the sycamore tree; a strong trunk but flexible branches. Don't worry, Genevra, he may be stern right now but if you truly believe you are right, he will come around."

"I hope so."

"Leave the Father alone now. Maria and Agata are chomping at the bit to get moving up the mountain."

"*Grazii* Marietta. I will find them so we can go home."

"No need to find them, *mia matri pìcciula*, my little mother, they are waiting at my house with that silly donkey of yours. Now *sciò, sciò*! Get yourself over there."

I hurried over to where Agata and Maria were waiting.

"*Mi dispiace.* I am so sorry I have made you wait."

Maria waved my apology away. "Have you wrapped Amadora tightly? It will be colder up the mountain."

"Yes, she is wrapped well and sound asleep–see?"

"Good." Maria responded. "Now climb up onto the donkey and we will be off–and no discussion from you, my dear. You have had a long day, as has Amadora, but at least she can sleep–you must stay awake until we are home."

I climbed on the back of Graziella. With Maria in the lead, the four of us, and our donkey, journeyed back to our warm cave home.

Chapter thirty

OLE STOMPING TOM

~AGOSTO 2011~

"DID ANYONE ELSE FIND OUT you were having visions?" Elena interrupted.

"What? No, I mean other than Agata and Father Nicolo, whom I told, no one ever did."

"So then you–hey, what do I call you?"

"Call me Genevra–that is my name after all."

"Okay, I wasn't sure if 'Genevra' was okay, or if I should be calling you '*Santa* Genevra' or 'Your Holiness' or something like that." Elena countered.

"No, people who write the history books or religious books call me that, but I've never thought of myself as a saint. I simply did the things placed in front of me–just like any other woman would do."

Elena paused to shoulder check before she merged into a larger autostrada with much faster cars whizzing by. Once settled onto the smooth but quicker highway, Elena opened her mouth to speak. She stopped, a frown crossing her brow.

"Go ahead, ask me. I already know what you want to say."

"Fine, tell me the answer." Elena retorted.

"No, you have to ask. Otherwise it is too easy for you. Ask."

"Well..." Elena took a deep breath and straightened her shoulders. "Okay, here it is. You said in one of your visions you saw one of your descendants and her name was Cristiana. Was that... was that... my mother?" Elena stuttered out the question.

"Ah, that is the $64,000 question, as they say." Genevra chuckled. "What do you think?"

"I don't know! You seem to know everything about me. And you are leading me to her, so maybe you are related to me–otherwise why would you do this? But you seem to know a lot of other things too, so maybe this is a coincidence. I don't know!" Elena paused to take a breath.

"So which one seems right?"

"I said, I don't know! For crissake, will you just tell me!"

"No, I think it's better if you tell me." Genevra answered.

"*Ufffa!!!*"

"Oh, and you may want to slow down a little. I know you are driving on an Italian highway, but 160 km/hour is rather fast, even for here."

Elena slowly braked, and brought her speed to a safer 130. Silence fell over the car and continued for some time as the low rolling hills approaching the coast sped past the little Panda.

"I think the Cristiana in your vision was my mother." Elena said quietly.

"As she was." Genevra answered. "What made answering that question so difficult?"

"I don't know what to think about you–this. If my mother came from you, this is all real–you are real–and I'm not sure I can believe that yet." Elena ran her hand through her hair.

"Does it matter?" Genevra asked. "If I bring you to your mother, does it matter if you believe in me or not? Have faith, *bedda mia.*"

Elena fell silent. In her mind, she struggled with the question. Was it important for her to know if this woman's voice from her crazy GPS was real or not? She had never had trouble with faith before, so why should this be different? Behind her thoughts she could hear Genevra humming something sounding vaguely familiar. Wait. Was that...?

"Oh my God, are you humming The Hockey Song?"

"What? Just because I'm an Italian woman from the 12th century I can't love Stompin' Tom Connors? I am also particularly fond of Elvis, Pavarotti, and Snoop Dog."

"Fine. That's it. I'm driving through Sicily with a disembodied saint humming Stompin' Tom Connors through my GPS. I give up. I have no idea if you are real or if I'm having a psychotic break, although my money's on the psychotic break." Elena growled her frustration, then she sighed, her shoulders dropping in defeat. "Well," she said, "I may be losing my mind, or you may be real, but I guess, as you said, how much does it matter?"

"Good girl!" Genevra cried out. "You are on your way!"

"On my way to what?" Elena grumbled

"On your way to becoming the young woman you were meant to be. Now, do you want to hear the rest of my story? It's still a while before we get to Palermo."

"Why not?" Elena answered. "This is all too Dali-esque for words. You might as well tell me the rest."

Chapter thirty-one

THE AGREEMENT

~1153~

MY LIFE AS A NEW MOTHER settled into a comfortable and happy routine. Amadora grew into a beautiful and healthy little girl, and she brought so much youth and joy to our lives both Agata and Maria seemed to become younger as well. By the time she was four, she could climb up and down our mountain like the goats and the sheep. She was a favourite with *Zzio* Enzo and his cronies. She merely had to open wide her dark eyes and whichever adopted *nonnu* she had targeted gave her the best piece of cheese, or sweetest desert. The older children gave her piggyback rides around the *piazza*, and she screamed with delight. She had my father's fair face but Landro's dark, emotional eyes. Both brought a nostalgic sadness to me at times, but her untroubled belly laugh quickly quenched any sadness.

Amadora was bright, and she mimicked us constantly. I had become well known for both the softness of my fabric and my embroidery. One day, as I was about to card the wool, Amadora stopped me.

"*Mamma*, let me try, *pi favuri?*" She gave me the same wide-eyed look, and I chuckled.

"Ah, Amadora, don't try that look with me, it doesn't work. I will let you try, but only because it is a good skill for you to learn. I held out the carders, and Amadora took them in her chubby little hands. Placing my hands over hers, I showed her how to draw the carders across each other to pull the knots from the wool. The carders were awkward for her to hold, but she kept trying.

"She seems to have your talent, Genevra." Maria stood over Amadora, watching her efforts with the wool. "Perhaps I will ask Giacomo to make her smaller carders she can manage more easily."

"*Grazii,* Maria. Do you think *Zzio* Giacomo would do that for me?" Amadora lisped.

"I think if you open your eyes wide like that he would do anything for you, *zitiduzza.*" Maria answered fondly.

~|~

I wish I could say our lives were always so carefree. There was a time, much darker and poisoned with jealousy. It was a lovely spring, and we were celebrating Easter and, in a much quieter way, Amadora's eighth birthday. Marietta and Maria had cooked all of Amadora's favourite foods, and I had made her a new dress to wear to church. I shook the dress to release any wrinkles, and Amadora stood in the centre of the room jumping up and down.

"Can I eat the cannelloni before I put my dress on? Please! I don't want to get sauce on my beautiful new dress." Amadora's eyes shone with excitement.

"Perhaps if you calmed down you wouldn't spill on yourself." Maria answered wryly. "And we don't eat in our underwear–not even on our birthdays."

Amadora huffed her feigned displeasure, but quickly changed to a wide grin as I held out the soft lavender-coloured dress.

"Oh *mamma*, it is so soft… and the colour is like the flowers in the field. Can I put it on now?"

"Yes, but only if you settle down. Your birthday falls on Easter Sunday this year, and your behaviour should match the day."

Amadora gave me a serious face for all of ten seconds before she broke into peals of laughter. I pulled the dress over her head, spun her around and did up the row of little buttons *Zzio* Enzo had taken great effort to carve. His eyes had become rheumy, and his hands shook more than I had ever seen before, but he still insisted on quietly spoiling my darling girl.

Amadora spun and the skirt flared out around her long, gangly legs.

"Oh *Mamma*, it is like a princess' dress! I look so beautiful!"

In my heart, I agreed with her entirely. She was lovely. But to her face I said, "You shouldn't be so vain, my girl. You are looking for bad luck."

"Oh, I know, *Mamma*. I won't say anything when anyone else is around, but I know you and Maria and Agata think I'm pretty too."

"Well, you won't be pretty if you don't eat. You will get all skinny, and no man will want you!" Maria answered as she put a plate of steaming cannelloni on the table. "Now, sit. *Mancia!*"

After our lunch, we made our way through the *piazza* and to the church. Father Nicolo still took care of Sperlinga's spiritual needs, but he was a little slower and more grey than the day he had baptized Amadora.

"*Ciau* Genevra! *Como stai*? How are you?"

"*Beni beni*, Father. And you? You are looking thin. I don't think you are eating enough. Your housekeeper, Concetta, is she cooking enough for you?"

"She is getting older and her hands are so crippled, she can't prepare food the way she used to. But what can I do? She depends on me for the few coins I can give her. Since she became a widow she has had so little." Father Nicolo placed his chin on his clasped hands and rocked back on his heals. "I don't know how to help her. It's a problem."

"Yes, *la vecchiaia e' una brutta bestia*. Getting old is a terrible thing. Let me think for a moment *Patri*." I turned my head and looked towards the *piazza* where I could see Amadora, giggling with three or four other girls a little older than her as several boys strutted by. She was growing up so quickly, and these silly girls who were her friends thought only about the equally silly boys. I wanted her to find some focus in her life, to develop some skills to help her later so that she wouldn't end up like the elderly Concetta. I didn't want her to rush into adulthood. A thought flashed through my mind–a brilliant thought! I caught my breath as the germ of this inspired idea took hold. I bit my lip and quickly turned back to Father Nicolo.

"Father, would you teach Amadora to read?"

He burst out laughing. "How, in our heavenly Father's name, will that help me with my problem?"

"Look over into the *piazza*. Watch Amadora with those other foolish girls–those *picciotti* are turning Amadora into a boy-hungry, dizzy girl. I know it is only a few years until we look for a husband, but I want her to be able to take care of herself and not run into a boy's arms too early like..." My voice drifted off. I didn't want to finish my sentence but the Father finished it for me.

"Like you? Is that what you worry about? It is a fair worry, Genevra. She is a lovely girl, and she will have many young men after her."

"Yes, that is my fear. If you were to teach Amadora to read, she would have a skill to fall back on–she could write letters, help in the church, and not have to always work her fingers to the bone! And if she came to the church for reading lessons, she could help Concetta with the cooking. Amadora is already a good cook, Maria made certain of that. We could tell Concetta it is payment for the reading lessons!"

Father Nicolo crossed his arms and frowned a little. I couldn't tell if it was from the bright sun or because he disapproved of the idea.

"It is unusual for girls to learn to read–normally I would only teach the three boys I already work with. But it would help Concetta, and I do like the idea of a girl being able to bring a few extra coins in to the family in case her husband is injured or falls ill." He paused for a few moments longer. His face relaxed, and he smiled at me. "Well, Genevra, I think you have found a good solution to a difficult problem. You may send her to see me next week. And I wouldn't say no if she came with some of Maria's good cheese." He chuckled.

"I will send Amadora to see you Tuesday morning?"

"*Perfettu*. Not too early *pi favuri*, I spend my early mornings in prayer."

"*Certu*. Of course. And she will bring some of Maria's cheese." I breathed deeply as a feeling of lightness settled over me.

The following Tuesday, I woke Amadora early.

"Come child, you need to get up and get washed and do your work."

Amadora flipped over in the bed she shared with me and pulled the covers over her head.

"Why? It's early. I never get up this early," she whined from under the covers.

I grabbed the edge of the blanket and with a quick flick of my wrist tugged it back from over her head. "Because you are going to see Father Nicolo today."

Amadora rolled back towards me with a frown. "Why? What does he want from me today?"

I could feel my brows pull together, and I reached out and smacked her leg through the blankets. "*Bambina irrispettosa!* You disrespectful girl! You should be grateful to Father Nicolo!"

She sat up and hung her head. Peering up at me from beneath her brows, Amadora responded in a contrite tone, "*Mi dispiace Mamma.* I'm sorry. Why does the Father wish to see me?"

I took the blankets to shake out and hang in the sunshine. "Father Nicolo has agreed to teach you how to read and write and in return you will help Concetta with the cooking for the Father."

"What!" Amadora jumped out of bed and stood on the stone floor facing me, her face screwed up into an angry fist, ready to fight. "I hate Concetta! She is mean and twists my ear when she thinks I've done something I shouldn't! And she smells like an old woman."

"Well, that's because she is an old woman, and she needs your help with the cooking–only two days a week. And you will become the only girl in Sperlinga able to read."

"Why should I learn to read? Could my father read?"

I sighed. Amadora had been asking pointed questions, and I had been trying to avoid them, but I realized that I would soon have to tell her something about her father.

"No, I don't believe your father could read, but I can, and I think every girl should learn to read. So does Father Nicolo, and he has agreed to teach you. Now, get washed, and dressed, and be grateful."

"*Mamma*, you can read? Why don't I see you reading?"

"Perhaps if we had a Bible in our house you would. But you must have something to read if you are going to read. Now, would you please get dressed." I put my hands on my hips–a sign Amadora recognized immediately. She grabbed her dress and pulled it over her head.

"But, why did you learn to read?"

"My father, your *nonnu*, also believed girls should learn to read."

"Did he teach you or did he send you to a priest too?"

"Neither, I had a tutor. Now, enough of this conversation. Get washed and come out for breakfast. We have already been talking too long." I turned on my heel and left the room, more to keep Amadora from asking more questions than anything else.

After her chores, I shooed Amadora out of the house, and sent her to Father Nicolo's house with a large wedge of cheese. I sat at the kitchen table with a sigh.

"She didn't want to go?" Maria asked.

"No, it wasn't that. She was asking questions about her father again."

"At some point she will have to know about her father and your family." Maria joined me at the table. She passed a bowl of olives towards me; a rare treat, and I placed one on my tongue, savouring the sharp, ancient flavour. "She should know where she comes from before she is betrothed. She may be only eight now, but in five or six years she will be wed, and a mother shortly after."

I nodded, my lips closed over the tart olive taste. "I know that is true, but it is not an easy story to tell. And what will she think of her mother chasing after a stable hand and having to run away?" I added with a sigh.

"She will think it was a great adventure, if I know your daughter even a little. It will only be important for her to understand she should be quiet about her family story if she wants to make a good match. Did you know that I saw her talking to the soldiers that came through our town last week? I gave her a scolding and a smack for being so foolish."

I nodded again. "*Sì*. I heard about it from Father Nicolo. She and those other silly girls. I gave her a smack over that one as well. But, I think I may have a remedy," I said hopefully. "Marietta came to me after the service on Sunday. She wanted to ask me if I had thought at all about a betrothal for Amadora. Giovanni's nephew, Mario, is now eleven and Marietta was thinking it would be a good match. Do you know Giovanni's brother well?"

"*Sì*! Michele! He is a good man, like Giovanni, and he has taught his son well. Amadora could do worse than to marry Mario. And by the time she is old enough to marry he will be sixteen or seventeen. Old enough to support a wife." Maria placed two cups on the table and poured us each a glass of her son's rich red wine.

"*Grazii*, Maria." I took the glass she offered me and sipped the deep red liquid–smooth with just an edge of bitterness.

"*Grazii*, Giacomo, for making such wonderful wine!" She raised her glass, and I joined her in the toast to her son. We drank in silence, both contemplating the news.

"What is this? Sitting about drinking wine when there is work to be done? Ah, such luxury!" Agata walked into the room carrying a wooden bucket, half filled with warm goats' milk.

"Giovanni's brother, Michele, is interested in creating a match for Amadora and his son, Mario!" Maria answered.

"That is good news!" Agata brought another cup to the table and Maria poured some wine for her.

"But how do we arrange this? What man do we ask to bargain with Michele?"

"Well, we could ask *Zzio* Enzo, but he is becoming frail. He may not be able to make a good arrangement." Agata answered.

"No." Maria interjected. "We need to ask a third party–someone with no connection to either family."

"But whom should we ask? It must be someone serious and well-respected. We cannot ask the *Patri*, that wouldn't be suitable either."

Even though I had lived in Sperlinga for almost ten years and knew almost everyone in the village, I could not think of anyone who was not related and held the kind of respect required. Suddenly Maria banged her hand on the table and grinned at the two of us.

"What Maria?" Agata cried out, startled at the loud sound.

"I know exactly whom we should ask! *Signuri* Rosso!"

Agata clapped her hands like a small child. "Yes! He is the perfect choice."

"*Signuri* Rosso? I've never heard of him. Who is he?"

"Oh Genevra, you will love him, I'm sure." Agata answered eagerly. "He doesn't live here but in Nicosia. He was the go-between for Marietta's family and Giovanni's. He is a skilled negotiator. When Marietta's father put down his foot about the dowry, *Signuri* Rosso managed to find a middle ground on which everyone could agree. He is well-respected, clever, and kind. He will do a good job for both families and especially for Amadora and Mario."

"Yes, and if we have a quiet word with Marietta, I'm sure Giovanni will send word to *Signuri* Rosso." Maria added.

"That is a wonderful idea, Maria. So, do you both think this would be a good match for Amadora?"

"Of course! I would never suggest a man for our darling girl that wouldn't be a wonderful husband. They are a good family, they have land, and Michele never beats his wife or his children. Mario has a sharp sense of humour that I think would match Amadora quite well." Agata answered.

"Yes, and if she is betrothed, she will have to become more serious about learning to be a wife–she will be less likely to spend time with those foolish girls who drool over the village boys." Maria added.

"Yes, I have been concerned about that. Well, it is settled. I will talk to Father Nicolo and Marietta the next time I go into the town." I raised my cup again, and Maria and Agata joined me. "To Amadora's future." We all drank and spat on the ground to keep her safe from evil.

Chapter thirty-two

IL MALOCCHIO

AMADORA HAD ONLY BEEN STUDYING with Father Nicolo for a few weeks when she returned home one afternoon in tears. Running past us, she hurled herself into the backroom and lay face down on the bed. Maria, Agata and I looked at each other with astonishment.

"Amadora, what's wrong?" I asked as I walked quickly into the back room.

"Nothing, leave me alone!" came her muffled voice from the folds in the down comforter.

"Don't be ridiculous. You can't lie on the bed sobbing and have me believe nothing is wrong! Now turn over and tell me what has happened."

Amadora lay still, her sobbing unabated, for a few moments more, and slowly rolled on her side, her stricken face turned up towards me.

"It was Concetta. Father Nicolo has been keeping me at my lessons longer than the first week. Today, Concetta told me I was a *buttana,* a whore, and soon my stomach would be fat with the *Patri*'s baby!"

I gasped at Amadora's shocking words. Unsure what to say or do, I did the only thing that I could think of. I crossed myself several times to protect myself against such evil words.

"But *Mamma*, that isn't the worst. After she said that she... she..." Amadora's sobs became louder and she hid her face in her hands.

I felt dread slip over me like a shroud. There was only one thing I could think of that might make Amadora lose control like this.

"Tell us, Amadora. Don't be afraid." came a calm voice from

behind us. It was Maria. She and Agata had come to the doorway of the room.

Amadora looked up. Her sobs quieted a little. "Concetta cursed me with *il malocchio*.

The room grew silent around Amadora's heart wrenching weeping. Agata's hand grasped my arm so tightly I could feel her nails leaving marks in my skin. I looked at Maria, my heart beating wildly. This was beyond anything I knew how to handle. *Zzia* Marcella had never covered how to break the curse of *malocchio* in all the lessons she had taught me, and I knew from Agata's grasp it was beyond her as well.

"Well, Amadora, it is good you are in this family." Maria answered breezily as she reached to straighten the counterpane Amadora had set askew when she threw herself on the bed.

Amadora wiped her eyes with the heels of her palms. "What do you mean?

"Well, my *nanna* taught my mother to break the curse of the *malocchio* and my mother taught me." Maria straightened up. "On Saturday afternoon we will do this, and on Sunday we will give thanks in church you are gifted with such a talented aunt!" Maria chuckled at her own joke.

Amadora frowned at Maria. "But it is Tuesday. That is four days away! What if I get sick or hurt before? Can't we do it now?"

Maria waved her hand and turned back towards the kitchen. "No, it must be done on a Saturday. Don't worry," she called over her shoulder. "Concetta is a stupid old woman. She doesn't know how to set *il malocchio* on a goat, much less a girl."

"*Mamma?*" Amadora's red-rimmed eyes searched my face.

"If Maria says not to worry, you shouldn't worry. She is the expert here." I patted her head, and squeezed her cheek.

"Oh, and Genevra?" Maria called from the kitchen.

"*Sì?*"

"I will teach you and Agata and Amadora how to break this curse. It is something all the women in our family should know how to do."

~|~

I woke up the next morning from a nightmare, drenched in sweat. In my dream, I had been working in the hot summer sun, picking up sheaths of dry yellow straw. Behind me was the devil himself, laughing and urging me forward, faster and faster, by poking my back with a large sharpened stick.

"Work, work!" he laughed. "Your child is waiting. She is calling for you! When you have piled ten sheaths you can go to her."

But every time I added another sheath to the pile, the previous one had disappeared. No matter how hard I worked, I couldn't make a pile of ten and as I worked Amadora's plaintive cries grew louder and louder. Suddenly the devil touched my back with his hand and burned me. I jumped and cried out and in doing so, I woke myself.

I lay in the bed and crossed myself several times to protect myself from such an evil dream. It was at that moment I heard Amadora whimper.

I sat up quickly and reached out to touch her shoulder. Before I had even laid my hand on her I could feel the heat coming off her in waves. I grabbed her and rolled her onto her back. She fell back limply. I touched her head. It was dry and the skin felt as if it were stretched tight across her skull. She whimpered again, but didn't open her eyes. I grasped her shoulders and shook her.

"Amadora! Amadora! Wake up!" When I let go, she simply fell back again.

I scrambled out of bed. "Maria, Agata! Come here!"

I could hear the rustling of bedding, as they climbed out of their bed in the kitchen.

"What? What is it?" Maria hurried into the room as Agata shuffled after her.

"It's Amadora. Feel her head!" I stood back, biting my knuckle on one hand and pulling on my hair with the other.

Maria placed her hand on Amadora's forehead. She frowned and glanced at Agata from under her brows. "Agata, put some water on to boil and add a handful of the dried herbs from the jar under the bed." She turned to me and said, "She has a bad fever but we will bring it down with this medicine. In the meantime, get a bucket of cold water and a rag. You will need to keep her forehead, wrists, and feet cool. Quickly." Maria opened Amadora's mouth and examined her tongue and gums. She pulled open her eyelids and checked her eyes. Under her breath I heard her whisper, "*Miu Diu*, if any serious ill happens to this child, I will curse Concetta with something far worse than anything she could ever imagine." I rushed to get the water.

I filled a basin with cool water. Grabbing a soft woolen rag torn from an old skirt, I carried both into the bedroom, trying my best not to spill while still feeling the pressure to get to Amadora's bedside quickly.

As I knelt beside the bed, Maria grasped my arm. "This is serious, Genevra. I won't pretend it isn't. But, it isn't hopeless. We have to bring her fever down and keep her clean. She will be sick for a time and it will be hard, but if the three of us take turns, we should be able to bring her around. Now, try to keep her cool as much as you can. Keep wiping her forehead, her neck, and her wrists."

I nodded, biting my lower lip between my teeth. Wringing out the cloth, I brought the cool rag to her head. Her eyes flickered.

"*Mamma.*"

"Shhh. You are sick, *carolina*. You need to lie still and sleep while I bath you." I whispered to her gently.

"*Mamma*, my head aches so. It's so dark–I can't see you."

Amadora moved restlessly, turning her head from side to side and moaning.

"Lie still, *mia bambina*. I need to cool your head. Please Amadora, please lie still." I begged her.

Suddenly she sat up and screamed. "No! No! Stop them!"

"Stop what? What do you want me to stop Amadora?" I was crying as I tried to hold Amadora from twisting back and forth. Just as suddenly she stopped and fell quiet back onto the bed, eyes staring wide. I grasped her hands, horrified. Had she died? Was she gone? But no, her chest still rose up and down, as I gazed into her unseeing eyes. I laid my head on the bed beside her, my tears creating dark wet spots on the blue counterpane.

Maria and Agata stood in the doorway. Agata came in and knelt beside me and pressed her bosom against my back, holding me close.

"Don't cry, Genevra. We will all take good care of her."

I nodded, sniffing, my head still on the bed.

Maria spoke from next to me. I jumped. I hadn't heard her walk into the room. "That was only the fever speaking. When the fever gets too high, the sick will see and hear things that are not there. That is why we need to get her fever down as much as we can." She squeezed my shoulder. "Genevra, you cannot break down. You must concentrate, and work to control the fever."

I nodded. I picked up the damp cloth and wiped her head, and wrists, and chest.

Maria gave me a small smile. "Agata is making a tea. When it is cool, we will try to get her to swallow some. That should help as well."

The next six days dragged on. Amadora cycled through periods of thrashing about and screaming over unseen monsters followed by stupor–nearly catatonic, with moments of lucidity when she cried about the pains in her head, knees, ankles, hips, and wrists. Sometimes she was so hot I believed the cool water would sizzled on her skin, yet at other times she shivered and moaned about the cold. Through all this, Amadora rarely slept. The closest she came to rest was the wide-eyed staring stupor would invariably follow the uncontrollable thrashing and screaming. Agata, Maria and I took turns staying up during the night with her; bathing her with cool water and trying to get her to take sips of Maria's herbal tea.

On the morning of the seventh day, Maria came in to let me sleep after a particularly difficult night. Amadora had fallen into a deep sleep–the first one since she had become ill. Maria pulled back the bedding and opened the front of Amadora's nightdress. I gasped. Her chest was covered with small red dots. Maria pulled up the skirt of her nightdress to examine her thighs.

"I was afraid this might be the case–the rash all over her legs and chest proved my fears."

"What? What is it?"

"We don't have a proper name for it, but some people call it 'jail fever'. When the soldiers pass through, sometimes they leave this illness here with us. This is one of the reasons we dread to see them. We have been lucky; they hadn't come through in many years until that day three weeks ago. It is not so strange Amadora has become ill with this pestilence."

"But she will get better?" I felt like a band was tightening around my heart.

Maria looked at her rough, work-worn hands. I could see tears dampening her lashes.

"Sometimes people will recover from this fever." She paused and drew a deep breath. "But Genevra, most people do not."

The walls of the room spun around me, and I dropped to my knees as a wail filled the room. I didn't even realize the cry had come from me until Maria grabbed me by my shoulders and shook me.

"Stop it! She is not gone yet." Maria crossed herself. "We do not give up until the last breath has come and gone. You are stronger than this. Pray for her, and pray for yourself. Now, go, lie in the other bed. Agata is bringing back water so it will be quiet for a time."

I left the bedroom and threw myself on the bed in the corner of the kitchen. I had been so busy trying to keep Amadora calm and cool I had not even thought to pray. How could I forget something so important? I tried to rise to my feet so I could kneel by the bed but my exhaustion was such it was impossible to even lift my head. Instead I rolled onto my side so I could see the sun shine through the window and I clasped my hands together and prayed.

"Holy Mother," I whispered so quietly only She and I might hear. "Holy Mother, my daughter's life lies in Your hands. She is so ill that I fear she might not live the week. You told me she was the next in the line of strong women that were to come from my loins. If she dies now, this line will die. Surely You must want her to live? Please, oh please, Mother, show me a sign she will be well. Help me to leave this burden in Your hands. Mother, I trust you, but I fear, too. Please help me." I squeezed my hands together so tightly they shook with the effort. Slowly, slowly, muscle by muscle I released the tension from my hands. By the time they had relaxed I had fallen into a dark and dreamless sleep.

I awoke hours later–the sun already drifting lower in the sky, casting late afternoon sun through our window. I pushed my shoulders up from the bed, shaking my head trying to clear my sleep-drugged mind. Neither the prayer nor the sleep had helped me.

"Ah, you're up. Maria and I thought you would never wake!" Agata stood at the table pounding dough, flipping it, and pounding it once again. She wiped her hands on her apron and reached across the table to grab the wine bottle and pour a generous cupful. "Here, you need to eat and drink something." She took a plate of *gnocchi* from above the oven and placed it beside the wine. "If you don't take care of yourself, you will be no good to Amadora."

I stood stiffly–I felt as if Graziella had kicked me all over before I had gone to bed. Every joint and muscle ached. Nursing Amadora had exhausted me more than I realized. I reached my arms out behind me and stretched my back and shoulders before taking a seat at the table. I was thirsty and gulped the wine quickly. I put one of Agata's *gnocchi* in my mouth. Usually so tasty, these were not up to Agata's high standard. I struggled to swallow the cloying taste and followed it quickly with the last mouthful of wine. Amadora's illness was taking its toll on all of us.

Agata had made a trip to the town to see Marietta and get new herbs to try with Amadora, and she told me of the latest village gossip, yet I could barely hear it. I was still so wearied. In the middle of a story, I rose and walked into the bedroom. I could no longer listen to the foolish trials of the people living at the bottom of the mountain. I did not care who was angry with whom, whose pig had died, and who had been drinking before church. None of those things mattered. It was time for me to release Maria and to take over the care of my dying daughter. That was the only thing that mattered.

Maria stood as I walked into the room. "Are you feeling more rested, Genevra?" Maria's voice sounded as if she were coming from a great distance. I ignored her. Instead I looked at my daughter.

Her eyes were closed in the sleep that had eluded her for so many days. She looked deathly thin with dark purple shadows under each eye, and her skin mottled with the red pinprick dots that had appeared earlier in the morning. How could she look this ill and still live?

I sat next to her and picked up the damp cloth from the bowl placed next to her on the bed and wiped her hands and face.

"I will bring you some fresh water, Genevra." Maria's voice was lowered, and she took the bowl and left the room. As I sat and stared at Amadora, I heard, somewhere in the back of my mind, Maria and Agata whispering in the other room. I did not pay attention to what they said, however, as I sat stroking Amadora's limp hands. After some time– how long I wasn't sure–I sensed, rather than saw Agata standing beside me.

"Genevra, you aren't well. You have been driving yourself too hard. I will take care of Amadora. Please rest."

The worried, insistent tone in her voice cut through my

consciousness, but all I could reply was, "Please bring me the fresh water. I need to bathe her." I did not take my eyes from my sweet daughter's ravaged face and I spoke no more. After a time of sitting in silence–I don't know how long–I heard Agata turn and leave the room. She returned with a fresh bowl of water, replacing the old bowl. Somewhere in the back of my mind, I was only minimally aware she was speaking to me. I heard the word "please" but I did not respond. My focus was all on my Amadora.

Over and over, I wiped her face and hands with the damp cloth. Dip the cloth in the bowl, wring out the extra water, wipe her forehead, face and neck. Dip the cloth in the bowl, wring out the extra water, wipe her forearms and her hands. I repeated these motions convinced this was all that was holding my girl to life. I knew if I stopped she would die. Over and over in my head I pleaded for her to live until the words became meaningless and all I could hear inside my mind was "*Pi favuri, mia Matri.*"

Outside of my mind, however, was another matter. As I bathed her, a battle had arisen over my head. While I was praying, my eyes intently on Amadora's sleeping face, I sensed, rather than saw, strange lights reflecting back and forth around the room. I glanced up and my heart felt as if the heavy leather band had tightened even more around it, squeezing and squeezing. The ceiling had opened to the sky and the room had become a battlefield. Horrible demons had appeared, from where I knew not. They flew about the room, their putrid bodies blood red and stinking. They cackled and gnashed blackened, jagged teeth and pulled at horrid, misshapen genitals. Yet, above my daughter flew angels, beautiful–as beautiful as the ones I had seen on the walls in the cathedral in Palermo–and terrible. Brilliant, golden light flashed angrily from their eyes. Silver light radiated from their hands, and faces, and robes. A dozen or so of the angels pointed at the demons, forcing them back with the powerful light, while the rest gestured over my daughter, casting their silver light in formidable waves over her body. These were not the gentle angels I imagined when I sat praying in church. These were God's soldiers whom He had sent to save Amadora from the *malocchio* that had brought this terrible illness upon her, and this was their crusade; a crusade for my daughter's soul.

My mouth dropped open, but I could not make a sound. In my

head, I held on to the words I had been praying, "*Pi favuri, mia Matri. Pi favuri, miu Diu.*" I watched in horror as the demons flew at the battalion of angels repeatedly, trying to break through their line. Again, and again, the front line of angels shot silver and gold light. I heard a rhythmic pounding and tore my gaze away from the demons in time to see the terrifying angels drive them back with the beating of their huge and powerful wings.

The battle raged on—it felt like days, yet as I could not take my gaze from it, it also seemed to pass, perversely, in the blink of an eye. Neither the demons nor the angels appeared to tire. Suddenly, a demon broke through—one of the angels had left a small hole open without the terrible gold and silver light to protect it. The demon had quietly stolen forward and was reaching his gnarled and twisted hand toward my Amadora. He made nearly inaudible hoots, unable to contain his glee, yet the sound echoed in my head. But, it was not the sound that alerted me to the demon. With his horrible, murmuring laugh, came angry, ragged rays of colour—an equally horrible dark yellow with edges tinged the same blood-red as the sagging skin of the demon. They shot across the room and into my head, swirling and mixing with my prayer.

I watched as his broken yellowed fingernails almost scraped across Amadora's face and still the angels did not seem to notice him.

"No! Look!" I cried to the angels, my voice a vivid deep purple, matching the intensity of my tone.

So quickly they responded, almost before I spoke. The angels turned on the demon and grabbed him. His hoots turned to screams as the angels tore holes in his skin and filled him with silver light. He writhed back and forth under the angels' firm hold. I could see the light tracing through the veins and pumping through his arteries. Through his chest wall, a light began to glow—it was his heart! Filling with silver light, I could see it pumping. The light spread to his other organs—liver, kidneys, lungs. His screams became more desperate. I clasped my hands to my ears and closed my eyes—his screams were black, the darkest black, and they spread jaggedly across the room, covering everything they touched. His screams still cut into my head, and I took up the prayers I had stopped when I cried out to the angels.

"*Pi favuri, mia Matri. Pi favuri, miu Diu.*" Silver tendrils stretched out at the sound of my prayers, comforting me against the demon's demented screams. I opened my eyes once more to watch as the light finally overcame the demon, and he exploded into silvery shards that fell across the room, the bed, and my daughter's face and hands.

This seemed to be a signal to the demons. Angry shrieks and howls filled and blackened the room. The freakish creatures moved forward–the largest demons moved to the front. With a horrid, ear-splitting screech, the huge demons dove onto the angels, and as each one fell upon an angel, the angel's touch filled the demon with silver light. Over and over they attacked, and over and over they were driven back leaving their evil foot soldiers screaming in anguish until they exploded with the silver light. The blackened screams of the terror and pain became so loud and the explosions of silver so bright I was amazed, but grateful, Agata and Maria, and in fact the rest of Sperlinga didn't come running into our little bedroom. The angels raised their terrible golden eyes, and beyond the screaming and dying soldiers cast their light upon the demons cowering and babbling behind. With a sharp crack, and the acrid smell of sulfur, the last of the demons vanished.

The demon army had been decimated. The angels had not one casualty. They circled around Amadora and caressed her body with their wings. The shards of silver covering her rose and curled gently in a sparkling mist above her head. The angels spread their arms and the silver mist drifted into their robes and they glowed brightly. Their faces had softened and were no longer terrible to look upon. They gazed on Amadora one last time, and with a flash of light they were gone.

I looked at my daughter's face as she opened her eyes. She moved her head slightly and her gaze, now clear, fell on me. "*Mamma.*" She whispered. The tight leather strap holding my heart in check fell away. I knew she would live. I collapsed onto the floor and knew nothing for a long time.

Chapter thirty-three

THE INHERITANCE OF COLOUR

~AGOSTO 2011~

ELENA LEFT A SMALLER REGIONAL HIGHWAY, followed an on-ramp, and merged onto the Palermo-Catania freeway. Instead of the quiet, local highways she had become used to, the freeway was clogged with traffic; each car jostling for any space slightly farther ahead than the car next to them. Ironically, the speed on the freeway was much slower than the local highways as they came closer and closer to Palermo. Eventually, they slowed so much Elena could take her hands from the wheel and gaze out at the glimpses of the pretty coastline to the right. Genevra had paused in her story and silence had settled over the car. Elena waited for Genevra to continue, but the silence continued unbroken until Elena could no longer stand it.

"Well?" she demanded. "Well, what happened next? Is that when you died?" With this question Elena realized she had become so enthralled in the story she had suspended all disbelief in the disembodied voice of the saint speaking so clearly through her GPS.

"No, I didn't die then, although I was told I came close."

"Was the battle real? Did demons really appear over your daughter?"

"It is not for me to say if they were real or not. They appeared real enough to me and that is all I cared."

Elena sat contemplating what she had heard. An air of expectation rose in the little Panda.

"I think you have another question." Genevra said. "Why don't you ask me?"

"One other question?" Elena snorted derisively. "More like one thousand other questions!"

"All right. I think you have a question in the forefront of your mind. Why don't you ask me?"

Elena paused. The answer to her next question could make the difference between believing the voice or believing herself to be stark raving mad. Taking a deep breath, she charged ahead.

"You mentioned about seeing colour when the demon laughed?"

"Yes?" Genevra answered.

"Can you tell me more about that?" Elena asked quietly, as if she knew what the answer would be.

"I knew you would ask me about seeing colours. In that moment, the moment that horrible demon broke through the angels' line, the shock of seeing my daughter so in danger I developed a skill—a secret skill I tried to keep only between Amadora and myself for a long time. I knew, as much as the people in Sperlinga loved me—Agata, Maria, Father Nicolo—they would think it came from the devil, and I would face something terrible. Perhaps stoning or burning—in the best case, I would be shunned. And Amadora, she would never marry if her mother had been possessed by a demon. I could see sounds. Sounds began, in that moment, to have colour and sometimes shape. Even now, without a body, I can sense the world as if I had ears and eyes, and sounds still swirl with colour. And just as oddly, Amadora woke from her fever with the same ability. We swore to each other no one else would know our secret, like you kept your secret between you, Lucia, and your father."

Elena hit the brakes. Fortunately, traffic was only creeping along.

"Wait! How do you know about the colours, and Lucia, and my dad?" Elena wanted to turn and face Genevra to ask her question, but there was no Genevra to turn to so instead she glared at the GPS.

"Haven't you guessed by now?" Genevra asked gently. "That long line of strong women? You are the most recent of my line. The gift of seeing colours started with the fight between the demons and the angels. It was our Mother's gift to the women of our line. It is a rare gift, one that comes from God, our Mother, and her Son. Only a few are so lucky."

"So... so you are my great, great... great a bunch more times grandmother?" Elena struggled to grasp the concept that this disembodied voice coming from the GPS was not just a voice but also a relative, an ancestor!

"That is exactly what I am saying. And I have come back to speak to all of my daughters, although usually in a dream. It hasn't been until the past 80 years or so there has been technology enough for me to make use of it. I spoke to your mother before you were born."

"You did? What did you say to her?"

"Ah, well. That is between her and I. If she chooses to share it with you, *va beni*. But that is her decision, not mine."

"Does she see colours as well?"

"Oh yes," Genevra chuckled. "It has made her a famous cake decorator. When someone orders a cake, she listens to the sound of their voice, sees the colours, and decorates the cake accordingly. The customers are always satisfied. In fact, more than satisfied because the colours vibrate with the same frequency as their soul."

Elena considered this. The colours had made her a better musician. She could plan the chords and harmonies based on what she could see. Gerry thought she was particularly talented and intuitive, but she knew without the colours she would not have been able to make the music she did. It had never occurred to her the colours could help with other talents too.

"Does she hide her... her, talent, too?"

"Yes. As I said, this is a rare skill, and few people would understand. She has shared it with only one other person."

"Who is that?"

"Again, that will be for her to decide if she will share with you or not, as it will be up to you to decide if you share your skill with her."

Elena felt a tightness in her chest and her belly constrict as she thought about meeting her birth mother and sharing such an intimate secret with this woman she didn't really know.

"This is making me nervous. Can you tell me more of your story? I want to know what happened, and it will keep me from thinking about what is up ahead." Elena asked.

"Of course." Genevra answered.

Chapter thirty-four

AMADORA'S REVELATION

~1153~

THE DREAD TIGHTENED AROUND ME, and I found myself struggling to breathe. The room split into waves around me, and I fell back into them. Floating in circles, I was drawn to a bright light above my head. Frowning, I was puzzled by the light. I reached up hoping to grab hold of the light so I could make sense of what I was seeing. Suddenly, before my hand, a beautiful, familiar face appeared. Who was this? I had seen her before.

"Do you not remember me, Genevra?

And with those words I knew, of course, who she was.

"I have been with you all along your journey. I am here to tell you your road is about to get steeper–much more *difficile*. But have faith, Genevra; I will walk with you each step you take. As your path rises sharply up before you, remember my words. You are the beginning of a line of powerful women. Your children's children will spread across all the land lit by the light of your Lord, and you will know each by the colours surrounding them. That fate is set in stone much harder than the sandstone of these caves. Harder even than the stone of the volcano that lies to your east."

"*Matri*, will there be reason for me to doubt?"

"No Genevra, there is never reason to doubt your Father, but you will. You are human and struggle, but you will come through your crisis to a faith equally strong and hard as this fate that is yours and the fate of the children that spring from your loins. Be strong."

Suddenly, the Virgin disappeared into a brilliant ball of golden light hovering over me, and shot straight at my heart. I gasped as the light struck me, forcing a sharp, exploding pain through my chest. From a distance, I heard familiar voices calling out but I could only concentrate on the intense pain I was feeling. The pain hit me over and over as if I was once again giving birth. I squeezed my eyes tightly, yet still tears managed to seep between. Slowly, slowly the pain abated and I found I could open my eyes once again. Maria and Agata were holding my arms and Amadora was crying out "*Mamma, Mamma!*"

I opened my eyes and shut them tightly again. The coloured light was too bright for me. I felt soft hands on my face. Squinting, I looked up to see Amadora's beautiful face, brows knit together with worry, floating above me.

"*Mamma,* oh *Mamma,* I thought you were going to die!" Great swirls of bright yellow circled her face as she threw herself across my chest. I tried to raise my arms to hold my beloved daughter but I was too weak.

"What happened to me?" I asked.

Agata's voice, golden with worry, answered from above my head. "You collapsed when Amadora woke up from her fever. You had exhausted yourself taking care of her, and you fell to the floor. It was as if you were possessed–your body shook, and your mouth foamed. Maria and I were terrified, and were about to get Father Nicolo but you stopped and seemed to sleep."

"Yes," Maria's low silver voice chimed in. "We lifted you onto the bed. You slept like the dead." Maria and Agata both crossed themselves. "You have been sleeping for two weeks now–but not peacefully. You have been crying out and mumbling in your sleep."

Amadora sat up, her face tear-streaked. "I tried to calm you, *Mamma.* But you wouldn't listen, and I was so tired."

I tried to get up and Agata grasped my shoulders. She helped me to sit.

"You must eat something, Genevra. We have some soup on the stove. But you must not get up–you are too weak." Maria said to me. "I will bring the soup to you."

"And you, girl," Agata added, pointing at Amadora. "I want you lying back as well. We will bring soup for you, too."

I didn't respond. I was too busy watching the colours swirl around the room with each sound I heard. I saw Maria give me a hard look and shake her head. She whispered to Agata. "I'm not sure if her brain has been addled by this or not."

~|~

It was three weeks before either Amadora or I were able to hobble our way to the door and out into the sunshine. Amadora's illness and my exhaustion had taken their toll on us, and we both felt an afternoon sitting in the sun would do us good.

"If you two are going to insist on sitting outside, I want you both to wrap up well. All you need now is to catch a cold, and you both will be for the grave!" Agata crossed herself several times and kissed her fingers. She spat over our heads to chase away any demons.

'We don't need to worry about demons now,' I thought to myself. 'Not after the battle over Amadora."

Agata wrapped the soft woolen shawls I had made around our shoulders.

"Now, don't you two stay out too long. I mean it." She turned quickly, but not before I saw the tears welling in her eyes.

We settled on a ledge near the door to our home. Amadora leaned into me as I leaned back against the sandstone rock face. It was so peaceful there. I looked up at the sky and watched an eagle circling. Her wide black-striped wings were stretched out; how far I couldn't tell. She was a large bird. I admired the feathers spreading like fingers at the end of each wing; a small adjustment of each feather could change the direction in which she flew. Suddenly she dove, wings tight to her sides, towards some prey in the grasses below. At the last moment, she dropped her yellow talons and widened her wings. She hit the grasses, and flew up immediately with a wildcat kitten in her talons. The kitten struggled as the eagle flew higher, but slowly the kitten's writhing lessened until it hung lifeless in the yellow talons now stained red. The eagle opened her beak and made a triumphant cry, "klu-kluklu-kluee!" I watched a brilliant orange stripe arc across the sky in concert with the eagle's cry. Amadora squeezed my arm tightly.

"Are you upset, *bedda mia*? It's just the way of things."

"No," Amadora answered slowly. "It's not that."

"Then what?"

"*Mamma*, I need to tell you something, but I'm afraid you will think the *malocchio* is still on me."

I felt a hand clutch my heart. We had suffered so much from Concetta's curse. Was there more? I tightened my arm that lay across her shoulders and held her close to me.

"Tell me, Amadora."

"Well, it's not that it's so bad, it's just strange."

Amadora paused and I sat quietly, my stomach flip-flopping as I awaited her words.

"When I hear sounds, any sounds, I... I see colours." Amadora dropped her head as if in shame.

I stared at my daughter, open-mouthed. Had she been gifted with the same thing the angels had given me? I laughed with relief. Amadora stared at me in confusion.

"Oh my girl, I am sure this is not from the *malocchio*. In fact, I am sure this is a gift from God." I crossed myself and kissed my fingers.

"But how do you know? How can you be sure?" Tears were filling Amadora's eyes.

I looked at her more seriously this time. How to explain this? How to tell her I saw the colours as well, and the Mother of God had been visiting her mother for the past nine years? Or should I go back farther, and tell her about how she had been conceived, and the family I had left behind? I looked into her eight-year-old face. She was young but before her illness we had been talking about her betrothal. It was time.

"Amadora, I have a story to tell you. It is a long story, and you may be shocked and angry with me after you hear it, but it is your story too, and you should know."

So, we sat in the sun, and my amber words swirled around us as I told her about her family; my father, how my mother had died, and how I had fallen in love with Landro. I told her everything, the visions, even the battle for her soul and mine that had taken place in the bedroom as she lay ill. Finally, I told her I, too, saw the colours.

"This is how I know the colours come from God. I watched the angels win their battle above you. And *Santa Maria* told me."

Amadora laid her head in my lap, and she began to cry. I felt her chest rise and fall with her tears. Her shoulders quaked as she sobbed uncontrollably. She sounded so desolate, but I knew these were healing tears–the blue that surrounded her was tinged with green growing brighter, the longer she cried. Finally, her sobs slowed and stopped. I had been stroking her head throughout. She reached around and grasped my hand, pulling it to her damp cheek.

"Are you all right, Amadora? Have your tears washed away your pain?"

Amadora sat up slowly, and turned her tear-stained face towards me.

I took her other hand and looked into her reddened eyes. "Can you forgive me?"

"Forgive you?" Amadora sounded puzzled. "For what, *Mamma*? You gave up everything for me! You could have been a princess! But you kept me, and now you live here in a cave instead of a palace. I'm so sorry, *Mamma*."

"Oh my darling girl!" I clutched her to me. "I could not have made any other decision, and I have never regretted it. I'd much rather a small cave with you, and Agata, and Maria, than the grandest palace in all the world."

I held her away from me and looked at her seriously. "But there is something you must understand. While Agata and Maria know about my past, they don't know about the colours nor the battle over our souls. They must never know. And no one in the town should know any of it. If we are to have you betrothed, and live a normal, happy life, no one can know. Not even Marietta nor Father Nicolo. Father Nicolo knows some of the story, but if he were to know more, he would have to contact the bishop. We can't have that. Do you understand? This is between us, and God, and *nustra Matri*."

Amadora nodded. "I understand *Mamma*. I am *la bastarda*." She hung her head.

I raised my eyes to the sky and sighed. I had been afraid she would see it this way.

"Look at me!" I said fiercely. "You are not a bastard! I loved your father, and if he did not love me in the same way, that is no fault of either yours or mine. Amadora, the Mother of God herself told me to keep you, and raise you, and love you! Do you think that in anyway makes you a bastard? You are blessed amongst women. The angels fought for you. *La Madonna* spoke for you. Elisabeth, Salome, Hannah, Rachel, Jochebed, Rebekah and Sarah helped me birth you! Be grateful, *bedda mia.* You truly are blessed."

Amadora looked back at me with a dawning realization crossing her face. "I am blessed! Mamma, I don't know why I have been chosen to be so blessed, but I will try to remember it in humility."

"That is all I could ask for, my darling daughter." My hand cupped her face gently. "Now, I think we should go back inside before Agata thinks we have died of cold out here on the ledge." And with my arm around Amadora's shoulders, we went back to our cave.

Chapter thirty-five

A WEDDING AND A SHRINE

~1160~

THE NEXT FEW YEARS went by relatively uneventfully. When the people of Sperlinga heard Concetta had cursed Amadora they shunned her. Amadora's sweet personality had charmed everyone in the town and most were outraged when they heard about the curse and the illness as a result, particularly *Zzio* Enzo and his cronies. Father Nicolo tried in his sermons, and in his conversations on the streets, to turn the tide of vitriol building against Concetta. Eventually, Father Nicolo, Amadora and I were the only ones speaking to her. Marietta was outraged when Amadora and I greeted her in the street, but we had discussed it, and together decided we would not hold resentment against her. What she had done had caused us a great deal of pain, but it had given us a great gift as well. In spite of our efforts to be kind, Concetta packed up her few possessions, and went to live with a distant cousin higher up in the mountains.

Amadora recovered fully. In fact, the conversation she and I shared seemed to give her more energy, more kindness, and a real willingness to do what she believed God would want her to do. She resumed her reading lessons with Father Nicolo, and she and I took over much of the work Concetta had done.

Once it was clear Amadora had returned to full health, she was betrothed to Mario with the agreement when Amadora reached 15 and Mario was 18, they would marry. Both families celebrated, along with Father Nicolo. As for me, I never truly recovered from the exhaustion and the fever that had gripped me after I had collapsed. I tired easily, my legs did not support me as well as before, and together with my back, my legs kept me in constant pain. But, I did not speak of it, even to Agata and Maria, although I suspect they knew.

Marietta and Giovanni had convinced *Signuri* Rosso to come and act as *sensale*, marriage broker, and conduct the negotiations. The negotiations were short. While we didn't suffer deprivation, neither did we have any elegance in our house. Mario and his family were better off. They had land and grew almonds, olives, and figs. They had herds of sheep and goats and made some of the best cheese in Sperlinga, although Maria would not admit her son's was not as good. Mario worked as a goatherd except when it was time to harvest from their trees. We had little to offer this family beyond my woollen goods with one exception. Amadora's bloodline. The story that I was a widow to a fisherman had taken root over the years. This gave her legitimacy. It also meant her bloodline came from somewhere other than Sperlinga. In such a remote village, it was common for cousins–even first cousins–to marry. If the opportunity arose to bring new blood into a family, it was considered a boon. This was the turning point in the negotiations, and *Signuri* Rosso took full advantage. In no time at all I was shaking hands with Michele and *ferme il parentado*, or sealing the alliance.

The day Amadora turned fifteen was an exciting one in our household. In two short months, she would be joined with Mario and there was so much to do in preparation. Amadora was glowing. Her voice had taken on a singsong quality with a golden light to it.

'So this is what pure joy looks like.' I thought to myself.

"*Mamma*, will you help me to pack my dowry into my new chest?"

Zzio Enzo had died three years before, but when Maria, Agata, Marietta and I had cleaned out his house, we found a large wooden trunk, ornate iron hinges on the side, and delicate, intricate carvings all over, complete with the name 'Amadora' on the top. This was obviously meant to contain her dowry. Inside there was a set of lovely dishes and cutlery, apparently handed down from his own family and intended to be part of Amadora's dowry.

Amadora ran her fingers lightly over the carvings of the chest.

"*Zzio* Enzo adored you." I said as I carefully folded the clothing, tablecloths, and other woollen items laid out on the bed. Two shirts for

Mario, two embroidered tablecloths, nightclothes for both Amadora and Mario, Amadora's baby clothes as well as maternity clothes from Marietta, all of which we folded carefully and lay in the chest. We laid the blankets and pillows on top of the other clothes and on top of that we placed a picture of *La Madonna*. Amadora carefully closed the chest and latched the top to the bottom.

"Look what Giovanni gave to you for your dowry!" Maria was carrying two shiny pots and a large knife. "They are not new, but they are in good condition and Marietta scrubbed them to a shine!"

Amadora jumped up and took them from Maria. "They are beautiful! And I think there is just enough space in the trunk for them."

Maria sat on the bed. "I have something I want to say to both of you," Maria patted the bed beside her and Amadora sat down. "Agata and I have been talking. She and I are getting old and the walk up and down the mountain to the town is getting harder and harder every time. And Genevra, I know it pains you too." She held up her hand. "No, don't argue with me. I know your legs and back have never recovered. So Agata and I went to speak with Michele. I know this wasn't part of the negotiation but Michele and Mario both have agreed. Agata and Genevra and I will move to *Zzio* Enzo's house, and you and Mario can have this house."

Amadora and I both sat stunned. Then Amadora jumped up with a joyful whoop.

"Maria, Agata, I can't believe you have done this for us." she said as she hugged them. "This is more than I could ever hope for. Michele is a nice man and I'm sure he'll be a good father-in-law but his house is teeny-tiny. There would be no place for Mario and I to be alone together. Mario and I will feel like the richest people in the village!"

"Amadora!" Maria said in a shocked voice. "Do you want to bring bad luck? A simple *grazii* is enough."

Amadora hung her head contritely and said, "*Grazii*, Maria, Agata." but the wide grin on her face belied her contrition.

I reached out and hugged Amadora. "Maria, Agata, what a wonderful start you have given Amadora and Mario," I released Amadora and turned to hug Maria, then Agata. "And, I will admit that you are right. After being ill, my body never recovered."

Agata returned my hug fiercely. "Amadora is the grandchild I could never have, and you are my daughter. How could I want it to be otherwise?"

The last two weeks arrived and ran by on Amadora's swift feet. She never stopped moving in her preparations for the wedding. Over and over she checked the beautiful carved chest. Were all the shirts in order? Did the picture of the Madonna need dusting? Were the tablecloths folded neatly? She pestered Maria about the food for the feast so many times Maria finally cried, "*Bastibili*! Enough of this constant chatter. The food will be what it is. Now off with you!"

As the day approached, Amadora became more and more fidgety.

"Genevra," Agata said to me in exasperation a few days before the wedding, "Can't you do something with this child of yours? She's driving us to distraction!"

"Of course, Agata. I'm sorry, I should have done something about this sooner. I've never been part of a wedding before, so I haven't known what to expect."

Agata stopped what she was doing. She turned to me with a surprised look. "This is your first wedding, isn't it? I had forgotten. I'm sorry Genevra, Maria and I assumed you would know what to do."

I smiled and placed my hand on Agata's and replied, "Don't worry, *càra*. I am learning new things everyday, and that keeps my mind young, even if my body complains."

I put down my sewing, and slowly and carefully, I unfolded my body until I was standing. "I'll go find her." With my knees and hips making their usual complaints, I walked to the door and stepped outside to an overcast day. Amadora was standing away from the door and looking up at the sky, tears running down her cheeks.

I sighed. Her emotions ran up and down like the mountains around us.

"What is it, *carina*? Why are you crying? Each tear falling before your wedding will bring you a day of sorrow."

"*Mamma*, look at the weather! It is cloudy and it may rain! What if it rains on my wedding day?" Amadora's arms waved about dramatically.

"Yes, it is cloudy, and yet the sun may come out. It may be sunny on your wedding day. But if it rains, it rains, and we will deal with that when the time comes. Besides, it will be the first day of June, and the weather is almost always good by then."

I turned her towards me and held her tightly by her shoulders. Looking into her eyes, I could see why she was so afraid. I had not been involved in a wedding, but neither had Amadora. And there was more.

"Are you afraid about becoming a wife, *sangu miu*?"

"A little. What if I do something wrong? What if I don't make him happy? What if... what if I don't give him a son?"

"Ah, Amadora, I should have talked to you about all this long before." I put my arm around her and led her to a stone bench Giovanni had recently put near the doorway so Mario and Amadora would have a place to sit together, to look out at the land of his father, and talk about... important things, trivial things, life. It was a bench on which they could sit in the evening as they got old and remember the footsteps of their lives. And today, she and I sat on it, so I could tell her some things I hoped would help her in her new journey.

"*Bella*, you have never lived in a house with a husband and wife, and I am guessing part of your fears come from that."

Amadora nodded emphatically, and I could see the words almost bursting forth from her mouth.

"Stop." I shook my head at her. "Something you must know when you go into any relationship is that there is a time to speak and a time to listen. You have wound yourself so tightly that I don't think you can listen." I put my arm around her shoulders.

"Look at the fields. Do you see the sheep and the goats? Somewhere there is your husband-to-be. He is sitting quietly with the sheep and goats. Do you know why?" I asked.

Amadora shook her head, and held her tongue.

"Mario sits quietly with his animals because if he gets agitated, so do they. If he is going to be a good goatherd, and a good leader, he must be calm when it is time to be calm. In the home, whether Mario realizes it or not, you are the leader. You must be calm when it is time to be calm. If Mario becomes angry or upset or...or..." I searched for the word.

"Agitated?"

I smiled. "Yes, *carina*, agitated. If he becomes agitated, you must be calm. If you are both in a dither nothing will be settled. Just as if you are upset, he must be calm so you can become calm as well. Over the past weeks, you have become more and more excited and fearful about the wedding and your married life. This has made you difficult to be with. Agata, Maria and I have been patient with you, but it is time for you to be a leader in your wedding preparations. Be calm, and we will be calm too.

"As for your fears, Amadora, you will be a wonderful wife. You have all the skills you need and more. You can keep a clean house, you can cook better than Maria, although don't tell her I said that. You can mend and sew. You have a sweet nature, if you don't get too excited, and you have a sharp sense of humour. All of these things together are bound to make any man happy. And as for sons, I can't promise you sons, but you are young, healthy, and beautiful, and you have wide hips for birthing children. And you can read, which means your children will be able to read. Perhaps one of your sons, if you have sons, will become a priest! This would bring honour to Mario's family. In any case, you will have many strong and beautiful children. Mario cannot help but want to bed you. Repeatedly, I would guess."

"*Mamma!*" Amadora's face had turned scarlet.

"Well, I only speak the truth, *bella.* I trust that I don't have to tell you what will happen on your wedding night. You may have lived with three old women for company, but you have seen the animals in the fields in spring. It is not much different than that. Mario is young, and he may fumble a bit. But give him time, and with some direction and encouragement from you, your nights may become... beautiful. Not to mention the many grandchildren you will give me!"

Amadora, who had hung her head in embarrassment, snorted a little and looked up at me with wide eyes and false innocence. "So, we should practice many times to get it right?"

I laughed. She would be fine, I had no doubt. "Calm down until the morning of your wedding. Then you can be a little flustered, and we will all understand."

Amadora threw her arms around me and gave me a tight hug. "Thank you, *Mamma.*"

~|~

Amadora was as good as her word. She spent the next few days calmly finishing all the tasks she needed to do before the wedding. And when she became a little anxious, she sat on the bench outside and watched the sheep and the goats below until she was calm again. Even on the morning of her wedding, when we woke and arose in what was once *Zzio* Enzo's house, she heeded my words, and calmly but firmly instructed everyone on what needed to be done.

Marietta, rarely at a loss for words, stood back, hands on her hips and with her mouth open. She slowly shook her head and turned to me.

"What have you done to your daughter? It is her wedding day—she should be in tears, or screaming at someone, or fainting away at the thought of her wedding night!"

"She seemed to have finished with all of that a few days ago. Believe me, she was not so calm or easy to be around on Wednesday," I chuckled. "But over the last few days, every time she felt nervous, she would sit outside on her own until she was calm."

Marietta snorted. "Well, that will work until the first child is walking and talking and then it is nothing but, '*Mamma* I want this, *Mamma* I want that.' And that goes for Mario too!"

We both stood laughing until Amadora looked at me with eyebrows raised. I hurried back to my job of filling the last few bags with candied almonds we had so fastidiously been making over the previous weeks. Marietta laughed again, and called to me, "Well, it is clear who has become the boss in this family!" I laughed as well, but I was pleased. Amadora was learning to be the head of her family. As long as she allowed Mario to feel he was the boss, everything would be smooth, I chuckled inwardly.

Soon, the food preparations had their final touches. The almonds and rice were in baskets to set outside the church for guests to throw at the new couple; the rice representing good fortune and money and the almonds for a quick conception. The ribbon had been tied over the church door, and the tables outside were groaning with covered plates of delicious delicacies the whole town had provided. It was time for Amadora to dress.

I had woven the finest wool that had ever come from my fingers. The carded wool was softer, the threads were finer, and the weave was closer. It was the colour, however, of which I was most proud. I had collected wild artichokes and lilac flowers during the spring and by boiling each of these separately, I had created dyes of two different but beautiful greens. Lilacs made a lovely delicate green, while artichokes gave a much deeper and richer colour. I had saved the rinds of the oranges and the lemons we had gorged on in the fall and had boiled them into a pale, yellow dye.

I had made all the clothes my daughter wore, so to get her size and shape right had been simple. What I struggled with was the style, but in the end I chose to make a dress in the modified Arab fashion that had been so popular when I had gone to King Roger's court. I had made a loose-fitting tunic with long delicate green sleeves, and pale yellow trim that edged the neck and ran a short way down the front, giving a suggestion of the young breasts beneath. A deep green cape, trimmed in lemon and, under the dress, for modesty, an underskirt to cover her ankles and a scarf to cover her neck. Finally, I had made a light veil using the deep green fabric, trimmed with yellow, to cover her head and held on with a cord of matching yellow. I allowed myself a small, internal gloat when I looked at the masterpiece I had created. But pride is ugly, so I put it aside and instead focussed on my daughter. When I lifted it out of the box, there were gasps all around, but it was to Amadora I looked. Would she like it?

"Oh, *Mamma*! It is... I can't believe..." And for the first time that morning Amadora's calm slid away.

"Do you like it?" I asked.

Amadora nodded her head, eyes glistening as she stared at the dress I had laid out on the bed beside her.

"Genevra, it is... beautiful is not strong enough a word." Marietta said, breaking the silence. "I never thought when I told you my secrets about working the wool, you would so thoroughly bypass me and my skills. Now, Amadora, wipe your face and get this work of art on you!"

Amadora was a beautiful vision of green and gold. She had inherited the golden tints from my hair now turned to silver. The light coming through the window fell upon her face, and her deep brown eyes seemed to absorb and reflect the beams. The dress fit her perfectly. It was, as I had hoped, a dress that showed both her modesty and yet the deep green hinted at the possibility of a fruitful marriage. But more than that, the dress seemed to reflect Amadora's nature. As she turned, the dress fanned out, and stopped when she stopped, with a humorous little flick. The dress was her.

"How do I look?" Amadora asked, yet the wide grin on her face told us she already knew.

"You look far too lovely for your own good." Maria said stepping forward. "But I would imagine Mario will be happy with the results."

"Yes," Marietta bustled around Amadora, brushing imaginary wrinkles out of the dress. "You should wipe your face; tears are not good before the wedding. And I suppose the dress will do."

None of us wished to bring bad luck with too much praise, but when Amadora turned to me, I stepped forward and took her hands in mine. I leaned forward and whispered to her so no one else could hear, "You are perfect." And she whispered back, "Thank you, *Mamma*. Thank you for everything."

"Quick, girl, it's time for us to head to church. Can't you hear the bells calling you?" Marietta said.

Sure enough, the bells calling the couple to the church were ringing. It was time. I turned to Amadora and hugged her tightly. "Go with God, my darling girl. Know the *Madonna* is watching over you."

There was a knock at the door. Giovanni, as Amadora's godfather, had arrived to accompany her to the church. As she stepped out into the sunshine, Giovanni caught his breath. "Are you ready?" he said as he offered his arm. With her nod, they set off for the church with the women following behind.

Mario had already reached the church door when we arrived. His face split into a huge grin when he saw Amadora and how lovely she looked.

"*Bon giornu.*" His chest puffed out like a pigeon as he looked at her.

"*Bon giornu.*" She replied coquettishly, gazing up at him through her long lashes.

The bells were ringing again. The whole town was being called to Mass and it was Mario and Amadora's job to greet each one as they came. Mario stepped forward and greeted me formally.

"Welcome, *Signura* Genevra. I am grateful you have come to our wedding." His eyes glinted with a hint of humour as the corner of his mouth twitched slightly. He leaned forward and whispered, "And I am grateful you have brought me such a lovely daughter." He stepped back with a much more serious look on his face, and gestured for me to enter the church. I made my way to the first pew.

Marietta sat next to me. "You know, Giovanni is enjoying every second of this." I raised my eyebrows to question her. "Well, we only had sons and he didn't have much of a role in those weddings. Show up and smile, is what I told him. He is as happy as a pig, giving away Amadora." Marietta shook her head. "They never grow up. They are always little boys hoping to have the attention on them. You know, you are lucky you didn't have to manage one all these years."

I snorted quietly at Marietta's words. I knew if anything happened to Giovanni, she would be devastated.

The church was filling up. I glanced back and saw the people filing in–some people I had not seen in church since Easter or Christmas. Some I had never seen in church.

"It's the feast." Marietta said derisively. "They can't come to the wedding feast if they don't come to the wedding. Maria's cooking is famous, and Michele is well respected. Everyone wants to be here."

Soon, every pew in the church was overfilled and people stood along the sides. The last parishioner entered and pulled the door closed behind him.

Father Nicolo, now greyer than when we first met, stood before the congregation and said with a hint of sarcasm, "I'm glad to see so many faces here I have not seen in some time. It is amazing how an empty stomach and the promise of good food will deepen one's faith."

A chuckle rolled across the congregation, in spite of themselves and the seriousness of the place and occasion.

I settled back for the familiar liturgy of the Mass. There were some days when it was just not possible for me to make the long trek to the church, although I had come to confess as often as my health would allow. I was so glad we had moved into *Zzio* Enzo's home and it was a short, straight walk to the church. I had come to confession the evening before. I felt, now, I could devote myself completely to this ceremony in which my darling daughter and Mario, a young man of faith, and humour, and honour, would give themselves to each other in God's grace.

I closed my eyes in prayer, but, like a flame bursting within me, I was overcome with a horrid, creeping feeling of foreboding and dread. I opened my eyes. The familiar calming azure of Father Nicolo's voice had not changed. The matching green tones as both Mario and Amadora answered were still as peaceful and hopeful as they had always been. There was not one hint in the words, or voices, or colours there was anything to cause me anxiety, yet there it was. I closed my eyes again and this time prayed directly to the *Madonna*.

"*Santa Maria*, please help me!" was all I was able to whisper in my heart when I felt familiar hands on my shoulders. Hands squeezed and communicated more import than words could have ever done. The day was warm, but it wasn't that warmth I felt. What I felt was an inner warmth–a hot crystal blue running from my shoulders to my chest, my chest to my stomach, on down my legs through my feet, finally shooting into the ground below. Behind closed eyes, I could see my heart beating bright orange in my chest. Every muscle, every organ, every blood vessel, every inch of my skin had been set alight by the hands… *Santa Maria*'s hands. I was being heated from within by God's love. I sat, eyes closed, feeling the anxiety and dread burn away until I was left with an empty, but peaceful feeling. I slowly opened my eyes, half expecting to see everyone staring at me. But the wedding Mass had continued.

Leaning back against the pew in relief, I set aside any worries and focused on my daughter. I saw only her shining face, and heard only how gently Mario answered each of Father Nicolo's questions. I knew there would not be a happier day for my daughter than this, except for the birth of her own children, my grandchildren. With that thought came the sudden, aching, horrid certainty I would never hold my grandchildren! How or why, I didn't know, but I was positive this was true. The calm *mia Matri* had given me, fled. Big, hot tears escaped from the corners of my eyes and I fought to hold back the sobs threatening to break free. Marietta turned her head towards me and lifted one dark eyebrow at me. She knew me too well, after all these years. Without saying a word, she handed me a clean handkerchief, put her arm around my shoulders, and pulled me in tightly. I leaned into her and felt the strength of a mother who had given up five sons to their brides. How lucky I was to have such a family of women to hold me up when I needed it.

The wedding ceremony drew to a close and with cheers from the congregation, Mario and Amadora turned to face the people they had known all their lives, this time as husband and wife. The crowd tumbled out of the church with much hand-clapping and laughter, and as the bride and groom exited the church, everyone grabbed handfuls of rice or packs of candied almonds from the waiting bowls outside the church and threw them at the happy couple until the air was a blizzard of white. I was pleased with the good fortune heaped upon them, but I had no fears about their futures. God would give them what they needed, would teach them the lessons to be learned and they would grow old together; of that I was confident. Yet, the anguish that had filled me in the church followed me outside.

With all the focus on Amadora and Mario, no one noticed my unease, with the exception of Marietta. Before we followed the crowd to the piazza for the speeches and celebration, Marietta pulled me aside.

"What is it?" she asked me bluntly.

"What do you mean? Everything is fine." I tried to brush off her question.

"Don't do that," she replied. "I have known you for more than fifteen years. I know when something is wrong. What is it?" she repeated.

"I had the feeling in the church I would never get the chance to see my grandchildren," I answered.

"What? That is ridiculous. Look, I know you still suffer from when you and Amadora were ill, but you are healthy now, even if your back and legs hurt you. You have a long life before you."

"Perhaps you are right," I answered to placate her.

"Of course I am. I always am. Now, today is your daughter's day and it is not for you to do anything to spoil it," Marietta chided me. "Come on. You have your daughter's wedding to dance at." With that she pulled me along to the *piazza*.

In the *piazza*, everyone was crowding around the food tables, filling their plates with *sasizza al ragù,* sausages floating in a full, dark red tomato sauce, *fagioli alla menta,* white beans cooked and marinated to give them a subtle mint flavour and *suppa di linticchia,* the thick lentil soup I had always loved. And the desert table! It groaned with *cassata,* the delectable *ricotta* cheese cake covered with *pistachio* icing and candied fruit, *gelu di muluni*, the sweet and rich tasting watermelon jelly, *pignolata*, fried dough covered with sugar, and of course, the ever-present *cannoli*, pastry rolls stuffed with sweetened *ricotta* cheese.

All chatter ceased in the *piazza* as everyone sat with their plates piled high with steaming, rich and delectable food. The only sounds were of spoons and forks touching the earthenware bowls and plates, and of groans of appreciation at the wonderful meal.

As the meal wound to a close, Amadora's new father-in-law stood and cleared his throat.

"*Scusari. Scusari tutti.* Can I have everyone's attention? I want to welcome Amadora to our family. Like every man, when I thought about having children, I always assumed it would be boys. And Giuseppina, my late wife," Michele and several other people in the crowd crossed themselves. "She gave me four healthy strapping boys. God bless her. But we had a secret, she and I. We both secretly wanted a daughter as well. I never complained about this to her but when I watched some of the other men in Sperlinga playing with their little girls, so pretty and so much more delicate than my rough-housing boys, I felt there was a missing piece in our family. Three years ago, my Giuseppina was taken from me." Michele's voice caught, and he cleared his throat noisily. He roughly wiped his eyes with the back of his hand and continued on.

"On the night she died, Giuseppina woke for an hour or so, and we were able to speak for the last time. We talked of all the wonderful things we had done in our lives. But then, she shared with me there was something she had always regretted. 'Michele' she said to me, 'you know I love our boys more than anything, but I always wished I could have had a girl. I knew in your heart you wanted one too, and I'm sorry I never gave you one.' My sweet Giuseppina, always thinking of everyone else. It was only minutes later she left us and joined our Lord." At this point, Michele could not hide his tears. All around the *piazza*, people were sniffling and wiping their eyes.

Michelle gave a rough cough, wiped his face and ran his hands through his thick grey hair. Turning to Mario and Amadora, he continued. "Mario, you are the first of my sons to marry, and Amadora, you are the first daughter to come into my family. I am grateful to have a woman back within our family walls, even if you two will be living in your own *grotto*. I know somewhere Giuseppina is smiling today. You are the daughter she wanted, that we both wanted, and I couldn't possibly be happier you joined our family." Michele kissed both Mario and Amadora soundly, as they blushed with eyes suspiciously bright, surrounded by raucous applause and cheering.

Giovanni stood up next. He had put on his best clothes for the occasion but as he tugged on his collar and put his hands in and out of his pockets, his audience shifted with sympathetic discomfort.

Giovanni cleared his throat to speak. "People of Sperlinga, this is indeed a joyous day." Behind him, Marietta snorted loudly. Sweat broke out on Giovanni's forehead, and he wiped it away with the sleeve of his suit jacket and jammed his hands back into his pockets.

"Um, as I was saying... People of Sperlinga, this is indeed a joyous day. Michele's family has been well respected in this town for many generations, and from his birth we have all looked forward to the day Mario would make a successful match."

Quiet conversations were breaking out around the *piazza*. Giovanni pushed his hands deeper into his pockets, and hunched his shoulders closer to his ears. He took a deep breath, pulled his hands out of his pockets again and gestured woodenly towards Amadora and Mario.

"When Agata returned to our little town, we were happy she brought such a pious young woman as Genevra to enrich our population." Giovanni strained in a pitch much higher than his normal voice as the conversations around the *piazza* grew a little louder. "When Amadora was born on that Easter fifteen years ago, Marietta and I rejoiced." Giovanni pulled hard on the tight collar around his neck and the top button popped off, shooting out and hitting Agata in the side of the head.

From behind Giovanni, Marietta's voice, exasperated beyond belief, rang out. "Oh for goodness sake, Giovanni!" Marietta jumped up, and stepped forward to stand beside her husband.

"What my oh-so-eloquent husband is trying to say is this; becoming Amadora's godparents was a gift we never expected but were overjoyed to accept. From the day Genevra arrived, and the day Amadora was born, they have both not only fit in to our little town, they have helped improve it. Genevra not only makes the best fabric–yes, I admit it, better than mine–she is generous with that fabric." Marietta scanned the crowds. Pointing out into the middle she cried out, "You, Gaetano!" An elderly man started and looked up at Marietta. "Didn't Genevra make you that woollen vest that kept you warm all winter?" Gaetano smiled and nodded. "And you, Giacomina, Genevra gave you all the soft woollen cloth you needed for your new baby, didn't she?" A shy young woman ducked her head and blushed after nodding in agreement.

"Amadora is just as generous. Father, who brings food to you almost every day?"

"Amadora does. But what is your point Marietta? We all know that Genevra and Amadora are wonderful!" A ripple of laughter crossed from one side of the *piazza* to the other.

Marietta joined in the laughter. "Everyone knows that Michele and Mario are an old and important family in Sperlinga. I want to make sure that Mario understands that he is also getting a gem in both his choice of wife and mother-in-law."

Mario stood and raised his glass of wine in the air and shouted, "I sure do!" Again, laughter spread through the crowd.

Giovanni stepped forward, pointed right at Mario, and cried out, "And make sure you remember that!" The crowd roared with laughter, and Giovanni, apparently surprised at his own outburst, flushed red, took a step back, and tripped, falling limbs all akimbo, onto the cobblestones of the piazza. Marietta turned and scolded Giovanni while pulling him to his feet. Her words were lost in the shouts of laughter, but his embarrassment and her annoyance were clear for all to see.

As the good-humoured laughter subsided, Agata stood. Genevra started. She had not expected Agata to speak in front of such a large crowd.

"One of the saddest moments in my life was when I realized I would never marry and have children." Agata paused. There was a soft rustling as many people leaned forward, straining to hear the soft voice that had replaced Agata's usually so strong and definitive tones.

"Many of you older folk might remember this. I was twenty-two? Twenty-three? And I realized my chances of marriage were growing slimmer and slimmer. I had a chance to travel to Palermo and work as a…, as a nurse to a rich family."

Genevra held her breath. Was Agata going to tell the town her real story?

"While I was working as a nurse, I met Genevra. She was newly married to a handsome fisherman; one with dark flashing eyes and black shiny hair. She loved him as much as I have ever seen a woman love her husband. When he… sailed off to sea and didn't return she was devastated." I let my breath out slowly. She had not betrayed me.

"It happened that my time with the family employing me had come to its natural end, so I suggested to Genevra she return to Sperlinga with me. In our time travelling together, I grew to love Genevra, and she became like my daughter. When she whispered to me one day she was expecting her own child, she asked me to be her baby's *nanna*. I was overjoyed. So, when I arrived, I returned to Sperlinga as a mother–an adoptive mother, but a mother nonetheless."

Agata walked over to Amadora and laid her cheek on top of my daughter's head and Amadora reached up to hug Agata.

"When Amadora was finally born, I thought I had fulfilled any destiny I might have missed out on. But I was wrong. The joy and love and desire to serve and teach I felt when I watch Genevra give birth to that sweet little baby has grown and grown as I have watched her become a little girl, take her first communion, and grow into such a wonderful young adult.

"And now, we are all here today having witnessed her marriage to Mario, a very lucky young man. My heart is complete. Amadora, Mario, be good to each other. Remember the little things. Say please, and thank you. Say 'I love you' everyday, even if you are angry. And take advice from those with more experience and time on this earth. Both Michele and Genevra have knowledge and understanding of this world they will share gladly with you.

"And Mario, I know it has been said, but you are a lucky young man. Amadora is accomplished, sweet-tempered and clever. Genevra will not interfere, but will help whenever you ask for it. Ask for it often. Amadora, you are also lucky. Michele is a kind and wise man. He has taught Mario to be the same.

"You two live in a town full of people willing to help you whenever you need it. Remember, *supra lu majuri si 'nsigna lu minuri.* We learn by standing on the shoulders of the wise."

With that, Agata sat down, and the crowded nodded and murmured to each other about the wisdom of Agata's words.

I knew it was my time. I rose to my feet and ran my eyes across the crowd in front of me, from one side to the other until they rested on Mario and my sweet girl. I stood before the crowd; I felt my palms grow damp. There was a lump in my throat and I struggled to swallow. I had been pondering for days what I should say at this moment, and had not come to any useful conclusion. I paused, waiting for inspiration. I opened my mouth to speak.

"Amadora. There was a time when I thought we would never see this day. When I wasn't sure we would make it through another night. But we did–you did, and you have grown to be a strong young woman. I could not have asked for more."

I saw tears glinting in Amadora's eyes, and I felt my eyes do the same.

"You are ready to be a wife, and to take care of this man who has chosen you, and whom you have chosen. There is nothing I can tell you today we haven't discussed already. There is nothing more for me or Maria or Agata or Marietta to teach you. Tonight will be the first night we have ever slept under different roofs." Amadora's tears turned into soft sobs and Mario gently put his arm around her shoulders. I held up my hand to her.

"I will miss you, but you should not miss me. It is my role to give you up, but it is your role to go to your husband with no reservations. May God give you a long and happy life together." I turn my gaze to Mario. "Mario, today I am passing on to you the best of all possible rewards for being the kind and honest young man that you are. Contrary to what some may think, even though she is now your wife, you cannot own Amadora. She is neither yours nor any other's to own. She is a strong and capable young woman, and, while other men may wish wives who will be obedient, you have chosen a wife who will challenge you to be a better man. Listen to her counsel; she is already a wise woman.

"Mario, I can see already that you care for my daughter, your wife. I am sure you will be a good husband and a wonderful father. Know that, in spite of the kind words of others today, the stories of the terrible mothers-in-law exist for a reason. I am not saying that I will be one of those mothers-in-law but..." and I left my speech hanging to the guffaws and laughter of the crowd. I sat with my heart breaking. I had done my duty as a mother and had given my daughter the best words I could manage with which to start her new life. Agata grabbed my hand

and squeezed it and Marietta smiled and nodded at me from across the *piazza*.

Speeches over, the marriage feast continued. The food and wine that all of our friends and family had provided was so great it almost spilled off the tables. All the guests–all of Sperlinga–ate until they could eat no more. Everyone who was baking brought braided bread coated with honey as good luck for the bride and groom, each one sure her bread was better than all the others. The dancing continued after the meal amidst more wine. Finally, I had a moment to myself. No one grabbed my hand to dance as I hobbled across the *piazza*. Nor would they. I sat in a darkened corner and watched the revelry. As the coloured lights from the music danced above the heads of the musicians, they swirled in a circular motion and I found myself slowly being pulled backwards into the darkness faster and faster until the colours spun farther and farther away.

I grasped for something, anything to hold on to but there was nothing for me to grab.

"Do not fear, Genevra." came a familiar Voice. Soft light rose above the horizon now stretching out in front of me. As the light grew and strengthened I saw the recognizable figure of Maria, the Mother of God, as she walked across the landscape towards me.

The dread I had felt since the moment in the church lifted, but the sorrow remained. Wincing, I slowly sank to the ground, my knees aching and sharp needles of pain shooting through my hips and back. *Santa Maria* reached her hand to touch my face and the pain lifted.

"It is our place to feel sorrow. All women do–even those who have never born a child. Genevra, you will never hold your grandchildren in your arms. No, you will not. But you will see them and all the women that will come from you. You are the anchor, and your children will do important things. They will do God's work. And so will you. Genevra, you are being summoned to do God's will. This will be the hardest yet the most joyous test of you yet. My Son will share with you his great sorrow and you will know His anguish and His rapture."

"But Mother, I am not worthy of His grace. I am a simple woman. I lay with a man who was not my husband. I gave birth to a child outside the sanctity of marriage."

"And for those things you have been forgiven. Do you not

remember the favour bestowed on the Maddelena? My Son forgave her sins. He has forgiven yours."

I reached out my hand to touch the cloth of her robe. I ran my fingers across the soft fibres–fibres softer than I could possibly create. "Mother, what shall I do?"

"You are to build a shrine in My name. But not here."

"But where, Mother?"

"You will know when you have found it. And I do not send you alone, Genevra. You will have help."

"When shall I leave? May I tell anyone?"

"You will know."

I threw myself to the ground, prostrate before her. "I will do what my Lord wishes. I will build a shrine to You, Mother."

Maria's smile beamed golden upon me. She drifted up and faded away in to the darkness.

I found myself sitting with my eyes tightly shut, hands clenched, head low. I crossed myself and opened my eyes. The music had stopped and Mario and Amadora's friends followed them up the hill as the couple made their way to their new home. The crowd of young people would stand outside the cave and shout and catcall until they knew the couple had consummated their marriage. Father Nicolo slowly crossed the *piazza* and sat beside me.

"A foolish custom," he remarked casually. "Yet, it marks a turning point in their lives, Mario and Amadora. And yours too." He turned his head towards me and I could almost feel the sharp look he gave me.

"Father, I need to speak with you. To confess. Are you too tired?"

"To take a confession? Never. Especially from the most pious member of the congregation." He chuckled and his eyes fell gently on me. "Come, let's go to the church."

It felt odd, entering the church again. My daughter's wedding had been that afternoon, yet I felt like I had not walked through these familiar doors in years. Father Nicolo led me to the confessional, but I stopped.

"Father, I don't need to hide my face tonight. What I need to tell you, I must say directly to your face."

"Very well, Genevra. Go ahead."

We both sat on the edge of the pews at the front of the church, facing each other.

"Forgive me Father, for I have sinned. It has been since yesterday afternoon that I made my last confession, but there are some things I have not told you. It is time for you to know all there is." With that, I told Father Nicolo everything; every visitation from the Virgin, the battle that took place over Amadora, and the colours both Amadora and I could now see as a result. And finally, I told him of the visit from the Virgin moments before he had come to me across the *piazza*.

Father Nicolo sat, hands clasped hard, head down.

"Father, there is one more thing."

"What? There's more?" He gave me a look, eyebrows raised.

I smiled at his discomfiture. "Just that I will be leaving in the morning."

"What? Where will you go? You can barely walk! No, I can't let you do that."

"Father, would you have me go against a commandment by the Virgin herself?"

Silence sat between us, biding her time, as Father Nicolo seemed to fight an internal battle. His face twisted–he would turn to look at me as if to speak, and hesitated only to sit back against the pew. I waited and watched the father calmly. As soon as I had spoken the words, "I will be leaving in the morning." I knew it to be what *Santa Maria* had intended for me. She had said I would know, and I did.

Finally, Father Nicolo sat up straight, as if coming to a decision.

"Fine. I cannot stop you from doing what The Blessed Mother has commanded, but I can stop you from going alone. Tomorrow morning, I will join you. No," he raised his hand as if to stop me although I had not tried to speak. "Do not try to stop me. I will send a message to the Bishop. Yes, Genevra, this I must do as I said I would fifteen years ago. I will send a message to him when we leave in the morning."

I nodded. I understood he was compelled to do this, and he had made the decision to accompany me after real internal struggle. But there was one request I had to make.

"Very well, Father. I will agree to have you join me, but I must ask you to refrain from telling the Bishop about Amadora. If he were to know that she had been given the gift to see colours too, her life would never be her own. If you cannot give me this, I cannot allow you to accompany me." I rose and stood firmly before the priest, my hands on my hips, looking at him.

He shook his head and sighed. "Fine, fine. You win Genevra. I will not mention Amadora to the Bishop."

Chapter thirty-six

LA STIGMATA

IN THE MORNING, AT FIRST LIGHT, I rose and packed a small sack with a few bits of food–bread, cheese, and some meat left over from the night before.

"Hmmmm, what? Genevra, what are you doing?" It was Agata. Rubbing her eyes, she rose, yawned, and came over to sit on my bed as I wrapped a shawl around my thin shoulders.

"I'm glad you're up Agata. There is something I need to tell you and Maria and Marietta, and most importantly, Amadora." I tied the top of the bag firmly in a knot after placing a sprig of fresh oregano inside to remind me of home. "Do you think you could you go across the *piazza* and wake Marietta and ask her to go collect Amadora for me?"

"Are you mad?" Agata stood, hands on her hips. "It was her wedding night! And you want her to get up, leave her bed and her husband and come to see you. Now. At sunrise."

"Yes, Agata. I wouldn't ask if it weren't so important I see her, and all of you, this morning.

Grumbling, Agata opened the door and jumped back with a little cry as she almost ran into Father Nicolo. "Father, what are you doing here?"

The father looked a little puzzled. "Well, I'm here to… don't you know?" He turned to me. "Haven't you told them?"

"Not yet, Father. I want to tell everyone at the same time. I just asked Agata to get Marietta to fetch Amadora."

The priest put up his hand. "No need to do that, I will go," he chuckled. "I suspect the last person she would expect to see this morning is her priest." He turned on his heel to jog the mountain path to the caves.

Agata stood looking from the door, to me, and back to the door. If the conversation we soon would be having were not so serious, I would have laughed out loud.

"Shouldn't you be waking Maria and Marietta?"

"Oh, yes, yes." Agata slowly and carefully climbed the stairs to where Maria slept.

I started to make breakfast. In a few minutes, there would be a crowd in the kitchen and, as much as I feared telling them my news, I knew it would go over much better on a full stomach. My back pinched and I groaned as I lifted a small bundle of kindling into the stove. Last night, when I spoke to Father Nicolo, I had felt so confident. Now, I looked at myself. I could hardly lift a small bundle of wood! Walking across the *piazza* caused me pain every time I did it. How could I possibly make any kind of journey in this shape? I took out the raw chickpea dough made the night before. Spread flat on a board, I quickly cut the dough into squares. I tossed them into a heated pan coated with *uogghiu*, olive oil, and fried them on both sides.

"The *panelle* smell wonderful, Genevra, even if it is far too early to be up after a celebration." Maria eyed me closely. "Why, may I ask, have I been woken so early?"

"Maria, I would rather say what I have to say only once, when everyone else is here." Avoiding Maria's eyes, I placed the *panelle* on to the table. "Sit, eat Maria."

" 'Sit' she says, 'eat.' she says," muttered Maria, hobbling over to the table. "At least you make a decent breakfast."

Just as Maria had made herself comfortable, there was a quick, sharp knock and Marietta and Giovanni walked in. Giovanni, always practical, sat himself immediately at the table to eat the hot *panelle*.

"All right Genevra, what is this all about? Does this have something to do with why you were upset at the wedding?" Marietta stood frowning, hands on her hips.

"What? Genevra was upset at the wedding? Why? Why were you upset, Genevra?" Agata came quickly to my side. "*Carina*, what was wrong?"

The voices of the three women all rose shrilly as they asked the same questions. I held my tongue until I could stand it no more.

"*Bastibili*! Enough! I will answer all your questions as soon as

Amadora and Father Nicolo return. Now, sit. Eat. The *panelle* are still hot but they won't stay that way if you all are chattering like *carcarazzi*, magpies."

Maria started to speak, but I raised my hand. "No, not one question until Amadora is here. Now, *mancia*. Eat."

The group sat in chastened silence, eating the hot *panelle*. Only Giovanni seemed pleased with himself, most likely because he had gotten a head start on breakfast.

After what seemed like an unending silence, the door creaked open and Amadora came in, hair mussed and with sleep still sitting on her shoulders. She frowned, a worried frown, and came to me asking, "*Mamma*, what's wrong? Father Nicolo came and told me you needed to see me right away. Are you all right?"

Mario, who had followed her into the room, came up behind her and placed his hands gently on her shoulders.

"Genevra, I think it is time that you explained what it is you are going to do," Father Nicolo said quietly to me. "Everyone is worried, and they need to know."

I nodded. "Everyone, please sit." Amadora and Mario joined the others at the table and Father Nicolo took a chair and sat back against the wall.

I stood before them, not sure how I was going to explain what it was I needed to do and why. I took a deep breath. "One or two of you already know I have been having visions of the Blessed Mother for a long time now–since before Amadora was born. She has appeared to me whenever I have needed guidance or strength, and I have learned to depend on what She tells me. Yesterday, during the wedding, I had a strong feeling that I would never have the opportunity to hold my grandchildren, and there will be grandchildren, Amadora. At least one girl." I looked deeply at my daughter and spoke tenderly to her. "And your daughter will give you a granddaughter who will give you a great-granddaughter. But I will never be able to hold my granddaughter nor my great-granddaughter. You see, I must go away from Sperlinga, today, this morning." As I said this to my daughter and to the other people who had become so close to me over the years, I was overcome with the sorrow of leaving them and my knees gave way as I heard a giant sob. I glanced around and was surprise to realize the sob was coming from me.

Giovanni, sitting closest to me jumped up and grabbed me by the arms and lowered me into a chair.

Amadora, Father Nicolo, Agata and Mario were on their feet. I waved them away as I collected myself. I wiped my eyes on my apron, and sat up straight.

"Yesterday, in the *piazza* while you all were dancing, our Sacred Mother came to me again. She has given me a task. And to accomplish this task I must leave you all. It is serious, what She has asked me, and I must go." Sobs rose again in my chest.

My head in my hands, I could feel the anguish *Santa Maria* had alluded to when She appeared to me last. Amadora, Agata and Father Nicolo were around me, and Maria and Marietta were standing next to them, all talking–shouting at once.

"No! You can't go!"

"What do you mean you are going away?"

"You aren't well enough to go!

"The Virgin has been appearing to you? When? How?"

"Father, you need to talk some sense into her!"

"*Mamma*, I need you to stay!"

"Genevra, are you all right?"

The last words came from the priest and the simple question gave me the strength to stand and stumble to the door. As I did, I felt sharp pain, the worst I had ever felt, in my hands, and feet, and at my side. I cried out, the pain was unbearable. But worse than the pain was a feeling of anguish and total betrayal filled my heart. Falling out into the street I curled onto my side, crying with the pain.

"Oh *Diu*! Help me! Please help me!" I called out. My vision narrowed smaller and smaller until I could not see anything. The pain had blinded me, and I felt as if I would faint.

"Oh *miu Diu*! Genevra, your hands!" It was Father Nicolo. He knelt beside me and grabbed me gently by my wrists. He turned my hands, palms up, to show both my hands had gaping holes in them and blood was gushing onto the street.

"*La stigmata,*" he whispered, almost inaudibly. He turned and grasped my feet–they were the same. He placed his hand to my side and pulled his hand away, fingers sticky with blood.

Father Nicolo crossed himself and, still kneeling, prayed in

Latin, arms raised to the sky. Agata, Maria, and Marietta fell to their knees. Mario and Giovanni stood and stared, and Amadora knelt by my head, cradling my shoulders and sobbing over me.

"Amen." Father Nicolo crossed himself and kissed his bent fingers. "Agata, get cloths to bind the wounds, quick. Mario, come with me."

I lay on the street, unknowing for a time, how long I wasn't sure. When I was able to open my eyes, I saw a small crowd of people–neighbours, friends, acquaintances–around me. Some stood with open mouths, some knelt, praying, some simply crossed themselves. Amadora still cradled my head, crying. Agata knelt beside me with a pile of clean cloths.

Agata took the cloths and wrapped them gently around my hands and feet, sobbing. "Oh Genevra, I never believed it would come to this. I should have stopped it!"

I clenched my teeth and she finished binding me. "Agata, you could never have stopped the visits, even if you had wanted to." The pain and the anguish had abated a little, but the sorrow stayed, as strong as ever. I looked up at my crying daughter.

"Amadora, you needn't cry," I whispered to her. "I have been blessed by our Virgin Mother, as have you! All of the line of women flowing from my womb will be blessed–you, your daughter, your granddaughter. You are the most fortunate woman in this village!"

In a louder voice, I said to Agata, "Help me inside. We need to bandage my side and I do not want to disrobe in the street." With Agata on one side and Amadora on the other, they lifted me upright. The pain in my feet was excruciating as I stood, so much I almost fainted again. I paused for a moment, my breathing heavy, trying to clear my vision. After a moment, I lifted my head and said, "All right, I am ready."

I hobbled, step by step, into the house, and sat in the closest chair. "Did everyone out there see?" I asked through clenched teeth.

Amadora simply nodded, but Marietta, who, along with Maria, had followed us into the house snorted.

"Did everyone see? They all saw and you can be sure the crowd out there is going to get bigger. If you want to leave this town, you will have to go soon." Her tone was almost sarcastic.

"Marietta, do you not believe me?"

For a moment Marietta glared at me. Then sighing, she answered. "Of course I believe you. It's just a shock to hear someone I love so much has been visited by the Virgin, is going to leave on Her command, and to see…that," she pointed at my hands, "all in the space of about 5 minutes."

I nodded. "Yes, for you I can see this is a shock. But for me, because I have lived with this for almost sixteen years, it is simply the next stage in my relationship with *Santa Maria*. Even Father Nicolo doesn't understand." I sucked in my breath sharply as Maria and Agata wrapped bandages around my middle to cover the wound in my side.

"How does it look? How big is the wound?" I asked.

"Not so big, about an inch, I would say." Maria answered. "It is not as big as the wounds in your hands and feet. The bleeding is already slowing." Maria knelt on the floor before me. "Genevra, before you leave, can you please bless me?"

I was confounded. I wanted to shake her but at the same time, I understood Maria's profound faith.

"Maria," I answered as gently as I could. "I am not the one to give the blessing, I am the one who has been blessed. But, I will give you this to share my good fortune with you." I softly kissed her forehead.

Agata knelt before me. "Please, do the same for me, Genevra. You truly are blessed. You have been since you were a baby. I knew you were special all the way back then."

I kissed Agata's forehead, then Marietta's. Amadora sat on the floor before me and laid her head in my lap. I had stroked that head so many times. I knew every bump and I knew the little cowlick that curled her hair so sweetly at the front. I tried to keep from crying, as I knew this would be the last time I would stroke her head. I leaned forward as far as my back and the wound at my side would let me, and I kissed her lightly on the head.

"*Bedda mia*. You are the light of my life. You are the reason the Holy Mother came to me. You are the reason I am so blessed. Thank you, my darling girl." I whispered to her.

Grief overwhelmed her. She sat sobbing into my lap as the other women, strong, sweet, wonderful women, closed in around her and laid their hands on her in comfort. We were like this until the door opened, and Father Nicolo and Mario returned.

Mario immediately went to his wife and placed his arms around her. I looked at him with grateful eyes. I cupped his cheek and leaned forward and placed a kiss on his forehead.

"Take care of Amadora," I said directly to him. "She is precious to me."

"Yes, I know *Mamma*. I will always be here for her. She is precious to me, too," Mario promised me.

I sighed with relief. I could leave now with a clear mind. I looked up at Father Nicolo. "Father, it is time to go." I stood carefully.

Marietta cried, "But you must have a clean shirt!"

"Why?" I replied. "This blood comes from wounds our Father gave me. I am proud to wear it."

Amadora handed me my bag and an extra bag of food, water and wine to Father Nicolo. Maria came in front of me and wordlessly handed me a walking stick. It had been *Zzio* Enzo's. It was not the ornately carved one he used on special occasions. It was his plain, but strong, everyday walking stick. I understood immediately. If I was to go humbly on this task, the things I carried must be humble as well. I looked at all of them with such love, I felt my heart would break. I turned, and Father Nicolo and I left the little stone house on the *piazza*.

Chapter thirty-seven

GENEVRA DEPARTS

WHEN THE FATHER AND I LEFT THE *PIAZZA*, and made our way on the road to the east, we were followed by some of the villagers. Some asked questions, and some followed in silence. I ignored the villagers, letting Father Nicolo answer their questions. Each step I took felt like an iron poker was being pressed into my instep. Using the walking stick was difficult as it hurt my already aching hands. It was agony as I hobbled down the road. 'But', I told myself, 'It is no more pain than our Lord suffered on the cross.' I tried to comfort myself with that. There were some moments, however, when that was not much comfort. The road we walked was dirt, which was easier on my feet, but it was just as easy to misstep. At one point, I stepped on a stone, which pressed right against the wound in my foot. I cried out and nearly fell. One of these villagers rushed forward and caught my arm to prevent my fall. He carefully made sure I would not fall again before he let go of my arm. I recognized him. It was Sergio, Mario's close friend. Sergio had been walking behind us, and I had not seen him.

"Thank you, Sergio. I appreciate your help."

"It is no problem. I am here to serve you, *signura*."

"Do you mean to walk with us a ways?" I asked.

"I intend to stay with you all the way on your journey." he answered. "Mario is my friend and I care for him. You are his wife's mother. That means I care for you too. And," he took my hands gently in his, "You have been marked by our Lord. I wish to serve Him in everything, and by serving you, I serve Him."

"Sergio has been studying with me. His family wishes him to join the priesthood," Father Nicolo commented. "I recommend that we keep him." The priest grinned. "He's pretty strong and could carry you if necessary!"

I smiled grimly. "It may come to that."

It was two full days of walking before the wounds in my hands and feet and side began to heal, but when they did, they healed quickly, almost as if it had never happened. I was grateful the pain had gone, but Father Nicolo wondered over the speedy healing.

"You know," he said to me as we sat in a farmer's field, eating some of the bread we had carried with us. "No natural wound could heal that quickly. From bleeding to closed in a few hours...and with you walking on those feet all the time! More proof that this is the *stigmata.*"

Sergio had cleared the area, and now sat listening to the priest.

I was bone weary. The pain had made the travel far more difficult and exhausting for me. I lay back on the ground.

"Do you wish to sleep, Genevra? We can stop for the night here."

"Yes, I think that would be a good idea, Father. I may fall asleep, but keep talking to me. It soothes my mind."

"Very well, but you may not find this so soothing. The morning we left, I took Sergio's brother back to the church. I gave him the letter I wanted to send to the Bishop. But before I did, I added an addendum, describing the *stigmata.*"

I looked at him sharply. Why was he telling me this?

"I gave him my horse so he could ride to Palermo and give the letter to the Bishop," he continued. "When the Bishop reads the letter, he may send soldiers to find you. He may want to question you."

I sat up. "What do you mean? In Palermo?"

"Yes," Nicolo answered. "That is my fear. But now the bleeding has stopped in your feet, I think we should take smaller roads, perhaps only goat trails, so we can't be found."

"Oh, Father. Why would you do this?"

"Genevra, I'm sorry. I was afraid–I should never have sent that letter."

I turned back to the priest. "When do you think this might happen?"

"Well, the letter will not yet be in Palermo, not for a few more days. It will take the soldiers less than a week to get this far. They have strong, well-trained horses, and they can ride quickly," the priest answered.

"I will carry you if your feet bleed again. That way you won't leave bloody footprints," Sergio said earnestly. "I am strong, and I could carry you a long way."

"Of that I have no doubt. Thank you, Sergio. If I need it, I will ask."

I lay back again. I was too tired to worry so much about this, at least tonight.

"I will decide where we go in the morning." And I closed my eyes and was asleep almost immediately.

Chapter thirty-eight

THE WORDS OF THE VIRGIN

I WAS WALKING ALONG A GOAT-PATH, close to the top of a mountain. My feet were hurting less and less, and it was pleasant to be able to walk freely. As that thought crossed my mind, I realized my knees and hips and back were no longer painful. I straightened up noticed my surroundings. The side of the mountain where I was walking was covered in rocky outcroppings and only a little vegetation covered the earth between. A slight breeze was blowing, and it was cool and comfortable. I was coming close to a small ridge. I leaned forward and almost ran up the last incline to the top. As I stood there, I could see a mountain, much larger than the rest with dark, thick smoke billowing in large clouds from the top. The mountain was grey, dark grey, and from where I stood, it seemed to have no vegetation at all. A heavy feeling of dread settled into my stomach. I was fixated on this mountain, as if my eyes were frozen, and I could not look away. Flocks of birds were flying past me, away from the mountain. The smoke got thicker, poured from the mountaintop and rolled across the sky like wild horses running before the wind. As I stood, fascinated, horrified, angry jets of fire flew from the mountaintop one after another after another until they were flying out so quickly it seemed to be a fountain of flame. And down this mountain ran rivers of fire, new rivulets dividing from the main stream over and over until the mountain was covered. Seconds after the first jets of fire flew, a loud boom echoed from the mountain of fire across all her waiting handmaidens, including the one upon which I was perched.

"It is a terrifying sight, is it not?"

I jumped. I thought I had been alone. I turned to see the Virgin Mother beside me, floating a foot or so above the ground. I dropped easily to my knees, something I had not done in any number of years, and prostrated myself on the ground before her.

"Rise, Genevra. I have much to say to you." Maria's sweet voice wrapped around me in a haze of azure blue.

"Yes Mother. I am ready to hear."

"As you walk, you will come to a place where you can see this mountain. It is has been known by many names: *Attuna, Aítnē, Inessa, Aetna.* The Arabs call it *Jabal al-Nār* but the people who live there call it *Mungibeddu.* It is a dangerous place. As soon as you see this mountain, turn to the north and walk until you reach a much smaller mountain with two spires resembling towers. You are to place my shrine between the two."

I gazed at Maria's face. Her words were clearly audible, yet she had not opened her mouth even once. My mouth too, remained closed, but my eyes were wide and I simply nodded my understanding.

She lifted her hand and raised it to God. I closed my eyes and I felt her love like a touch, running across my cheek. "Genevra, you will need help in this and it will come from unlikely places. You must have faith when it comes and open your heart to it."

"How will I know, Mother?"

"It will come with a sign, a sign from your past. Look for it with open eyes and an open heart."

I bowed my head. "Yes, Mother, I will. I promise."

With my words the mountainside faded, as did the angry mountain and the Virgin. The last thing I saw was Her gaze shining on me."

~|~

"Genevra, Genevra! Wake up–the sun is rising. We need to start." Father Nicolo's words woke me from a deep sleep.

I sat up, rubbing my eyes and running my hand through the mess of hair covering my head. "Father, I cannot keep this hair clean and neat while we are on the road. Do you have your shaving knife with you?"

"Yes, I do."

"Can you please rid me of all this hair? I believe we have time."

Father Nicolo dropped his head to one side and eyed me. "You are too calm for one who was told last night soldiers of the Bishop might be following her. What is going on in that mind of yours?"

"Shave my head and I will tell you."

The father and Sergio listened quietly as I told them of my dream. At the end, Sergio seemed willing to accept the directions from my dream, but Father Nicolo was more sceptical. He stepped away to look at me. He turned on his heel and paced away and back.

"An angry mountain? A fountain of fire? This is crazy! What if this one was a dream? Do you know where we are going?"

I turned towards the priest, ready to scream in frustration. Instead I screamed in pain and total anguish. The pain in my hands, feet and side had reappeared. I fell again to the ground and blood pooled on the path under my palms and insteps. My shirt, once again, became wet with blood. Sergio ran towards me. Grabbing for his bag, he pulled out clean bandages he must have brought with him from Sperlinga. Tenderly, carefully he wrapped my hands and feet to help stop the flow of blood.

"Here, more clean bandages." He handed them to me and turned away. I realized they were for my side. I tried to sit up, but I was overcome with the agony. Father Nicolo came to me and held me up by my shoulders.

"Here, you can bandage your side now. I will not look." I lifted my shirt and wrapped the bandages around myself, fumbling and dropping them on the dusty road. Sweat covered my face with the effort and the pain. Finally, I collapsed back against the Father, spent.

Father Nicolo knelt in the dirt for a while, holding my shoulders tightly. "I'm sorry I questioned you, Genevra. We will go east until we see the mountain of fire and then we will go north. But for now, I think you should let Sergio carry you and we need to watch for a village where I can go and beg for some food. We will have nothing soon."

I was too exhausted and weak to argue, so as Sergio lifted me into his arms, I lay limply, shorn head against his shoulder as we started out on our next day of walking.

Chapter thirty-nine

NEWS OF HER FATHER

THE NEXT FEW DAYS CAME AND WENT with spectacular similarity. I would check the wounds in my feet, yet everyday they would still be bleeding. Sergio would carry me on his back so I would not leave a bloody trail for the soldiers to follow. If we came to any villages, Father Nicolo would go and beg for food. Most people would feed a priest and give him food to take on his way. We picked sweet, wild strawberries growing along the pathways and drank from crystal streams. It was a pleasant, quiet lull. I felt the need for less and less food as we went on our way, preferring to leave most of my portion to Sergio. On the fifth day, when I checked my feet, I saw that my wounds were healing. I walked again.

The morning was glorious. The sun was white hot in a glowing azure sky, yet there was a breeze through the mountains, dancing around the sun-bleached rock outcroppings. The mountains gave us spectacular views, and were dotted with dark green pine trees. The morning was wonderful. And then came the afternoon.

We came to a tiny village–too small for their own church. As usual, Sergio and I hid along the trail while Father Nicolo went to beg for food. The father would usually be gone for an hour or so and would return with a bag of food we could share for the next two days, until we came across another village or small farmhouse. Sergio and I passed the time talking about home. Or, I should say, Sergio talked about home and I listened. For me, the chapter of Sperlinga was finished, the page was turned and I could not think about what I had left behind for if I did, I would not be able to move forward.

Suddenly, we heard the sound of horse hoofs on the path behind

The priest jumped at those last two words. I felt as much as saw the probing look he gave me. "Of course, Genevra. I trust you in all things."

It took some convincing for Beppe to join us. More than anything, it was Sergio, who sat comfortably after making sure I had my food and drink, that swayed him. Sergio leaned back on one arm, legs stretched out, picking at the wild *cèusi* berries we had gathered earlier that day. He grinned up at Beppe and offered him a berry from his brightly red-stained fingers.

Beppe hesitantly stepped forward, took the mulberry and ate it. He sat next to Sergio and looked at me warily.

As we ate the bread, cheese, and berries, and drank some of the wine Father Nicolo had brought back from the village, I told Beppe the whole story of how and why I had left, and what had brought me to this place on the road. Father Nicolo had heard it before, but Sergio's eyes became wider and wider and he sat up and leaned forward as my story progressed. Beppe also leaned in to hear what I would say next. When I spoke of the *stigmata,* Beppe gasped. I held out my hands so he could see the white round scars that had developed since the *stigmata* had begun.

"But, if you are travelling on the commandment of the Holy Virgin, why does the Bishop wish to have you returned to Palermo?" Beppe frowned, "I don't understand."

"Beppe," Father Nicolo answered, "The *stigmata* is almost never seen. The Bishop will likely never have another opportunity to witness it. It is a miracle, and how often does anyone have a chance to witness a miracle?

"But now, Beppe, there are some things we must ask you. Are you planning to take Genevra to Palermo?"

Beppe fiddled with the strap on his boot. It took him some time to answer, but finally he lifted his head and said, "No, I don't believe I will."

The sigh of palpable relief from the priest rose into the air, a violet cloud, circling into twists until it faded away.

"The next question. Are there anymore soldiers coming this way?"

"No," Beppe answered. "Most of the soldiers continued along the main road even after we lost your trail. A few of us were sent off in less likely directions to search the countryside. I am the only one that came this way."

Father Nicolo leaned back against a tree, grinned and took a large mouthful from the wine skin we were passing back and forth. He looked a good deal younger than he had at the beginning of this conversation, almost playful.

"I have some questions, Beppe." I paused for a long moment while he looked at me expectantly. I knew if I waited too long, I would lose heart and not be able to ask the questions I needed to ask.

"How is my father?"

"Your father, *signura*, passed away several years ago. When you disappeared, he spent his time riding through the hills and searching the caves, travelling farther and farther. One day, he stopped looking. After that he, I don't know, seemed to surrender. He stopped riding. He sold all the horses but two – his own and Bella. He divided up much of the farmland and the orchards and gave each of the servants enough land to support themselves and sent all away but three–me, the cook, and one housemaid, Anna. Anna–she is now my wife–told me he would lock himself in his room for days. Finally, a neighbour came by with a rumour you had been seen in Castelvulturo. It was the middle of winter but he came out to the stable like a crazy man and saddled his horse. He was wearing only his nightclothes. Your aunt and Anna and I all tried to stop him, but he would have none of it. When *Signura* Marcella tried to grab his arm, he threatened to hit her. We could do nothing but let him ride. We did not hear anything from him or about him for two weeks. And then, a rider came to tell us your father had died. By the time he had arrived in Castelvulturo, he was already ill. He had a fever and was delirious. He ran from house to house searching for you. But when he realized you were not there, he climbed back on his horse and rode away at breakneck speed. He was found later, lying on the road with his horse nearby. He had fallen and hit his head. He likely died before he felt his body hit the ground. I'm so sorry, *signura*, to bring you such terrible news."

A burning fire had settled in my gut and I sat with my shaven head in my arms sobbing with anguish over the pain I had caused my father, and that he had fallen to his death because he was searching for me. Sergio moved next to me and put one arm around my shaking shoulders. I pushed him away, crying as I had never done before in my life. Overcome with nausea, I turned and crawled, sharp stones pressing painfully into my hands and knees, over to the bushes and vomited over and over as if my body were trying to rid me of the guilt and shame of being such a reprehensible daughter.

Finally, I lay spent. I was empty. This was something for which I could never forgive myself. The only grace there would be for me would be to finish this quest *Santa Maria* had given me. I felt a hand on my shoulder, turning me. A damp, cool rag wiped my face, head and neck. I looked up into Beppe's gentle eyes. There were a few more things I needed to know. I struggle to sit, Beppe's arm supporting me.

"What happened to *Zzia* Marcella?"

Beppe sighed. "After your father's body was returned to the house, she organized a small funeral and Mass to be said over him. After that, she closed the house and joined a convent. I heard that she is at rest now too. She passed peacefully, or so I was told."

A few more tears squeezed out of the corners of my eyes. *Zzia* Marcella had been strict, but she had always loved me and she had stepped in when my mother had left. I would always be grateful.

"What about Bella?" I asked.

"*Signura* Marcella gave her to me before she left for the convent. She asked Anna and me to stay and take care of the house and the land, so we did. We kept Bella in the stable there, and I rode her everyday. About a year after your... after the house was closed, I had her bred. She has had two foals, both as beautiful as she. One is still at the house with Anna, and the other... well, this is the other." Beppe stood and walked over to the nose of his mare and stroked it. She nickered at him and pushed her delicate head against his hands. "Her name is Zita. My daughter named her."

"You have a daughter." I said. I looked at him. He was not the little boy who had been afraid to brush Bella so many years before. He was a grown man with a child and many responsibilities. I had not foreseen any of this. How could I? The road of my life had twists and turns no one could have foreseen, and why should Beppe's be any different?

"So, how did you end up as one of the Bishop's soldiers?" Sergio asked curiously.

"I heard the Bishop was looking for good riders to help escort his emissaries along the roads to different parts of *Sicilia*. The money is good and it is only when they send for me. Otherwise I can stay home with Anna and Isabella."

"You named your daughter Isabella? That was Bella's full name you know." I said.

"Yes, I remember. And Isabella has asked for the story every day of how she was named for a horse."

"Has she ever seen Bella?"

"Of course, she walks out to feed her a carrot or an apple or some other treat almost every morning."

I was stunned. "You mean Bella is still alive?"

Beppe grinned. "Yes, she is old and is turning grey, but she is very much alive."

I crossed myself. Out of so much grief, at least there was this one piece of grace.

Silence fell over our little group. I sat and grieved for my father. Sergio helped Beppe brush Zita. Father Nicolo watched me closely.

"*Signura* Genevra."

I looked up to see Beppe standing over me.

"I would like to join you and help you finish your journey. I will never have another opportunity to serve Our Lord so directly again. Please let me come with you." His words tumbled out, one over the other, as if he were afraid I would say no.

Placing my hand on Father Nicolo's shoulder, I struggled to stand. I looked up into the pleading eyes of this young man who I had known so long ago and nodded. He knelt before me and took my hand.

"Please Beppe, I have not been Lady Genevra in a long time. You do not need to kneel before me.

"I don't kneel because you were once Lady Genevra. I kneel because you are the handmaiden of the Holy Mother."

I knelt awkwardly in front of him. I placed both my hands on his shoulders and quietly said, "Thank you Beppe. I am glad to have you on our journey."

Chapter forty

FATHER NICOLO'S CONFESSION

NOW THAT WE WERE NO LONGER WORRIED about the soldiers, we moved more quickly, more openly. We walked longer days and took shorter breaks. The *stigmata* came on me once again during that time. The pain and anguish I felt did not diminish with each episode. When it happened Sergio and Beppe helped me up on Zita and she and I rode together. I had not sat on a horse since I left my father's house at fourteen, and I had never ridden astride a horse. But Zita was a calm, well-trained mare, like her mother, and she gave me an easy ride.

As each day of travelling went by, I became more and more distant. Or perhaps distant is not the word. I withdrew into my soul. With each step Zita took, each swaying motion, I felt the arms of the *Madonna* buttressing me. All the words she had ever spoken to me swirled around in my head and I spent more and more time with her and less with my companions, although they walked beside me step for exhausting step. After two weeks of walking and riding this way, I looked up to see a steep, rocky slope leading to the top of a sharp ridge. The sun's rays shone out like the silver the angels had used in their battle with the demons so many years before. The sun lit the edge of the ridge and brought it into sharp relief. My heart leapt at the sight.

"It's this way!" I cried out. I urged Zita forward and together we led the way up the slope. Before we had climbed far, Father Nicolo stopped and peered up at the mountain ridge, hands on his hips.

"Shouldn't we try to go around this mountain, Genevra, or at least find another spot to cross? That ridge looks unstable at the top. I think it is too dangerous," Father Nicolo questioned.

"No, we must climb here. I'm sure this is the way. Don't worry

Father, the *Madonna* said I would know, and I do. It will be fine and we will be safe," I replied as patiently as I could. Not waiting for a reply, I turned forward on Zita and drove her on. Even she seemed to doubt my judgement, but nonetheless, I felt compelled to climb to the top.

Beppe clapped Father Nicolo on the shoulder, and said with a grin as he passed, "Have faith, Father."

Sergio simply nodded, clapped his other shoulder and walked on by.

Father Nicolo shook his head and slowly followed along behind.

The closer we got to the ridge, the steeper and rockier it became. I climbed from Zita to help her find her footing along the narrow path taking us up to the ridge. We used rock outcroppings to hold and pull ourselves up. Zita struggled behind me and I could hear the laboured breathing of the men and the horse as they climbed.

Finally, I reached the top. It was a narrow rock shelf. Before taking the time to look around me I turned to help Zita and lead her onto the shelf. I reached down to help pull each man up to the top. They flopped onto the path, panting and sweating. I turned to look. It was spectacular.

"Look, look!" I cried pointing to the east. I had been searching for this sight. The men quickly sat up to see what I was pointing at. I heard them gasp.

Before us was the mountain in my vision. The angry mountain. Clouds of dark grey smoke billowed from the top and rivers of fire ran down its slopes. I sensed rather than saw all three men cross themselves.

The angry mountain held my gaze for several minutes. I turned to look to the north. The top of the ridge was a well-established goat path. We could safely travel along the ridge. I followed the path with my eyes and at the end I saw…

"It's the two spires! I can see them! Look!" I shouted.

The men turned. Father Nicolo turned and fell to his knees, crossing himself. I watched him clasp his hands together, a shocked look on his face. His eyes rolled up into his head and he fell forward, shaking.

"Quick, grab his head!" It was Beppe.

The three of us grabbed the Father, trying to hold him as he threw himself against the hard stones. Over and over he shook until suddenly he stopped, and lay still as death. I laid my hand on his back, checking for any sign of breath. At my touch, he sat up with a gasp.

He fought for breath, tried to speak, gasped, and tried again.

"Oh, forgive me Genevra. I didn't believe you when you told us to look for an angry mountain and two spires. And when you took us up this ridge, I was exasperated, sure we were going, if not on a fool's errand, at least the wrong way. I was certain it was too dangerous. Please forgive me."

I placed my hands on his head and replied, "You are forgiven, Father. Does not Our Lord give us forgiveness in all things as long as we come to Him with a repentant heart? You taught me that."

Sergio and Beppe knelt next to Father Nicolo.

"Please, Genevra, give me the Lord's forgiveness as well," Beppe said. Sergio simply nodded beside him.

I smiled gently at the simplicity of their understanding. "The Lord's forgiveness is not mine to give, but be assured if you truly wish it and are repentant, it is given to you already." I reached to touch each of their heads.

We had silence for a moment, broken only by bird chatter. I sat down on the ground next to them.

"I know it is a little early for us to stop, but I think here is a good place to rest. It may be narrow, but it is enough. We have accomplished much today. Let us eat our supper here," I said. Looking at Father Nicolo, I added, "I think tonight we should give confession and receive the Host." The priest simply nodded.

Sergio and Beppe and I set up our simple camp. After his fit, Father Nicolo sat away from us and looked at the mountain of fire for a long time. The sun was making his dip towards the horizon. The priest knelt facing the mountain, clasped his hands before him and bowed his head in prayer. He stayed that way for several minutes, stood and returned to us.

"I am ready to hear confessions now," he simply said, and turned and walked back to his spot.

Beppe stood, drew a deep breath and said, "I will go first."

Sergio and I sat in silence and tried not to watch what was happening along the ridge, but we could hear Beppe's sobs and the murmur of Father Nicolo's response. It was not a long confession, but obviously an emotional one. He came back to sit with us, trying to hide shiny, watery eyes and a red face.

"Sergio, he wants you next."

Sergio looked terrified. His face was white and his usual grin was gone replaced by a pinched mouth, as if to open it might mean he would spill out all he had to say too quickly. He walked to the priest as if he were dragging a heavy cross. He was with the father for a long time. 'What could he possibly have to confess?' I wondered.

Finally, Sergio came back, still serious but with a lighter step. He knelt before me.

"*Signura*. I have been so worried I was not worthy of this holy journey, that my contemptibility would bring dishonour and failure. I was ready to turn back, but I was afraid you would need my strength. I didn't know if I should stay or leave."

I took his hands and said, "Oh Sergio, you have been more than helpful. The times you carried me when I was unable to walk... I am not sure if I would have even been able to make it here without you. I do not know what made you feel contemptible, but in my eyes, you are pure–you have been forgiven."

"*Grazii, Signura, grazii.*"

I turned to rise and saw Father Nicolo waiting patiently for me. As I approached him, the last few weeks ran through my head. What to confess? There seemed so much, yet nothing at the same time.

Father Nicolo smiled kindly at me. This was Father Nicolo, the priest. I realized on this journey, we had been travelling with Father Nicolo, the man.

I knelt before him. "Forgive me Father, for I have sinned. As we have made this journey, I have been so single-minded, I have not remembered to consider other's struggles. I have not looked into the hearts of my fellow travellers. I have not seen their pain. I have been impatient and short-tempered. Even when I have not expressed it, it has sat in my mind like an evil seed, ready to sprout its black vines. And Father, I have been guilty of the sin of pride. There have been times when I have felt special and proud I was the one chosen. Instead, I should have been always only humble and grateful."

"Is that everything, my child?"

"Yes Father, I believe it is."

"And do you repent yourself of these sins?"

"Oh yes, completely and wholeheartedly."

"Then my child, you are completely and wholeheartedly forgiven."

I glanced up and saw a grin on Father Nicolo's face. Father Nicolo, the priest, was indeed back.

I sat back and looked at the glowing mountain. "What about you, Father? You have no one to take your confession."

"Yes, that is a problem all priests face at least sometimes in their lives."

"Father, I know I can't take your confession, but I can listen if you wish to talk," I offered.

The father thought for a moment, and seemed to make a decision. "Yes, I think I will take you up on your offer." Father Nicolo sat quietly and I waited for him to order his thoughts. We both sat watching the rivers of fire run down the mountain.

Without moving, Father Nicolo spoke. "When I first became a priest, I longed for an experience that would act as a catalyst for my faith. I knew I wanted to serve God but I didn't have the same fervour I saw in some of my brethren. I thought if I could find something that would make me burn with the same passion, my faith would rise like a phoenix from that experience. But, as I am sure you can guess, that never happened. It is not to say I didn't have faith. I did. It was just a quiet faith deep in my heart. I was sent to Sperlinga and fell comfortably into my duties there. Then you came.

"From the beginning, you tested me. I was shocked–you were so young, unwed and with child. But you were so repentant and your faith was so great I had no choice but to forgive and accept you. I learned what a joyous young woman you were." Father Nicolo paused, turned away from me, put his head in his hands, and was quiet for several minutes. He straightened his back, and without looking at me he spoke again.

"You tempted me, Genevra. I had never been tempted by a woman. Some of my brethren, before they took their vows, made their way to the back streets in Palermo to visit the dark women who sell their bodies for money. They were afraid of taking final vows without having ever experienced lying with a woman. I never wanted to do that. But, you, Genevra, you were different. I fought with my desires every night. I begged for forgiveness, but it was not forthcoming–I wasn't repentant, you see. When you asked me to teach Amadora how to read, I thought by giving to your daughter, it might be my penance, but when the two of you fell ill, I believed I was being punished.

"I have battled with this for years, Genevra. Years. But when the *stigmata* hit you for the first time, a different demon joined desire. It was jealousy. God had given you the catalyst I had been praying for all my life. The Virgin Mother came to you. You had visions. You watched a battle of good and evil play out over your head. You had everything I wanted. So, when you set out on this journey, my motives in joining you were two-fold: I wanted to be near you, but I also hoped that some of your "specialness" would rub off on me–by being with you I might become that phoenix.

"As we journeyed, I found myself becoming less and less of a priest. I let you lead because that was easier to do. I was no longer a leader of men, I was a follower of a woman. I experienced petty annoyances–where did we make camp, how long we would walk each day. And, while I believed you had been chosen to make this journey, I didn't always believe your intuition was taking us in the right direction. So, instead of standing up like a leader, I whined like a stray dog. The last of those moments came with this ridge. When you insisted we climb the ridge, in spite of my misgivings, I believed you were being reckless, and I was angry. But when we reached the top of the ridge, and saw that," he nodded towards the mountain, "I felt I had brought myself to the gates of hell. In the moment when I was insensible, I too, had a vision. The Mother came to me, and showed me in a fleeting moment, all of the sins that I had committed because of my desire and jealousy. My anguish was terrible. I writhed on the ground and cried out as if I were already in hell. I begged for relief. She watched me suffer for–I don't know how long. It felt like a lifetime. She placed her cool hands upon my head and told me if I truly wished to repent and to follow a path of goodness, Her Son would forgive me. Instantly, I was delivered from my pain. But not only that, I was delivered from my desire and jealousy too. I became the phoenix! And this I owe to you. If you had not ridden into Sperlinga on that cart sixteen years ago, I would not have found my catalyst. So, thank you Genevra.

"And in answer to your question of who takes my confession–I believe this time, the Holy Virgin did." Father Nicolo turned his face back towards me with beatific smile.

I expected to feel shock, disbelief, anger–something at the telling of this tale–but I didn't. I found myself feeling grateful Father Nicolo was back and I felt an unbreakable bond had formed between us. The Virgin had reached out and touched us both.

"We are both blessed, Father. Our Holy Mother has, once again, taken care of us.

Chapter forty-one

A FINAL FAREWELL

THERE WAS NO WATER ON THE RIDGE so we had to share what we had with Zita. This would be the last meal we would have unless we could find something to eat along the path to the spires. Each of us ate slowly, lost in our own thoughts, watching the sun disappear below the horizon. The moon was full, that night. It was one of those moons that seemed much larger and closer to the earth. As each one of us finished, we lay down, our heads on our bags and slept.

I had not been asleep long when I woke up screaming. It was the *stigmata* again. This time it was far worse than it had been before. I curled up in a ball, covered in sweat and blood and I thought I would faint. I prayed I would faint, so I would be released from the surging pain and anguish of such unknown depths, I truly believed I would never recover.

Father Nicolo held my head and prayed over me. Sergio pulled the bandages out of my bag and wrapped them around my hands and feet. He paused.

"Do it, man. Don't be a boy about this. She needs you," Father Nicolo barked.

Sergio looked at me with such pity, and said, "Forgive me *signura*. He lifted my shirt, eyes averted from my thin breasts and pressed a bandage against the wound in my side.

I screamed with pain. This must have shaken Sergio, but I could feel him press the bandage even harder while saying the words, "*Mi dispiace.* I'm sorry." Beppe helped him to secure the bandage on my side and lowered me to the ground.

I was almost insensible with pain. For the rest of the long, sleepless night, I tossed and turned, trying to find a way to be comfortable, but nothing helped. I believed I would not survive the hole of red-hot darkness in which I lay. I looked up–it was the burning mountain! I was in the burning mountain! The smell of sulphur caused me to choke and cough. I moaned at the heat, the burning of my flesh. I was caught at the gates of hell; I was being tested for my faith.

I prayed to Maria, to Jesus, to God, to release me from my pain–to release me so I could climb to the spires and build the shrine to Maria. I screwed my eyes together until all I saw was red and the muscles of my face hurt. I repeated over and over. "Thy will, not mine. Thy will, not mine." It seemed endless, the prayers, the pain, the torment. Finally, the heat abated. I opened my eyes. I was not in the fiery mountain, but lying on the ridge with my friends.

Before the sun had crossed the horizon, I was awake. I crawled from Father Nicolo to Beppe to Sergio to wake them so we could make our way along the narrow goat path. There was no food or water left so we wasted no time on breakfast.

"How do you feel, Genevra?" Beppe asked me.

"Every moment is excruciating, but the pain is less than last night. If I am well enough to move, I don't want to waste time, in case the torment of last night returns."

"You need to ride Zita. You cannot walk and the path is too narrow and precarious for any of us to carry you." Beppe answered.

I knew it was the truth, so I let Sergio and Beppe lift me onto Zita's strong back. I leaned down and place my forehead on her great neck. "Forgive me Zita." And as if she understood, Zita nickered back.

We moved carefully along the path. All I could see, all I could focus on were the spires ahead. All day I whispered, "Oh Holy Mother, help us to reach the spires today." Blood was still seeping generously from my hands and feet, but particularly from my side. I tried using the bandages and my skirt to wipe the blood from Zita but it only made my hands and side bleed more. My head felt light, as if it were floating around my body, and I was afraid I might fall. I lay forward onto Zita's warm neck and tried to hold on though it was now slippery with my blood. I had given my walking stick to Father Nicolo to use and I could hear him–tap, step, tap, step. It was hypnotic, the sound was. I nearly fell asleep to the sound, holding on to Zita. The sound seemed to slow–tap…

step...tap...step.... Finally, it stopped altogether, as did Zita. I raised my head and looked up. We were at the spires. The ridge had opened to a large ledge. At the back, next to the wall of the mountain, was a small spring. Zita walked toward it and I gave the beautiful mare her head. When Zita stopped, Sergio lifted me and lay me on the ground in view of the climb to the spires.

I was exhausted. My head was still spinning, but it didn't matter. I was here. I tipped back my head and smiled up to the sunlight. '*Grazii* Maria. Thank you for getting me here.' I thought to myself. I was so focussed on the spires, I barely noticed the three men talking quietly to each other. I closed my eyes and drifted to sleep in spite of the pain.

I awoke to hear footsteps approaching me. Father Nicolo was standing over me.

"Genevra, can you rise?"

"Oh, I think perhaps with some help..."

"No, Genevra. You can barely sit. We have been talking. Sergio and I could climb up between the spires and build the shrine while you and Beppe wait here."

I looked at the climb. It was, perhaps, twenty feet up and I knew there was some truth in what Father Nicolo said to me. But I also knew it was to me, Maria had given this task, and it was I that had to make the shrine.

"No!" I tried to yell, but it came out as a whisper. "No." I crawled along the ledge until I reached the start of the climb.

"No Genevra, please stop. You can't do this, it will kill you!" The voices of Beppe and Sergio came to me as if we were all underwater. The words, muffled, came to me and floated away. I reached up the steep climb. I felt hands holding me, lifting me up to the next level. I knew it was Father Nicolo. His renewed faith would hold me up.

It was a long, slow hard climb. We had reached an outcropping requiring me to stretch up high and grab hold, swinging my legs up and over. I might as well have had to fly.

"I'm sorry, Genevra. I don't think I can get you onto that outcropping. It is two high for me to lift you. I am so sorry, but I think this is the end."

"No! This cannot be the end!" I lifted my arms in spite of the pain. "Mother, I beg you! Help me find a way to reach between the two spires." I peered up to the ledge.

"Look," I whispered.

Father Nicolo looked up and gasped. "No, it can't be." Beppe and Sergio followed the priest's point, and both fell to their knees. The *Madonna* was floating in a glowing light, above the ledge. *"Santa Maria."* Father Nicolo whispered, and he too fell to his knees.

Maria reached out to me. As she did, I could feel the wounds in my hands and feet heal. I reached back and I felt light, lighter than I had ever felt in my life. Father Nicolo let go of me and I drifted away. At the same time Maria glided closer. I kept my eyes on Maria. As my feet touched the ledge, I realized I had floated up to her. I knelt before her. *"Grazii, mia Matri."*

"It is not Me that has lifted you up, Genevra, it is your faith." I dropped my head and closed my eyes, awash with gratitude. When I looked up again, Maria was gone.

"Genevra! Genevra! Are you there? Are you all right?" It was Father Nicolo.

I crawled to the edge and peeked over. "Yes, yes. I'm fine."

"Wait, I will make it up there!"

I crawled away from the edge and lay back with my eyes closed. My hands and feet had healed but the wound in my side had not. It was still seeping blood and it ached.

I must have drifted into a dreamless sleep. It was to be my last sleep. I woke to the sound of Father Nicolo and Sergio scrambling up and onto the ledge. Sergio climbed over, held out his hand and pulled Beppe up after him.

"Genevra, you floated! You floated out of my arms and up to the ledge! Up to where Maria was waiting for you!" Father Nicolo was almost shouting.

I put my hand up to my eyes to block out the sun, and replied wryly to the good father, "Yes Father, I know. I was there." I sat up gingerly and looked around. I was still lightheaded, but I felt better than I had earlier. We were sitting on a ledge, deeper than it was wide. In the centre, there was a circular depression. At the back of the ledge, there was a pile of stone that seemed to be the remnants of an earlier rockslide. I crawled on hands and knees to the pile and sorted through stone by stone. I ignored the tender scars in my hands as I picked up each stone. This one was large and brick shaped–it could be part of the base. That one was rounder and smaller–it could go on the top. Sergio and Beppe came to help, and after a moment to gather himself, Father Nicolo came too. Lifting the stones was heavy work but after the past few weeks, it seemed like nothing to us. As we slowly finished sorting the piles, an oddly shaped large blue rock caught my eye.

"Look at that stone, quick, help me uncover it!" We pulled the last twenty stones from the bigger rock and sat back in amazement. The large blue stone had taken the shape of *Santa Maria* when it had broken off in the rockslide! This would be the centrepiece of the shrine.

Father Nicolo shook his head. "I think after this, I will retire to Rome. I do not believe I know of any other priest who has witnessed so many miracles in so short a time. Sergio, if these events have not made you sure about entering the priesthood, nothing will."

Sergio grinned and replied, "The *signura* convinced me many days ago."

"Well," Beppe interrupted, "We are here to make a shrine. Let's make a shrine!"

We pulled the stones, one at a time, to the depression in the ledge. Laying them end to end, we formed a circle and then sat back panting. The pain in my side had worsened, it was sharp and the blood was flowing more freely. The sun was a sliver of gold behind the mountains but its light was being replaced by the silver of the moon.

Beppe sat up. "Okay, we are almost done. Come on, come on. Let's finish before the moon sets, then the Madonna can watch the sunrise!" He climbed to his feet and put his hands around the head of the stone. Sergio rose and took the feet. Father Nicolo and I took the centre positions.

"On three," cried Beppe. "*Unu, dui, tri!*" We lifted. I felt a sharp pain as something tore in my side. Blood gushed over my torso, but I couldn't put down the *Madonna,* not now. We shuffled a few inches at a time until Sergio had reached the circle platform. Slowly, slowly he lowered the base of the stone into the circle platform. The father and Beppe and I held the giant stone upright while Sergio filled in the space between the base of the large stone and the edge of the circle platform. As quickly as he could, he grabbed large and small stones until the space was filled.

"Slowly, slowly let go. We don't want the Madonna to fall in case some part of the stone is knocked off," Beppe instructed.

Carefully we let go of the stone, and stepped back. She was standing.

The three men let out a cheer that echoed through the mountains. I wanted to join them but no sound would come out of my mouth. Slowly, slowly, like we had carried the *Madonna*, I fell to the ground.

I opened my eyes expecting to see Father Nicolo, or Beppe or Sergio. Instead I was in the cave in Sperlinga where I had raised Amadora and lived with Maria and Agata for so many years. I jumped to my feet. Jumped! I had not jumped to my feet in a long time. In fact, I had not moved without pain since waking after the battle over Amadora's head! I looked back and forth around the room. Some things looked a little different–a different table and chair, a newly braided, brightly coloured rug–but mostly it was familiar. I heard something even more familiar. My heart stopped. It was Amadora's voice. I had not expected to see her ever again! I could hear her approach the door–she was coming in from outside, chattering away to Mario. I watched her enter. Everything seemed to be moving more slowly, as if through water. She was looking back at Mario as she walked in. When she turned back and saw me, she screamed. It was a bolt of ice blue shooting across the room followed by shards of cornflower blue when she dropped the bowl she had been carrying, breaking into several pieces. Mario slid to a stop as well, lost his balance, and wind-milling his arms, fell back onto the floor. I peered at their faces–both mouths had dropped open and Amadora's face had gone white. I didn't understand. I wanted them to know how happy–grateful, I was to see them both. I smiled and reached out my hand towards my girl. Amadora reached back for me, crying. At first, her hand went right through mine as if it were mist.

'No!' I could not speak the words but they echoed through my head nonetheless. 'No! I must hold her, I must say goodbye!' Immediately I felt each bone and muscle in my body harden and I knew I had become solid. She reached out again and touched my hand–this time it was firm–and threw her arms around my waist. Slowly, slowly, I lifted my arms up. I stroked her hair softly, my cheek resting on the top of her head. I whispered my love for her. I was content to stay that way forever, for the moment to last indefinitely, but once the thought entered my mind, I could feel her fading away. I looked up to see Mario receding into the distance.

"No!" This time my voice was not just in my head. Amadora lifted her eyes and looked at me. "It's too soon! Amadora, I love you. I will always love you!" And with those words Amadora, Mario and the familiar cave-home faded into nothingness.

Chapter forty-two

ELENA IN PALERMO

~AGOSTO 2011~

"WHAT? WHAT DO YOU MEAN 'faded into nothingness'? Where did they go? And how did you get there from the ridge? Dammit, you can't leave the story there." Elena grabbed the wheel tighter, fingers white.

"Well, they were gone. Or rather, they were gone from me. I was dead. But I think the Holy Mother, in thanks for following her instructions and building the shrine, gave me the final gift of saying 'I love you.' to my daughter." Genevra's smooth sienna voice had a sad undertone.

"You were dead. You mean, you went all that way and did what you were told and you died in the end? But, that's not right! Oh my God, if your life were a movie, it would be French."

Genevra laughed. "I had never thought of it, but, yes it would be. It certainly wouldn't be Hollywood." They were silent for a moment, each sitting with their own thoughts.

"Now, take this off ramp; it will take you into the heart of Palermo," Genevra said quickly to Elena.

Genevra gave Elena swift and accurate instructions through the centre of the city. Turning quickly here, driving down a back alley there, Elena avoided all of Palermo's notorious traffic.

"How are we missing all of the gridlock?" Elena asked.

"It's one of the perks of having a saint in your GPS," Genevra chuckled. "Here, turn on Via Roma. In a few blocks you will see Corso

Vittorio Emmanuel. Turn left there. Watch out for those pedestrians. Now quick, into that alleyway! At the end is a courtyard. You can park there."

"So, where are we?"

"Where are we? Where have we been heading all day? This is the back door to *Panificio Cristiana.* Your mother stands behind that door. The *panificiu* is closed but if you knock on the door, Cristiana is still there."

"Will you be here when I get back to the car?"

"No, I have done for you all I can do. The rest you must do on your own. But, tell Cristiana I have sent you and my greetings."

"I don't know what to say to you. I wish I could give you a hug goodbye…" Elena's voice trailed off.

"You don't need to say goodbye to me. I am always watching you, all of you who are my daughters. I am not a patron saint of any place because I am the patron saint of my girls. I am the anchor, and each one of you is a link in the chain. It is my job to protect you."

"Thank you, Genevra. *Grazii mille.* I won't ever forget this."

The GPS crackled and was silent. Genevra was gone.

Elena sat, holding the door handle, trying to stop the shaking in her hands. "Okay, if I'm going to do this, I've got to do it now."

Elena climbed out of her car as the back door to the *panificiu* opened and a middle-aged woman stepped out. She was dressed in a white baker's jacket and had a streak of flour across her cheek. She dropped a pile of cardboard tied neatly into a package next to her door and straightened up, looking directly at Elena.

The woman nodded at Elena. *"Bona sera."*

Elena stared at her, until, uncomfortable with Elena's stare the woman asked, *"Sì? Che cos'è?* Yes, what is it?"

At first the words would not come out, but she finally croaked, "Are you Cristiana? Are you? Genevra has sent me. She said to say hello."

The woman's face went white. *"Ccà?* Who did you say?"

"Genevra. Genevra from Sperlinga. Maybe I've got the wrong person." Elena replied.

"No…" the woman said slowly. "You have the right person. I am Cristiana and I know who you mean by Genevra, but who are you?"

"My name is Elena. I've come to Sicily from Vancouver, in Canada." Elena paused for a moment and shook her head. "Look, I don't expect you to believe me and I know this sounds *pazzu*, crazy, but when I got here, Genevra started talking to me through my GPS."

Elena waited for Cristiana's reaction. Cristiana just stood, watching her, listening.

"Okay, like I said, she started to talk through the GPS. At first I thought I had lost my mind, but she led me to Sperlinga, and I met several people on the way that are probably your relatives."

"You went to Sperlinga?" Cristiana interrupted sharply. "Whom did you talk to?"

"Um, well, first of all there was Francesca in Punta Grande. She told me to see Angelina Lo Bianco. So, I went to Sperlinga and saw Angelina. She was helpful and gave me lots of information, including this photo... of you." Elena finished hesitantly. She pulled the photo out of her purse and handed it to Cristiana.

"And I stopped in a field to sit and eat and I met Annabelle and Aldo. It was Aldo who found out you were in Palermo. After I left for Palermo, the voice on the GPS told me she was Genevra and she told me her whole story."

"But why have you come to see me?"

"Okay, there is no easy way to say this, so I'll just say it. I was born on April 16th in 1980. My mother was a young Sicilian woman who had been taken advantage of by an older man. She gave birth to me, gave me up for adoption, and she went back to Sperlinga to live with her grandmother. I didn't even know I was adopted or that my birth mother existed until March when my father, my adopted father, died. I have followed that woman all the way to Sicily so I could meet her. I don't want anything from her. Just to meet her, and perhaps know her a little. Do you understand what I am saying? After everything, I think, perhaps, you are my birth mother." The words tumbled out of Elena in a rush.

Cristiana stumbled back against the bakery door and crossed herself. Her face had turned as white as the flour smudge across her cheek. She put her shaking hands up to her face. Her knees buckled and Elena had to step forward quickly to catch her.

"Should I get you inside here? Is there a chair for you to sit?" Elena grabbed at the doorknob awkwardly and pushed it open. Holding

Cristiana up with her right arm, she walked her into the back of the bakery and to a stool by the sink. Elena grabbed a cleanish looking rag, ran it under lukewarm water and rang it out.

"Here, let me wipe your face and neck. You'll feel better." Elena mopped the back of Cristiana's neck, her forehead and finally her wrists.

As Cristiana revived, her eyes ran over Elena as if she were a glass of cold, clear water. "Is this true? Is this really true?" she asked.

"I think so. I mean, everything I've been told makes me believe you're my mother. If I'm wrong, I'm sorry, but I hope that I'm not."

Cristiana struggled to sit up a little straighter, and Elena let go of her shoulders.

"I have thought of you every day since you were born, and I've cursed myself for having given you up. I've never forgotten you," she cried out fiercely.

"I believe you. I've never doubted you. Look, maybe we should go somewhere to talk, somewhere more comfortable than a stool in the back of your bakery."

"Yes, of course. I live upstairs. We can go up there."

Elena helped Cristiana to her feet, holding her elbow tightly as she wobbled across the floor and outside to another door. The courtyard was small and dirty and smelled of rotting garbage. The second door, like the first, was rusty and squealed as it was opened and they stepped through into an air-conditioned foyer.

The foyer was large by Sicilian standards, and directly across from the door was a staircase – not at all what Elena expected when she was out in the courtyard. It was a gleaming, white marble spiralled piece of art. The railings had graceful wrought iron curves in the Arab style. A skylight four flights above allowed streaming beams of sunlight to bounce off the marble steps. Portraits in oil of ancient Sicilians circled up the walls.

"Only one flight and we will be in the sitting room."

At that moment, a singsong voice, a delicate marbled peach, floated down the stairs. "*Sei tu, cara*? Is it you, darling?"

"*Sì*." Cristiana said to Elena in a quiet voice. "Please go in and sit. I must explain this to… to someone first."

"Of course." Elena walked into the elegant room and sat on a brocade divan. It hadn't occurred to Elena that Cristiana might have a family, but of course it made sense.

The room was perfect. The ceilings were tall, with pale mouldings and swirled confectionary-like ceiling medallions surrounding bronze and Venetian glass chandeliers. The walls had been papered with green and gold stripes, top to bottom, and the furniture reflected the beautiful colours. These pieces were clearly antiques, but Elena had no idea of their ages. All she knew was that the room and the pieces in it were overwhelming, and she was afraid to touch anything.

Outside the room, she heard voices, quiet yet underscored. She waited as patiently as possible, and was about to stand and carefully wander the room when the door opened.

Before Cristiana walked a woman. No, not walked. This woman was much too elegant to simply walk. Head tipped to one side, smiling pleasantly at Elena, she entered–glided. It was difficult to guess her age but Elena tried at fifty. She wore a pale pink sleeveless top over a grey skirt. She had matching grey pumps, not too high, but stylish. Her hair, bobbed at the shoulder, had a few streaks of grey but her face wore lines suggesting perhaps her life had not been so easy. She held out her hand gracefully to Elena and said, "*Piacere*, I am so pleased to meet you. I am Maria Antonella."

Elena touched the proffered hand carefully and answered, "*Piacere*. My name is Elena. I am here from Vancouver."

"So I understand. You and Cristiana have so much to talk about. Why don't you get acquainted and I will arrange for some snacks to be brought in. Would it be all right if I joined you shortly?"

"Of... of course. It's fine with me." Elena answered, a little confused. Who was Maria Antonella?

"*Perfettu*. I will be back shortly, *carina*." With a peck on Cristiana's cheek, she turned and left the room.

Silence filled the room as Cristiana and Elena looked at each other. Cristiana was the first to break her gaze. She looked uncomfortably at her work-roughened hands, scarred with small burns, and said, "You probably are curious about Maria Antonella."

"Only if you want to tell me," Elena answered gently.

Cristiana sat on the edge of a matching brocade chair and looked across at Elena. "She is my partner. Not business partner... girlfriend is the correct word I suppose, although it is difficult to apply the word 'girlfriend' to someone like Maria Antonella." She paused and waited, watching Elena expectantly. When Elena said nothing, Cristiana added, "Are you shocked?"

Elena shook her head. "Not at all. You're lucky to have someone who obviously cares about you so much."

Cristiana smiled, "Yes, she does care about me, more than I deserve sometimes."

At that moment, as if on cue, the door opened and Maria Antonella returned. "Excuse me for interrupting. There will be coffee and *panini* shortly. Please, don't let me disrupt you."

Cristiana stood and took one of Maria Antonella's graceful hands in hers. "No, I want you to be here. You have heard this story so many times, if I miss anything, you will be sure to tell me."

Maria Antonella, sat, crossing her ankles, and looked expectantly at Cristiana.

Cristiana stood and walked to the window. In spite of the white baker's uniform, the late afternoon sun created a silhouette so Elena could only make her out in shadow. Without turning to face them, Cristiana began to speak.

Chapter forty-three

CRISTIANA'S NEW JOB

~MARZO 1980~

THE SKY HUNG GREY LIKE OLD DISHWATER, over the mountains to the north, waiting for God's whisper to rain on the city. The exhausted, dark-eyed family walked through the doors of the airport and out into the first fresh air they had breathed since they had left Sicilian soil the day before. The sky, foreboding as it appeared, was unfamiliar to Cristiana's teenage eyes. It weighed heavily on her and everyone in her family. Even her little brothers–Onofrio and Benedetto–usually so rambunctious, stood soberly, holding tightly onto the handles of the suitcases. With her one hand, Cristiana grasped onto her little sister's shoulder. She reached for her mother's hand with her other, and held it tightly. All around her, English words swirled and dipped, dancing in between the waves of yellow and gold, just out of the way of her understanding.

"*Bona sera! Bona sera!*"

Cristiana turned in time to see her father embraced in a tight hug by a huge wolf of a man–shaggy grey hair shook all over his head as he pounded her *Papà* on the back, and kissed him on each cheek.

"Alfonso! *Benvenuto*! Welcome to Vancouver. Not much sun today but you will get used to this. No, no. I will take your bags." His booming words broke like a brilliant yellow sunburst against her retinas and Cristiana took a step back and blinked.

"Children," *Papà* said, "This is *Zzio* Silvio. Say hello."

Anita, the baby, stared at the big man, while Onofrio and

Benedetto peered at their scuffed shoes and mumbled some unintelligible sounds. Only Cristiana stepped forward, and held out her hand in the North American way.

"*Piacere, Zzio* Silvio. I'm pleased to meet you."

"Well, you must be Cristiana, this other little one," he ruffled Anita's hair, "is much too small to be seventeen! Welcome to you too." Pushing her hand aside, he grabbed her by the shoulders and kissed her soundly on each cheek. She squeezed her eyes together. It would take a little time to get accustomed to the brightness of his voice.

Marta, Cristiana's mother, stepped forward as well. "*Bona sera,* Silvio. It is so good to see you after such a long time." She spoke quietly, seriously and Cristiana watched the gentle ribbon of creamy mint swirling around her head. The long travel had written across her face with its quill, her eyes circled by dark smudges and lines tightly etched.

Silvio held her by her shoulders, and looked piercingly into her face as if the lines written there would tell him some secret the family had not shared. "*Benvenuto.* I am glad you are all safely here." he said, kissing her much more gently on each cheek.

~|~

Zzio Silvio put each of the two suitcases firmly under his thick arms and grabbed one end of the old-fashioned travel chest that had been owned originally by their grandfather. Alfonso lifted the other end and followed Silvio to a 1960 Ford Falcon that had seen better days. Scratched and banged up, it was still grander than the few ancient Fiats they had seen on the narrow cobblestone streets of Sperlinga. The boys' eyes were like saucers as they stared from the big man to the Ford Falcon and back again.

With a flourish, Silvio opened the door to the backseat and the boys, their energy returned at the thought of a ride in a big American car, scrambled across the cracked, wine-coloured leather, giggling and poking each other. Marta lifted Anita in, next to her brothers and slid her own bony backside across the seats. She lifted Anita onto her lap to make room for her eldest daughter to follow. Instead, Cristiana watched her *Papà* and *Zzio* Silvio struggle to fit the travel chest in the trunk of the car. Finally, Silvio pulled out a length of bright yellow rope and tied the top of the trunk tightly over the travel chest.

"Jump in the car, girl!" Silvio roared. "We need to be off!"

Cristiana jumped at the brilliant lightning zigzagging across between them. She scrambled into her seat and sat tight up next to her mother. As she pulled the door closed behind her, she sharply hit her ribcage with the handle for the window. Tears sprung to her eyes with the pain, but stayed with the exhaustion and the strangeness of it all. *Papà* had taken the spot of honour; the front passenger seat was the best seat in the car, after the driver's seat of course. Silvio pulled away from the curb and made his way out onto the road leading them from Richmond, where the airport stood, and into Vancouver where their new home waited.

Cristiana pressed her forehead against the cool window and wept silently. Her father wouldn't hear; he was too busy asking *Zzio* Silvio question after question about work and their new home and whom he might know. Cristiana wasn't worried about her father, how he would do in Canada. He would be fine, he always was. It was her mother that concerned her. Marta had been reluctant to leave Sicily. She had not said anything to Alfonso, but when Cristiana had accompanied her mother to the church at the end of the *piazza*, she had heard her mother's whispered supplications to some secret saint, begging her to take care of her family on this terrifying journey. Not wanting to place any more care on her mother's shoulders, Cristiana bit her lower lip and let the pain of it distract her from the sobs, now lying colourlessly silent in her chest.

When they had ridden the bus to Palermo to catch the first of their flights to Vancouver, the March weather had been bright and warm. The fields were green with new sprouts and the almond trees were blooming. As she sat in the bus winding its way through mountain roads, Cristiana could not imagine there was anywhere in the world not bathed in sunshine. Of course, she understood winter–there was rain, and even sometimes snow, in the mountains of Sicily in January and February. But it was spring and of course the sun was out, warming the newly planted fields. The letters from *Zzio* Silvio had told how beautiful Vancouver was but all Cristiana could see now was grey... grey sky, grey roads, grey buildings... grey, grey, grey. This was not beautiful–not like the beautiful azure of the Mediterranean, the brilliant green hills of spring, the dry orange fields in the summer. Even in the winter the skies were often clear and blue, even if the cave-homes were cold. And here it was cold. It was a biting damp cold cutting through her clothing and her flesh and settling in her bones.

As if reading her mind, Silvio spoke. "It rains a lot here, but when the sun comes out, this city sparkles! The rain keeps it clean and keeps the trees green–even in the middle of the summer!"

"What about work?" Cristiana's father stretched his arm along the wine-coloured seat back of the old '60 Ford Falcon. "Is there any work here for me, brother?"

"Sure, I got you a spot along side me working on a farm on Lulu Island. We can drive out together so you don't need to buy a car right away." Silvio quickly darted in and out of highway traffic, one hand on the wheel, the other waving at his brother. "I found a big apartment. Three bedrooms! It's on Commercial Drive–Little Italy they call it–big enough for all of us." He winked at Alfonso. "You won't have to share a bed with your *bambini*. The boys will have a room, the girls will too. I will sleep on the couch. Alfonso opened his mouth to speak and Silvio simply waved his objections away. "*È nenti*, it's nothing."

"Is there space for a garden?"

"Well, there is a small *tirrazza*. We could grow some beans and tomatoes there."

"No land?" Alfonso frowned. "How do we feed the family?"

"Brother, you are in a big city here! Not little Sperlinga anymore. Land is expensive, not like at home. But, not to worry. We can bring home the produce on the farm they think can't sell–these Canadians must have everything *bello*, it must look perfect or they won't buy. They leave perfectly good fruit and vegetables behind. But, I don't mind. More for us!"

"So, together we can make enough for our family to do well?"

"Of course. But wait, I haven't told you the whole thing yet!" Silvio's chest puffed out as a self-satisfied look crossed his face. "I have found a job for Cristiana! A good job, in a shop. She won't have to work outside or break her back washing clothes for some rich Canadian."

"What kind of store, Silvio?"

"It is an Italian goods store. You know, pasta, sauces, cheese and sausage from the old country. Fruits and vegetables from here. She will be able to get all of those things for a discount. The owner was born in Sicily–a little town in Agrigento called Cianciana–so he speaks Sicilian. Not from Sperlinga, but still a good man." Alfonso turned his head to the back while still accelerating along the city streets. "What do you think Cristiana? *Va beni?*"

"Sì, *Zzio* Silvio. *Grazii.*" Cristiana barely heard her uncle. She was already becoming accustomed to the brilliant yellow his voice shot across her mind. She had laid her head on her mother's bony shoulder and was drifting to sleep watching the grey streets of Vancouver rush past her slowly closing eyes.

"Hey, girl! Wake up!" Cristiana opened one of her eyes to see the car had stopped and her father and *Zzio* Silvio were already out of the car. Onofrio was rubbing his eyes but Benedetto and Anita were already scrambling across their mother's lap to climb out the door.

Cristiana saw her mother's pained face as Anita's little boot struck Marta's bony shin. Cristiana's hand came up and smacked Anita's head–not hard but enough to get her attention."

"*Fai araciu!* Be careful! You're hurting *Mamma*, little *ancila*, you little guttersnipe." But when Cristiana saw Anita's crestfallen face, she ruffled her hair and smiled.

"*Scusassi Mamma.* I'm sorry." Anita wrapped her arms gently around Marta's neck and squeezed tenderly.

Marta hugged her softly back, laying her cheek on Anita's soft mahogany curls. "*Va beni, picciridda mia.* Don't worry my love. You didn't hurt me." Marta's exhausted face softened as she gazed at her youngest girl. "You will never hurt me." She turned to Cristiana, "nor will you." She stretched her arm awkwardly around Cristiana and included her in the hug.

The family stood with mouths gaping as they looked around their new home. Cristiana and Marta had found the kitchen and Marta was running her hand along the edge of the refrigerator handle–the refrigerator was easily triple the size of the little one they'd had at home. The stove was electric with a fan that hummed, shooting little dots of goldenrod across kitchen.

She turned to Alfonso and said, "How can we ever afford this? Even with all three of you working, this must cost a small fortune?" Marta's lower lip trembled. "We will be on the street in a few months!"

"What, woman?" Alfonso growled warningly. Cristiana stepped

forward–her father's voice was the same menacing slate colour it always became whenever his anger bubbled dangerously. "You don't believe I can take care of my family?" Alfonso drew his hand back to strike Marta across the face when he was stopped by Silvio's hand on his arm.

"Stop that Alfonso. It's natural Marta would worry. Have you ever lived in a home with a kitchen like this?"

"Hmmph, how would I know? I don't pay attention to the kitchen."

Silvio turned to Marta. "Listen Marta, in Canada, there is nothing special about this kitchen. Many rich people have much larger and grander kitchens than this. I would never put us in a home I thought we couldn't afford."

Marta nodded contritely.

"Hey *bambini*, how would you like to see where you will sleep?"

The boys raced each other to the bedrooms, their giggles silver tinkles streaking behind. Little Anita took *Zzio* Silvio's hand and chattered away to him in a comforting pink as he led her to her new room.

Cristiana held back and stood around the corner from the kitchen, listening. She held her breath, shoulders tense. Her eyes were closed and her clenched fists were tight to her breast, waiting.

"Alfonso, forgive me. I did not mean to question you." Marta whispered.

"You will never, ever, question me in front of my brother and my children again. Do you understand?" Alfonso's angry words swirled, shifting between black and the dark slate colour behind Cristiana's closed eyes. She heard a thump and a small cry from her mother. Alfonso stepped roughly out of the kitchen but stopped when he saw his eldest daughter standing by the door.

"What? Are you snooping? You will mind your own business if you know what's good for you, girl." Alfonso snarled. He pushed past her and followed Silvio.

When he was several steps past her, Cristiana turned and rushed into the kitchen. Marta was on the floor, leaning against the lower cupboards.

"*Mamma!*"

"I'm fine, Cristiana, I'm not hurt." Her mother's soothing tone floated the soft mint green across the space, calming Cristiana as it always did.

She hurried over and knelt beside her mother. "Let me help you up, *Mamma*." Taking Marta under her arm, she let her mother lean on her as Marta struggled to stand.

"My girl." Marta whispered. "What would I do without you? Don't mind your *Papà*, there is tremendous responsibility on his shoulders and he doesn't need me putting doubts in his head. I should have said nothing, and trusted he knew what he was doing." Marta glanced around. "I never imagined we would have a kitchen like this!" Her hushed voice sounded astonished.

Cristiana nodded. "I know *Mamma*. I can hardly believe it!"

Marta gave Cristiana a little hug and giggled. "I feel like a queen in this kitchen! Now, let's go see these bedrooms. Maybe they have gold doorknobs!"

As she looked around the apartment, Cristiana found her step had lightened a little and she was curious at what she would find. The bedrooms, Cristiana thought, were nothing special, but the beds were softer than she could ever have imagined. She and Anita were to share a bed, 'I don't think I could sleep without her little body keeping me warm.' Cristiana thought gratefully as she gazed at the double bed her uncle had bought second hand from the family of the elderly man who had passed away downstairs.

Anita was bouncing on the bed and singing, "A big bed, a big big bed!"

Zzio Silvio turned his head toward Cristiana and whispered, "Don't ever tell her a dead man used to sleep in this bed. She will get nightmares and keep you awake all night!"

Cristiana grinned at her uncle. "Anita get nightmares? I may get nightmares!

Silvio snorted. He opened his mouth to speak when he was interrupted by the sound of angry young voices shooting barbs at each other from the next room. He strode out the door to find Onofrio and Benedetto arguing fiercely about who would get the top bunk.

"I am the oldest, I get to pick first!" Benedetto declared with all the force of an indignant eight-year-old.

"Not fair!" Onofrio cried. "You are only three minutes older, but I am stronger and I can sit on you until give in!"

Silvio stood, hands on his hips, chuckling as he watched the twins. Cristiana, always the peacemaker, slipped past him and took both boys by their arms.

"Shame on you," she said as she knelt between them. "*Zzio* Silvio had gone to all this trouble to find us a beautiful home, you each get your own bed, and all you can do is argue? Well, I have a solution. Benedetto, you are the oldest so you will sleep in the top bunk tonight."

Onofrio opened his mouth in outrage but Cristiana interrupted him before he could speak.

"Onofrio will get it tomorrow and you will change back and forth like that every night. And..." Cristiana lifted up one finger imperiously into the air, "if either of you complain, I will take the top bunk, my suitcase will go in the bottom and you will both sleep with Anita."

"But she kicks!"

"She pees the bed!"

"She does not pee the bed anymore, but she does kick. So, if you don't want to be kicked all night, no complaining!"

The boys stopped their arguments, but Cristiana grinned inwardly as she watched the boys frown resentfully at each other.

"Well done, Cristiana. You handle those boys like a mother. Better than a mother! If your *Papà* and I had fought like that, your *nanna* would have taken a switch to both of us!" Silvio chortled.

"*Zzio* Silvio, this is a beautiful home. Thank you for finding such a place for us," Cristiana said earnestly.

Silvio smiled. "I know this is so much better than the caves in Sperlinga, but after you have been here for a while you will find this is not the palace you and your mother think it is." He took Cristiana's face between his two work-roughened, bear-sized paws and gazed into her eyes so intently she found she had to look away. "Listen to me, niece. There are much better places than this. That is why we all must work hard, and perhaps one day we can own our home and not have to live at the whim of the landlord."

Cristiana nodded seriously. "I won't disappoint you, *Zzio*."

~|~

The next morning was Saturday. *Zzio* Silvio woke them all early.

"This is your first full day here. Today, we will go for coffee and *cannoli* at Bar Catania, my treat. After, I will take you to church to meet the *Padre*. He is not Sicilian. He is from the north, from Padua, but he is a good man and I think we can forgive him that one flaw," Silvio laughed. "After that, I will take all of you home, and Cristiana, I will take you to meet your new boss, and where you will be working. Sound good to you, girl?"

At 1:30, Cristiana stood outside Market Via Palermo on the north end of Commercial Drive. It took up the ground floor of an old, dirty-grey concrete building. The windows were also dirty, and through the grime Cristiana could see disorganized piles of coffee, pasta, canned goods and kitchenware. On the street in front, however, were carefully organized rows of tomatoes, aubergine, zucchini, cauliflower, potatoes, and garlic. A handsome man, bushy black hair swept back from his face, with the beginnings of stoutness suggested on his square frame, bent over to restock the vegetables.

"*Ciau*, Antonio!" *Zzio* Silvio shouted. "*Como stai*? This is my niece, Cristiana. You have work for her, *si*?"

"*Ciau* Silvio. *Sì, sì.* Come in girl and I will show you around." He held the door open and swept them inside with a grand gesture. "This is where I need your help." Cristiana stared in disbelief. She wasn't sure if she were more compelled by the gentle intertwining of rich magenta and silver that Antonio's voice had released in soft ribbons, or the incredible mess of the shop. It looked even worse from the inside than it had from out. Goods were piled haphazardly on the shelves. There had been order at one time, Cristiana could see, but any semblance of order had been relinquished to a kind of chaos barely held at bay by some vague attempt at shelving. The floor had not been swept in days. A bag of flour had fallen, broken open and white trails and footsteps criss-crossed the shop. Oddly, however, to the right of the disorder, boxes of fresh fruit and vegetables were neatly stacked waiting to be emptied into refrigerated display cases.

"Colourful, isn't it?"

Cristiana jumped in shock. Could he tell she was seeing the colours from his voice? She worked so hard to hide this shameful thing.

Was it written on her face?

"It's such a mess, all the broken bags of herbs and spices. My wife took care of all this…" Antonio nodded towards the mess.

Cristiana breathed out with relief.

"I was never much interested in the dry goods." Antonio continued. "She insisted we should stock them. I only wanted to have a fruit and vegetable shop. She… she hasn't been well the past couple of months. This part of the business has gotten away from me and I need someone to clean up and organize this part of the store. You'll also need to keep track of what we need to order and also to help out customers. You speak English?"

Cristiana shook her head.

"Doesn't matter. Most of our customers speak Italian or Sicilian. The broom is in the back. Start with this mess on the floor."

Silvio turned with a quick wave at Cristiana. "Pick you up at 6:30," he said. He was out the door and gone.

Antonio followed him without another word and went back to restocking the vegetables. Cristiana stood still for a moment, unsure about what she should do. The thought of helping out with customers terrified her, especially if they came in expecting her to speak English. But hard work had been Cristiana's companion ever since her twin brothers had been born, so she went into the back, found the broom and began to sweep.

As 6:00 approached, Cristiana held her breath as she watched Antonio inspect the four narrow aisles she had spent the afternoon organizing and cleaning.

"Not bad. Not bad at all," he said with a slow nod. "I didn't expect you to be this far along today."

Cristiana breathed out slowly, and felt her shoulders drop with relief. She had kept herself busy all day, but sitting in the back of her mind, waiting to snap at her heels if she slowed even for a moment, was the thought she wouldn't be good enough and Antonio would throw her out on her ear, disappointing both *Zzio* Silvio and her father on her first full day in Canada. As the tension drained away, it was replaced by exhaustion. She had been fighting sleep, her body still believing it was on Sicilian time. She swayed a little on her feet.

Antonio stepped forward with concern. "Here, sit down before you fall down." He pushed a wooden vegetable crate in her direction with his foot. She gratefully sank onto the hard, wooden surface. The box creaked and wobbled but held as she leaned back against the end of the shelf.

"I'm going to make you a coffee. I always make a coffee for my wife when we close the store for the evening. I can make you one too."

Antonio locked the door and moved to the back of the shop. He filled a little *espresso* pot with cold-water and dark brown–almost black–coffee grounds that smelled richly like home to Cristiana. Setting the pot on the hot plate, Antonio pulled out a tin and emptied a few biscotti onto a plate. Cristiana heard the water spluttered an angry orange/black as the coffee perked into the top of the pot. Switching off the hot plate, Antonio poured the steaming liquid into tiny espresso cups. He carried them out to the front of the store where Cristiana, eyes closed, listened for his footsteps. As soon as she heard the sea-green tapping of footfalls walk towards her, her eyes popped open and she jumped up, rocked on her feet and fell back to her seat on the crate, her head spinning.

"Whoa, whoa!" Antonio said. "You stay right where you are." He set the coffee on the desk next to the register and stirred a little sugar into each of the cups. "Here, drink this," he said handing her the sweet coffee, "and eat this." He followed up with an almond *biscotto*.

She accepted them both gratefully, realizing she had not eaten anything since the coffee and *cannoli* that morning. "*Grazii, Signuri...*" She paused realizing she didn't know his family name.

"Antonio, call me Antonio." he replied.

~|~

Over the following weeks, Cristiana and Antonio fell into a comfortable habit. Cristiana would almost always arrive before Antonio so he had, after a few days, presented her with a spare key. From Monday to Saturday, she would open the shop, set the *espresso* pot to brew, and sweep the sidewalk in front of the store if it was fine. If it was not she would unroll the large mat inside the door so customers would not leave wet footprints on her clean aisles. By this time, Antonio would have made his entrance, growling about whatever politics or soccer game or bit of gossip had raised his ire that morning. He invariably brought some pastry from home, something that his wife had made, and he and Cristiana would begin their day together with an *espresso* or *cappuccino* and the pastry. Antonio would talk to her about the shop, the world, or the little town where he had been born. Cristiana listened, rarely answering or contributing to the conversation. Antonio never spoke of his wife to Cristiana, other than to mention her baking. She did not even know his wife's name. Cristiana thought it was odd how Antonio kept the two parts of his life so separate, but she did not question him. It wasn't her place.

Cristiana's English remained nearly non-existent. She spoke to the middle-aged Italian women when they asked her questions, but only then. To their daughters, who wore fashionable clothes and conversed easily in English, she spoke not at all. For them, she was a part of the shop–a bag of rice, a box of salt. She blended with the cloth sacks of semolina and the brown bags of pasta lining the shelves. Cristiana's whole world became her conversations with Antonio, and the time she spent at home, helping her mother with the cooking and the cleaning.

Onofrio and Benedetto had both started school. After *Zzio* Silvio, they became the translators for the family, as their English improved with leaps and bounds.

"Onofrio, go see who is at the door." *Mamma* cried.

"It's the lady from across the way. She wants to know if she can borrow some milk!"

"Benedetto, answer the phone." growled *Papà*.

"It's the lady from downstairs. She says we are thumping on the floor."

"Onofrio, Benedetto, go to the bank and pay this bill for me!" *Papà* would hand them the money and off they would go, feeling important *Papà* because trusted them with these necessary jobs.

After a particularly long day at the store, Cristiana came home exhausted to find Marta in bed with a headache. Dropping her coat over a kitchen chair, Cristiana picked up the tomato sauce-stained apron Marta always wore and tied it around her waist. As she dropped the *rigatoni* into the boiling water she called out, "Anita, Benedetto, Onofrio, come and set the table!"

Anita scrambled into the kitchen and opened the cutlery drawer– her special job each day. Benedetto and Onofrio, however, sauntered nonchalantly into the kitchen.

"Come on boys, I need your help here. Get the table set!" Cristiana ordered.

"Huh," scoffed Benedetto. "You can't tell us what to do. We are men in this family. You can't even go to the bank."

"That's right," scowled Onofrio. "When was the last time you went to the post office to buy a stamp? Never! You can barely say your own name in English."

"Listen, you mind me or I will box your ears and then you'll be sorry." Cristiana said firmly, hands on her hips.

From the living room, Cristiana heard her father call out gruffly, "Leave them alone! They aren't hurting anyone, Cristiana. They are being boys. Leave them be."

Both boys smirked and stuck their tongues out at Cristiana and ran away to their room, laughing.

And so, with their father's blessing, Onofrio and Benedetto ran wild. Neither Cristiana nor her mother were able to control them, both women drifting deeper and deeper into their own dark caves of sadness.

Chapter forty-four

LOVE IN VIA PALERMO

~MAGGIO 1980~

EVERY DAY, CRISTIANA THOUGHT MORE AND MORE about Sperlinga, how much she missed her family and friends back home, particularly her *nanna,* her grandmother. As each day passed, more and more she wanted to leave Vancouver and fly back to Sicily, back to the dry, comfortable little cave in which her *nanna* lived, in which many of her ancestors had lived. The cave into which she had been born.

The only bright spots for her were in the morning and at the end of the day when Antonio would sit with her and talk while they drank their espresso, and munched on whichever treat Antonio had set out for them that day. The days themselves became longer and more unbearable. Cristiana felt more isolated as each day passed. It didn't help the weather had been particularly wet and grey–all she could think of when she looked at the dark, wet clouds was the brilliant blue of the sky stretching above the Sicilian mountains.

One day, when she was particularly low, *Signura* Montalbano came into Market Via Palermo. Cristiana dreaded the days when this citron-shrill, high-heeled woman paraded into the store with her little entourage of friends, daughters, and daughters' friends in tow. Without fail, the *Signura* would demand some item from Cristiana, change her mind and berate Cristiana for bringing her the wrong thing. Her daughters would simply ignore Cristiana, which was much preferable to the sharp tongue and spitefulness of their mother.

This particular day, *Signura* Montalbano had come shopping with two of her friends and all of their daughters together. The shop was small at the best of times, but eight women added to the two or three others already in the shop made the aisles almost impassable.

Cristiana sighed. As much as she feared the *Signura*, she couldn't help but be a bit envious of her style. Cristiana's own dress was covered by a dingy white apron, but underneath it was wrinkled and sacklike. As usual, Signura Montalbano was wearing the best of everything. The heels of her black leather shoes were narrow and not for the first time did Cristiana wonder how anyone could balance in them. Her dress was beautifully tailored, if tight, and emphasized the round breasts and bottom framing what looked like a girdled waistline. Her blue-black hair was permed and the perfect curls were held in place, contrary to gravity, by a good deal of hair spray. Her make-up was, to Cristiana's eyes, gorgeous. Long eyelashes had been glued to her natural ones and underlined violet eye shadow. Her lips were bright crimson, the colour helping to emphasize the scowl she usually wore.

The two friends were new; she had not seen them with the *Signura* before. Both of them were also decked out in the spiked heels Cristiana admired, but instead of the tailored dress, the tall one wore a beige-coloured pantsuit topped off with large amber bracelets and earrings. Her hair was short-cropped and her legs were thin and spindly and together they served to emphasize her height. She towered over Cristiana. The other woman wore a tight fitting black skirt and a yellow blouse showing a deep cleavage framed by large ruffles. Her hair, dyed a soft auburn, was swept back and held in a chignon by a large, rhinestone clip.

Signura Montalbano turned her scowl on Cristiana as if she were expecting Cristiana to do nothing but anger her.

"I want fresh buffalo mozzarella–the proper kind. Not the shit they sell in the supermarket."

Cristiana cringed. She had been through this with *Signura* Montalbano over and over again. It was almost impossible to get fresh buffalo mozzarella like you could find back home. To be truly creamy and blindingly white, it had to be made with unpasteurized milk and the Canadian government didn't allow them to sell anything unpasteurized.

"*Mi dispiace'*, *Signura*. I'm so sorry, but we cannot get the fresh mozzarella you asked for."

"You stupid girl. I told you last week I needed fresh buffalo mozzarella today. Why didn't you get it for me? I gave you a whole week's notice!"

"I'm so sorry *Signura* Montalbano, it isn't possible to get the kind of fresh mozzarella you want."

The *Signura* turned to the tall friend in the pantsuit and said, "Honestly Gina, she is quite stupid, don't you think. I am going to have to get my husband to speak to Antonio about her. He needs to get rid of this one, and hire a different girl. Even his wife was better than this worthless thing."

Cristiana flushed deep red. The daughters, usually so good at imperiously ignoring her, were sniggering openly. She felt hot pinpricks behind her eyes and she dropped her head to hide her discomfort.

The pant-suited woman laughed derisively and replied, "You know, I think we should stop shopping here altogether and go to Rosso's Food Market. Obviously, you can't get the same kind of service here." She turned on her heels and called out, "Mimma, girls, let's go. It's dirty in here, and I don't want to touch anything." She pushed the door with her fingertips as if it were covered in grime and swept out.

Signura Montalbano followed just as imperiously but Mimma, the third woman with the yellow blouse, paused on the way out. She had the good grace to look embarrassed. She opened her mouth as if to speak, but stopped herself, turned and she was out the door.

A tight knot was forming in Cristiana's stomach. She was ashamed. She had asked Antonio about the mozzarella, but he had brushed it off, saying it was impossible. Perhaps if she had asked again, pushed a little harder he might have thought of some way to get it for *Signura* Montalbano. Now, not only had she lost three customers for Antonio, *Signuri* Montalbano would be calling Antonio to complain. The Montalbanos had been customers since Antonio had opened the store, he would certainly be loyal to them. She would lose her job and there would be nothing else for her to do. Stupid girl! Why hadn't she tried harder to learn English? Cristiana felt the hot prickles of shame spread across her chest, up her neck and into her face. How could she face Antonio? How could she face her father or *Zzio* Silvio? Even her mother would be disappointed–they needed the money she brought in every week, and the discount Antonio gave her at the store helped them to put dinner on the table every night. Tears filled her eyes and a small sob escaped her lips.

So much shame. This was one more hot coal piled on top of so many others in the pit of her stomach reminding her at every moment how desperately unhappy she was in Canada.

Antonio had gone out to do the bank deposit as he did every day before closing the store, but Cristiana could see him coming through the windows she so painstakingly washed every other day. She couldn't let him see her crying. She ran to the back room of the shop and tucked herself onto the floor behind the big wheels of hard cheese stored there. She covered her face in her apron and the tears came.

Antonio pushed open the door and called out, "Cristiana, I picked up some of those *biscotti* you like!"

Cristiana pushed her face into her knees and sobbed even harder.

Antonio called again, "Cristiana, where are you? I brought you some chocolate *biscotti*!"

Cristiana tried to stifle her sobs and still her tears so she could answer him but before she could do so, she heard and saw his footsteps approach and stop right next to her.

"Cristiana, what's wrong? Are you sick?" Antonio's voice sounded concerned.

Cristiana simply shook her head, her face still covered.

"What is wrong girl? Get up! Let me see you."

Still, she didn't move. She saw the bright sea-green starbursts as Antonio's footsteps move away across the floor of the shop. That was it. Surely he was going to phone *Papà* or *Zzio* Silvio now to come and get her. She was done here and there was nothing to do but face her father's anger. But instead of the telephone, she heard the deadbolt slide across the latch and she felt, more than saw the lights at the front of the shop go out. Cristiana held her breath.

The footsteps returned and she felt Antonio's leg brush against her foot as he sat on the floor next to her. What was he doing? They sat without speaking. She could hear the loud tick of the clock hanging above the entrance to the store and saw it shoot its sharp barbs of gold across the ceiling. Dammit! Why couldn't she be ordinary? Maybe if she didn't see these stupid colours all the time she could be plain Cristiana and have no one notice her. She growled to herself when she could see the small purple hiccups that were all that were left of the sobs that had finally slowed and stopped. But mostly, she could hear Antonio breathing beside her. In and out, in and out, soft magenta floating between them. He said nothing. Finally, she lifted her head a few inches from her knees and stole a quick glance at Antonio. He was not looking at her. His eyes were focused on some invisible point on the wall in the back room. He didn't look angry, or disappointed or worried. He looked mainly thoughtful.

Cristiana sat all the way up and leaned against the wall, as Antonio was. They continued to sit wordlessly surrounded by the sounds of their own breathing and the ticking of the clock.

Cristiana was not sure how much time had passed when Antonio said, "I was the first one in my family to come to Canada. Did you know that?"

Cristiana shook her head

"Of all the brothers, I was the one who had excelled in English in school and so it was decided, I would come first and prepare for the other brothers to come after me. But when I got here, I discovered my English was not nearly as good as I thought, and besides, I landed in Montreal. English isn't so useful in a place where most people speak French." He chuckled. "And the winters were so cold. I had never seen so much snow in my life! This is no life for some Sicilian boy, I thought to myself. So, when the weather finally warmed up–which took a long time, I can tell you, I hitchhiked out to Vancouver. I would travel for a while and stop and work on someone's farm until I had enough money to go on. The farms they have on the prairies are so big, some of them, I'm sure all of Sicily could fit inside them! When I got to Vancouver, I found a job on a farm in Richmond. I was picking beans, and broccoli, and cauliflower, squash, and strawberries, and blueberries for my room and board, and a little cash on top. But I was the only Sicilian working on that farm. A Chinese family owned it, and the workers were all Chinese or Indian–all I heard around me was Chinese or Punjabi! The food was plentiful but we never ate pasta or had cheese with our meals. There was no good fresh bread in the mornings. I ate mainly with the Indian workers so I learned to like curries and spicy food.

"I was lonely. I missed my family and my friends. I missed speaking Sicilian and Italian. I missed our church. I missed my mother's cooking. I almost packed up and went back to Italy. But, they had sent me first. If I returned, I would have disappointed my whole family.

More importantly, I would have disappointed my father." Antonio paused.

Cristiana was mesmerized. It was as if Antonio had looked inside her soul and described what was there. "I... I'm lonely too."

"Wait." Antonio said. He stood and held out his hand to Cristiana. "This is a conversation that deserves to be at a table and not on the floor." He motioned Cristiana to sit at the table he used for his desk. He disappeared into the store and returned with some good *tumazzu* cheese, a knife, and some antipasti. He waved Cristiana towards a box under the table where she found some homemade red wine Antonio saved for when he brought his cronies back into the store to play scupa on a Saturday evening. Cristiana, utterly confused at this point, placed the wine on the table followed by the two glasses Antonio pointed at.

As for Antonio, he had dialled the phone and was waiting for someone to pick up on the other end. Cristiana stared at him, bewildered.

"Silvio? Antonio here. Look, I got swamped with a shipment at the end of the day. Do you mind if I keep Cristiana here late? I'll pay her overtime. *Va beni*? Okay? *Grazii*, old friend. I'll make sure she gets home safely."

Antonio hung up the phone and paused before he turned around. Cristiana had no idea what was going on. Not two minutes ago she had been sitting on the floor sobbing. Now she was sitting at the table with wine and food in front of her, and why had Antonio said they had a big shipment when clearly nothing had arrived? She shook her head, trying to make sense of it all.

Antonio poured out the dark purple wine into the two glasses and pushed one across at Cristiana. He leaned back in his chair and stared at Cristiana.

Cristiana felt hot under his gaze. She wanted to squirm but she resisted the urge. Instead, she waited, looking at the glass of wine she held in her hands.

"I think," Antonio said slowly, "You have many things you would like to talk about."

Cristiana nodded.

"I also think," Antonio added, "You have had no one to talk to since you came to Vancouver."

Cristiana nodded again.

"So, I have closed the store and your family is not expecting you home until later. You heard maybe I know a little of what you are going through. I will listen. *Dimmi*. Tell me."

Cristiana was dumbstruck. Her father never listened to her mother's troubles. Even her uncle, who was so kind and seemed to understand, never had a conversation of any length with her. It had never occurred to her Antonio would be willing to listen to the problems of his 17-year-old shop assistant. She opened her mouth but had no words and no place to start.

"*Allora*, Cristiana. What happened today that made everything seem to be so much more than you could bear?"

And Cristiana, for the first time since she had sat at the knee of her grandmother, began to talk. Really talk. She told Antonio about *Signura* Montalbano and the buffalo mozzarella. She told him of her fashionable daughters and how much she missed her girlfriends from back home. She told him how her whole life had become the time at this store, that Onofrio and Benedetto no longer heeded either her or her mother and, when *Zzio* Silvio wasn't at home, her father would shake her mother, or strike her in places that wouldn't show. She talked about how she was afraid of her father, and she was afraid Onofrio and Benedetto were growing up like him. She told him there had been a boy back home who had liked her but her father had packed them up and moved them to Canada before the boy had had a chance to approach her family, and she told him how she was afraid because she couldn't speak English, she would never meet some boy here who would love her and marry her so she could have her own family and move away from her father.

All this came out in a rush. Cristiana found herself speaking faster and faster until the last line... meet some boy who would love her and marry her and take her away from her father... exploded from her on a rush of air. Her arms fell to her sides and she sat drained of all emotion. When she looked up at Antonio there was an odd expression on his face. Sympathy? Maybe. If Cristiana's father had been a different man, she might have said fatherliness. What she was seeing was Antonio, the white knight. Antonio, her rescuer and saviour. Whatever it was, the look not only comforted Cristiana, it threw her into a small whirlwind of new emotions.

"You poor girl," Antonio said. And with those few sympathetic words, a new torrent of tears arrived but these tears were different. Cleaner. These tears washed away the remaining venom of anger, and fear, and loneliness that Cristiana had been holding in all these months.

Antonio quickly moved his chair around beside her. He placed his arm around her shoulders, pulled her to his chest and stroked her hair. He whispered soft pale words of comfort into the long black velvet tresses covering her head and, even though Cristiana was shocked at this intimacy, it felt so good and so right she allowed Antonio to continue.

As her tears subsided, Cristiana heard the words Antonio was whispering. They were words of love. They were the pale pink words she had not heard since they had left her grandmother behind in Sperlinga. Yet these words were unlike any her grandmother had uttered. They were emotion-charged and made her feel differently than she had ever felt before. Once the boy in Sperlinga had, in a solitary moment, grabbed her hand and stolen a kiss before disappearing into the town. She had thought that must be love, but this? This was something new.

Every gash, every scar, every wound her exhausted psyche bore, screamed out for the love Antonio seemed to be offering her. The emptiness she had felt from the moment they had stepped off the plane in Vancouver was being filled, filled with the sweet and tender promises dripping from Antonio's lips to her waiting ears. He whispered the words, '*t'amu, t'amu*, I love you', and she lifted her unexpected blue eyes to his and whispered back, "*T'amu*, Antonio." His lips covered hers with a kiss and together they were gone; lost in caresses, and desperation, and lust.

Chapter forty-five

A BLACK STORM

EVERY DAY CRISTIANA WOULD ARRIVE early at the shop, make the coffee and set out fruit and cheese and sausage and the fresh bread she bought for him each morning at the neighbouring Italian bakery. And every day she would add something or change something to make the back room of the shop look more homelike until one day Antonio looked around and joked, "Cristiana, we could almost live in this room!"

Cristiana felt her chest expand at those words and a warm, prickly flush spread across her chest. This is exactly what she had been imagining as she worked so hard to make the backroom a comfortable place for Antonio. She dropped her head in a confusion of embarrassment and pleasure that he had seen through her efforts.

Antonio watched her discomfort and quietly reached out his hand to pull her to him. Seating her on his lap, he wrapped his arms around her and looked into her face. Long and intense, it seemed to Cristiana that hours... no seasons... passed in that moment. She was terrified by the look. For all of her playing at house in the back room of the shop, for all of their lovemaking, no matter how tender, after the door had been locked for the evening, Cristiana had been aware their moments together were fragile, they could be slashed with a wrong word, a bitter look, an angry thought on a knife's edge. She caught her breath and waited for the cruel cut.

"*Amuri,* I have never spoken to you about my wife."

Cristiana turned her head away and closed her eyes. The exciting prickling sensation in her chest had turned to a heated and heavy stone in her stomach.

"There was a reason for that. I never wanted to distress you with fears about my feelings for you. But, now, I think it is time I share a little."

Cristiana held her breath. She felt Antonio's arms tighten around her. This was it... she could feel the end of this beautiful time rising like a black, furious storm, about to crash over her. She held herself still, as if by staying motionless, this dark tempest would miss her and move on to its next poor victim.

"My wife has left my house. I don't think she will be back. She has had a miscarriage. Two, in fact. The first was simply God's will. There was nothing she nor I could have done, it simply ended." Antonio paused. "But the last one. The last one she blamed me for. I have been spending so much time here..." Antonio did not say the words 'with you' but Cristiana heard them nonetheless. "...so much time here, and she was doing so much work on her own, she lost the second baby."

At this, Antonio stopped. He took a deep breath, and another and dropped his head into Cristiana's lap. Great, shuttering sobs shook him. At first, Cristiana was astonished. No man in her family, particularly her father, had demonstrated such grief. Anger, yes. Grief, never. Tentatively, she raised her hand and placed it on Antonio's head. Softly, she stroked his hair, like she did for her sister, Anita, when she was prostrate with sorrow over some childish slight. When he did not push her hand away, her confidence grew and she whispered soft, consoling words into his hair.

Antonio's grip around her tightened. The sound of his sobs subsided but he continued to breath deep gulping breaths. His hands reached up and gripped her shoulders and he pulled himself up, a man drowning in his anguish and fighting for the surface in order to breathe. His hands grabbed the sides of her face and he pulled her into a violent kiss. Their teeth hit and caught her lower lip and she tasted blood. He stood and pulled her to her feet, their lips still pressed together, his tongue invading her mouth. Surely, he could taste her blood as well. Half carrying, half dragging her, he pulled her to the little mattress at the back of the room and threw her down and himself on top. He entered her quickly and hard. Cristiana was not ready for him. She smothered a cry with the back of her hand as Antonio forced his way in, over and over. This violence from Antonio frightened her but at the same time, she understood anger and violence and loved Antonio all the more for it.

It was over in a few seconds. Antonio collapsed on her and rolled to the side. Cristiana didn't move. His roughness had hurt her. She felt bruised and sore but exalted. She had been filled with the joy of his love since that first moment together weeks before, but now she truly felt glorified by his love. This love she understood. This love she trusted. This love was all she'd ever known. They lay silently for a while. Then Antonio spoke in a low voice.

"I'm sorry."

Cristiana turned and kissed him. "*È nenti, miu amuri*. It was nothing."

Antonio took her in his arms. "Cristiana, I don't believe my wife will come back. She has said she wants to divorce me. After some time, a decent amount of time, I want you to move into my house with me."

Cristiana laid her head on his chest and smiled peacefully to herself. "Of course, Antonio. Whatever you want."

Chapter forty-six

THE AMBULANCE RIDE

~GIUGNO 1980~

VANCOUVER WAS AWASH IN SUMMER. The sky was that lovely pale blue that stood out against the green sea and dark blue mountains. Cristiana was learning to love the city, in spite of its differences from Sperlinga. She would stand at the kitchen window and breath deeply, the fresh air filling her lungs; the oxygen thrilling every cell in her body. The days came and went. Her life had not changed, yet it was entirely different. Her father's anger did not frighten her as much as it had once. She knew she would be leaving the apartment soon and it altered her attitude towards him. She still obeyed him. She still served him his breakfast and handed over the money she made from Antonio's shop, but the fear she had always felt when speaking to her father was gone and she could see he knew it.

One morning, as she was pouring coffee for her father, she spilled a little on the table. Before she wiped it away, she finished pouring for *Zzio* Silvio and her mother.

"Girl!" Alfonso growled, "Clean up this mess."

Cristiana, her thoughts miles away and humming to herself, turned and placed the little *espresso* pot back on the stovetop, took a cloth from the sink, ran water through it, wrung it out, and calmly wiped the coffee from around her father's cup. She looked up to see her father's black scowl. Surprised, she asked, "What is it, *Papà*?"

Without giving Cristiana even a moment to flinch, Alfonso jumped to his feet and drew his hand back, but as he was about to let it fly, his arm was blocked.

"Don't be an idiot, Fonso." Silvio had grabbed his wrist and stood, toe to toe with his younger brother. "You blacken her eye, and Antonio will be at the door wanting to know why his customers are asking what happened to Cristiana. We need the money she brings in."

Turning her gaze from her father's livid face to her uncle's stony one and back, Cristiana was certain her father would strike *Zzio* Silvio instead. She heard her mother gasp. That small whisper of air was enough. Alfonso turned on his wife.

"This is your fault she has become so arrogant!" he railed at Marta and he let his hand fly. The crimson shotgun sound of the slap, and the crack as Marta's head hit the floor echoed around the room. Cristiana couldn't move; couldn't believe. The silence in the room had become thick, motionless, holding her fast. She and her father and *Zzio* Silvio stood, a picture frame around the image of her mother, white-faced and still on the black mottled linoleum of the kitchen floor.

A small white whimper skirted around the heavy silence. Cristiana looked up to see tiny Anita standing in the doorway, her brown eyes wide, her lower lip trembling. Behind her, Benedetto and Onofrio had come from their beds. Benedetto stood, mouth open but Onofrio, rubbing his eyes sleepily, bumped into his brother.

"Hey!" he cried, grumpily. "What are you doing?"

The moment was broken. Cristiana dropped to her knees at her mother's side. She heard her father's footsteps as he strode from the room and she felt *Zzio* Silvio as he knelt beside her.

"Take care of your mother. Only get Onofrio to call for an ambulance if you think it is necessary, but make sure he tells them she slipped and fell in the kitchen. I'll go after your father." he whispered to her.

Cristiana didn't answer. She held her mother's hand, patting it and murmuring, "*Mamma? Mamma?*" After a moment, Zzio Silvio rose and left her.

Marta began to stir. Cristiana gripped her hand tighter. "*Mamma*, are you all right? Can you hear me?" Marta groaned but didn't answer.

"Onofrio, call for an ambulance."

"But *Zzio* Silvio said to call only if it was necessary."

Cristiana turned on her brother, eyes flashing dangerously.

"And I said, call for an ambulance."

Onofrio shrank back a little, staring at his sister, and scrambled for the telephone.

~|~

The paramedic that had banged on the door now knelt beside Marta who still lay on the kitchen floor. His hands gently probed the back of her head, her neck, and made notes on a clipboard. Marta's eyes had opened and they darted back and forth between the attendant and Cristiana. Benedetto had taken Anita into her bedroom and Onofrio quietly answered the questions the paramedic asked him.

"Make sure you tell him she slipped and fell," Cristiana said to Onofrio with a quiet intensity even the attendant understood.

"But, Cristiana…"

"Onofrio." Cristiana cut him off. "There is too much at stake here. They don't think about this as a family matter. Do you understand? Tell him she fell."

Onofrio nodded and translated quickly. The paramedic frowned and replied. He looked at Marta and asked her something in slow, loud English.

"*Mamma*, he wants to know if you slipped and fell."

"*Mamma,* you must tell him yes," Cristiana whispered. Her eyes were downcast but she gripped her mother's hand tightly.

Marta's eyes fixed on her daughter's face. Slowly she answered, "*Sì.* I fell."

Cristiana raised her eyes to meet her mother's. A look of understanding passed between them.

The attendant watched the interaction between mother and daughter and shook his head. How many times had he seen this scenario played out, Cristiana wondered. How many times had he seen children covering for their violent fathers? Cristiana gritted her teeth, hating her father in that moment. But what could they do? Onofrio, crouching next to the ambulance attendant, and Benedetto were the only ones in the family who could speak English, other than *Zzio* Silvio, and they were not even old enough to think girls were more than annoying hindrances to their play. The money Cristiana made working for Antonio helped pay the rent and bills, but it was not enough to support her mother, brothers and little sister. And *Zzio* Silvio, as wonderful an uncle as he was, understood this was a family matter and it was not for him to step in between a husband and wife even if it were his brother and sister-in-law. They were stuck. It was in that instant Cristiana realized their salvation lay in Antonio's hands. She could see the only way out would be to take her mother and Onofrio, Benedetto and Anita to live with her at Antonio's house. Surely Antonio would understand.

Cristiana whispered to her mother, "Don't worry *Mamma*, I will take care of you. I know what to do."

Marta looked back at Cristiana, a smile briefly crossed her lips but her frightened eyes did not change.

Cristiana sent Benedetto and Anita to tell Antonio she would not be at work, she had to go with her mother to the hospital, and she and Onofrio rode with her mother in the ambulance. In spite of his worry, Onofrio sat wide-eyed looking at all the instruments and equipment in the back of the ambulance. He asked the attendant a question, who gave him a long answer.

"What is it?" Cristiana asked.

"I asked him how to get a job driving an ambulance. He told me I had to finish high school first and I could go to another school to learn how to be a paramedic."

"I think that would be a very good thing, Onofrio. I would be proud of you, if you could help people that way."

Onofrio nodded. Cristiana was certain if her brothers could focus on something positive, and had a goal like this to work towards, it might help them follow a different path than her father had taken. She tucked this thought away to consider later, when she was not so worried about her mother.

As they pulled into the hospital emergency bay, the attendant spoke seriously to Onofrio.

"He said we are to stay in the waiting room, they have a nurse who speaks Italian and we shouldn't worry. He said *Mamma* is going to be okay, but they want to check where she hit her head to be sure."

Cristiana nodded and squeezed her mother's hand.

"Don't worry *Mamma*. We will be waiting for you. We'll be fine."

Marta smiled back wanly. "I know. I will see you soon."

As they climbed out of the ambulance, a large nurse in a tight pastel pink uniform came outside, spoke to Onofrio and took him by the shoulders and led them in.

"We are supposed to go with her," Onofrio called back over his shoulder to Cristiana.

She sat them in a corner of a large waiting room filled with people. Some were comforting crying children; others were holding their arms or hands or stomachs or were holding bandages or ice packs to different parts of their bodies. Some had fallen asleep. Most, however, had the blank look of people listlessly waiting to be seen. All around them swirled language, words Cristiana did not understand. Most were English, but Cristiana could hear several other languages as well. On the faces of those speakers she saw the studied fearful looks of those who did not understand. It was a look she had caught in her own reflection more than once.

Time passed painfully slowly. She watched the sick and injured waiting. Did the slow passage of time make the physical pain of the people waiting worse? Or did the physical pain focus time moment by moment so its passage went by unnoticed? Cristiana shifted in her hard plastic chair. Onofrio had found a stack of magazines filled with pictures of cars that kept him entertained for at least part of the morning. Cristiana was grateful for that. She didn't much feel like amusing her younger brother while she fretted over the thoughts of her mother. The worry was so much worse because she had no picture in her head of what was happening to *Mamma*, and what they were doing to her somewhere in this huge, confusing building.

Onofrio had tossed the last magazine onto the table and was becoming restless when the large pink nurse walked across the waiting room. Immediately, the blank eyes of the waiting awoke and turned on mass to follow her as she made her way from the secret place behind the door to the far side of the crowded waiting room. As she stopped in front of Onofrio and Cristiana, the eyes turned back to staring unseeing at the floor, the walls, each other.

The Pink Nurse, as Cristiana thought of her, spoke to Onofrio.

"She wants us to go with her. She has someone who can talk to you in Italian, she said."

Cristiana nodded and stood. They followed behind the Pink Nurse whose pantyhose made a soft 'scritch scritch' sound as she made her way across the room. She took them through a smaller door to the right and Cristiana found herself in a room with two institutional-style sofas covered with orange vinyl–armoured against any unwanted fluid unintentionally spilled. The Pink Nurse pointed to the sofas and spoke loudly in English to Cristiana and raised both hands and pointed twice at the floor while looking at her intently. Cristiana understood 'wait here' from the hand gestures, if not the words, and nodded. The Pink Nurse smiled at them kindly, patted Onofrio on the shoulder and spoke a few words before leaving the room.

"What did she say?" Cristiana asked.

"She said not to worry, and we could go see *Mamma* soon."

Onofrio sprawled across one of the sofas with a huge sigh and a groan. "How looooonnnnng is this going to take?" he moaned.

"I don't know," Cristiana answered. She sat on the sofa across from him, crossed her arms and leaned forward. "Onofrio, were you serious when you spoke to the man in the ambulance about becoming an ambulance attendant?"

"I think so. I liked the ambulance, and he was nice to me."

Cristiana looked seriously at her brother.

"I want you to listen to me carefully, Onofrio. You and Benedetto are standing in a place right now, and you can go left or you can go right. I've been watching you two since we came to Vancouver. Every day, I see you become more and more like *Papà*. You know, I don't mean that in a good way. He is our *Papà*, and while we live in his house we have to obey him, but you have seen the way he treats *Mamma*. He is so angry all the time. Look at *Zzio* Silvio. He is so much kinder and funnier with all of us. The people who come to visit in our home respect him. They fear *Papà* but they respect *Zzio* Silvio. Respect is so much better. You must follow *Zzio* Silvio's example. Be like him. Obey *Papà*, but in your heart and in your actions, be like *Zzio* Silvio. One day, we will all leave *Papà*'s house, and what we take with us will make us the kind of people we will be for the rest of our lives. You and Benedetto must finish school. I think working in an ambulance would be a good job for both of you. It will help you remember to be kind and helpful to people. You will be able to make enough money to set aside some for

Mamma to have a few nice things from time to time. Things she never gets from *Papà*." Cristiana reached out her arms and grabbed Onofrio by his shoulders. Onofrio's eyes were wide. His older sister had never spoken so forcefully to him before, except when he and Benedetto teased Anita to distraction and made her cry.

"You must be a better person than *Papà*." Cristiana continued. "You and Benedetto are better people. Don't waste it by becoming angry like *Papà*. Be happy boys, be good boys. Help people." At this point Cristiana was shaking Onofrio, both sobbing.

"I won't. I won't be like *Papà*!" Onofrio's face screwed up in anger and anguish.

"That's right. It's never okay to hit a girl. Not even Anita. Not even when she gets into your things and makes you angry. You must be better than that! *Papà* might be the man in the family, but he will never take care of *Mamma* properly. You and Benedetto must do that. I won't be in that house forever." Cristiana stared hard into Onofrio's face through her tears.

Onofrio stared at her. "Are you leaving? Are you going to leave us?"

Cristiana bit her lip. "Onofrio, I'm a woman. One day I will marry and start my own family. When I do that, it will be up to you and Benedetto. But until that day, I will be at home to help." She saw relief spread over her brother's face.

"That won't be for a long time. You don't even have a boyfriend." Onofrio said.

Cristiana didn't contradict him. She pulled him to her and hugged him hard. "Remember what I've said, Onofrio. Remember, and tell your brother the same."

He hugged her back and promised. "I will." The door to the room opened a crack and they heard voices on the other side. They pulled back from each other and wiped the tears from their faces.

A small, sturdy woman with a wild tangle of frizzy brown hair and flashing blue eyes walked in the room carrying a dozen or so messy file folders, dog-eared papers poking haphazardly from inside them. She dropped the files on one of the two hard backed chairs standing against the wall and pulled the other one up so she sat almost between the brother and sister.

Flashing a broad smile full of teeth at the two, she said in perfect but slightly accented Italian, "*Buon giorno*. My name is Pina. I am a social worker here at the hospital and the doctor has asked me to come and speak to you." Without giving either of them an opportunity to answer, she continued. "The doctors wanted to know how your mother got hurt."

"She slipped and fell in the kitchen," Cristiana answered.

"Are you sure? The doctors think it looks like someone hit her."

"No! I told you. There was water on the floor and she slipped and fell. It... it was my fault. I spilled some water and didn't clean it up right away."

The woman's sharp eyes peered at Cristiana. Onofrio shifted uncomfortably and Cristiana inwardly willed him to keep his mouth shut as she held her chin high and hardened her expression.

"You know, sometimes we have women and girls come in here and their husbands, or boyfriends or fathers or brothers have hit them and they are afraid to tell anyone. But we can help them, protect them, from getting hit again." The woman leaned forward, arms on her knees.

For only a fraction of a second, Cristiana let herself imagine what it would be like to live without the fear of her father, but pushed the thought as far away as possible.

"I told you," Cristiana said firmly. "She fell in the kitchen."

The woman leaned back in her chair and sighed. "That's what your mother said too. I just have to confirm with everyone." She picked up one of the files and flipped through the papers inside. "So, here is the situation with your mother. She is fine. When she hit her head, her brain sloshed back and forth a little in her skull. She has what we call a 'concussion'. She will have headaches for a while, but those will go away in the next few weeks and she will be as good as new."

Cristiana held herself erect, even though she felt like slumping in relief. She stood and said, "*Grazii, Signura*. May we take our mother home now?"

The social worker eyed Cristiana up and down for a few moments. "How old are you?"

"Seve... nineteen," Cristiana answered.

"So, that would be seventeen then?" The social worker said with one eyebrow raised and pen poised over the file.

Cristiana nodded reluctantly.

"I'm sorry, Cristiana, isn't it? I'm not trying to make things more difficult for you but you are too young. I can't send your mother home with you."

"I am capable of taking care of my mother!" Cristiana bristled.

"Oh, I have no doubt about that. In fact, I'm pretty sure you could take care of her, your siblings and half the neighbourhood if you needed to. That's not the point. You shouldn't have to take care of your mother. At seventeen, you should be in school."

"I finished school in Italy, before we moved here."

"And yet here you are, you are living in a country in which you can't speak, read or write the language, depending on your little brother to do the translating for you."

"We are fine, *Signura,*" Cristiana answered through gritted teeth, hands balled into fists at her side.

The woman sighed. "My name is Pina. Look, my job is to make things easier for you, not harder. Let me help you. Is there another adult in your home?"

"There is my father and my uncle."

"Do you have a phone number for them?"

"They are at work."

"No phone number?"

"No phone number."

Pina ran her hand through her frizzy hair and sighed. She looked back up at Cristiana.

"Okay. When do they get home from work?" she asked.

"Six, seven o'clock. It depends on the day." Cristiana answered.

"Can you at least tell me where they work?" Pina asked.

"They work on a farm in Richmond. I don't know which one."

"All right. Let's try this. Are there any other children in the home?"

Cristiana said nothing. She looked defiantly at the social worker. Pina sighed again. She turned and replaced the file on to the pile of papers and leaned back in her chair.

"Sit, Cristiana." She waved her hand in the direction of the sofa. "No, sit down. I just want to talk."

Slowly, Cristiana sank onto the hard, industrial couch.

"That's better. Would you like a drink? Maybe a coke or a root beer?"

Cristiana gave an almost imperceptible shake of her head.

"No? I want to explain something to you. The hospital pays me to come here every day to help people. They hired me because I speak Italian, and I can work with the Italian families here. But that's not why I come to work everyday. I have seen everything here. I have seen families–miserable and afraid. Occasionally, I see ones that are happy. I've seen families at their worst. Fathers and grandfathers who hit their children and the women in their lives; mother's that starve their children; people shot by their neighbours; babies that are addicted to heroin; teenagers strung out on any kind of drug that you can name. I come to work because sometimes, when I offer help, they take it and sometimes they leave here a little better off than when they came in.

"Sometimes there are people who come in here and don't want my help, or don't want it now. From time to time, these people who say no come back later. Their situation gets worse, and they don't know what else to do. I am not saying you will be one of those people, but, just in case, I want you to take my card. It has my pager number on it, and you can call me anytime you need to. Even if it is in the middle of the night. The most important thing is, I'm here to help you." Pina reached out with the small white card. When Cristiana made no move, she thrust it closer to the girl. "Take it! Hell, even if you can't use it, maybe your mother or someone else you know can."

Slowly, Cristiana reached out and held the card, her index finger almost touching Pina's. Her hand paused there for a moment. She took the card, and slipped it into her pocket, almost surreptitiously without looking at the print.

Pina sat back with obvious relief. "Excellent. Now, I can't send you home with your mother but what I can do is get someone to go and get the other children at your home and bring them here." Pina waved away the surprised look on Cristiana's face. "When you didn't answer me, I knew there would be others. We will bring them here and you can look after them until we can bring your father and your uncle here." Pina's sharp eyes scrutinized Cristiana's stony face as she mentioned Cristiana's father and uncle.

"Now," Pina said, turning to Onofrio. "You look like you could use a hamburger and some french fries. The food at this hospital tastes like cardboard but there is a good burger place across the street. What do you think?"

Onofrio nodded vigorously, and vaulted to his feet.

In spite of herself, Cristiana smiled. The speed at which her brothers could go from one emotion to another was masterful, and she envied it at times.

"Come on, you two. You've had a rough morning. Let's go drown all your difficulties in a milkshake." Pina grinned toothily at them and held open the door.

Chapter forty-seven

THE WORD OF THE SAINT

PINA WAS AS GOOD AS HER WORD. Over the next few days, Cristiana came to trust what Pina had said to her. She was wonderful with Anita, making sure the little girl had lots to occupy her while they waited at the hospital. She joked with Onofrio and Benedetto, and distracted them from their worries about their mother–particularly Benedetto who had needed some extra reassurance. When the police, who had waited at the apartment, brought her father and *Zzio* Silvio to the hospital, it was Pina who stood between Cristiana and her father and prevented him from taking out his anger on Cristiana for involving outsiders in their family matters. But most importantly, Cristiana had watched Pina pull her father aside, along with one of the police officers, and stand toe to toe with him in a conversation, the subject of which Cristiana could only make an educated guess. All she knew was after that conversation, while her father's anger had not diminished, the back-handed responses to her mother stopped altogether and any worries Cristiana might have had about leaving her family and moving into Antonio's house were gone.

Antonio had seemed suitably shocked when Cristiana had told him the story of the day at the hospital.

"What a terrible thing for you to have to face!" he said as he held her close to his chest. "I was worried when Benedetto and Anita came to tell me you had taken her to the hospital."

The unbidden thought, 'Not worried enough to come and help me,' rose up in Cristiana's mind, but she pushed it away. Instead, she held on to him tightly, head on his chest, and whispered. "It doesn't matter. It is all fine now." Antonio gave her a quick squeeze, and released her.

"I'm glad to hear it." he said and nothing more. She watched in stunned silence as he, whistling, picked up a box of onions, and carried them to the bin outside the front of the shop. She picked up the price-tag gun, and blindly priced out a box of capers Antonio had left for her to do.

From that moment, Cristiana carefully kept the problems of her home from her life with Antonio in the shop. Otherwise, her time there continued on as it had before. Every morning, Cristiana went to work hoping today would be the day he would tell her she was to move into his house, but every evening she would think to herself, "It must be too soon. He will tell me when it's the right time." And every day after work had finished and the door was locked, they would come together in the back room of the shop.

One day, as Antonio was taking the key from the register to close for the evening, the little bell on the door tinkled, announcing a customer. From the back aisle, where she was sweeping up the dust from the day, she heard a familiar, lively voice. Setting aside her broom, Cristiana walked to the register to see Pina talking to Antonio.

"Cristiana! *Ciao! Come stai?*" Pina's big, familiar toothy grin met Cristiana's surprised look. "I needed some fresh aubergine to make *caponata* tonight and thought I would stop by and say hello at the same time."

Cristiana stood dumbfounded, not sure what to say as the two orbits of her life came crashing together.

Pina held out her hand to Antonio. "My name is Pina, I met Cristiana when she took her mother to the hospital a couple of weeks ago. *Piacere.*"

Startled, Antonio shook her hand and replied with his own, "*Piacere.*"

"Look, I know you probably have more work for Cristiana to do, but I was wondering if I could steal her a little early? I want to check and see how her mother is doing, and I thought I might take her out for coffee." Pina's frizzy hair bobbed as she bounced up and down on the balls of her feet.

"Uh, certainly." Antonio, a little flummoxed by Pina's straightforward request, looked at Cristiana and said, "You go on. I'll see you tomorrow."

Cristiana, carried on by the force that was Pina's unprepossessing smile, mumbled, "*Va beni. Nni videmu* Antonio. See you tomorrow."

Cristiana followed Pina out of the shop. She glanced down at the cracks along the old sidewalk as if the lines running back and forth, crisscrossing under her feet, would give way to a map, instructions to help her get away from what she feared would be a conversation full of questions she didn't want to answer. Her shoulders hunched up around her ears, Cristiana tried to hold back, her eyes darted back and forth, but Pina would have none of it. Pina grabbed her by her elbow and led her around the corner and away from the Italian neighbourhood of Commercial Drive, the whole while chattering about how she had seen the quarter change; which shops had closed, which one's had opened, and where was the best place to buy *gelato, ricotta,* and *prosciutto.* Finally, she turned and directed Cristiana into a most decidedly un-Italian coffee shop.

"Coffee? Or maybe you would prefer a hot chocolate?"

"Coffee please."

Pina went to the counter and returned with two large steaming cups of coffee and a plate with two doughnuts.

"I know this Canadian coffee is..." Pina shuttered. "But I wanted us to go somewhere we could speak Italian and not have everyone in the shop understand your business." Pina squeezed four little creamers into her coffee and at least as many spoonfuls of sugar. "Nothing makes this coffee taste like anything but dirty water, but at least now it is sweet and creamy dirty water." She chuckled at her own joke.

Cristiana picked up the cup, and held it between her clammy hands. She stared as the surface of the coffee rippled with the shaking of her hands. What did Pina want?

As if she had heard Cristiana's thoughts, Pina said, "Cristiana, you needn't worry. Honestly, all I wanted was to find out how you are, and how things are at home."

Cristiana hesitated, still unsure if she could speak frankly to this little whirlwind of a social worker.

"Look, I understand. 'It's good to trust, it's better to not trust.' I get that whole Sicilian thing. I've been doing this job too long to not have come across this before. How about I ask you some questions, and you can answer or not as you like?" Pina mumbled around a mouthful of doughnut, powdered sugar obscuring her lips, and dusting the tabletop. "Okay, first question. Has your mother 'fallen' again since the last time?"

Cristiana shook her head.

Pina wiped the sugar from her lips. "Good. A police officer and I had a word with your father about the consequences of her 'slipping and falling' again. How are your brothers and sister doing? Has it been difficult for them since your mom went to the hospital?"

"No, they are all fine. Benedetto and Onofrio are working hard at school, and *Zzio* Silvio is helping *Mamma* find a nursery school for Anita. Onofrio wants to become an ambulance attendant now, and if Onofrio wants it, so does Benedetto." Cristiana answered.

"Good! That's wonderful. If they decide they want to stick with this, down the road I can help them with applications for school and to get scholarships. Which leads me to my last big question. How are you? Your father and uncle, were they very angry at you for calling the ambulance?"

Cristiana hesitated. Could she trust this woman? She wasn't family, and she had the ability to create untold havoc for them. But, she had made things better, and done it without causing any great disruption to their family. Cristiana felt something turn and shift inside her, and, almost without a conscious decision, her mouth opened and unexpected words came tumbling out.

"My father was angry, but I think he is a little scared too. I don't know what you and the police officer said to him, but he has said nothing to me about that day. In fact, he has said nothing to me at all since that day. Honestly, I like it much better this way."

Pina scrutinized Cristiana's face closely. "I can see you are telling me the truth, but I think that you aren't telling me the whole truth, are you? There is something else, isn't there?"

Cristiana blushed. She had tried to push her thoughts about Antonio to the back of her mind when Pina began to ask her questions, but her undercurrent of disquiet was palpable.

"There is one other thing, but it doesn't have anything to do with my father."

"Go ahead, I'm here to listen." Pina encouraged her.

"Well, there is a..." Cristiana hesitated, not wanting to say to Pina there was a man in her life.

"Is it a boy?" Pina asked.

Relieved to not have to say 'man', Cristiana nodded.

"Do your parents and uncle know?" Pina continued.

Cristiana shook her head.

"Are you sleeping with him?"

The blunt question shocked Cristiana. She turned bright pink and covered her face with her hands.

"So, that's a yes." Pina answered herself matter-of-factly. "Are you using birth control?"

Cristiana grasped for the crucifix hanging around her neck and blurted out, "Of course not!"

Pina sighed. "So, there may be another problem. Cristiana, I think I should take you to have a pregnancy test.

Cristiana froze. Her chest tightened and she couldn't breath. Pregnant? But it had only been a few weeks! She couldn't be pregnant!

Pina looked at Cristiana's face. The colour had all drained, and she was suddenly as pale and grey as the dirty, sun-bleached sidewalk. Pina took Cristiana's hand across the table and said gently, "You hadn't thought about pregnancy, had you?"

Cristiana shook her head numbly. "It's only been a few weeks. I, I don't think I could be pregnant, could I?"

"*Cara mia*, it can happen on the first time. Did no one tell you this?"

"No, never." Tears welled up in Cristiana's eyes. She turned her desperate look towards Pina. "How will I tell my mother? Oh, *miu Diu*! My father will kill me!" Cristiana crossed herself.

"Calm down Cristiana! You don't know you are pregnant. When did you have your last period?" Pina asked.

"I, I'm not sure. Maybe a month ago?"

"One month? Are you sure?"

"No, it was more. The last time was before we... before he and I..." Cristiana's head began to swim and the room seemed to pitch back and forth. "I think I'm going to..." Cristiana leapt to her feet and ran to the back of the coffee shop and into the washroom where she fell to her knees before the toilet and vomited up the coffee and doughnut. She stayed kneeling on the floor retching until there was nothing left but sweat beading on her forehead, and her upper lip, and running down her back. Her hands were clammy, and she shook violently as she tried to calm her breathing. She closed her eyes, and leaned the side of her head against the wall of the bathroom stall. Behind her she heard footsteps.

"Cristiana, are you all right? Can I help you?" It was Pina.

Cristiana didn't answer right away. She was too busy trying to keep from retching again, trying to slow her breathing.

Pina knocked softly on the door to the stall. "Do you need anything?"

"No." Cristiana answered weakly. "Please, give me a few minutes."

Pina's footsteps moved away, and Cristiana was left alone in the bathroom.

'How could I be so stupid?' she thought to herself. 'Of course I could get pregnant! What made me think I could be different?' She leaned her head on the back of her arm and held her breath as another wave of nausea rolled over her. When it had passed she slowly sat up, and breathed again.

"That's just it." she whispered to herself. "I didn't think." Cristiana gripped the toilet seat, and slowly got to her feet. She wobbled her way to the sink and washed her hands and ran cold water over her wrists. Her face felt hot so she moistened some paper towel with the cold water and patted her forehead and temples with it. She swished water around in her mouth and spat it into the sink. She looked at herself in the mirror. She knew, she just knew she was pregnant, had known the moment Pina mentioned the possibility.

Another thought intruded. Tears welled up in her eyes and spilled over onto her cheeks. This was a mortal sin. She had committed a mortal sin. She would have to confess as soon as possible! She had not been to confession since she had given up her virginity. She had known Father Ignazio would make her promise to stop and she hadn't wanted to. But now? This she couldn't leave on her conscience.

Cristiana still felt light-headed, but no longer thought she would be sick. She swayed as she made her way out of the washroom, and across to the table where Pina sat.

"I need to go to confession." Cristiana's voice wavered. "I need to tell the priest about this."

"Cristiana, we don't know for certain if you are pregnant. You might be, but until we get you a pregnancy test we won't know. And there are other tests you should have–gonorrhoea and syphilis at the very least."

"What are those?" Cristiana asked nervously. The words themselves sounded frightening.

Pina took Cristiana's hands in hers. "They are diseases that you can catch from having sex," she said gently.

"You can catch diseases from... from, doing that?" Cristiana's voice dropped down and ended in a whisper.

"Yes, but most are not serious if you find out and treat them in time."

Cristiana sat dumbfounded. For several seconds her mind was blank. This was too much to take in. She stared, unseeing, through Pina and across the coffee shop. She could catch a disease? And, like an elastic band, her thoughts snapped back into place. A disease. Sex could give her a disease!

"Pina, please. I must confess before I do anything else. I need to see Father Ignazio right away." Cristiana's voice was high pitched and desperate. If she had caught a disease she had to make her confession. What if she became too ill to go to confession? What if she died without making confession? The thought was too horrible to consider. No, the only solution was to go, now. Immediately.

Cristiana strode out the door. She broke into a run. Pina jumped up and ran behind her.

"Cristiana, wait. Let me take you to the clinic first." But Cristiana was already out the door and half a block ahead of Pina. "At least let me come with you to Queen of Angels Church! I can drive you to the clinic after." Pina's words broke through Cristiana's panic. She stopped and waited for Pina, puffing hard, to catch up.

"My car is over here. I'll drive you to Queen of Angels." Pina opened the door to a boxy old VW, dented and scratched, and Cristiana climbed in clutching at the dashboard in front of her.

Pina pulled carefully out into the constant traffic of 12th Avenue. She glanced over at Cristiana, and saw how alarmingly white the girl's face had become.

"Don't worry, Cristiana. I'll get you there as quick as I can."

Queen of Angels Church was a tall, square, brick building. It had none of the grace of any church Cristiana had known in Sicily. The pictures and sculptures of the saints were all modern images and for Cristiana and others like her who had come from Italy, they did not have the same gravitas the much older works held in the Italian churches, even in a small village like Sperlinga. The doors were open and there was a short queue of people, mostly elderly, waiting for their turn at confession.

Cristiana mindlessly dipped her fingers in the holy water and crossed herself before she made her way down the aisle and along the pew to sit next to a silver-haired woman in black. The woman had her eyes closed but her lips moved silently as she counted off each prayer on the beads of her rosary. Cristiana had not put her rosary in her purse that morning so instead she clasped her empty hands before her and knelt to pray but no words came. Instead she whispered her story to God.

"Lord, I was so unhappy when we came here. I missed my grandmother and my friends. This place was so strange and no one understood me. I was afraid you had abandoned me." Cristiana pressed her forehead against her white knuckles. She bit her lip, trying to hold back the sobs threatening to accompany her tears.

"That day when those women were so horrible to me in the shop, and Antonio held me and comforted me, it felt so wonderful and right after feeling so wrong for so long, I told myself anything that... that breath-taking must have been given to us by You. It had to have been, it was so beautiful. But now, please forgive me Lord. I can understand all the veiled warnings from *Mamma* and Father Ignazio and all the nuns from school. Now, not only am I pregnant, I am certain of it, I could be sick as well. And if I'm sick, my baby could be sick too. I brought all this on my baby and myself by sleeping with Antonio. This is a sign from you, God. I understand. No more men. I will have no more men in my life." Cristiana raised her hand, palm out, and pushed at the air, as if thrusting all men away.

"*Bastibili.* Enough," she said out loud.

Cristiana raised her eyes to the angular glass crucifix at the front of the church. She was empty, empty of all words but the promise she had made; a promise that rose from a place so deep inside her, Cristiana recognized she had never opened the door to that place—the place in her in which God lived—since she had left Sicily.

Cristiana bathed her face in the light from the abstract glass image of the crucified Christ at the front of the church; her heart lifted as she felt His light fall upon her. She closed her eyes. The exaltation of the moment was so powerful, so overwhelming and so complete she felt as if God Himself had reach down, grasped her soul and was lifting her heavenward. Every fibre, every drop of blood, every cell was filled with that perfect exaltation. She was floating. And, as if it were the most natural thing in the world, a beautiful woman appeared before Cristiana, although Cristiana's eyes were closed. The woman too, seemed to be floating. On her hands and feet there were wounds, terrible gaping wounds, but there was a light in her face like none Cristiana had ever seen. She smiled and spoke to Cristiana in the Sicilian of her childhood.

"Cristiana, you have come here to confess, to make yourself right with God."

"Yes, Mother." Cristiana whispered.

"I am not Maria, but Maria comes to you through me. I am called Saint Genevra. I am the one sent by God to watch over you, and every woman in your family." She reached a hand out towards Cristiana and made the sign of the cross over her forehead. Cristiana felt drops of blood from the saint's dripping wounds on her forehead, and her heart leapt.

"Cristiana, you carry a child within you. This girl is blessed as you were, as your mother was. But it is not for you to raise her. You must return to the land of your birth. She will stay here and you will go. There is work for her here, and work for you there. Know I walk with you, and with her."

Behind the saint, in the glow of her light, other women, appeared. Each one stepped forward and made the sign of the cross over Cristiana, and with each one Cristiana felt her heart expand. And as each one blessed Cristiana, the women, one by one, stepped back and faded away. Finally, it was only Saint Genevra that was left.

"One day, this child will come to you. She will come to find you and your story. You will tell her about me and you will tell her about her father. And through this she will create something beautiful." And with those words, Saint Genevra stepped back and faded as well.

Cristiana eyes flew open but Saint Genevra remained. She

stared without blinking as the saint disappeared into the background. She did not want to take her eyes off of Genevra even for a moment.

Once the saint was gone from her view the floating feeling disappeared too. She glanced around, surprised to find she was still kneeling in the same pew, her hands still clasped together but the fear and confusion was gone. It had been replaced by a feeling of adoration–one the saint's visit had created in her soul. She was transfixed in place, afraid to move in case she lost it. How long had she been gazing upon Saint Genevra's face? It felt like a moment, yet it could have well been forever.

A shuffling sound to the side broke her reverie and she glanced over to see the silver-haired woman was leaving the confessional. Cristiana rose to her feet a different person. Instead of fearful she was happy; happy to be confessing, and happy to be carrying this child.

Cristiana sat in the tiny cubical, crossed herself and said, "Forgive me Father, for I have sinned. It has been perhaps six weeks since my last confession. I have come to confess a mortal sin."

Father Ignazio jumped. He recognized Cristiana's voice, but she had rarely confessed more than having angry words for her brothers. She had never even been close to having committed a mortal sin in the past. He cleared his throat and said sternly, "And what is that sin?"

"Father, I lay with a man. An older, married man. In fact, I did this more than once–many times over the last four weeks. And now I am carrying his child."

There was a long pause as Cristiana waited for the Father to respond. She was convinced he would be disappointed, even shocked with her behaviour. She knew she needed to confess in a spirit of contrition to be forgiven and she should feel ashamed, yet instead she felt centred, as if everything she knew, everything she was, and everything she understood had been revealed to her by Saint Genevra's visit. She recognised what she had to do, and she was at peace.

Finally, Father Ignazio replied. "That is a serious thing, Cristiana, with any man, but one that is married is far worse. Are you still sleeping with him?"

"No Father. The last time was yesterday, but I realized today there can be no more. I have come to the decision no man will touch me again. Not ever."

"I'm glad to hear you have made that decision. Do you understand what you were doing was wrong?" He asked seriously.

Cristiana considered this for a moment before answering. "I think, Father, I fooled myself into believing what this man and I did was a gift from God, but I understand now that was not the case. I was unhappy here and confused and it seemed to be the only thing that would make me happy again. I recognise now how wrong it was."

"Cristiana, I will give you penance for your sin, but I want to meet with you outside the confessional. There is so much here, it is a dangerous labyrinth you are following my child, and you will need some good counsel."

"Of course Father." Cristiana. "Whatever you think."

When Cristiana left the confessional, and walked to the back of the church, Father Ignazio followed her. Pina looked up and stood as they approached.

"Father, this is Pina. She is a social worker I met at the hospital when my mother... was hurt. She wants to help me."

Pina looked at the teenager standing before her, but Cristiana's bearing had changed. She was no longer the terrified seventeen-year-old girl of an hour before. There was a firm line to her jaw and her eyes flashed. No longer was her skin pale and grey. Rosy spots had risen high on her cheeks.

"*Molto piacere.* I am Father Ignazio. I assume you know what Cristiana shared with me?"

"Of course Father, but the situation may not be what you think." Pina reached out and grasped his arm. Father Ignazio raised an eyebrow and turned to Cristiana.

"I have no doubt I am pregnant, Father."

"But Cristiana," Pina said in a low voice. "You haven't even had a pregnancy test. You can't know yet."

"Okay." Father Ignazio placed his hands on his hips. "It seems we have some things to discuss. Cristiana, *Signora* Pina, please, come into my office." Father Ignazio stepped back and gestured for both women to go ahead.

Cristiana had never been in the back of Queen of Angels Church. Grey cinder-brick walls balanced a low white-tiled ceiling, which hung oppressively over the hallway. She watched each footfall land on the patterned orange carpet as she and Pina made their way down the hallway to Father Ignazio's office.

The office was not what she expected. In spite of the modern architecture of the church, Cristiana walked into the office prepared for dark wood panelling, a large wooden desk, and a largish crucifix, gruesome and terrifying. Instead, Father Ignazio's office was bright. White walls were covered with framed Chagall and Picasso prints. The crucifix, a stylized silver cross, hung on the wall between two windows through which the sun beamed onto Father Ignazio's cluttered desk. The chair next to his desk was piled high with books—books on theology, sociology, psychology, and detective novels in Italian by Andrea Camilleri. Two padded Ikea rattan chairs sat, one on each side of the room, pointing from the corners of the red Persian rug into the centre of the room.

"Please, *Signora* Pina, Cristiana, sit down," Father Ignazio leaned against his desk.

Cristiana sat back and let the words of the priest and the social worker wash over her as they discussed what would be the next steps for her. She was vaguely aware they were laying out a course of action, however it was of little interest to her. Cristiana already knew what her action would be. It was only when she heard Pina mention her father did she pay closer attention.

"Father, I don't know if you are aware, but the situation with Cristiana's father is… well, problematic." Pina said gravely.

Father Ignazio nodded, just as serious. "Yes, I have noticed he is, shall we say, physical with Marta."

"Yes, and I'm afraid if he discovers Cristiana may be pregnant, he will be physical with her. I know she is still under age, but we need to find some way of protecting her from her father."

"Cristiana is only under age for a few weeks more, isn't that right, Cristiana?" Father Ignazio turned to her.

Cristiana jumped a little and nodded. "I'll be eighteen in three weeks."

"Well, that simplifies a good deal of things." Pina answered. "But the first thing is to get you a pregnancy test. Then, we can decide what to do from there."

"But I know what to do."

Both the priest and the social worker gazed at her in surprise. Cristiana's eyes didn't waver as she looked back at them, her expression serious but calm.

"What? You've already decided? But... We haven't even discussed anything yet!" Pina said.

"It might be better to get some advice, child." Father Ignazio knelt down before Cristiana so they were looking at each other eye to eye. "If you are pregnant, this is territory you have never walked through. *Signora* Pina and I have both counselled girls in your circumstances."

"I have already had good counsel. I know I am pregnant and I know what is the right thing for me to do." Cristiana's words were quiet but firm.

"Cristiana, who could possibly have counselled you? You hadn't even entertained the idea of a pregnancy until less than an hour ago!" Pina said, hands firmly on her hips and exasperation written across her face.

Cristiana held her breath. She was committed. She had to share what she had seen, but she knew how unlikely it would sound. She let her breath escape slowly through her teeth.

"Before I gave my confession, while I was waiting, I closed my eyes to pray. I promised God I would never let another man touch me. As I prayed, I saw a woman floating before me. She spoke to me and told me what I needed to do. She told me I will have a daughter. She has work to do here, and I have work to do in Sicily.

"Once I have my daughter, I am going back to Sperlinga, but she must stay here. You can find someone to take care of her?" Cristiana asked Pina.

"Uh...yes. There are a lot of families wanting to adopt a baby. But, are you sure? Who will you live with there?"

"My grandmother is still in Sperlinga. She is old and I will go back and take care of her. As I said, there is work for me to do there." Cristiana answered calmly.

Father Ignazio frowned, tilted his head as he looked down at the carpet. "Is this something you imagined, Cristiana," He lifted his head and looked back into her eyes. "Or are you saying you had a vision?"

"I don't know if it was a vision or not, but it wasn't my imagination. She was a saint I had never heard of before."

"She was a saint?" Father Ignazio gaped.

"She called herself Saint Genevra, and she had the *stigmata*."

The priest moved the pile of books from his chair and onto his desk two or three books at a time. Near the bottom of the pile he pulled out a large blue leather bound volume, opened the book and flipped through the pages.

"This is a book of lesser known saints. It was Genevra?"

"*Sì*."

Father Ignazio turned a few more pages, stopped, and ran his finger slowly down the page. He looked up at Cristiana with a frown.

"What town did you say you were from in Sicily?"

"Sperlinga. It's a tiny town in the centre of the island."

"And you had never heard of Saint Genevra before?"

"No, never." Cristiana looked at the priest, puzzled.

Father Ignazio sat in his cushioned desk chair and leaned back. He lifted the book and translated so Cristiana could understand.

"Saint Genevra is a little-known saint who lived in Sperlinga in the 12th century AD. Genevra was visited numerous times by the Holy Mother who gave Genevra instructions to build a shrine approximately 100 kilometres from Sperlinga in the direction of Mount Etna. Genevra walked the 100 kilometres while suffering the *stigmata* on her hands, feet and side. The shrine was created by the erection of a large blue tinted stone resembling the Virgin Mary in shape. The shrine can still be seen near the Ciancio Forest. In 1221, Pope Honorius III declared her a martyr. Miracles that led to her beatification and canonization include: an attestation of a divine message in the visitation by the Virgin Mary, *stigmata*, levitation at the sight of the Virgin, appearance after death over 100 kilometres away from her place of death. Her feast day is June 24th, however, she has not been adopted as a patron saint by any town."

Pina leaned forward. "She was from Sperlinga?"

Father Ignazio nodded.

"Then," Cristiana stated, "I must do what she said."

Father Ignazio nodded his head in agreement. "I can't say if you had a visitation or imagined what you saw. You may not remember having heard of Saint Genevra, or you may truly have never heard of her. Either way, I think your plan is the best course of action," he turned to Pina, "… assuming you can find a Catholic family to adopt the child."

"And the story for her father? We cannot tell her father the truth. I can't guarantee Cristiana's safety in that house or the safety of the young man if her father were to know the facts."

Cristiana looked up, "I will tell him I was forced." She looked at the priest. "I know it is a lie, but can I do that much, Father?"

"It's stretching the truth, but you did fall into the hands of an older man, so, yes, I think you can say that." Father Ignazio slowly answered.

"Wait, you know who the father is?" Pina sat up straight and shot the question at the priest.

"No, I only know he is older and married."

"Older and married? Cristiana, you didn't tell me any of this. If you tell us who the father is, maybe he can take the baby to raise it. I mean, if there is a baby, that is." Pina rubbed her eyes–the situation was rapidly becoming more and more muddled.

Cristiana considered this and shook her head. "I will tell him, he deserves to know, but he is in no position to raise a child. My daughter must go to a family. A family in which everyone will want her and give her the best. He can't do that right now."

"Why not, Cristiana?" Pina leaned forward.

"You must trust me on this, Pina. I won't tell you who he is. I know he can't take care of a child, any child, right now."

Pina opened her mouth as if to argue but Father Ignazio raised his hand. "I think we should leave this here. We have a plan and it includes finding a good situation for the child, if," and he gave Cristiana a hard look, "there is a child. For now, I think you should go home. Your family will be worried–I know you are later than usual. Pina, can you drive Cristiana home?"

"Of course," Pina answered. "And tomorrow, I'm taking you to the clinic."

Cristiana stood. She looked from one to the other and said, "*Grazii mille*, both of you. I know you are both worried but it will all be fine. I know it will." She smiled at the two adults, both of whom stared at the teenage girl who was comforting them, rather than the other way around.

~|~

Cristiana climbed out of Pina's boxy little VW in front of her apartment building..

"I'm going to come inside with you." Pina raised her hand to forestall Cristiana's objections. "No, don't try to stop me. I want to make sure your father knows I am still around and keeping an eye on things."

Pina strode forward, head down, towards the front door and Cristiana came trailing along behind.

At the apartment, Cristiana turned the key and swung open the door.

"Cristiana! You're home!" Marta came running out of the kitchen. "Where have you been? I've been so worried." Marta threw herself at Cristiana and hugged her tightly.

"*Mamma*, I'm only a couple of hours late!"

"You've never been late before!"

From the kitchen Cristiana heard her father growl, "Girl, you are late. What do you mean making your mother worry like this?" Heavy footfalls came toward her from the kitchen. Alfonso rolled into the hallway like a locomotive, hand raised. Pina stepped out from behind Cristiana and looked at Alfonso with one eyebrow raised.

"*Buona sera, Signor.*"

Alfonso skidded to a stop and lowered his hand.

"I bumped into Cristiana at her work and offered to take her out for coffee. I wanted to make sure everything was going well here, and there hadn't been anymore… falls."

Alfonso grunted, and turned back into the kitchen.

"No, no more falls. I'm fine and Cristiana is fine. The children are all fine too." Marta's hands played with her collar as she looked past Pina to the wall behind.

"I'm so glad to hear that, *Signora*. Remember, you can call me anytime if you need me for anything." Pina turned to Cristiana. "I will see you in a couple of days, Cristiana. We can have coffee again."

"*Certu*, Pina. I'd be happy to see you again."

Chapter forty-eight

THE SECRET IS SHARED

"CRISTIANA, WE SHOULD TALK about how you will tell your family." Father Ignazio had invited her and Pina to meet with him when Pina had called with the confirmation of the pregnancy. His elderly housekeeper, a stout Polish woman named Edna, delivered a steaming pot of tea and Father Ignazio thanked her and poured the scalding liquid into heavy earthenware mugs.

"You could wait a little, Cristiana." Father Ignazio said. "There is nothing that says you have to face your father right away with this news. I can't imagine this is going to be easy, knowing what your father is like."

"I disagree Father," Pina interjected. "Cristiana is still a minor for another two weeks. I know it isn't long but I could get into a great deal of trouble for sitting on this information."

Father Ignazio opened his mouth to answer, but his words were stayed when Cristiana put her hand on his arm.

"Father, I think Pina is right. Whether I tell my father today, or tomorrow, or in two weeks, nothing is going to make this easy. I only need a couple of days to talk to my baby's father first, and I will be ready. Or at least as ready as I can be when it comes to *Papà.*" Cristiana gave a resigned little smile. "There are three things I'd like to ask of both of you. I'd like to tell my parents here, in the rectory, if you don't mind Father? I think *Papà* is less likely to make a scene if we are here, and there is someone he doesn't know like Edna around to hear. I'd like both of you here with me and I'd like a promise you will keep checking on my mother. I'm sure *Papà* will blame her for this and when no one is around he might take his anger out on her."

"Of course Cristiana," Father Ignazio answered and Pina nodded vigorously from the other side of the study.

"Thank you. I think *Papà* will not let me come home after we tell him, so I will pack a suitcase and leave it here, in case." Cristiana ticked off the things she would have to do on her fingers. "And I will have to find another place to live. Also, I will have to phone my *nanna*. I know she will be happy to have me back, no matter what, but I need to call and tell her I will be coming."

"I can call her if you know her phone number," Pina interjected. "And I already have a family willing to take you in, if your father won't let you go home. If that doesn't work, I you can come and stay with me. You will not be homeless," Pina added fiercely.

"I will need some clothes to wear as I get bigger. But the most important thing is to find a family for my daughter. They must be Catholic and it would be nice if they were Italian," Cristiana said.

"Yes, Catholic is essential," Father Ignazio added. "As for clothes, I'm sure the women of the parish can put together some clothes for you and for the baby when the time comes."

"Don't worry about the family. That is my job. Finding an adoptive family for an infant is easy. I may even be able to find you an Italian Catholic one!"

"*Grazii milli*, both of you. You are making this so much easier for me."

Pina came forward and hugged Cristiana impulsively. "Of course we will help you!"

Father Ignazio cleared his throat. "So, I'll tell your parents to come in on Friday. Will that give everyone enough time?"

~|~

Cristiana peeked through the curtained window into Father Ignazio's study. She could see *Mamma* nervously pulling at her sleeves, and glancing at the door. *Papà*, sitting erect in the chair directly across from the priest's desk, was holding himself still but his eyes glanced left and right as if looking for an escape route. Father Vincenzo, the priest in Sperlinga had been quite different than Father Ignazio; far more stern and forbidding. A call to his study had always been followed by the uncomfortable and inevitable dressing down, particularly for the guilty youth of the village. Cristiana watched Father Ignazio sit calmly, quietly studying a book on his desk. Even through the tiny window, Cristiana could feel the stillness in the room grow palpable as the tension in Cristiana's parents became more and more visible. Marta and Alfonso both seemed to hold their breath.

"Come on, Cristiana. It's time." Pina lifted her fist to the door.

The sharp rap shot through the silence and Cristiana could hear Marta let out a small squeak.

"Come in." the priest called out evenly.

The door opened and Edna ushered Pina and Cristiana into the room. Cristiana glanced at her mother and down at her hands as she blushed right into the roots of her hair. She had never wanted to hurt *Mamma*. Marta gaped, a dawn of pre-understanding and distress seemed to cross her face. It was Alfonso, however, to whom Cristiana looked next. She knew there would be no surprises from her father here. For her father, yes, but from him, no, and she was ready for what she knew was coming. She and Pina sat together on the old, red leather couch, worn and cracked.

"Ahem," Father Ignazio cleared his throat. This small sound focused all their eyes on him and, with a master's touch and years of practice and experience, he began his orchestrated minuet through the potential minefield laying before them.

"I think we should start with tea. Edna, can you bring us a pot please?" Edna's face, profoundly ugly with grey eyes hiding behind a flat nose and skin wrinkled and scarred from an unfortunate childhood brush with chickenpox, seemed impassive and dull, but anyone who chose to look closely enough would have seen those grey eyes twinkle slightly as she nodded and left the room. She had, many times, watched Father Ignazio deftly guide unsuspecting parishioners into decisions, and to conclusions they would never have made on their own.

He looked back down at the papers on his desk. He seemed to be absorbed, once more, in their content. The silence that descended once again over the group was electric, but he would not relieve them of their discomfort. Instead, he picked up a pen and rapidly moved it up and down as if he were about to tap in on the desk, but at the last moment each time he stopped himself. Every eye in the room was transfixed by the movement of this pen. It was as if he were no longer there, the pen moved up and down of its own accord. And when they had all but forgotten about his presence, he shot a question through the room that made each one jump in surprise.

"Marta, are you well?" Each of them looked up to see Father Ignazio's clear gaze, piercing through the room at Marta. "Any more falls?"

Marta glanced fearfully across the room at Pina, and sideways at Alfonso. She had tried hard to keep her hospital visit from the rounds of church gossip and was shocked to hear the priest mention it.

"Ah, no. No more falls Father."

"Good! I'm glad to hear it." He turned his penetrating gaze on Alfonso. "It must have been most distressing to hear your wife had injured herself. I'm sure you have taken every precaution to make sure it never happens again."

Alfonso stared at the priest, unsure where the priest was leading him, simply nodded.

"And of course," Father Ignazio continued, "I know you would never want one of your children to slip and fall either, especially not a lovely girl like Cristiana."

Alfonso, confused, looked at his daughter. "No, of course not." Alfonso answered.

"And you would do everything you could to keep her from, oh, say, slipping and giving herself a black eye, wouldn't you?"

"Yes, of course Father."

"*Bene, bene.* Good, good. Just making sure, that's all. Ah, look. Here comes Edna with tea for all of us."

Edna pushed the door to the office open with her elbow as she balanced a large tray covered with a teapot and cups and saucers. She placed it carefully on a coffee table sitting in front of the large leather couch.

"Thank you so much Edna. Pina, would you mind pouring for us?"

Pina stood and poured the scalding liquid. The cups, each fine bone china, had a thin slice of lemon on the saucer next to a tiny silver spoon.

"When I was a young man, just out of seminary, I was sent to assist in a large parish in Manchester. The hope was I would improve my English skills. I also picked up the habit of a cup of tea with a little slice of lemon, every afternoon. I find it relaxes me."

Pina handed the first cup to Father Ignazio who placed it on the desk in front of him and stirred the lemon into his tea. Cristiana also placed hers on the coffee table and followed the priest's actions. Marta and Alfonso, however, were forced to balance the tiny fragile cups on their laps, Marta's thin fingers holding the edge of the saucer, and Alfonso's large work roughened hands trying desperately to hold the handle of the teacup without breaking it. Alfonso, in particular, sat hunched forward on his chair, staring uncomfortably at the unfamiliar scene of blue Edwardian ladies walking in their blue English garden on the side of his teacup.

"Now, since we are all comfortable, I think we should begin our... oh, conversation." Father Ignazio leaned back in his chair and put his fingers together as if creating a church steeple with his hands.

"Sometimes," he continued, "As a priest, one of my flock will confess something to me they may wish to share with some other people around them. Cristiana has something she confessed to me she needs to tell you. She has done her penance, and is now right with God so I am going to ask, as we proceed, that you remember this.

"Unfortunately, Cristiana was taken advantage of by an older man. She now finds herself in the unfortunate situation of being, how should I say it? Well, with child, I suppose, would be the most delicate."

As the priest had been speaking, Cristiana found herself looking at her mother. Marta had stopped fiddling with her teacup and had turned her eyes towards her daughter. Her face had gone white and her lips were parted in a slight 'oh'. The dark circles always below her eyes seemed deeper and more purple than usual. Cristiana's gaze met her mother's. Cristiana could see she knew. A light of realization dawned on Cristiana. Even before the priest spoke the words Marta knew. Even as Alfonso sputtered and swore, Marta knew—knew about Cristiana's pregnancy and knew about Cristiana's vision as surely as Cristiana had seen it herself. The room disappeared as the mother and daughter gazed into each other's eyes. An arc of understanding reached between them. In the background, Father Ignazio was explaining to an enraged Alfonso, held into his chair by the fine bone china in his hands. Pina was grasping Cristiana's shoulder. None of this mattered. Cristiana mouthed the words, "*Tu sai? You know?*" at her mother who nodded and whispered back, "*Io so.* I know."

From that moment, her father's bluster meant nothing to her. She broke the gaze with her mother and interrupted the priest.

"*Papà*," Cristiana spoke sharply. "Save your breath. This has nothing to do with you. Pina," Cristiana gestured in the social worker's direction, "Has found a family to take me in until my daughter is born. Once she is born, she will be adopted into a Catholic family here, and I will go back to Sperlinga and live with *Nanna*. As Father Ignazio said, I have made my peace with God. It is time for me to move on. I was never meant to stay in Canada. My life is in Sicily."

Alfonso opened his mouth to answer but he felt a hand on his leg. It was Marta. "*Miu preju*," she said using the pet name she had not uttered in years. "It is done. She does not belong here. Let her go."

And as if he were a balloon suddenly deflated, Alfonso sagged back into his chair. Pina grabbed his teacup and Alfonso placed his large farmer's hands over his face and sobbed.

Chapter forty-nine

"YOU HAVE SAVED ME"

~FEBBRAIO 1981~

CRISTIANA KEPT HER PROMISE to the priest that no man would touch her again, but she did visit Antonio once more. Her pregnancy was far enough along she had developed the waddle marking the walk of all pregnant women, and she climbed on a bus taking her to Commercial Drive. She wandered up the familiar street, listening to the rolling blue sounds of Italian flowing around her. She stopped a few hundred feet away from Market Via Palermo and watched Antonio stock the fruit and vegetables in the display outside the store. She no longer felt the same flip flop in her stomach when she looked at him. Instead, she felt a fondness, a gratitude for what he had given her. She needed to tell him.

"Antonio."

Antonio turned in surprise. "Cristiana! What? I thought I would never see you again!"

"I wanted to visit you one last time. There are some things I want to say."

"Come in! Come in the shop! I'll make you coffee." He stopped and turned back. "Can you drink coffee?"

Cristiana smiled. "Yes, of course I can drink coffee. I would love one."

Antonio found her a chair and fussed around making *espresso* and putting out *biscotti* for them to eat. Once he poured out the scalding, dark liquid, he sat down opposite her.

"I must tell you something, Cristiana," he said a little shamefacedly. "My wife, and I have gotten back together and... she's pregnant too." The last bit came out in a rush.

Cristiana smiled. "That's wonderful, Antonio. You will make a superb father when the time comes."

Antonio gave her a relieved grin. "I thought you might think the worse of me, going back to my wife after… well, after everything."

Cristiana put her coffee cup down. "Antonio. The day I told you I would never be touched by a man again, I gave up any hold I might have had on you. You are free to be the man you are meant to be, and I am glad you have found what it is you want. I came here today to thank you. This is not what I had planned for my life, but it has given me so much. I would never have had any of these experiences if it were not for you. You were so kind to me when I needed it. I can only say thank you." She smiled at Antonio and they sat quietly for a few moments as they sipped their coffees.

"There is one other thing, Antonio, I want to ask you." Cristiana looked seriously into Antonio's eyes.

"Anything, Cristiana. What can I do?"

"Father Ignazio is going to make sure my baby is brought up Catholic, but I am so afraid that she won't end up with people who will love her the way that I already do. Can you watch over her and make sure she gets to a good family? A family to truly love her as if she were their own?"

Antonio grasped the cross that perpetually hung around his neck and kissed it.

"I swear to you on my mother's memory I will make sure your baby–our baby–is loved as if it were with you."

Cristiana sat back and smiled. She trusted him.

"Thank you Antonio. I knew that you would watch over her for me."

~|~

Marta, Alfonso, Silvio, Onofrio, Benedetto, and Anita all stood awkwardly at the airport security gate. Pina stood next to Cristiana holding a boarding pass as the girl turned to each member of her family and hugged them one by one. Beside Cristiana was a small carryon bag. There was no baby carrier, no diaper bag, no bottles or stuffed toys. But in her purse, tucked into an envelope, and wrapped carefully in tissue paper, was a small collection of Polaroid pictures of a tiny baby. Each one had been cried over; now and always they would be Cristiana's most treasured possessions.

There was little to be said to each family member. Every important word had been shared over the previous nine months. Cristiana's pregnancy had brought some healing to the family. Marta, encouraged by her daughter's strength and with the support of Pina and Father Ignazio, began to stand up to her husband. In turn, Alfonso had stopped hitting Marta, and had made his peace with his daughter. As Marta held Cristiana, she whispered in her daughter's ear, "You have saved me, my darling child." Tears filled Cristiana's eyes. She knew what her mother meant. She had whispered the same words to her daughter when she held her for the last time.

Without another word, she took the boarding pass from Pina, hugged her tightly and strode toward the security gate, carry-on bag in one hand, the other wiping tears from her cheeks.

Chapter fifty

ELENA'S FATHER

~AGOSTO 2011~

CRISTIANA HAD STOPPED TALKING. The room was silent. Elena sat motionless, her cheeks wet, her mother's story still washing over her in waves. Cristiana came and sat next to Elena on the divan.

"I hope you can understand why I gave you up. I hope you can forgive me."

Elena took Cristiana's hands. "There is not one thing to forgive. If you'd done anything differently, had made any other decisions, I wouldn't be here. Your... my birth father did live up to his word. A Sicilian family adopted me, and I was raised in a big family–lots of cousins and aunts and uncles. I had no brothers or sisters, but I had so many first and second cousins that I didn't need them. My mother died when I was ten. I loved her and missed her, but my father was wonderful, and he made sure I never wanted for anything, even though we weren't wealthy."

Now Cristiana was crying. "I am so glad. My whole life I've been worried that you ended up with a family that didn't love you as much as I did."

Elena put her arms around Cristiana and the two cried into each other's shoulders, grieving the loss of so many years and grateful the lost years were done.

Finally, the two women sat up, wiping their faces and laughing.

"It is like watching mirror images of you two." Both Elena and Cristiana jumped. They had almost forgotten the third woman in the room, she had been sitting so still. "Elena, did you bring any photographs of you from your childhood?"

Elena smiled and pulled a fat envelop out of her purse. "Of course. I thought you might want to see some."

Maria Antonella stood and poured the coffee the housekeeper had quietly brought in and joined the other women on the divan.

The pictures were full of images of Elena growing up: a few with her mother, many more with her father. There were pictures of picnics, days at the beach, picking strawberries on Lulu Island, riding the ponies, and playing at concerts. Cristiana exclaimed over each one.

Elena picked up one of the last of the pictures. It was a picture of her and Lucia about age four. *Zzio* Tony held them, one sitting on each of his strong arms. She handed it to Cristiana. "I saved this one to the end. It is one of my favourite pictures. It is my cousin Lucia and me and my *Zzio* Tony at the beach."

"Cristiana, what is it?" Maria Antonella asked.

Cristiana face had, once again, gone white. She gripped the edge of the picture so tightly she had creased it. "This, this man is your uncle?" she asked incredulously.

Elena frowned at the unexpected response. "Yes, that is *Zzio* Tony. My father's older brother."

Without taking her eyes from the photograph, Cristiana replied, "Elena, that is your father."

A dark grey swirling whisper grew in Elena's ears louder and louder. The grey swirl moved faster and grew larger until Elena could barely see. She leaned forward gasping, trying to clear her vision. What was that sound? The ocean? No not loud enough. A plane? No. It was a train, a locomotive. It sounded like the steam engine she and her father had taken once from Vancouver north to Squamish and back. Why was there a train? She couldn't understand. She seemed to float off the sofa and drift to her knees. In the distance, behind the locomotive's roar, she could hear someone calling her name. She slumped to the floor and, feeling sick, lay still, hoping that both the train and the swirling grey mist would leave.

"Elena! Elena! Can you hear me? Wake up!"

Elena felt hands grip her shoulders and shake her until her eyes and ears had cleared and she could see again. She looked up into the worried faces of Cristiana and Maria Antonella. She lay still, trying to sort out what had happened.

Uncle Tony. Her father. Elena, gasped and struggled to breathe. No, Cristiana must be mistaken. Her father must be someone who looked like *Zzio* Tony. But Tony had been a shopkeeper, too. She struggled to sit up. Cristiana's strong arms cradled her back and supported her as she climbed her way back into the moment.

"He can't be my father, he's my Uncle Tony! You must be wrong. What, what did you say was the name of the shop? Where did you work? Was it on Commercial Drive?" Elena peppered her with questions.

Cristiana struggled to answer. "Yes, I think so. I don't know." She shook her head as if trying to clear her head.

Maria Antonella answered this time. "But *carina*, you do. You have one old photo in the back of your linen drawer." she said gently.

Cristiana stared blankly at Maria Antonella for a moment. She jumped to her feet and rushed out of the door. Both Elena's and Maria Antonella's eyes raised to the ceiling as they listened to Cristiana's footsteps dashing up the stairs. There was a pause, a slam and rushed footsteps coming down the stairs.

"Here," she panted as she thrust the picture to Elena.

"You look, I can't look." Elena answered

Cristiana hesitated before holding her hand out to take back the creased photograph. "Commercial Drive. Market Via Palermo. It was the name of the street where Antonio grew up." She handed the picture back to Elena.

Elena looked at the picture in disbelief. In the picture was Cristiana, another grinning man that must have been Cristiana's *Zzio* Silvio, and *Zzio* Tony. And above them was the same storefront sign that she and Lucia had walked under so many times. Market Via Palermo. The store that her uncle had named after the street in Cianciana where they had grown up. They…*Zzio* Tony and her father. Or rather her father and her father. Oh, she was so confused. This couldn't be right. She looked up into her mother's eyes and she knew that Cristiana was telling the truth.

Elena blinked and a lone tear, harsh like a secret, crept down her cheek. She looked away and swept the back of her hand across her eyes. She nodded. There was nothing more to be said.

Chapter fifty-one

THE HOME OF HER FATHERS

~SETTEMBRE 2011~

ELENA SLID HER HEAVY SUITCASE into the trunk of her Fiat. Cristiana handed her a bag filled with wine, dried oregano in glass jars, and ripe figs. The wine and the oregano were to take home; the figs were for her to eat on her drive to Cianciana.

Closing the trunk with a solid thump, Elena stood for a moment, hands still on the back of the car, eyes squeezed tight. Two tears wedged between her red-rimmed lids, slid out and made their way slowly down her cheek. She had been with Cristiana and Maria Antonella for two weeks. They had talked late into the night, every night, sharing glass after glass of deep red Sicilian wine. Over the wine they had talked of the important things: Elena's life and family, Cristiana and Maria Antonella's relationship, Genevra's story, how Cristiana had become a baker, Elena's life with music, the colours each could see, their hopes and plans. They also talked of inconsequential things: the best places for seafood and pasta in Palermo, the direction of fashion in Milan, where they would go on Elena's next visit to Sicily. And there would, Elena assured her mother, be a next time, and another next time, and even more after that.

One night, Maria Antonella unearthed an ancient guitar and the two of them, Maria Antonella on the piano, and Elena on the guitar, serenaded Cristiana with the same Sicilian folk songs Elena had learned from her father. She had packed more into her two weeks with Cristiana, and had learned more about her than she had ever believed possible. As she stood at the back of the car, Elena felt a soft hand on her shoulder. She turned into the arms of her newly found mother and they held each other closely for a long moment. Cristiana broke the hug and stepped back, wiping her eyes with a white hanky pulled from the sleeve of her lightweight summer baker's uniform.

"Please drive carefully on your way to Cianciana. The interior roads are so winding and dangerous. I wish you were going to stay here." Cristiana gripped Elena's arm as she spoke.

"I am a careful driver, Cristiana." Elena replied. "You needn't worry. The past two weeks with you and Maria Antonella have been more than I ever imagined. I feel like I truly know you now. And the story Genevra told me helped me to see Sperlinga as one of my homes. I am so grateful to the both of you for everything, but part of my reason to come to Sicily was to visit Cianciana to see where *Zzio* Tony and *Papà* grew up. I need to see that part of my family too."

Maria Antonella smiled graciously at Elena. "Of course you must visit Cianciana, but come back to us some day."

Elena reached out and hugged Maria Antonella much more carefully than the long, tight hug she had shared with Cristiana.

"Thank you for everything." She whispered into Maria Antonella's ear. "Thank you for taking such good care of my mother."

Maria Antonella cleared her throat. "Go with God, *carina*. Be safe."

Elena climbed into the little Fiat and started the engine. As she drove slowly down the narrow street, she waved and called out the window, "*Arrivederci al prossimo anno!* See you next year!"

~|~

The drive to Cianciana was neither as long nor as dangerous as Cristiana had suggested. Two hours through rolling hills, wild-looking fields, and rocky outcroppings left Elena regretting she would be leaving Sicily in less than a week.

Cianciana appeared suddenly on a hilltop as she rounded a corner. She slowed as the pot-holed road curved into the village. The mid-afternoon sun glinted off the stained-glass reflections of *San Antonio* in the *chiesa matri,* the mother church, momentarily blinding Elena as she drove through the empty cobbled streets until she found a narrow parking spot next to the boutique hotel into which she was booked. Grabbing her carry-on bag, Elena entered a lobby that was surprisingly luxurious.

"*Buon giorno.* Welcome to the *Albergo San Antonio.* You must be Elena Alcamo, from Canada, I believe." A beautiful young woman with dark eyes smiled warmly at Elena. "Please sign the register. Here is your key. You are in room three upstairs."

Elena picked up the pen and signed the register with a flourish. "*Grazii.* Can you tell me where *Via Palermo* is? I want to go there once the *pisolino,* the afternoon nap, is over."

"*Certo.* Let me give you this map of the town. We are here and *Via Palermo* is only a few blocks away, here."

"*Grazii milli.*"

"*Prego.* If there is anything else you need, please let me know."

Elena walked the steep slope of *Salita Carmelo* once again on her last day in Cianciana, past the church, up to *Via Palermo,* the street on which both her fathers had grown up. It was a short, narrow street, cobblestoned and lined with tall houses, either stuccoed or stone; typical in Sicilian mountain villages. As with most villages, people were curious, but Cianciana was unusually friendly and open. Her father used to say in a typical Sicilian manner, 'It is good to trust, it is better to not trust', but this didn't seem to be the case in Cianciana as far as she could see. People greeted her warmly on the small back streets–on *Via Palermo,* time seemed to have stopped. The *Ciancianese* sitting outside their doorsteps said *bona sera* and asked where she was from. As soon as she explained who she was, they were excited to meet Salvatore Alcamo's little girl. She was astonished to find out she was related to most of them in one way or another. They peppered her with questions about her father, and it only felt awkward when they asked about her *Zzio* Tony. They gave her bags of figs and oranges and lemons and ignored her protestations she wouldn't be allowed to carry them into Canada. She said her final goodbyes to her newfound relatives with promises to email when she got home, and turned once again up the hill. She walked all the way to the top to *Calvario,* or Calvary, where the tall cross had been standing, protecting the town for how long, Elena didn't know.

From there Elena could see the whole of Cianciana, in fact, the whole of the Platani Valley and the other villages and towns surrounding it–Sant'Angelo Muxaro, San Biagio, Ribera, and, because it was so clear, she could see all the way down to the sea at Eraclea Minoa. Her father and *Zzio* Tony and her mother and her siblings had all played at the top of this hill. In truth, her grandparents and great grandparents had played here too and many more generations before that. Her father had told her the Alcamo family had been there hundreds of years.

She sat in the shade of the cross and had a private word with her mother and father. She never shared with anyone what she had said there. She packed up her fruit and camera and made her way back to the Panda and to the road to Trapani.

Chapter fifty-two

A PRAYER OF THANKS

AS THE PLANE MADE ITS FINAL DESCENT into YVR, the Vancouver International Airport, Elena was still struggling with what to say to her family. Should she hide what she found out? *Zzio* Tony would know she knew. Should she tell Lucia? Would it destroy their family? She couldn't imagine that *Zzia* Laura would put up with infidelity. Finally, as the landing gear locked into place, she gave a little prayer to Genevra.

"Genevra, please guide me through this because I haven't got a freaking clue what to do." she muttered to herself. All she could do was to trust Genevra to take care of it, as she had taken care of Elena all through Sicily. She tucked her tablet into her carry-on. In it was the beginning of an overture to an opera–an opera she would call "Saint Genevra". The three weeks she had spent in Sicily seemed like an entire generation–more in fact. She had lived the lives of Genevra and Cristiana vicariously and these experiences were calling her to immortalize them in music.

~|~

Immigration was relatively quick and for once her suitcase arrived early and unscathed. She handed her stamped entrance card to the officer standing at the door, which opened to dozens of waiting friends and family. For her, it was opening to her sister, Lucia.

It took Elena several scans of the crowd before she saw Lucia standing at the back. She waved, and Lucia gave what seemed to be a half-hearted wave back. As she walked closer, she was stunned to see that Lucia's face was haggard and drawn. Dark shadows smudged below red-rimmed eyes. And she was thin–thinner than Elena had ever seen her. Elena wove her way in and out through the crowd. Had *Zzio* Tony told Lucia? Elena could scarcely believe that. Yet, the tragic waif Lucia had faded into, told the truth. When Elena reached Lucia, she was shocked how she could feel every bone when Lucia threw her arms around Elena crying. Elena held her for a moment, her heart in her throat, and stepped back, holding Lucia by her shoulders.

Cautiously, Elena asked, "What's wrong? What's happened?" eyes intent on Lucia's face.

"Oh my God, you don't know? You must know! You found her, didn't you, Cristiana?" Lucia cried.

"You know?" Elena was dumbfounded. "But, how could you possibly know? I didn't even know if I should tell you."

"Dad told us. When I read out your email to him and to Ma, that you had met your birth mother, I guess he realized you must have found out he was… Well, Ma pitched a fit. She threw all his clothes out on the lawn and he's living with Guido from the café on Commercial Drive. Ma won't have anything to do with him, but she told me she doesn't hold any of this against you. She wants me to bring you home." Lucia sobbed. "Oh, Elena, how are we going to get through this?"

Elena grabbed her suitcase with one hand and put her other arm around Lucia. She steered her out of the terminal and towards the parking lot.

"Don't worry, Lucia. We can get through this. We have people to help us." And to herself she gave a quiet prayer of thanks to Genevra for being the one to help her through.

As always.

The End

Glossary

Most of the words in italics in The Bastard of Saint Genevra are Sicilian. Today, in Sicily, most people speak Italian with only the older generation speaking Sicilian with any regularity. Sadly, many of the youth in Sicily cannot speak Sicilian, and in some cases, can't understand Sicilian either. I have included Sicilian vocabulary here as an homage to the Sicilian people and their wonderful language–earthy yet beautiful. I have used some Italian when a character would not have used Sicilian, when the Italian and the Sicilian are the same or when the Sicilian word has escaped my research.

I also need to acknowledge that Sicilian is different in the wide range of cities, towns and villages all across the Mediterranean jewel that is Sicily. Most of the Sicilian I have included comes from the province of Agrigento, some from the province of Messina and some from Palermo. I want to thank the following people for their help in my search for the correct terms:

My neighbours in Cianciana, Antonio Vaiana and his mother Anna Pendino.

Art Deili and his excellent website at
http://www.dieli.net/SicilyPage/SicilianLanguage/Vocabulary.html

And my ever patient and ever helpful husband, Nick Cacciato.

Sicilian	Italian	English
	agriturismo	a farm B&B
allura	allora - allura	then, well
amuri	amore	love
ancila	angela	angel
bastibili	basta	enough
bedda mia	cara mia	my dear
beddra	bella	beautiful
beni	bene	well, good, okay

buttana	puttana	whore
bon viagiu	buon viaggio	have a good trip
bona notti	buona notte	good night
bona sera	buona sera	good evening
carabunera	carabinieri	National police force
carcarazzi	gazze	magpies
	carolina	little dear
càru	caro	dear
ccà	qui	here
certu	certo	certainly
cèusa	gelso	mulberry
	che cos'è	what is it?
chìesa matri	chiesa madre	mother church
chiusu	chiuso	closed
	Ciancianese	someone from the town of Cianciana
ciaramedda	cornamusa	bagpipe
ciau	ciao	hi, bye
como sta/stai	come sta/stai	How are you?
	desco da parto	birthing tray
drevo/dreva	bambino/bambina	child or baby
è nenti, miu amuriè love	niente, mio amore	It's nothing, my love
emuninni	andiamo	Let's go
famigghia	famiglia	family
fai araciu	fai adagio	go slowly
	ferme il parentado	sealing the alliance
friscalettu	flauto	flute
	gnocchi	dumplings
grazii a Diu	grazie Dio	thank God
grazii milli	grazie mille	a thousand thanks
grazii pi tutti cosi	grazie per tutti	thanks for everything
ma va scusari signu	scuzi signora	excuse me, ma'am
maccu di San Gnuseppi		"Saint Joseph's Soup"

maistra	maestra	mistress
malocchio	mal'occhio	evil eye
mancia	mangia	eat
marranzanu	scacciapensieri	jaw harp
	mi dispiace	I'm sorry.
mia matri pìcciulu	mia madre piccolo	my little mother
minchia		cock or dick
(vulg.)		
miu Diu	mio Dio	my God
miu maritu	mio marito	my husband
miu papà	mio papà	my father / dad
miu preju	mio gioio	my joy
nenti	niente	nothing
niputi	nipote	granddaughter
nni videmu	c'è vediamo	see you later
nanna	nonna	grandmother
nonnu	nonno	grandfather
nustra Matri	nostra Madre	our Mother (of
God)		
	panelle	fried chickpea
bread		
panificiu	panificio	bakery
passaru	passero	sparrow
pazzu	pazzo	crazy
perfettu	perfetto	perfect
pi favuri	per favore	please
picciotti	ragazze	girls
picciridda mia	piccolina mia	my little one
	pignolata	fried dough
pinsione	pensione	inn
	pisolino	afternoon nap
pregu	prego	you're welcome
pupa	bambolina	little girl
sangu miu	il mio sangue	my blood
sciò		shoo
scupa	scopa	card game

cusassi	scusate, scuzi	excuse me
	Sei tu, cara?	Is it you, dear?
	sensale	go-between
	sfincione	type of pizza
signura	signora	Mrs., ma'am
signuri	signor, signore	Mr., sir
signorina	signorina	Miss
sugnu	sono	I am
suppa di linticchia	zuppa di lenticchie	lentil soup
stupennu	stupendo	stupendous
t'amu	ti amo	I love you
	tarantella	traditional dance
tirrazza	terrazza	terrace
tumazzu	pecorino	sheep milk cheese
	uffa	Ugh, expresses frustration
unn c'è mali	non c'è male	not bad
unnè	dov'è	where
uogghiu	olio	oil
va beni	va bene	okay
vatinni	vai	go
vene ccà	viene	come here
vivi	bevi	drink
zitiduzza	ragazzaccia	diminutive for girl
zzia	zia	aunt
zzio	zio	uncle